IN THE
CROSSHAIRS

ALSO BY JACK COUGHLIN

NONFICTION

Shooter: The Autobiography of the Top-Ranked Marine Sniper
(with Capt. Casey Kuhlman and Donald A. Davis)
Shock Factor: American Snipers in the War on Terror

FICTION

Kill Zone (with Donald A. Davis)
Dead Shot (with Donald A. Davis)
Clean Kill (with Donald A. Davis)
An Act of Treason (with Donald A. Davis)
Running the Maze (with Donald A. Davis)
Time to Kill (with Donald A. Davis)
On Scope (with Donald A. Davis)
Night of the Cobra (with Donald A. Davis)
Long Shot (with Donald A. Davis)

ALSO BY DONALD A. DAVIS

Lightning Strike
The Last Man on the Moon (with Gene Cernan)
Dark Waters (with Lee Vyborny)

IN THE
CROSSHAIRS

A SNIPER NOVEL

GUNNERY SGT. **JACK COUGHLIN,**
USMC (RET.)

WITH **DONALD A. DAVIS**

ST. MARTIN'S PRESS ✠ NEW YORK

IN THE CROSSHAIRS. Copyright © 2017 by Jack Coughlin with Donald A. Davis. All rights reserved. Printed in the United States of America. For information, address St. Martin's Press, 175 Fifth Avenue, New York, N.Y. 10010.

www.stmartins.com

Designed by Omar Chapa

The Library of Congress Cataloging-in-Publication Data is available upon request.

ISBN 978-1-250-10353-6 (hardcover)
ISBN 978-1-250-10355-0 (ebook)

Our books may be purchased in bulk for promotional, educational, or business use. Please contact your local bookseller or the Macmillan Corporate and Premium Sales Department at 1-800-221-7945, extension 5442, or by email at MacmillanSpecialMarkets@macmillan.com.

First Edition: August 2017

10 9 8 7 6 5 4 3 2 1

IN THE
CROSSHAIRS

Prologue

THE CIA SNIPER TEAM huddled unseen in a shadowy crevice that had been created when an earthquake scrambled the Pamir Mountains of Afghanistan four years earlier. Luke Gibson and Nicky Marks were eyes-on the scruffy home of old Mahfouz al-Rashidi, warlord of the Wakham Corridor.

They had been there for almost twenty-four hours, having been dropped by a helicopter onto a high plateau six kilometers away and then humping the hills beneath a cold and cloudless black sky spangled with bright stars. The terrain was so silvery that the night-vision goggles weren't needed. The chopper's racket, which had pounded their ears during the flight, had given way to silence as their ears adjusted, and all their senses finally clicked into sharpness. Along their quiet way the two men, dressed in local garb, made frequent stops just to look and listen and smell the surroundings. A dog in the nearby village of Girdiwal yelped as if it were being whipped. The stalk was sweaty work, even on the chilly night, but they had found the predetermined slot without difficulty, converted it into a hide in the scrub bush, done a soft radio check, and, with rifles zeroed and telecoms set before the sun rose, had burrowed into position. It was no big deal. The pair of seasoned veterans had been in this area before, for a CIA safe house had been set up there many years ago. It would not be used this time, so the strike couldn't be traced back to them. The loose shale covering the hard rock on which they lay was as familiar as an old couch.

At about 0800, there was a buzz in the heavens and a lightweight AS550 Fennec scout helicopter belonging to the Pakistani Army popped over the horizon. Gibson heard it first and pointed as the dot grew larger and the bird found a landing spot near the front gate of the house. The snipers had been expecting it, as had Mahfouz al-Rashidi, for this was a regular payday for the master of the Wakham.

"Right on time," Gibson said softly as he watched the camouflaged rotary-wing aircraft shut down, its rotors revolving slower and slower. An officer climbed out and was escorted through the gate while a soldier and the pilot unloaded freight and lugged it in.

Nicky Marks unzipped a satchel that he had brought with him and powered up an electronic array of miniaturized snooper technology, pushing buttons to start recording. "We're green across the board, Luke. The audio is five by five, and we should be getting a picture any minute."

AL-RASHIDI PUT DOWN HIS cup of mint tea when he heard the sweep of the blades, anticipating the homage that would come to him on this special day. The host welcomed the courier from Islamabad and bade him sit and visit with the family, as was the custom with strangers.

Outside, Luke Gibson watched the swirling dust settle from the helicopter landing to gauge the wind speed between the hide and the house. He was as still as a sleeping snake. Nothing bothered him.

The warlord had a peculiar relationship with the ISI, Pakistan's intelligence service, and it had been fruitful. The Islamabad government provided cash in return for information about what was happening along the long valley in neighboring Afghanistan, particularly at the point where it met the closed Chinese border. The first gift from the officer today was a black nylon suitcase filled with shrink-wrapped bricks of American greenback dollars. The second was a huge flat-screen television set with powerful receiving capability that could pick up broadcasts from around the world, almost everything from the Sky Network to Netflix, plus a built-in CD player. The technician, a lowly enlisted man, was ignored as he set up the amazing equipment, burying his real purpose in the maze of wires and controls that only he understood.

The TV set, the receiver, and the suitcase also communicated the other way, for it contained a hive of mini-microphones and sophisticated spyware. Within a few minutes, Nicky Marks and Luke Gibson could see and hear as if they were sitting inside with Mahfouz al-Rashidi and his sons.

The old guy had an unkempt beard and looked comfortable in loose trousers beneath a long tunic. He was totally at ease, feeling quite pleasant, not just about the courier and the gifts but because all four of his sons had come together for the first time in months to celebrate their father's seventieth birthday. He also had two daughters, both devout and placed beneath the veil early in their teens, then married off to worthy men and gone from his life. Soon the ISI officer, his men, and the helicopter were gone, and the warlord turned to the business at hand. The TV set was not even turned on, for it was a mere entertainment trinket and of no true substance, just a gift from an appreciative customer to mark the first day of Muharram, the start of the Islamic new year.

The four young men sat with their father in a circle, paying close attention to his words. Together, the family of Mahfouz al-Rashidi formed a jihadi terrorist cell whose five members were known only to one another. With family, there was no worry of betrayal.

The clan originally came from the Egyptian intelligentsia in long-ago years when Islam existed in the shadows and, in the opinion of the old man, the people strove not to exalt God, as was proper, but to be ever more like the infidel Westerners. Had not his own father and uncle amassed wealth from an international import-export business created by their own forefathers along the Nile? Mahfouz had been born into a life of privilege just after the war in 1949. But for the grace of the Prophet, praise be unto him, he would also have been lost to the secular temptations prevalent in his formative years.

Instead, he had puzzled out deep meanings of the Koran, befriended radical mullahs, and fallen under the hypnotic sway of Osama bin Laden, Al Qaeda, and the dream of jihad. It was with bin Laden's advice that al-Rashidi migrated with his family away from secular Egypt to this forsaken place on what had once been a trade route to China. That heathen nation had closed the border at its end of the Wakham Corridor, making it a dead end for official trade but creating a thriving black-market haven, a valuable pipeline for information, and a prosperous place for the cultivation of hillside hectares of opium poppies.

It provided the priceless isolation in which al-Rashidi raised his own den of lions. His religious mentors and the billionaire bin Laden kept him going as a special project, almost cut off from the world, tediously making ready for a strike at some unknown future date when the tawdry Western world would cower in fear.

"Tell me of our purpose," the old man said, addressing his eldest son, Mohammed.

"To destroy America," came the answer. Mohammed was a forty-year-old architect who now lived in Paris.

"Ali. Our mission?" The watery dark eyes of the old man passed to the second son, a year younger.

"To grind fear into the heart of the United States! To make them eat ashes!" There was no hesitation from the skilled attorney, who was a prosecuting lawyer for the Afghan government.

The old man nodded again. Very good. "How do we do that, Kalil?"

"Follow the teachings of Osama bin Laden and make a memorable strike to glorify the Prophet, whose name be praised." Kalil rocked back and forth, as he had done as a child while memorizing the Koran. He was employed as a petrochemical engineer by a British company and spent much of the year aboard North Sea rigs.

"And who among us shall do this thing?" He turned to the last of the four.

The youngest spoke with the same certainty as his brothers. "Why, Father, that will be me," replied the smiling and clean-shaven Stephen Rush, who ran a reputable industrial real-estate business in Houston, Texas.

The father felt as though he might burst with joy, and rolled his eyes heavenward as he said softly, "Allah be praised." It had been a very long and hard journey raising this family beyond the reach of so many enemies, keeping them pure, educating them at fine universities, and placing them in strategic occupations. Sacrificing them all simultaneously was a tragic decision, but it was a promise he had made to Osama. He knew that after coordinated attacks were made in Texas, Pakistan, France, and London the honored house of al-Rashidi would be hunted down like rabid dogs and extinguished from the face of the earth. They would reunite as martyrs in paradise. Who could ask for more?

GIBSON DECIDED THAT HE had heard and seen enough of the Rashidi boys. They had just confirmed the intelligence gathered over the past few years. "Put up our radio link," he said over his shoulder to Marks without taking his eye from the powerful spotting scope that was poking through the tumbled foliage. When Marks confirmed that the encrypted signal was available, Gibson said, "Tell them it's a go on this end." Then he made some final minor scope adjustments to his old-school M24 (SWS) sniper rifle and chambered a 7.62×51-mm. NATO cartridge.

The house, five hundred meters distant, loomed large in the magnified image, and Gibson scanned left to right, then up and down. Al-Rashidi should have heeded the Prophet's warning against becoming arrogant, for it had been his undoing. The Egyptian prided himself on his relationship with Osama bin Laden, who had left notes about him and the special project in his private files. Unfortunately, when an American commando team killed bin Laden and found that information the careful and loyal Mahfouz al-Rashidi stood exposed. The little warlord in the small house in the no-name wasted valley became a person of interest. He had reached too far.

Then he was groomed as carefully as a teenage girl tends her hair and eye makeup. Money began to flow in exchange for information about who was doing what in his valley. He liked the new power and importance, and his sons had been happy to get out of the Wakham, with money to spend.

Mohammed developed a liking for the whores of Paris. Ali enjoyed the perfumed boys of Islamabad. Kalil was up to his neck in gambling debts to London bookies, and young Stephen Rush, whose real name was Syed, was a cocaine freakazoid. The boys had all gone Western, but told their jihadi father what he wanted to hear, not necessarily what was true. All hated having to come back to this crude shack and were about as capable of planning a coordinated attack as a herd of turtles.

No matter, thought Gibson, who knew their backgrounds. It was time to end this game and take all five of them off the map. He slowed his breathing and steadied the rifle. Forty thousand feet above him, an MQ-9 Reaper drone had been loitering for two hours in sky circles on sixty-six-foot wings under the control of a pilot and a sensor operator back in the United States. When Gibson passed along the permission from Marks, the drone slid into a straight path above the target and jumped up as it released a pair of GBU-38 Joint Direct Attack Munitions, smart bombs that weighed five hundred pounds apiece. The JDAMs rode the laser beam flawlessly directly through the roof of al-Rashidi's home and exploded with a thunderclap that rolled far down the valley.

Gibson had been expecting it, but it was still quite a show. With the thud of detonations, the building actually blew apart in a canopy of debris and dirt. A tower of smoke rolled up and fire flashed horizontally. He kept his eye on the scope as the concussion pushed against the mountains.

He had been doing this kind of thing for a long time, and it still surprised him that anyone could live through such an attack, but, invariably, someone did. Even Hitler walked away from a bomb blast that killed or wounded almost everybody around him in a closed room. And, sure enough, down in the smoking rubble a figure stirred. An arm—not much more than a claw in Gibson's scope—was raised, and then fell, and rose again. A man was digging out. The head emerged. It looked like Kalil, but the sniper couldn't be certain because the face was so badly burned. It really made no difference. The torso wiggled and struggled and emerged from the ruins. It stood slowly, holding on to a torn wooden beam for support, and Gibson shot him through the chest. The target fell and there was no more movement.

Gibson pulled the rifle back. "Tell them mission completed." Marks passed along the message to send the drone back to its base and bring in the extraction chopper. There was no hurry to get away. No cavalry would be riding to the rescue for the al-Rashidi gang. Gibson pulled out a packet of chocolate, took a sweet bite, and thought, Happy New Year, Mahfouz, old buddy. That thought was followed quickly by Damn, I'm good at this.

SAN LUIS DE LA PAZ,
MEXICO

THEY WERE BURYING COLONEL Francisco Miguel Castillo of the Mexican Marines today. The funeral was a peculiar affair, because the dark secrets of Mickey Castillo were no secrets at all. His business was known throughout his hometown of San Luis de la Paz, a small city that straddled the old Spanish Silver Road in Central Mexico. The people had eagerly followed the career of the popular local boy who had become a Special Forces hero and his nation's star operator in the war against the deadly drug trade. He was their champion, descended from the Chichimeca warriors who were never defeated by the Europeans.

The Castillo family owned several homes, including one in the capital and another on the Gulf, but Miguel had chosen to live at a spread of his own within ten miles of the ranch house in which he was born. It was to this place that he had come in later years to escape the pressures of his job, a place where he could be at ease. But more than cattle branding went on out at the old ranch beside the Manzanares River, and strong men other than vaqueros were regular visitors. Neighbors often heard the *bap-bap-bap* of rapid gunfire and the *whumps* of explosions out on the private acres where Castillo and his mysterious friends trained and practiced at all hours. Those sounds were comforting lullabies to the townspeople, for they made them feel safe and protected. The crime rate always went down when the colonel and his friends were at the ranch and arrived to check out the restaurants and bars in the evening. It was a mutually beneficial relationship. The residents who provided sanctuary for the colonel didn't share information about him with outsiders.

The impossible happened. The colonel had been gunned down during a raid against a cartel headquarters belonging to the powerful narcotics kingpin Maxim Guerrera, near Juárez. It was just a lucky shot by a cowardly thug whose submachine gun continued to chatter bullets even as the man holding it fell mortally wounded by marine fire. Two bullets hammered Castillo just above his chest armor and below the helmet, severing his brain stem, and he died. He was thirty-five years old.

THE INFORMATION WAS INCLUDED high in the morning briefing of Martin Atkins, the director of intelligence for the Central Intelligence Agency. Atkins always approached his office at the CIA headquarters in Langley, Virginia, with a sense of trepidation in the mornings, for his coffee invariably arrived at his desk with a little taste of 2 percent milk and an avalanche of bad news from around the globe.

The Sandbox was usually at the top of the list, with bombings, assassinations, and assorted outrages committed by jihadist organizations ranging from the big boys like Al Qaeda to some loner with a bomb and a car and a death wish. That was a staple.

Then his team would shift focus to the real players—China and Israel, a nuked-up North Korea and Russia—and the stalwart allies, such as the United Kingdom and Western Europe. Things were generally quieter in those channels, although more long-range and serious, for the stakes were so much higher. His briefers had worked throughout the night to prepare his early-morning checklist of horrors. Atkins would help whittle it down to be combined with similar top-secret material from other intelligence agencies that would be given to the director of National Intelligence, who, in turn, would brief President Christopher Thompson.

The gruesome menu seemed fine, overall. Routine. Atkins winnowed out a few items, then approved it to be passed up the chain. It was the item from Mexico that disturbed him most on this fine April morning when the cherry trees were blossoming all over Washington. Others would brief the president. Atkins had the more onerous task of informing his best field operative that Mickey Castillo was dead. Even as he dialed the number, he understood that he was unleashing a whirlwind.

A FEW DAYS LATER, the small cathedral of San Luis de la Paz was crowded as the shocked citizens gathered to say farewell to their hero. A sturdy wind blew out of the mountains and through the forests and along the valleys, and after the proper words were said by the priests the coffin was loaded into a hearse by six strong marines. The funeral procession wound through narrow streets filled with people who believed the unusual wind on this day heralded a gloomy change for their quiet world. For with the colonel gone, who would be their shield?

The drug-cartel lords everywhere in Mexico were glad to see him go, none more than Maxim Guerrera. Castillo was called Big Poison by the criminal giants, because when Mickey and his boys appeared at some processing plant, shipping point, or hidden house, they brought death and disruption with them. He was poison to their business, and they could not touch him in return. They tried, even posting a healthy bounty on him, but always failed, and his retribution for any such attempt had been so fast and furious and certain that it was best not to anger him as long as the overall profit picture remained strong. It had taken what was little more than an accident to finally bring down Miguel Castillo. Now Guerrera sought to make it a death that would be remembered.

Police officers and marines escorted the small procession past the colonial-era buildings and out to the cemetery, where an honor guard stood ready among the tombstones and crosses and stone statues of the Virgin and the sorrowful angels. Generations of San Luis de la Paz families had been laid to rest in that garden of marble headstones.

From the black Mercedes that had stopped behind the hearse stepped Castillo's mother, in midnight mourning from head to toe, a dark veil covering a swollen face tracked with tears. The marine who had opened the door took her gently by the arm and led her to the gravesite, where several rows of chairs had been arranged. She sat in the front row, staring across the open grave, still in shock.

Then a man emerged from the car. He was wiry, with brownish fair hair, and wore an expensive black suit. Some mourners recognized him as the colonel's close friend, an Anglo named Kyle Swanson, who was often at the ranch. He was always polite and deferential to the locals, never said much, and it was obvious that he and the colonel were in the same line of work. The man had the deep and restless eyes of a wolf, and those suspicious eyes swept around the limousine like a slash of radar. Then he leaned back in, offering his hand.

Finally, out came the colonel's lady, the señora, and the respectful crowd quieted even more. She also was an American, petite and beautiful and caring and funny. She threw great parties at the ranch and moved among the poor in the slums of San Luis with confidence, bringing help and understanding. Her blond hair glowed in the sun around the edges of a small black hat and veil. It was said that Elizabeth Castillo had once also been a soldier, but that was never confirmed, and the couple didn't talk about it outside the family. What was discussed openly, by those who had seen her do it, was that the tiny woman was a *mago*—a magician—with firearms. She had won money from many men in impromptu shooting matches at the ranch, and they loved her for it. It was sad that she had not yet been blessed with children, the women said.

"You okay, Coastie?" Kyle Swanson whispered as she rose and took his arm. "Hang on. Not much longer."

"I will kill the bastards who did this, Kyle," she whispered. "I will personally send them to hell."

"Focus, girl," he ordered. "Let's put Mickey to rest." He took her to the front row, where she sat beside her mother-in-law. The women held hands. Swanson went to a chair in the second row, directly behind them. Swanson wasn't grieving for Mickey, and hadn't shed a tear from the moment he received the awful news from Marty Atkins. By the time he ended that call, Swanson was already in a zone of resolve. A lifetime as a top U.S.

Marine Corps sniper and his status as a CIA operator had prepared him well for such moments, and personal feelings only got in the way. His day job and cover story was being the executive vice president of a global company called Excalibur Enterprises. After the call from Marty Atkins, he had immediately arranged for the corporate jet to fly to Mexico. As everyone else mourned, he watched the crowd.

The police had established an outer perimeter, and all roads into the cemetery area were blocked. Mexican marines in combat gear were in strategic positions. They all knew that an attack was unlikely, but with the drug thugs no one could be sure. Terrible things happened in modern Mexico, and it was best to bury Big Poison as soon as possible and retreat to the ranch.

The polished coffin of handcrafted cherry wood was placed on the webbed straps of a lowering device that straddled the grave. The hole had been prepared the night before, and a small pyramid of dirt was covered by a mat of green artificial turf a hundred feet away, beside a yellow backloader that would finish the burial after everyone had gone. The heavy vault that would hold the casket was in place below, ready to accept its eternal burden.

A priest said some more words, and in the distance a somber mariachi group sang of loss and rebirth. The honor guard dipped its flags, and the marines saluted as Colonel Castillo was lowered into the waiting grave.

A glint of gold in the bright sunlight drew Swanson's attention, his subconscious tactical mind grinding at its own work even while his friend was leaving forever. The blink had come from some object worn by a man standing beside the little tractor at the dirt pile. An earring? He appeared tall for a Mexican, and was clean-shaven but for a sharp, pointed goatee, which indicated that he cared about his appearance. His jeans were clean, as was the long-sleeved Western-style checked shirt. Gravediggers normally didn't look so clean or wear jewelry while on the job. A straw cowboy hat was tilted forward, shading his face.

The colonel's mother began to shake with another spasm of emotion. The widow wrapped an arm around the older woman, but kept her head up proudly, her attention fixed on the disappearing coffin. "I'm going to miss you so much, Mickey," Beth Castillo whispered.

In the row behind them, Kyle Swanson was suddenly alert. Nothing had happened, but after so many years in dangerous spots around the world he had a sixth sense that he obeyed without question. As the coffin of his pal kissed the cement of the vault, Swanson once again saw the distant blink. The man was on the move, walking away. Fast. Why would a gravedigger leave his machine only minutes before he had to do his job? Swanson grabbed the backs of the pair of folding chairs directly in front of him and gave a mighty pull as he shouted a warning: "Bomb!"

Both Castillo women screamed as they spilled backward, and Swanson dived to cover them with his own body an instant before a device planted beneath the vault detonated with thunder and a dazzling flash of light. The explosion erupted from the hole with a roar and was followed by a fireball that seemed to rise from the depths of hell. People toppled like tin cans as the explosive beast ravaged the area. Swanson covered his head but felt the air being sucked from his lungs, and then debris began to rain down on his back.

The rectangular shape of the grave had saved them, by channeling the main power of the blast straight up into the sky. Still, the strike was awful. People were down all around, stunned and shaken or wounded or dead. Swanson coughed for air and wiped his eyes, then rolled away, a sharp pain at his back.

He knelt and checked the women. Mickey's mother was unconscious. Elizabeth had scrabbled to her knees on the littered ground, and they stared at each other for a moment as the stunned silence gave way to a commotion.

They concentrated on helping the older woman, checking her air passages and making sure there were no broken bones. Sirens were sounding. People were yelling. "Mama will be okay," Beth declared. "How could they do this?" Looking at Kyle, her face filled with a mixture of sorrow, rage, and hate, she swore, "I will make whoever did it pay! I want back in!"

SWANSON REMAINED STILL AS chaos spread to allow things to settle enough to get past the buzzing ears and the instant headache and the showering dirt and debris. He had to assess the situation and get the hell out of this mess.

People were fleeing toward perceived safety. Others stumbled about in shock. The desecration of the grave had been complete, and with no regard for the innocent. Castillo's enemies had struck a horrendous blow that would stand as a warning of the fate awaiting anyone who opposed the cartels. Even death would not end the punishment.

First things first. He was okay. Beth was okay. Mama Castillo didn't look so good. Her skin was gray. A trail of blood that trickled from one eye was probably just a vitreous hemorrhage. No broken bones were apparent, but her pulse was weak. She would live, although Swanson didn't think she would like the world into which she awoke.

"She's good enough to move back to the ranch," he said. "Best we avoid the hospitals and bring in our own medical care. It will be safer out there."

"Yeah," Beth agreed. She barked a string of instructions in fluent Spanish to a young Mexican marine, who took off at a run to organize an escape convoy.

"Get one of the cops over here and translate for me," Swanson said, and she waved to a policeman with a sweaty face and a missing cap. He recognized her and loped through the rubble.

"Señora Castillo? Are you hurt?" He was studying them, looking for injuries.

She nodded and held up a finger to silence him. "Kyle, this is Sergeant Rey. What do you want him to do?"

Swanson was on one knee. He pointed across the debris field to where the backhoe had been toppled to one side by the blast. "We need to secure that tractor. The man who was beside it may be involved in the bombing. Rey, you take charge of it—and don't let anyone else even touch it until the machine can be checked for fingerprints and other evidence."

"Yes, sir," the policeman said, not needing a translation. But he wanted to do more than just stand by a tractor. He wanted to shoot somebody. "Is there anything else?"

Swanson spoke directly to him. "Tell your guys to locate the regular gravedigger. Likely he's dead somewhere nearby and another man took his place. That would probably be the bomber."

The cop seemed a bit wobbly, dealing with the vestiges of his own shock. "Help is already on the way. Can I take you to your car, señora?"

Beth shook her head. "Rey, listen closely. Start the search, then stand guard at the tractor. It is very important. Thank you for your concern, but we will be fine. Now go!"

"You saw the bomber?" she asked Swanson.

"Maybe. I saw somebody who didn't belong," he said. "No need to speculate until we see what the cops turn up. Now let's get Mama out of here."

THE RAGTAG CONVOY SLICED, bumped, and burrowed its way through the old streets of San Luis de la Paz with a police escort of SUVs mounted with machine guns, blaring sirens, and flashing warning lights. Swanson felt absolutely naked. He had flown out of Washington upon getting the news about the fatal shootout. To avoid airport and customs hassles and delays, he chose to leave his personal weapon at home, because he could always borrow one from the substantial armory of the Castillo ranch. Then he got caught up in the emotional funeral arrangements and decided to let the security detail do its job while he provided comfort and support to the widow and the mother of his friend. After all, what could go wrong at a funeral? *Stupid. Stupid. Stupid.*

Now everywhere he looked he saw potential kill zones, and all he had was a heavy six-shot .375 Magnum revolver that he'd borrowed from the driver of the Mercedes. The long-barreled weapon wasn't even the real deal but a knockoff of the Smith & Wesson made famous in the *Dirty Harry* movies. Not even close to a modern Desert Eagle. While checking the load, Swanson discovered that the gun had been manufactured by a Chinese factory that was in the cheap mail-order gun business. He kept it pointed down beside the seat as a safety precaution. The heavy car rocketed across a curb.

He was in the front seat and both Mrs. Castillos were in the back, with Mama still out cold and Beth cradling her in her arms. "Keep your Beretta handy," he said over his shoulder. She always kept the small weapon in her purse.

"I can get to it if we need it. Do your own job." Her voice was tight. She resented being told something so basic.

They weaved through a traffic roundabout and were well away from the cemetery, headed for open country. Swanson didn't breathe easier until he saw the first cow in a field. There were few places for death to hide in open pasture. He glanced back and caught Beth staring at him, and he shrugged and went back to watching the livestock.

Elizabeth Ledford Castillo was one of the most interesting people he had ever met, and they went back a long way. A corn-fed American blonde from the Midwest, she had been a remarkable sharpshooter from girl-hood. Nobody could explain the uncanny gift, other than that she was like a child-savant pianist, only she was a prodigy with firearms. It was almost as if she didn't even have to aim at a target to punch it out. Her protective family shunned publicity when the reporters came knocking after hearing tales about the new wunderkind Annie Oakley.

She remained on the quiet farm throughout high school, but excitement beckoned, and to make her gift something more than an oddity she joined the U.S. Coast Guard, because at the time it was the only service branch that allowed women to really shoot. It didn't take her long to qualify as a sniper who could take out live targets, stinging them from the open door of a helicopter, which meant that both she and the targets were moving when the trigger was pulled. Bandits, pirates, and drug smugglers all suffered beneath the cool, methodical aim of Beth Ledford.

She was satisfied with her assignments until her brother, a physician, was killed by terrorists during a flood-relief mission of Médecins Sans Frontières, Doctors Without Borders. Beth was devastated, and would not let the situation rest. Instead of the cooperation she expected from her superiors, she ran into a buzz saw of official opposition and trouble from people with other agendas. That was when she appeared on the radar of Kyle Swanson's old team, Task Force Trident, an élite black-ops unit. The small, pretty young woman, who was only about twenty-five at the time, started out almost as a mascot. They called her Coastie.

But she soon proved to be a valuable tool for the team, because she really could shoot as good as, or better than, any of them. Well, Swanson thought, she wasn't better than him, although that was never tested, because he might not like the answer. Beyond the absurd marksmanship, Coastie carried a touch of murder in her soul and the uncompromising determination of a backwoods preacher. Beth Ledford developed into a stone-cold killer and a smooth Trident operator, someone Swanson was always happy to have as a partner. In fact, she had even saved his life. There had been romantic opportunities that never bloomed because of Kyle's emotional isolation. Then she fell in love with Mickey Castillo instead and retired from the game so that they could get married. Swanson knew he could have had Beth himself had he just been able to say, "I love you," but he couldn't. He had said that before to other women, and those words packed too much hurt, so he settled for being best man at their wedding and a good friend to both.

Swanson adjusted his sunglasses and again made sure the safety was secure on the hand cannon at his side. The driver was doing a good job on the road. He was built like a fire hydrant, with the jowly face of a bulldog, and drove as if this were a NASCAR tryout.

Swanson used the moment to reflect on what Coastie had blurted out at the cemetery: she wanted to come back into the secret world. But three years had passed since she had retired to the easy life of a wealthy family in Mexico's upper middle class. It was too soon for her to make this kind of decision, or any major decision. Nobody should make a life choice during such emotional moments, but Coastie wasn't like everyone else. If it was revenge she wanted, Swanson knew that he wouldn't be able to stop her. She hadn't been asking permission. He shifted in the seat. The tension was miles behind them now, and the ranch was five miles of smooth road straight ahead.

BY THE FOLLOWING AFTERNOON, Swanson was no longer at the ranch. Word had come down directly from Marty Atkins, the only man in the CIA to whom Swanson answered directly, and the word was to get up to Mexico City immediately. He wasn't sad to go, because he could postpone dealing with Coastie for at least a little while. He knew that she wasn't going to give up.

It took most of the day to make the trip to the capital, but the sun was still high and hot in a cloudless sky as he boarded a helicopter to take him above the horrendous traffic of the city and the dirty smog that hugged the tops of the tall buildings. More than eight million people lived in Mexico City, and it seemed that most of them were on wheels of some sort, clogging every avenue.

The chopper set down lightly on the helipad atop an inconspicuous office building, and a guide showed him to an elevator. A reception desk was directly in front of the elevator door when it opened, and Swanson understood that the young man seated there was also a guard, despite the blue sports coat and the tie and the bright manner. Swanson handed over his cred pack, and the man nodded up at a camera. "Just a moment, sir. Mrs. Johnson is coming out to escort you."

Swanson was looking for the pinhole cameras that surely covered the area when a knobless door buzzed open. "Mr. Swanson. I'm Irma Johnson, the executive assistant to Mr. Wright. He's expecting you." Her voice was calm and smooth, because she was used to the crisis mode that always existed in these offices. This was just another day in the heart of the CIA in Mexico.

Everything about her was neat, from the graying hair to the polished nails. She was the unflinching gatekeeper of the dark world, and professional to the core.

"We have to walk a bit because he's in the secure communications suite." The hallway was narrow and built to provide niches in which staff members could take cover in case of an attack. The zigzag route made it impossible for a gunman at one end to shoot all the way to the other.

Neither remarked on the unusual architecture, which was pretty standard for important outposts around the world. Outwardly, it had the bland look of an insurance company, including potted plants and tasteful wallpaper that seamlessly hid the firing ports.

At a dark-mahogany door, Mrs. Johnson activated a touch panel and the portal opened. She stood aside and Swanson moved into the communications center of the CIA's home away from home in Mexico. Glitzy new computers and old file cabinets intermingled in what seemed to be a continuation of the haphazard layout. In reality, it was an efficient way to do business, to loop tomorrow back to yesterday. In the information age in which teenage hackers could attack a government computer system just for the hell of it, paper copies had come back in style.

Timothy Wright, the station chief, gave Swanson a brief handshake and had him sit down. There was a thick black notebook peeled open on the desk, and he said, "Let's get straight to it, shall we?"

"Sure. What's going on? I shouldn't be here." Swanson took a straight-backed chair. "Such a direct link with the company could destroy my cover."

"I've just gotten off the scrambler with Director Atkins, who briefed me on your background: illustrious career in the Marine Corps as a sniper, Medal of Honor winner, and now you're the executive vice president of

Excalibur Enterprises, a private corporation." He spoke in a slow voice that carried a hint of Nebraska twang. His white sleeves were rolled up on his forearms, and his demeanor was that of a stern grandfather. "You work for us on the side as a special operative. Marty Atkins is your boss, and he cleared this meeting because we have ourselves a bit of a problem, Mr. Swanson."

"Kyle," he responded, mindful that it was usually best to keep one's mouth shut.

Wright smiled. "Fine. I'm Tim." He put on a pair of rimless bifocals and read from a single sheet. "Here is the trail of breadcrumbs, Kyle. You flew in a couple of days ago from Dulles to attend the funeral of your friend, Colonel Castillo, right? No advance contact?"

Swanson shook his head. "I hadn't spoken to either the colonel or his wife, who is also a close friend, in about three months. Not even texts."

"Right. Then you go to the cemetery and almost get blown up by a bomb in the grave."

This time Swanson didn't reply at all. The man was spinning a chronology that he already knew.

Tim Wright continued. "Grab a bottle of water from the shelf, if you want some. We can have real drinks later. Anyway, you told the police that you saw a suspicious character moments before the blast."

Swanson bought a little time by getting a bottle and concentrating on opening the cap. It was room temperature, but at least he wouldn't catch Montezuma's revenge. Dirty water going in one end usually resulted in diarrhea exiting the other.

"I had a session with a police artist yesterday afternoon to help construct an Identi-Kit likeness. He nailed it pretty well with a full-face image. Still, I only got a glance."

Wright reached into the notebook and pulled the sketch from the clear protective sleeve. "This it?"

"Yes." Right down to the pointed goatee.

Wright pursed his lips. Swanson wasn't making this easy. "The local cops pulled some prints from the tractor that was used to dig the grave.

The cemetery employee who had that job was found dead in a work shed, with his throat cut."

"So you have an ID?" Swanson raised his eyebrows.

"The prints match those of the man in your sketch, Swanson." The CIA station chief whistled a puff of air and took out a photograph that mirrored the sketch. "His name is Nicky Marks."

"Not Mexican?" Interesting. "Never heard of him."

"The real name is Nikola Markovitch. He's Russian. And he's one of ours."

"Humph." Swanson cleared his throat, thought it over. Had a drink. "A Russian CIA operator? What does that have to do with me?"

Wright slid the sketch and the photo back into the plastic and closed the book. "Are you aware that Colonel Castillo did occasional favors for us?"

"No surprise." Mickey had said nothing about it, but then why should he? The CIA and the Mexicans obviously often worked in tandem on intelligence matters, particularly on the volatile drug front. "That raid on which he was killed, a joint op?"

"Yes, but that's beside the point."

"Then, Tim, just what is the point? Why am I here?"

Wright closed the binder and gave Swanson a kindly look that a teacher would show a child who was slow to pick up on the lesson. "Mickey Castillo is killed during a CIA operation. We can presume that Nicky Marks, whom the agency also used on occasion, attacked Castillo's grave. In turn, Marks is identified by you, Kyle Swanson, another CIA special operator. To say that Atkins wants to know more about this situation would be somewhat of an understatement."

Swanson remained cool. "I'm a shooter, Tim. I deal only in high-value targets who pose a direct threat to the United States of America and believe they're beyond our reach. I'm neither an investigator nor an espionage agent."

Wright got to his feet and put his hands in his pockets. Grandfather, lecturing. "Consider it this way, Kyle. On some unknown day in the future, you may be sitting in a congressional hearing room having to answer questions about this under oath. We will cover it up, but nothing is airtight.

There are legions of snoops and spies and leakers and hackers and con-
spiracy weirdos and oversight committee members who are always out
there chewing our asses, and one of them may find this trail. Then they'll
all want TV time and will sell the information to prove they have the balls
to attack us. By then, you had better know some answers, don't you think?"

Swanson had the sudden feeling that he had entered some twilight
danger zone, on a path that was dark and shadowy. He had no illusion
about what he had just learned: the CIA would feed him to the wolves in
a heartbeat. "I'll talk to Marty when I get back to Washington," he said,
rising from his chair.

"Do that. You're booked to leave here tomorrow morning," Wright said.
"Marty will give you the full file on Nicky Marks." He extended his hand,
shook with Swanson, then walked out.

Mrs. Johnson walked in, somehow having been silently signaled that
the meeting was over. She said goodbye and, in a softer voice, added, "A car
is waiting to take you to your hotel for the night. Please don't dally about
with this assignment, Mr. Swanson. We can all hear a clock ticking."

SWANSON CANCELED THE HOTEL booking and directed the driver to go to the Four Seasons hotel in the Paseo de la Reforma. He was glad that his cover job didn't require him to be poor. Money had advantages. He used his cell phone to check into the posh hotel, and put the charge on the Excalibur Industries credit card, an American Express Centurion.

Once in the suite, he stripped down, showered, and pulled on a soft robe, then called room service to get his clothes cleaned and pressed and back to him by six o'clock the next morning. Looking over the menu, he ordered a steak, rare, with potatoes and vegetables. "Add a bottle of Jack Daniel's and bring up a bucket of ice, too," he said. That should take care of his overnight stay. Now, for the hard part. He dialed Coastie.

Her voice was strained. Yes, she said, she understood that he couldn't make the round trip in a single day, only to then turn around and fly to Washington. Some places, such as San Luis de la Paz, are just hard to reach. No, Mama wasn't improving. The blow to her head was serious and the doctor wanted to get her to a hospital. Yes, they were safe. The ranch looked like an armed camp.

"How about you? Are you all right?"

"No, I am most certainly *not* all right," she snapped, her temper rising. "My husband is dead and his grave has been desecrated. Mama is in a bad way, and I feel helpless and crushed. Why aren't you here with me, Kyle?

You're supposed to be my friend." The voice rose louder, then she broke off into sobs.

He looked through the big window out toward the purple mountains as he listened to her weep. "I am your friend, Beth. You know that. You need some time to deal with your grief and take care of Mama Castillo. And I haven't forgotten what you said."

"I want back in."

"I'll be straight with you, Coastie. Keep in mind that this is an unsecure connection. You're way out of shape after three years of marriage and a life of ease. There's no way you could go into the field yet, so if you're serious you have to start a hard PT program and knock off some weight."

"Are you saying I'm fat? I run a mile and work out every day!"

"Not nearly good enough, and you know it. Then get your shooting eye back."

"I can outshoot you right now," she said, fighting.

"This is not a contest between the two of us, Coastie. If everything comes together, and you clear the physical conditioning and a round of psychiatric exams, and if the organization decides it even wants you, then maybe you can come back. Big maybe, girl."

There was silence, and a deep inhalation of breath. "How long would it take, Kyle?"

"At least a year." He hated doing this. This wasn't the sort of support that a knight in shining armor gave a maiden in distress. This also was no fairy tale, and life wasn't fair. "That would be the official deal, so don't say you haven't been warned."

"It sucks." Her growing anger was palpable before she caught what he had said. "The official deal? Are you thinking of something else?"

Ever since his briefing that afternoon, Swanson had been unable to shake the feeling of how alone he really was within the CIA. All special operators were the same in that respect, close to no one and far from God. Unknown bureaucrats would turn on them without a second thought if it was deemed convenient. Their loyalty was to the country and the company, not the individual. He often thought of the old Jabberwock poem about a beast with jaws that bite and claws that catch. He would sound paranoid if he tried to explain it, but facing unknown terrors all by himself had always been a hard, twisting road. He trusted Coastie to remain alongside him if the Jabberwock, the Jubjub bird, or even the frumious Bandersnatch came lurking.

Kyle kept his voice even. "How about this? You stay down here with Mama as long as you need. Then you come up and work directly for me at Excalibur. I think we can have you ready in three months. You interested?"

Beth soaked up the surprise and replied, "Yes, of course."

"Okay, then. Give Mama my best, and we'll stay in close touch. A final question, Coastie. Was Mickey on the payroll of that other outfit that I work for? Careful how you answer."

She thought about it. "He worked with a lot of similar organizations, mostly coordinating efforts, but with your company he actually did some specific tasks now and again. He never gave me details."

Damn. So Mickey was a spook, too. "Keep your head down and your marines close until you leave. Stay strong on the emotional front, too. Time will help."

"It's hard, Kyle. I miss Mickey so much. I can't just sleep and cry all the time."

"I know. We'll talk later." He ended the call, satisfied at having bought another three months before he had to make a final decision.

WASHINGTON, D.C.

THE MEMORIAL TO AMERICA'S third president, Thomas Jefferson, was waterfront property on the National Mall, and a favorite meeting spot for the director of intelligence, the number two man of the Central Intelligence Agency. The Mall was anchored by the needle obelisk of the Washington Monument at one end and the domed Capitol building at the other, with a brooding, iconic Abraham Lincoln dominating the panorama. People by the thousands strolled the Mall daily from one end to the other, but few broke away to trek the mile from the White House to visit Mr. Jefferson's five-ton statue in the neoclassical memorial on the southern bank of the Tidal Basin that was fed by the waters of the Potomac River.

Martin Atkins was on a stadium seat cushion for comfort on the stone steps. Swanson approached, nodded to the security detail, and was allowed through the protective perimeter. At a bit over sixty, Atkins was still a handsome man, but Swanson could see that the job weighed heavily on him. The hair was still thick and full, but it was graying fast. Atkins was an old-time iron pumper, and while his chest remained thick, the shoulders were slumping owing to age, the law of gravity, and the woes of the world. Swanson didn't have a cushion, but sat beside Atkins anyway. The chill of the shaded stone was immediately felt through his jeans. "Hello, boss," he said.

The director folded his *Washington Post* in half, and then in half again. "Dirty business down in Mexico," he said, and blew out a breath.

"Yeah," Swanson replied. It had been an observation, not a question to elicit details. Atkins probably knew more about it than Swanson did.

"We're at war," Atkins declared as he gazed out over the rippling Tidal Basin. "We have the biggest and best intelligence service on the planet, and can barely keep our heads above water."

Swanson remained quiet. The boss would get to the real message in his own time, in his own way.

"The Russians, these ragtag terrorists, the rebellions, the North Koreans, the Los Angeles Dodgers, and those petty African tyrants—and did I mention the damned terrorists?"

"Yes, you did."

"Add in the Congress and the current administration and our budget rivals and the mud-headed media talking heads."

"Sounds like you've had a full day."

"Yes." Atkins stuck the newspaper under his arm. "Which brings me to you, Young Skywalker. I have to deal with all this other shit from morning till night, and I damned well don't need another problem like the one you've handed me."

"Wait a minute, Marty. I didn't do anything but go to a friend's funeral."

"Bullshit, Kyle. Somehow you're involved in this thing, and that places the agency in jeopardy from an unexpected quarter. I've ordered an internal investigation to see what they can figure out."

"You want me to talk to them?"

"Of course. Private and confidential. Moreover, I'm assigning you to personally resolve this matter, whatever it is. Clear it up, try not to leave too many stains on the carpet, and turn this problem into a solution. I have enough problems of my own."

Swanson shook his head slowly. "I was told you would give me a file on that guy down in Mexico."

Marty Atkins stood and turned to look at the statue of the man who wrote the Declaration of Independence. "That Tom Jefferson was one smart fellow," he observed. "JFK once told a group of Nobel Prize laureates having dinner at the White House that the place had never seen such brilliance except for when Jefferson dined alone."

"The file, sir?"

"Tommy J. also warned that our nation must continually change to keep pace with the times. He had no idea what he was forecasting." Atkins looked down at Swanson. "Change is happening at light-speed all around us, and we're struggling to stay in front of it or risk getting run over. I really don't need this Mexico thing on my plate, Kyle. Take care of it. Read this newspaper." The director leaned over and picked up his cushion and walked away, drawing the three-man security detail with him.

He left the folded newspaper on the steps.

Inside, Swanson found a plain manila folder sealed with tape.

NICKY MARKS WAS ONE sick puppy. Just reading the CIA dossier was hard work. Swanson had gone to a pub before delving into the information, and was glad to have a strong drink at hand as he leafed through the documents.

Nikola Markovitch had emerged from the Soviet Union as it fell apart. He leveraged his knowledge of several languages and his military training to become a hired gun for one of the Russian mobs for several years.

Apparently pretty good at doing dirty work for the new-blood billionaires, Markovitch saw that job as having a limited future because there was a very high mortality rate among the enforcers. At that point, he found a job in which he might not be murdered in his sleep by a friend, and became a mercenary about the time the invasion of Iraq opened respectable horizons for homeless and stateless soldiers. Markovitch was soon wearing desert-class sunglasses, a big mustache and camouflage uniforms, and being paid well by a private security company based in the United States. He didn't shy away from the occasionally messy work.

It was in Iraq that he first popped up on the CIA's radar. Leafing through a few pages of photographs, Swanson saw a man who clearly enjoyed his work. The guy loved a good battle, was merciless toward his enemies, and extraordinarily efficient. Swanson also saw another picture developing: that of a man with absolutely no loyalty, not even to his own name.

Ten years ago, Marks stepped completely into the shadows and became a special contract operator for the Central Intelligence Agency. Here was a man who would do anything, and without a second thought. No clandestine operator could be asked to do more than that. The agency rewarded him with full American citizenship and a personal history that included a Social Security number and a bank account into which deposits were made directly, discreetly, and legally. He threw away the old name and became Nicky Marks because it was easier for his paymasters to write and pronounce, and to convince themselves that he was a true-blue, faithful U.S. citizen.

Swanson was halfway through a fresh bourbon and ice when it dawned on him that Nicky Marks was no longer a spring chicken. The years had passed in a hurry, and the enthusiasm that had stamped his early career seemed to have abandoned him, as had his two wives and three estranged children. According to the assessment of his profile, the personal troubles didn't interfere with his work. He still got his jobs done with a minimum of fanfare. His handlers kept him around because he suited their requirements like a domesticated cat with sharp claws. He did what he was told. No more, no less.

Swanson closed the file. If that was so, then why was Nicky Marks with that tractor in Mexico? The simple answer was that he was there because someone paid him to be there. Maybe some event had changed his style and he needed money, and the cartels were calling. Maybe he missed the old days. Maybe he wasn't tame at all.

Swanson concluded that the guy was a killer who had fallen in love with the power and the money, a double whammy that possessed him as tightly as religion grasps a fanatic. That was all there was in his world, he was good at it, and nothing else gave the same buzz and satisfied him as much as being a paid assassin. Swanson ticked off some indicators: the total disregard for laws or the rights of other people, no feelings of guilt or remorse, and a tendency toward violence—all apparently masked by a charming personality. It was all there in the paperwork. Bottom line was that Nicky Marks was just a garden-variety, run-of-the-mill psychopath.

Alongside a tractor.

T HE HUNT FOR NICKY Marks began with a thorough electronic scrub of the massive computerized U.S. databases, where hits on the name popped out like pimples on the face of an unlucky teenager. Signs of Marks were all over the place. Cell phones, landlines, frequently visited Web sites, personal contacts, a passport, bank accounts, credit-card buys, and even a pair of overdue parking violations in Charlotte, North Carolina. It all led nowhere. Each address led to a post-office box in Washington, D.C., in ZIP code 20505, and the listed phone number was 703-482-0623. Both were public contact points of the Central Intelligence Agency.

The scattered information was all just the debris of a false life, bread-crumbs spread carefully over the years. It was an elaborate personal cover story, probably concocted with the help of the CIA itself, and proved nothing. Marks had become a Nowhere Man. The thick dossier didn't contain a résumé of jobs that Nicky Marks had performed with government authority and permission.

However, just because someone wanted to vanish didn't mean he could. Nobody lived in a post-office box. The real trail had to begin within the CIA itself. Marks obviously didn't punch a clock, so someone had to be his primary contact—if it wasn't his boss at the top of the food chain, which would be Marty Atkins, then at least the intermediary between a plan and the man.

Marty had included an abbreviated history on the field operative who dealt with Marks. The CIA identification photo showed a man of thirty-three, with a square jaw and a slightly sloping brow that seemed bigger because he made no attempt to cover the creeping baldness. Instead, his brown hair was cut very short, very exact, with the touch of a stylist. The face was deeply tanned. It was not a Florida tan or the product of a tanning booth or a liquid spray but, rather, the product of months of working outdoors beneath a hot desert sun. Squint lines burrowed at the corners of brown eyes that looked straight at the camera lens. The name was Lucas Gibson. The thing that leaped out was that he had no military record. Swanson flipped back through the pages and there was no mention of Gibson serving. Why would Atkins leave out something so important and basic?

Swanson puzzled over that as he finished his drink, then went into his room to start packing. Arrangements had been made, and he would be on a plane across the Atlantic first thing tomorrow.

BERLIN, GERMANY

THE GRAY GERMAN SKY began leaking as night fell, dragging a curtain of light rain up the River Spree, along with white blades of lightning and the smell of burned ozone. Pedestrians ran for cover to wait it out. Kyle Swanson paid the fare on the taxi meter and dashed across a sidewalk and up the stone steps of the Restaurant Äpfel. He brushed away drops clinging to his coat as he stepped inside. A tiny Asian hostess, tightly wrapped neck to knees in a crinkly black dress, smiled with emerald eyes. "Guten tag."

"Hello," he responded, peeling out of his damp topcoat. "Do you speak English?" Her nametag read "Aurora." He was guessing Filipina.

"Of course," she bubbled in silky reply. "Do you have a reservation?"

"Yes, I'm meeting another gentleman. The reservation is for Herr Schmidt." That was one of the most common surnames in Germany, and similar to using Jones in America.

"Herr Schmidt is already waiting at table, sir. Please follow me." She spun and walked confidently down the aisle, her doll-like figure pulling all male attention away from other matters. She pushed through the potted palms that lined the back wall and opened a set of pocket doors to reveal a private dining area. Luke Gibson was sipping a drink.

The Berlin rendezvous was frequented by foreigners who enjoyed dining later than the average German. The menu mirrored eateries in New York or London. Marty Atkins wanted the men to meet at a neutral site and keep things as far as possible from Washington. Swanson had flown in via London, with time to spare. Gibson was spirited out of Afghanistan aboard a private plane of the Air Branch of the CIA Special Activities Division, the latest incarnation of the infamous Air America from the Indochina days. Reality does not die; it just changes names, and the agency always needed its own birds for special work.

"Ah," Gibson said with a grin. "So you're Kyle Swanson. From everything I've heard, I expected you to be about nine feet tall."

Swanson sized him up. Usually a soldier's lifestyle slides inexorably away when he becomes a civilian and sheds that skin. The demanding military schedule, the regimentation, the automatic authority, the chain of command, and even the physical bearing erode, for his life no longer depends on such things. Luke Gibson was way beyond that. He was squared away, but in a totally civilian manner, as if born to wear a trooper's uniform without ever having done so.

They didn't shake hands. Swanson gave his coat to Aurora, who withdrew and closed the doors. A low cello melody oozed from hidden speakers and the lighting was subdued, a combination that provided a sense of isolation in the huge city. He eased into a chair and got down to business. "Where can I find Nicky Marks?"

Gibson took a slow sip from a heavy crimson drink, savoring it. "Well, hello to you, too. They create a helluva Bloody Mary here. Finlandia vodka, the usual veggies and crumbles of bacon. Bacon improves everything."

Swanson leaned forward and put his elbows on the table. "I'm not here to talk about bacon, and it's too late in the day for a Bloody Mary. Director Atkins said you're the Marks contact."

Gibson avoided the challenge by raising his glass again and drinking before he answered. "It's a good drink, no matter what the time or place. You remember in the *MASH* movie, about Korea, how the new surgeon demanded an olive in his martini? Some things make the world a better place." Gibson took the slice of celery from his drink, bit off a piece, and crunched. Swanson remained silent.

Finally, Gibson spoke again. "Yeah, Nicky was one of mine; apparently, he's decided to go out on his own. He's a very talented boy, and with a high market value. You won't find him."

Swanson felt a sudden jolt of anger, remembering the cemetery explosion that desecrated the grave of his good friend. "Can you still contact him?"

"Let's hypothesize about that for a moment, Mr. Swanson. If you went rogue and did something horrible, would you ever let anyone find you?"

Swanson studied the calm man across the table and was reminded of the proverb that the eyes are windows to the soul. Gibson was unflustered, outwardly open and friendly, but if the old saying was accurate, then Swanson was looking at a rat's nest of a soul, a place filled with spiders and screams. "Maybe you didn't understand me, so I repeat: Can you still contact him?"

Gibson pushed his drink aside and folded his hands as the grin vanished. "Don't patronize me, Swanson. Nicky is in the wind. As the boys and girls at Langley probably told you before you left, all his accounts have been closed, his apartment was abandoned after being wiped clean, the hard drive on his company laptop contained nothing of value because it had been drilled multiple times, and none of his friends have a clue where he went. His girlfriend says he dumped her two weeks ago. There has been no activity on cell phones, because he only uses burners. Nicky is in the fucking wind."

Swanson filtered that. If Marks had dumped the girlfriend two weeks ago, that meant the assassin had laid out his getaway before even showing up in Mexico. That suggested meticulous planning. "I'm getting tired of you dancing around my question, Gibson. Can you or can you not contact this shitbird?"

"I tried right after I got the summons from Atkins. No luck." He shrugged. "I was out in the middle of Afghanistan at the time. I don't know where he is."

"Or why he bailed?"

"Probably money, because it sure as hell wasn't out of loyalty or idealism, or any flag or religion. As I said, Nicky is gone." Gibson spread his empty hands palms up.

"Then we have both wasted trips to Berlin." Swanson prepared to rise but stopped at a passing thought. "What was his hook to Mexico?"

"Unknown. To me, the whole thing smacks of drugs. Maybe some cartel hired him. Those people throw around good paychecks for this line of labor. He had done some enforcer work before, back in the day."

"When was the last time you saw him?"

"About six weeks ago, in Kabul. Nicky was cool then. He seemed perfectly normal. At least, as normal as he ever was."

Swanson disagreed about the cartels. "The drug lords in Mexico keep whole death squads at the ready; plus, they have local cops and military on their payroll. Why reach all the way to Afghanistan to bring in an expensive specialist?"

Gibson regained his pleasant attitude. Swanson noted that the strong shoulders had relaxed. "No fucking idea, other than that Marks is very, very good. Somebody knew somebody who knew somebody who knew somebody else who recommended him. His name has gotten around quite a bit among the jihadis and they put a reward on his head, with no luck. If they couldn't kill him, why not just get him a new job somewhere else? Like I said, Nicky is a great mercenary. He would go to a high bidder. I can't blame him for being tired of Afghanistan. I am, too."

Swanson sighed with frustration and started to get up from the table. "I'll ask him all that when I find him. And I will find him, eventually."

The easy smile remained. "Maybe I misspoke, Swanson. When I said you wouldn't get him, I really meant only that you will never find him by yourself." Gibson shifted his position, leaning forward, switching gears as a negotiator. "Look, I'm as pissed off as you are about this. A recruit I brought in and trained has bolted over to the bad guys and did an abominable thing to your friend in Mexico. Nicky has dirtied my own reputation, and the agency will hold me responsible for allowing him to go off the reservation. Hell, I may lose my job."

Swanson sat back down. "You have my attention."

The tanned face turned serious, and the crow's-feet deepened as he squinted. "I suggest that we work together. We'll use every tool the company has available, every trick in the book and some that aren't in any books, trace Nicky to his hidey-hole, wherever it may be, and then blow the fucker away."

"We should partner up?" Swanson was surprised by the suggestion. "No way."

"It makes sense. You and I are probably the tops in our weird game, and Nicky isn't far behind with his skill set. Director Atkins wants him off the board and buried. So do you. So do I."

"I work better alone," Swanson said.

"Snipers work best in teams. You know that. How many shooters have you taught that rule?" Gibson had spent a lot of time doctoring this pitch before making it. Could Swanson deny his own doctrines?

That was a cold fact, and Swanson knew it. Was it not the reason that he was even considering bringing Coastie back to work? The difference was experience and trust. She had proved herself repeatedly as being able to cover his back in combat, and they made an excellent team, while he had just met Luke Gibson. There was no foundation here.

Gibson went on, "I just finished a gig up in the Badlands, and my partner was locally trained by the Green Berets. Asshole nearly got me killed. I think the damned mule we used to carry the gear was smarter. For me to work with a guy like you would be a privilege; plus, it would increase the odds of bringing Nicky down."

That made some sense. "Tell you what, Mr. Gibson. I'll think about it overnight and run the idea past the director. Meet me back here tomorrow, same time. And, if I agree, you be ready to tell me everything you know about Marks. Maybe we can work something out."

Gibson's smile broke out again. "Okay, you got a deal. Hey! Since we're done here, you want to go have some dinner or a drink?"

"Maybe tomorrow. My body clock is messed up after the long flight. Enjoy the rest of your Bloody Mary."

"Nah, I don't like drinking alone. The company booking agent said you didn't approve of their low-range hotel and upgraded to the Radisson Blu on your own dime. They did the same with me, so I changed over to the Hilton. Bureaucrats have strange priorities. He'll be pissed that both of us ignored his picks."

"Our meeting was supposed to be secret," Swanson observed.

"Good luck with that. Every time I go on a job I worry about the long logistics tail. How many people were involved in just getting us together tonight? Dozens? No such thing as a secret."

Swanson had to agree. "Yeah. Well. Anyway, I'm out of here."

"I'm going in the same direction for a few blocks. If the rain has stopped, I'll walk with you. Maybe I can find a nice warm bar with friendly women who are eager to please."

Swanson retrieved his coat from Aurora and the two men exited onto a broad sidewalk that meandered along the River Spree and sloped down beyond a protective hedgerow to the water's edge. They turned north. The rain had passed, leaving a misty overcast that dulled the glare of the city lights. Cars and trucks were a steady ribbon of illumination. On their left, the broad river flowed dark and swift. Boat traffic was minimal, because the Spree was too narrow to be a significant maritime route.

"What was it about Marks that made you recruit him in the first place?" Swanson shoved his hands deep inside his coat pockets as they walked.

Gibson, in a climber's coat, fished out a cigarette and lit it with the practiced flip of an old metal Zippo. "I had watched him work a couple of times when he was attached to merc units. He was so cool under fire that he made it look easy. I checked his records and thought he showed some promise, so I brought him aboard in starter work like recon. Within six weeks, I knew I'd found a winner." Gibson exhaled and the breeze snatched away the ribbon of smoke. "Langley loved him because he didn't worry about unusual assignments. He would push the envelope without changing his heartbeat."

"So they took over? Trained him up?"

"Yeah." He inhaled deeply, then exhaled and flicked the butt. It twirled away like a little spinning torch. "You know the drill. Time passed and a lot of bosses punched his ticket. I was just the middleman."

"If that ticket has a lot of fingerprints, then it's no wonder the agency's nervous. There might be a lot of blame to go around for him going rogue," Swanson said, then paused. "So somebody back in the States was actually running him?"

Gibson looked up at the tall buildings, then down to street level. Snipers always kept their eyes moving. "Don't know, man. Beyond my pay grade."

A cream-colored automobile with a glowing yellow taxi sign on top abruptly broke from the line of oncoming traffic. The engine revved and the front wheels cut toward them. Swanson noticed that the passenger window was sliding open just as Luke Gibson hit him with a shoulder block that took them both to the ground. They fell to the left, over and through a waist-high border of shrubs and flowers, then down the grassy slope toward the water.

A small oval object flew from the window of the car, hit the pavement, bounced once, then caught in the hedgerow and exploded.

Swanson and Gibson were slashed with dirt and leaves, while the hot shrapnel of a hand grenade trimmed the greenery. By the time they raised their heads, the car had disappeared.

"You okay?" Swanson was brushing off his hair and face. The blast had gone over them, but the dirt and grass had showered down. His ears were ringing.

Gibson was on his hands and knees, coughing. "Yeah." The man from Afghanistan wiped at his clothing.

"The good news is we didn't get our dumb asses killed. The even better news is that we're not going to have to look far to find Nicky Marks. He threw that grenade. The bastard was laughing as he went by."

A GAIN?" MARTY ATKINS, BACK at CIA headquarters in Virginia, was on an encrypted call to Berlin, his voice incredulous. "You were attacked again by the same guy? In another country? Impossible!"

"Not impossible, Marty. I just picked a shard of metal out of my coat. It was about as hard and real as I care to get."

Luke Gibson was also near the speakerphone. "Positive identification, sir. I saw him clearly. It was Nicky Marks who threw the grenade."

There was a pause while everyone digested that information. "I also think it was a bullshit piece of playacting, sir," said Gibson. "If Nicky had really wanted to kill us tonight, we would be dead meat. Instead, he flips a grenade from a passing car—almost like a kid with a firecracker."

"Why?" Atkins remained confused.

Swanson said, "To get our attention? To send a message? Who knows? The point is, Marty, that, once again, all three corners of this incident have CIA connections, just like in Mexico."

"With you as the common link," the director of intelligence said.

"He knew exactly where we were. That means there's a leak in the information stovepipe, boss." Gibson rubbed his palms, but showed no other sign of concern.

The director of intelligence knew that a bad situation had just gotten worse. "I'll tighten the information flow on this end and try to deal directly with the two of you from now on," he said. "This new incident may be a break we can use. Right now, you're all in the same city. Kyle, I want you and Luke to work together until we nail this guy and find out what he's up to. Swanson is the lead."

Swanson tensed. He had just been saddled with a partner not of his choosing. "Yes, sir."

"Gibson, are you on board with that?"

"Yes, sir. We'll find him. We have to work with the Germans, though."

Atkins was somber about that idea. The incident had happened on German soil, so there was no way to remain totally independent. And Gibson was right: they would need help. "Very well, I'll contact the GSG Nine and you work with them. Keep it away from the locals."

Over the years, Swanson had forged a good relationship with the élite counterterrorism and special-operations unit known as the Grenz-schutzgruppe 9 der Bundespolizei, which was always shortened to GSG 9. It was excellent, but the promised stoppage of information at the Washington end had just as quickly been opened on the other, and the short hairs began to tickle his neck. How could they hope to keep the incident away from the police when GSG 9 was technically a police unit and not a military team?

"Marty, I don't like the way this is going," he said. "This guy has tried to kill me twice in a week and I'm getting pretty tired of him, but we're moving too fast. I want to work alone; no cops, no partner—particularly someone like Gibson here, whom I just met—and with much less bureaucracy. It will be impossible to close the information channels, but the fewer people involved the better."

Gibson looked across the table. "I saved your life tonight."

"I appreciate that, and no offense intended, Luke, but it changes nothing. We are not a team."

Atkins stopped them. "With no backup, you'll be a sitting duck for Nicky Marks. It's an order, Kyle. You and Luke work it out. And you have to be debriefed by the GSG Nine people. It's not exactly a secret that somebody threw a grenade in the middle of Berlin tonight. They'll want answers."

Swanson scratched an ear. "What's happening is that we're playing by rules being set by Nicky Marks. He tried to kill me twice and failed, because I was sloppy. If we throw a full deck of operators at him, he'll just run away. If we don't, then he'll be emboldened to try again, whatever his reason. Next time, he loses. If you want me to be the lead on this, let me lead."

"What do you think, Luke?"

"If Swanson wants to take that chance, fine by me. He's hung up on the whole 'partner' thing, but that's okay. I can be his backup and his single contact with the agency. He doesn't want a high profile, so I can deal with the cops and the stuff he might need. After all, I'm the one who knows Marks best."

"Done, then. You guys make it work. Let's find out what's making Nicky Marks tick."

YUCATÁN, MEXICO

THE SNIPER COULD SMELL the green of the subtropical jungle of the Yucatán Peninsula. The playground of Cancún was on the toe of the north-facing boot, but outside the tourist haunts the ancient forests still ruled. An underlying stench of rotting vegetation was the predominant odor, and everything was so green the color was almost tangible. It was a palette that spread from bright harlequin to somber avocado, accented by the shadows of the sunlight that fell through the leaves in graceful lines and the long vines that crept around the jungle floor. The sniper's clothing matched the tangled surroundings. A handmade Ghillie suit stuffed with twigs and leaves and vegetation belied any telltale sign that a human being was underneath it all. Even the skin of the rifle and the optics tube were camouflaged.

Perched among the curling roots of old trees, the shooter felt invisible to the target, Ramiro Delgado, who hadn't even glanced toward the brush line in the past hour. He was too busy selling drugs and making money. The Mexican cops wouldn't arrest an American for carrying or using a small amount of almost any drug, but a dealer wouldn't be as lucky. A vehicle would come along the busy main road out of Cancún and turn left at the crossroad that led south toward El Naranjal, making two more turns onto roads even less traveled until it found Delgado's mighty GMC Sierra pickup parked in a clearing.

The informant had said that young Ramiro was rich for his age because he operated an all-service drug emporium on wheels, complete with a sophisticated communications suite. He alerted his clientele of the day's marketing location by Wi-Fi message. The informant was to be one of the day's customers.

The drugs that Ramiro Delgado carried in the spacious truck bed would be dealt out on a cash basis, cut and resold on the streets of Cancún and Cozumel and up and down the Yucatán coast. Business had been brisk. The sniper waited, not wanting to attract attention by having to contend with collateral damage. Not that killing two dealers instead of one mattered. It's just that it was an unnecessary complication.

The slender Delgado spoke with the latest arrival at his truck, as he carefully counted through the wad of U.S. bills, then stuffed it in his pocket and walked to the back of the truck to pull out two cardboard boxes. He sliced one open with a knife and handed a small plastic bag—a *bolsita*—of cocaine to the buyer, who also took out a knife and opened the baggie.

The customer liked what he tasted and stuffed the tiny bag into a shirt pocket, gave his supplier a fist bump for luck, took both boxes, and drove away. Ramiro had cut the coke earlier, and the contents would be diluted even further in a final bit of processing before being peddled at a price of about half a gram for ten U.S. dollars. By then, the product had been reduced to a point that bore little resemblance to the original pure syrup but still packed a powerful kick.

It made no difference to the sniper. Heroin, syringes, cocaine were all part of the drug food chain that would slake the thirsts of partying tourists and Mexicans alike, and maybe even reach up into Texas and farther north, with the price escalating at every step. What was ridiculously cheap for an American tourist in Mexico would be borderline expensive in Connecticut.

The sniper watched him go, then returned the scope to young Mr. Delgado. How old? About twenty-one? Not even shaving yet. Fuck him.

The wind was quiet as the sniper made the final adjustments on the Leupold Mark 4 scope, the distance exactly lasered, and it was time to shoot. Delgado made a note on a little pad, put the money in a safe beneath the front seat, then started punching information into his computer to summon his next customer. He sat very still in the front seat, concentrating on his work.

The sniper inhaled a soft breath, keeping things calm, let it escape, and barely felt the tightness of the trigger as it began to depress, ever so slowly, until it tripped and the M110 rifle fired, its bark reduced thirty percent by the stainless-steel suppressor on the end of the barrel. Even so, creatures were surprised and began their flights and chatter even as the 7.62×51-mm. round took Delgado in the left side, pulping the heart and spinning around the rib cage when it crunched bone. The body spilled across the seat like Jell-O poured from a mold.

Elizabeth Ledford Castillo took an easy aim and shot a second time, the bullet going into the drug dealer's butt and up the torso. One shot, one kill—and one more just for the hell of it. No arrest, no trial, no Judge Judy to arbitrate—no mercy for the little worm.

"Enough, señora. We must leave now," said the former Mexican marine who had been her spotter for the job.

She wanted to rush the other way, across the clearing and to the body, where she could dip her fingers in the blood of Delgado and scrawl THIS IS FOR MICKEY on the truck. Instead, she nodded and began to slide backward out of the hide. "Yes."

While the marine stood a cautious overwatch nearby, Coastie peeled out of the Ghillie rig and changed into a modest faded blue top, old jeans and boots, then pulled her blond hair back into a ponytail. She washed her face and hands and came back to the real world. It would not do for the grieving Señora Castillo to be seen as some sort of alien creature. She felt good, even a bit bouncy, as she cranked up the four-wheel-drive vehicle and headed off. Not bad for the first time out, she thought.

A bit ragged, but not bad at all. The marine stayed behind to clean up the site.

AFGHANISTAN

THE DEMISE OF MAHFOUZ al-Rashidi, warlord of the Wakham Corridor, not only left a sizable hole in the ground but also threatened to disrupt the tattered nation's largest industry: opium. Under normal circumstances, the eldest son would have stepped into the breach and kept the chain intact. With all four of the old man's heirs also killed in the attack, things in the Wakham Corridor were in disarray.

The entire area was not the common desert color of brown. At this time of year, it was a shiny bright poppy pink. The fragile ecosystem and the semi-arid climate had created a landscape that was almost perfect for the cultivation of the drug, and far enough away from the war zones that farmers could till their crops in relative safety. The righteous al-Rashidi had turned a blind eye to the trade, for the growers had paid tribute to the warlord who kept them safe. He, in turn, shared the tax upwards with the current reigning power in the region, whether that was the United States, the Taliban, ISIS, the Chinese, the Pakistanis, or the government in faraway Kabul. Over the years, the policy had been mutually beneficial, as the opium trade soared in importance and outstripped the next most successful crops by a three-to-one ratio. Millions of dollars were made by the time the product reached the addicts on foreign streets. Farmers could not only survive; they could get rich.

Now it was springtime, the cold of winter warming to a gorgeous temperature, and as the snow melted in the mountains to spill into the rivers and feed the poppies, al-Rashidi was no longer at the rudder to steady his peculiar ship. Nature did not abhor a vacuum any more than did the flourishing opiate economy of Afghanistan, which furnished ninety percent of the entire world supply.

Qari Abdul Razaq shook his head in worry as he read the reports of a small unit of Taliban fighters that had investigated the attack in the

Wakham. There was no doubt that the entire circle of adult males in the family had been wiped out, and the villagers of Girdiwal were already disorganized. Some farmers eyed the situation as an opportunity to settle old scores or grab new land for cultivation, or both. Opium money propped up the Taliban, and couldn't be ignored.

"We have to make a new alliance," Razaq said as he spread the two-page document on his desk. He wore clean robes, but his beard was long and ragged, in accordance with Taliban rules that forbade shaving. Razak was hundreds of miles away from the Wakham Corridor, seated in his neat and spacious office in Doha, Qatar, the tiny Gulf State oil boomtown that provided the Taliban with a diplomatic window to the world. Razaq was much closer to the Al Udeid Air Base than he was to the battlefields of his home country, where the U.S. military was still at war with the Taliban, and the ISIS usurpers. The American troops were run by the U.S. Central Command headquartered out at the Al Udeid base, not far from his front door. Qari Abdul Razaq had gone full circle. He had been part of the mujahideen delegation that visited President Ronald Reagan at the White House in 1983 to show solidarity against the Soviet invaders of Afghanistan. Then in 1989, when the Russians left, he chose to work in the Taliban rebellion, which did stupid things in the name of religious law. The 9/11 attack on the Twin Towers was carried out by Osama bin Laden and Al Qaeda, although the Taliban had granted them safe haven in the Afghan wilds. So the Americans came charging in, only to quickly spin away to invade Iraq and topple Saddam Hussein, then allow ISIS to grow in his place. In Afghanistan today, the U.S. and the Taliban were bitter enemies; in Doha, they were neighbors. It was an international house of mirrors.

"I agree," responded the civilian-clothed army colonel who represented the Pakistani intelligence service. "And the sooner the better."

They were speaking English for the convenience of the third man in the meeting, who asked, "And if we put a lid on it nothing changes?"

"Exactly," answered Qari Abdul Razaq. "We will figure out the loyalties later, but right now we need to put a successor in there so as not to lose the whole crop. We will support him for a year and see how it goes."

"Avoid a flash point," said the colonel. His English had a clipped flavor to it, like that of many Pakistani military officers, a unique accent left over from the days of the British Raj and training at Sandhurst.

"Do you have somebody in mind, Qari?" the third man asked.

"Yes. He is a middle-aged mullah of the same village, and his eldest son is a rather shy fellow who would much prefer the safety of the Wakham Corridor with his family than continuing to fight a war in which he is certain to be killed. With our combined backing, they can pick up right where al-Rashidi left off."

"That should settle things for a while. Let the poppies grow in peace for another season," said the Pakistani.

"Yeah. All right." The third man rose and straightened his blue suit. "Do it, and I'll inform the Prince."

The Taliban minister threw a verbal jab along with a polite smile. "We would not have this problem at all if your people had not killed al-Rashidi and his boys in the first place."

"Fat chance. We're not going to allow a new Osama bin Laden to rise. They shouldn't have been mucking about with ideas of taking out the Houston oil complex and Hollywood with biochemical weapons."

"Yes. We had our eyes on him from the start," said the Taliban negotiator. "We also were not going to allow him or the boys to actually carry out a strike, but had to let them play at a doomsday catastrophe to keep them happy. After all, who gave you the human intelligence on the plan?"

"You did, my friend, indeed you did. In your debt on that." He started toward the door. "And one last thing: I was never at this meeting."

"Of course not," Qari told his American friend from the Central Intelligence Agency. "Please give my humble regards to the Prince."

BERLIN, GERMANY

LUKE GIBSON ARRIVED AT the Alexanderplatz Radisson Blu Hotel only to discover that Kyle Swanson had checked out and departed last night. No note had been left. There was no forwarding address. After wrapping up the grueling GSG 9 debriefing, they had agreed to meet for breakfast at nine o'clock, then hire a private car to take them out to the Berlin Tegel Airport for their Lufthansa flight to Washington. "Well," Luke muttered to himself, standing in the lobby and staring blankly at the giant aquarium. "This sucks."

He went to a little café nearby and took a table, gave the snotty waiter his order, then opened his phone. No message from Swanson. Where was he? Gibson called the local CIA. They had nothing other than that Swanson was due in Washington that afternoon via Lufthansa to Dulles. That ain't gonna happen, Gibson mused, but didn't say anything. He looked out over the broad avenue. It was a beautiful morning in Berlin, and even the abrupt service by the waiter couldn't really put Gibson in a foul mood, because he was learning things.

Working with Kyle Swanson was going to be difficult if Swanson didn't want him along. That was why Gibson hadn't put up a fight over being dismissed as a partner. The fuckin' super-sniper works alone. Okay, so be it. There would be less resistance when Swanson had to reach out for beans or bullets and Gibson would be there to help. It wasn't as if Swanson had a lot of choice in the matter if he wanted to keep the operation secret. And in the background lurked the evil specter of Nicky Marks. Gibson willed himself to be patient, to ride it out. Good things would eventually happen.

Gibson bit into a monster of a *Berliner*, the mother of all doughnuts, and felt the sugar rush. Tourists wandered by, maps in hand. Gibson drank coffee, which perked him up even more. He should be mad at Marty Atkins, if anyone. The director of intelligence had turned to him for the premier assignments until Swanson came along. Nowadays, he was lucky to get a high-value job at all, and the new guy got the best assignments. There was no use trying to convince himself that Swanson wasn't a great shooter, but Gibson doubted that the former marine was actually better overall at the job. For one thing, Gibson was younger, and trigger time wasn't the only measurement. He believed Swanson had lost his edge, a victim of age who was pulling along the clanking debris of a long and difficult military life. Swanson was almost a dour old prisoner in a golden cage, while Gibson considered himself to be a free spirit who was current with the times and in his prime.

The bottom line was that Marty Atkins worshipped the guy. Gibson was number two. It was a hard place to find himself after being number one for so long. He finished his breakfast, flopped some bills on the table, and walked back to the hotel parking lot to retrieve the rental car. Like any good hunter, the sniper knew the secret was patience; he would just let Kyle Swanson come to him. Meanwhile, where the hell was he?

ABOARD THE EUROSTAR

SWANSON WAS HALFWAY TO London, relaxed in a premier seat aboard the Eurostar train that was dashing beneath the English Channel. He had left the Radisson Blu and caught the 10:14 PM City Night Line overnight sleeper to Paris. The train rocked him to sleep in a deluxe cabin, and less than fourteen hours later he was transferring to the Eurostar for London, and enjoying *un petit déjeuner* of strong coffee and a warm croissant. He wasn't hiding, exactly, but he also hadn't told anyone where he was heading. No use in advertising his whereabouts unnecessarily.

After reading a newspaper, Swanson plugged in his laptop, hooked up to the train's onboard Wi-Fi, and from that to a private server, to send a text message to Beth Ledford. France was seven hours ahead of Mexico, so it was midnight for her. The Skype app remained off because he didn't want to be overheard, and she probably wouldn't want to be seen.

You awake? If not, call me first thing in the morning.

He hit the Send key and waited. There was a ping of response as Coastie came online, and they slid into a silent conversation.

Hi. I'm still up. Can't sleep hardly at all. U kno?

I know. Where are you?

At Mickey's cousin on the Yuc Peninsula. Secure. Mama C is still hurting, but will pull thru. Where u?

In Europe on business. I wanted to check on you. Remember that job offer?

Sure. Sounds good. I'm not quite ready to come up yet. Tying up some loose ends down here. It is hard, Kyle . . . I miss Mick so much. Cry a lot. I'm still training, tho.

Natural to cry. You're just about where you're supposed to be in the grieving process, Coastie. Staying busy will help. I want to move up your timetable. Things have changed.

????

I need a bodyguard. Can't give details by text.

WTF ?!?

Same guy from the funeral tried again in Berlin. Situation urgent. Please get up to Washington SAP. Excalibur pays well.

OK. Just a few more days here.

Good. See you in Washington. Tnx and bye. Get sleep.

Swanson closed the laptop with a sense of quiet satisfaction as the train rushed through the Chunnel on its two-hour-and-fifteen-minute journey. The iPod music fed a playlist through the earbuds and helped him calm his mind.

He thought about Luke Gibson, how he seemed to be a nice guy and how he was obviously good, or else Marty Atkins wouldn't be using him. And he had proved his fast reflexes in the grenade attack. Swanson was already ducking away when the device was thrown, but Gibson had moved even faster. Age? So, yes, maybe they could work together, as long as Swanson got to make the decisions.

The real problem wasn't with Gibson as an individual. The Marine Corps had been Swanson's home for many years, and that meant he could always trust his fellow marines. It was automatic. It was why after moving on to other pursuits in life marines always had a bond with other marines. The brotherhood was tight. Luke Gibson wasn't a marine. He may not have been anything.

Coastie wasn't a marine, either, not really. Task Force Trident was mostly a marine special-ops outfit when she came aboard from the Coast Guard. It was a tight family of equals, all superior at their jobs, and she had fit right in and might well have worn the Corps' eagle, globe, and anchor insignia. The big thing at the moment was that she wasn't with the CIA, either. Swanson intended to cross up whoever was the behind-the-scenes master of this morbid game by bringing in a ringer.

More out-of-the-loop help was waiting at the other end of this train ride. Gibson didn't need to know any of that.

MEXICO

BETH LEDFORD TURNED OFF her cell phone and put it away for the night. She would never carry it on a mission, because the accidental push of a button might result in unwanted beeping or lights flashing at the worst possible time. She checked herself in the full-length mirror mounted behind the door of her bedroom. It was good that Kyle hadn't wanted to Skype, because she would have had to refuse, claiming modesty or some other lame excuse. He probably would have wanted to know why her face was striped in nonreflective green and black camo paint, why her yellow hair was tucked beneath a black knit watch cap, and why she was dressed in a black shirt, jeans, and boots. That made her smile as she gave a final check to the Sig Sauer P226 handgun that she had chosen for the night. It was a bit big for her hands, but it was reliable. Having personally polished each of the dozen .40 S&W cartridges, she pushed in the magazine and locked one in the chamber. No need for a holster. Coastie shoved the pistol into the waistband of her jeans.

Another one of Mickey's boys, a sergeant, was waiting for her with the car and made no comment when she climbed inside. The entire squad backed the señora's quiet campaign of revenge for the death of her husband. The little woman was a serious warrior.

The first hit in the forest had taken out a middleman distributor belonging to the Villareal Organization. Tonight she would dispose of a leader of the rival Beltran Brothers tribe. Neither gang was a major cartel, but they were growing and were always ready to protect their turf through bullets, knives, acid baths, or beheadings. Coastie wanted to spark a fight and let them kill one another rather than her having to do it. She figured she could do her new job with Kyle in Washington and still get down to Mexico on vacation. After all, she had family here.

As they drove away from the city, Coastie started breathing deeply and shutting down her emotions, letting her body and mind slow down and focus. It took only fifteen minutes to get to the beach road, and the car slowed for a curve. "Good luck, señora," said the driver as he tapped the brakes once and Coastie rolled out the door and into soft sand.

A side road fed off toward the water, and she jogged down it quietly, unseen in the shadows. The house was straight ahead now, with no lights burning. Manuel Beltran was asleep. Beth made herself comfortable in a ditch, pulled on some night-vision goggles, and watched the single guard make his rounds. The man was so bored that he hardly looked beyond his feet. There was no movement inside the house. By about two o'clock, the fat guard was nodding off in a sagging beach chair on the patio with his weapon across his knees. Coastie moved like a black cat, a shadow lost in the other shadows. A hop over the rail put her on the patio. A few more steps and she was behind the guard, pulling his head back to stretch the neck and slashing fast, deep, and hard at the arteries to leave as much of a mess as possible.

Inside the house, she paused and took a note from her pocket. Written by one of the marines so that it looked as if it had come from a man, it was a warning to the Beltrans to stay in their own territory. Ramiro Delgado had powerful friends, it read, and tonight was a night of revenge.

She moved like a wraith down the hallway and into the bedroom area, checking each room until she found Manuel Beltran sound asleep, with his right arm thrown across a woman. Slowing even more, Beth assumed a proper shooting stance and brought the pistol into position, even taking a moment to aim. As time stood still, she felt in complete control of her world, and a burning hatred for the man in the bed.

Shooting had always seemed so easy and natural to her, and she gently gave Manuel a triple tap in the head, two in the chest, and one in the groin. The noise awoke his bed partner, and Beth stepped forward and clobbered her twice with the pistol. She wouldn't be able to remember a thing.

Beth bailed out, avoiding the guard's blood on the patio, and jogged back down the road, tasting the sweet night air rich with its salty ocean smells. By the time she was back in the car and moving off, she had decided to leave for Washington on Sunday.

PARIS, FRANCE

IT WAS EASY TO hide in France in the springtime. The annual flood of tourists was rising fast, and no stranger drew a lot of attention. For the freshly shaved Nicky Marks, it was easier to blend in as a somewhat lost and overwhelmed American sightseer than to sneak around like the killer he was. As that wise old Chinese Communist dude Mao Zedong preached, the revolutionary should mingle among the people the way a fish swims in the sea. Marks was no revolutionary, but he got the point.

The girl he picked up last night was the real deal, a freshly divorced American lawyer out to experience the wonders of Paris, and hooking up with a handsome French-speaking escort like Nicky was a find. Sylvia White of Montgomery, Alabama, spoke with a funny southern accent, and he let her do most of the talking in public as she struggled with her maps and guidebook and laptop. Her holiday was more like a military campaign, from the food at a certain sidewalk café, to the artists on the Left Bank, to the Louvre and a list of at least twenty must-see artworks. At least Nicky could have a nice dinner in the evening and an energetic bout of sex while Sylvia commented that her former husband—also a lawyer, name of Reginald—had never done *that* to her in bed, or *THAT*! Nicky would put up with it for a while, for being with Sylvia meant that he was safe. Terrorists normally run. Her accent, however, was driving him crazy.

He hadn't spent much time thinking about throwing that grenade back in Berlin. He did it and got his money. Planning wasn't his responsibility. He was puzzled about why he hadn't been instructed to make sure of a kill. Setting off a loud boom and doing nothing else seemed rather pointless. The thing in Mexico had been equally nonsensical, to his way of thinking. However, the Prince was working out another one of his master schemes.

"I want to go visit that big Versailles place tomorrow, and see where Marie Antoinette lived," Sylvia had announced in bed, making the name sound like Marie-Ann Tawnette. "Would y'all like to go along?"

"The Château de Versailles," he said, gently correcting her mangled pronunciation. "Sure. Let's do that." In fact, the choice pleased him. The monstrous complex of palaces, gardens, and museums would swallow him from sight for an entire day, just another tourist fish.

The Prince would signal when it was safe to come out of hibernation. The lawyer from Alabama was in France for two more days, after which she would move on down to Italy to absorb the colors of the golden Tuscan sun. That was a whole different set of guidebooks, and he had already politely refused to accompany her, claiming important pending business meetings. She would be able to find another sleeping dictionary down there, he told her, and she giggled.

By then, the Prince would probably have him on the move anyway.

SIR GEOFFREY CORNWELL RELAXED in a lawn chair that sagged in the shape of his butt. The warm sun baked on his face while his wife, Lady Patricia, puttered nearby in a patch of flowers. She could have had the gardener perform that chore, but Pat delighted in helping the earth come to life again in springtime, after the frosts, and she was thinning her perennials. Beside her lay a pyramid of fifty bulbs that needed to be planted today, and those *Gladioli acidantera* didn't care that she was rich. If her ladyship wanted their gorgeous summer flowers, she needed to get them into the ground.

Kyle had arrived the night before, in time for a family dinner with these two people who were his surrogate parents. They had known one another for years. The gods of fate had gambled freely with Kyle's life until he got a winning hand with the Cornwells. Merely being around them was a calming balm. He threw a pebble at a duck in the pond and missed.

"Quite a conundrum, my boy," opined Sir Jeff. "You and this Nicky Marks fellow being tied together in two attacks on different continents." Kyle had laid out the situation in a late-night session with them, then let them sleep on it before having any real discussion.

"So the bad man is after you personally? It has to be you, doesn't it?" added Pat.

"I don't know." He threw at the duck again, skipping the rock past its tail. The bird quacked annoyance. "It's too early in the game, Pat. I don't have enough information."

"It cannot be a coincidence," Sir Jeff observed.

"No. Maybe I killed somebody's cousin at some point back in the day and they're out for revenge. A lot of people hold grudges against me."

"Sit down and stop molesting our livestock, Kyle." Lady Patricia shook her dirt-scabbed trowel at him, put it down, and lit a long, thin cigar. "We haven't seen a thing on the news or in the papers about either of these incidents."

"Different stories in Mexico and Germany. Nobody has tied them together yet."

She was cross-legged on the grass. "Our poor Coastie. That was a beastly thing to do. She and Mickey were a wonderful pair. I called her yesterday and we had a long talk. She's not very steady yet."

Sir Jeff nodded. "In her condition, are you seriously considering bringing her to work? She may be too fragile."

"I think I'll need help that nobody knows about. I'll make up my mind after I see her. Fragile, she ain't. You know that."

Lady Patricia released a stream of smoke. "Oh, poof. You can't make that decision to keep her out of things, Kyle. If trouble begins, and you're involved, she'll want to be right there, and you know it."

"Only time will tell," he said, lowering his voice to mock a television reporter. "When this is done, I'll send her packing over here for you to take on holiday. Out on the boat, maybe. Go shopping. Woman stuff."

"There's a leak in the CIA?" Sir Jeff interrupted. "Of course there is. So who benefits from this? There are a lot easier ways to take you off the board than by concocting some complex scheme involving the Central Intelligence Agency. You may be the link, Kyle, but it might be bigger than you."

"Again, I don't know enough yet."

Sir Jeff had a frosty glass of lemonade. "What's the one thing the CIA, or any intelligence service, truly fears?"

"Losing its secrecy. Inner workings coming to light. Outsiders getting a look at what it's doing and planning," Kyle replied. "They even warned me that someday this might come before a congressional hearing. None of us want that."

"So there you go, my boy. Perhaps the question should be not who has the most to gain but who has the most to lose. And why? Isn't that interesting?"

Kyle nodded. He had first met Sir Jeff and Lady Pat years ago when he was a Marine Corps sergeant and Jeff was a medically retired colonel in the British Special Air Services. Sir Jeff used his savings to start a weapons-development business, and the U.S. Marines lent him their best shooter to develop a world-class sniper rifle. They had warmed to each other right away, and created the Excalibur, the best of its kind in the world. After that first success, Excalibur Enterprises never looked back.

That seemed so long ago now. Sir Jeff had found that he was even better in the business world than he had been as a commando, and the company had grown and expanded until it became a major player in the weapons game. And he had brought Kyle along for the ride, persuading the Marines to allow him to borrow the young marine whenever his special experience was needed, which was often. That closeness eventually led to Kyle's becoming the executive vice president of a huge enterprise, leaving the Marines, and becoming heir apparent to Sir Jeff, with an obscene salary and benefits program.

The flip side and hidden fuel behind the success was that the Pentagon and the British government, the CIA and MI6 were able to cloak many delicate operations behind a front that was willingly supplied by Excalibur. Somewhere along the way, the aging British couple formally adopted Kyle Swanson, who had grown up as an orphan in the States, to be the child they never had.

Like all families, they had disagreements, the major one being that Kyle wasn't yet married. Lady Pat wanted grandchildren, and Sir Jeff wanted whatever she wanted. Coastie had once been a candidate, and, as Lady Pat often reminded Kyle, it was his own fault that she got away.

"Tell me more about this Gibson fellow?" Sir Jeff brought the conversation back to life. "Can you work with him?"

Kyle shrugged. "I have no real choice in that. He seems capable enough, and the Berlin incident proved that he has balls."

"Watch your language, dear. The ducks are listening." Lady Pat smiled. "You were lucky that Mr. Gibson was there."

"No such thing as luck, my dear." Sir Jeff finished off the lemonade, put his feet up on a garden bench, and closed his eyes. "Check him out thoroughly, Kyle. Your life may depend on it."

THE PRINCE WAS NOT a prince at all, in the traditional sense of the word. His father was a king in name only, and neither of them carried a drop of royal blood. Others had bestowed the title on him, and he kept it because he liked it.

He was alone in a booth at Joe's Stone Crab in Washington, pondering the next move in protecting his drug kingdom, a vast enterprise that extended from the poppy fields of Afghanistan to the refineries in Mexico, and, finally, into the noses and veins of willing American customers. It was very profitable. It was also powerful, which was why he was at one of the favorite restaurants of the men and women who ran the nation's capital. This place was a fund-raising heaven, allowing political figures to wheedle campaign donations while enjoying excellent food.

He spotted Congresswoman Veronica Keenan the instant she entered. Tall, dark-haired, and attractive, the freshman legislator was trolling for support and her aides had set her up with the moneyman waiting in a private booth. She hated begging, but it was the name of the game. It took a lot of cash to stay in office, to which she had only recently been appointed upon the death of her husband, who had held the seat for three terms. The campaigning never stopped; she had a lot of bills to pay, including thousands of dollars in dues to her political party.

A waiter escorted her to the table, and she followed with a confident walk. She extended a hand and a high-wattage smile. "Mr. Prince, a great pleasure to meet you." She measured Harold Prince carefully. A mane of thick black hair was swept low across the forehead like a rock star from the eighties. The teeth sparkled. Glasses with tinted lenses kept his eyes in a bit of shadow. There was a small flesh-colored Band-Aid on his cheek that drew her eyes away from his other features. He was in his thirties and was totally unremarkable in any way. Wig, caps, dark glasses. Phony, she thought.

Prince welcomed her, and when a bottle of wine appeared at the table they each had a glass and the waiter poured and withdrew. He had seen this dance hundreds of times; members of Congress did not come to Joe's just for the food.

They clinked glasses, and Veronica Keenan said in a low voice, "Let's get the nasty part of this meeting out of the way, Mr. Prince, then we can have a nicer chat. I appreciate your generous donation to my campaign."

The Prince had a delivery service take an envelope to her office that morning. In it were a check for $9,999 and the supporting paperwork to show where it came from. Donations below $10,000 didn't draw close scrutiny. "Congresswoman, my firm admires your work and we are happy to support you."

"The people of my district thank you, sir. As do my party and I. Every little bit helps." Ten grand wasn't big league enough to buy special favors. The congresswoman could probably find that much money in the cushions of her office sofa after an important lobbyist visited. She thought that Prince was smart enough to know that. It was enough to get a lunch.

The Prince smiled. "I know. I know. It isn't much," he said. "It is a gesture of goodwill and gives me this chance to have your ear for a moment. "It is information, not cash, that I bring to your table today."

Veronica Keenan suddenly grew attentive. The handsome man had undergone a change of expression and his eyes had sharpened. Behind those shaded lenses, she couldn't see their actual color. The waiter came back and took their orders, then left again, not wanting to witness whatever was about to be discussed.

"You want to be a crusader, Congresswoman, but you have not yet been able to grab an issue that will vault you into the limelight. That is the assessment of my friends, at least."

"That is candid, rude, and wrong," she sniffed, taking a sip of white wine. "My work is forcing the big pharmaceutical companies to make major concessions in the pricing of their drugs."

The Prince laughed softly. "Sure. No matter what you do, those companies will not be hurt, because America is a nation of pillheads and cocaine freaks, and you, madam, have no real clout."

She inhaled and let the air out slowly. "Fuck you," she whispered, her eyes flashing with anger. "Who the hell are you, anyway?"

"Just a new friend who would like to give you that breakthrough moment to put you on the Sunday shows for a year. God knows you'll need the help if you want a second term."

"How dare you talk to a member of Congress like that!" She was growing a bit worried. Mr. Prince wasn't bowing to her power in Washington.

"Let me be quite frank about this, Congresswoman. You are a flea. You were appointed to your seat when your husband died, never elected. You represent the Third District of Nebraska, some sixty-five thousand square miles of nothing, and it sprawls over three-fourths of the state. Challengers are lining up in your own party to bring you back home."

She didn't answer, just moved her wineglass around on the napkin.

"The one thing you have in your favor, the reason I'm here, is that you're considered harmless enough to have become the lowest-ranking minority member of the House Permanent Select Committee on Intelligence. A rubber stamp for others to use. That is where I want you to consider your efforts."

"I cannot and will not discuss anything concerning that committee, Mr. Prince. For you to suggest such a thing to me is enough for a felony charge. You vastly underrate my status." That was a lie. Her colleagues had made certain from the start that the new girl at the Capitol understood that she was only one of four hundred and thirty-five members of the House of Representatives, which was only half of Congress, which, in turn, was only one-third of the United States government. A very little fish.

The Prince smiled genially and waved away the rancor. "I would ask nothing of the kind. It's just that something has come to my attention. What you do with the information is up to you."

The food began to arrive, an appetizer of the famous stone-crab claws.

The conversation stayed on hold while they ate, and resumed again over coffee.

"What, exactly, is it that you do, Mr. Prince? I'm still unclear on that."

"I have a number of businesses involved with international commerce, Congresswoman. I run around checking on them, and I learn quite a bit that's never on the record." It was a non-answer, and he looked around the dining room as if he were concerned about being overheard. "Here's what I have for you. Once again, something has gone wrong inside the CIA, and they're covering it up. As a person of power, you can bring it to light."

"What?" She was interested. Mr. Prince may be useful after all.

"There was an attack recently on the funeral of a Mexican military officer who had been killed during a botched drug raid. It was a CIA mission using foreign troops."

She leaned back against the cushion, taking her coffee. "I remember something about that. Tragic, but so what?"

The Prince knew she was hooked. He explained how there were three CIA connections in the Mexican atrocity, which made her raise her eyebrows. Then he added the Berlin ambush, which also had three CIA links, with two of them having been involved in Mexico.

"They haven't reported the one in Germany to us yet," she observed, warming to the idea of knowing something that was being kept under wraps.

"In both cases, the attacker was a known CIA assassin by the name of Nicky Marks. Also, in both cases, another CIA hard case, name of Kyle Swanson, was the possible target."

"What about these other men you mentioned—the late Colonel Castillo and Luke Gibson?"

"Both were also on the agency's payroll. As I understand it, they were not directly involved. This is between Marks and Swanson. Marks is a very bad guy, but this Kyle Swanson is equally dangerous and just as dirty. My guess is that they might be rivals in drug trafficking on the CIA dime."

"It does sound like more than a coincidence." She finished off her coffee and put the cup down. "How do you know all this, when I don't?"

The Prince laughed aloud. "I have to protect my sources, ma'am. Anyway, there it is. You run with it however you choose. Something is about to hit the fan over at Langley, and your committee might want to keep an eye on things. Put yourself on the map, Congresswoman. Get ahead of the curve. You can be a player."

She wished she could see his eyes. "I must get back to the office now," she replied. "Thank you for your kind donation, and for a delicious lunch."

"My duty as a patriot, ma'am. I doubt that we will meet again, but I will be in touch. Best of luck."

When she left the restaurant on Fifteenth Street Northwest, Veronica Keenan believed that her chances for reelection were a lot brighter than they were an hour ago.

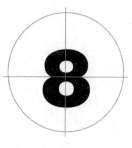

THE WAKHAM CORRIDOR
AFGHANISTAN

THOUSANDS OF YEARS BEFORE the birth of Christ, opium seeds bloomed in the warm, dry, welcoming lands of Mesopotamia. The poppy seemed almost magical in its dual gifts of being a pain reliever and a bringer of great pleasure. Once that genie of easy joy escaped, it would never be capped back in the bottle. Wars would be fought over opium and its derivatives, and thousands upon thousands of addicts over hundreds of years would pay or do anything to maintain their habit. In places such as the Wakham Corridor of Afghanistan, farmers of the twenty-first century planted the little flowers as their primary crop, and every spring their fields sprouted with the pink-and-purple blossoms that were the basic building blocks of the incredibly lucrative dope chain.

Farida Mashaal had had an excellent year with his four acres on the slopes of the Corridor, thanks to late rainfall that had cleared just in time for the poppies to dry. Using his own family and itinerant workers, he had gathered the harvest without a problem. The Afghan government's army had reduced its impotent campaign of eradication, and the Taliban not only left him alone but even furnished extra men to help milk the rubbery drops of raw opium from gentle slices on the pregnant bulbs. So today he stood in his field beside a bearded man carrying an AK-47 slung over his shoulder and scribbling in a notebook. A battery-powered calculator made by Texas Instruments did the math.

"I make it probably very close to ninety pounds," declared the Taliban taxman. "An excellent crop."

"Allah be praised," replied the farmer. "I can feed my family for another year."

"Cash or product?" With the figuring done, it was time to collect the tax. "Four hundred American dollars or two bags."

The ill-educated Afghan farmer did some number-crunching of his own, playing the futures market for this strange gold. Farida didn't need a calculator because he had been doing these calculations for years and could feel the answers in his bones. Prices had shot up, almost doubling, in the past year, and raw opium of the purest, virginal kind was currently selling for about $150 per kilogram. There are 2.2 pounds in a kilogram, so his 90 pounds worked out to roughly 41 kilos. He grimaced as he did the multiplication—41 times $150—and the grimace gave way to a smile. His harvest so far would be worth more than $6,000, a small fortune for the humble farmer. A hundred dollars per cultivated acre.

"I will pay money this time." His decision was not hard. He was betting that the price of opium would continue its steady climb. The farmer pulled a clump of hundred-dollar bills from a pocket of his baggy trousers and counted off four for the Taliban taxman, who made a note in his book.

"Do you still need our men for your harvest?"

"No. You can take them now, with my thanks for the assistance."

"It is our wish for you to succeed," said the taxman.

Farida remained silent. Of course you do, he thought. You support your crazy revolution by taxing me for something that is not yours, and your men in the fields spin tales of battlefield glory to recruit a few workers before the season is over. Just take the money and the boys and leave. The farmer gave a small bow and backed away. He had to load bags of his pasty product aboard his truck and get it to the village before nightfall. At least the Taliban could provide protection along to Girdiwal.

LONDON, ENGLAND

KYLE SWANSON WORE CAUTION like an outer layer of skin, as strong and protective as the shell of a Texas armadillo. Think. Analyze. Plan. Take care.

Look at what the enemy sees. Remain flexible. Slow is smooth; smooth is fast.

He was being pushed toward something. He didn't know what the destination might be, but his sails were filling and the wind was fair and he was being moved, though not by his own hand. The Cornwells had no answers, not that he expected any, because the full extent of the problem was unknown. Swanson thought that by talking about it with them some moment of clarity might shine through. Two days of talking, looking at it every which way, and they'd found nothing.

In his room, the sheets were fresh, the pillows soft, and he had some jazz playing softly to counter the sounds of the big city. Any metropolis is filled with nighttime traffic, abrupt screams or loud laughter, the animal sounds of cats and dogs, and piercing automobile alarms. Swanson wanted sleep. He would fly back to Washington tomorrow, and go out to CIA headquarters and make a decision concerning Luke Gibson. Coastie would be arriving soon. Nicky Marks might come creeping around. He turned off his mind and closed his eyes.

As he slid deeper into the unconscious abyss, a heavy darkness engulfed his mind, with ominous gray clouds that rolled about the sky like volcanic marbles. A screen of raindrops dappled an unseen ocean, followed by the roar of thunder and a thirty-knot wind of an instant storm that ground the surface into waves that blotted out the horizon and swallowed the little sky that was faintly visible. The smells of sulfur and ash came to him. He was about to get clobbered, and he didn't even have time to batten down the hatches. Oh, no. I don't want to do this; I don't want to see the Boatman.

But there he was, stringy in dirty rags and standing at perfect ease aboard a long, narrow boat that bobbed in a puddle of calm while the maelstrom roared about. "We need to talk," came a hissing whisper from the nightmare figure.

"You are not there. You are just a PTSD hallucination." Swanson saw himself standing at the end of a long pier, soaked by the waves that surged up all around. He was in uniform, with an M27 IAR across one shoulder and his boonie hat tilted low.

The figure gave an evil smirk. "Of course I'm a hallucination. You really should get some help from a psychiatrist about seeing me all the time."

"So why are you bothering me?"

"Because, as usual you're in trouble and you've summoned me to prepare for what's ahead." The Boatman leaned on a long oar to keep his craft steady and waved a bony arm. "My little boat is empty for now. You will bring me some souls to ferry across."

"I don't think so." Swanson shifted the machine gun. Maybe he should just rip a couple of bursts of 5.56-mm. rounds through that stack of rags and be done with him. But you cannot kill something that is not alive.

"I know it's true. You're already on the path."

"I'm going after only one man. You don't even have to make a separate trip for him. Leave Nicky Marks here to rot for a while after I kill him. Let the crows work on his eyes and innards. He's a worthless piece of shit."

A cackle of laughter. "This cannot be done alone. You can keep the body. His soul belongs elsewhere."

Swanson stiffened. "I'm not alone. I will have help."

The black hood shook from side to side. "No. Again, you see the signs, now I have told you, but you neither listen nor see."

"How, then? Why? Tell me how this comes down."

The winds spiked the surrounding waves into sharp peaks of foam. The Boatman's black robes spun out like wings as he leaned on the oar and pointed the bow back into the storm. Over his shoulder, before the darkness swallowed him, he called out, "I will save a place for you."

"Wait! Don't go yet! Tell me more. Give me something!"

The little craft vanished, and Swanson tossed and turned in the bed, sound asleep and troubled.

PARIS, FRANCE

NICKY MARKS HAD A fine time showing his American lawyer lover around the treasure domes of France. From the Louvre to Versailles to churches and élite collections, she was dazzled by the gold, jewels, and masterpieces.

When the emperor Napoleon went trekking about conquering countries, he assigned teams of experts to accompany the armies. For centuries, the common practice of a conquering power was to loot the victims. However, Napoleon wanted more than just money hidden in a farmer's potato bin. When the dust of battle settled, the French specialists had first crack at the important thievery. Their systematic gathering of valuable plunder brought back paintings by the Masters and scientific wonders spawned by foreign genius. The result was a France awash in antiquities. That lasted until the Nazis came along and stole most of it for themselves. One thing that was left behind by both of them was an established illicit trade in antiquities.

While the Alabama attorney took a long shower back at their hotel after a grueling day of sightseeing, Marks logged onto her laptop, as he had done every day that they had been together. Using her IP address, he went to an international search-engine site that specialized in fine art and was given a choice of more than thirty million possibilities. The top-tier index was a long list of paid placements by museums and auction houses, and Marks quickly filtered out items being offered by private parties. With hundreds of kilobytes per second, it did not take long.

There it was, in plain sight, the header line in dark blue:

FOR SALE: *Early translation, Italian to English, of* The Prince, *by Niccolò di Bernardo dei Machiavelli. Private estate. Provenance established. Serious inquiries only. Reply this address.*

It was a bogus, nonsense ad that any serious collector would dismiss out of hand, because it contained no dates, no price, no details, and no verification of any sort. An obvious forgery. Many scam artists sharked the art world, and they were very adept at gulling rich amateurs.

The ad had been created by a talented hacker to draw little attention, but, just in case, it had some specific defenses. An embedded malware virus switched any potential customer without a password to a hard-core porn site. The simple, nondestructive shield virus easily discouraged most of them from going further. Any attempt to break through that firewall would result in a meaner virus attacking the snooper's system.

That was fine. The advertisement was aimed only at him. Using the password, he went through the corrupted site to a relay point that bounced him to another site.

Up popped up a generic picture of the marketplace in Kabul. He recognized it instantly. No words, only the single color photograph. It meant that Marks had to go back to Afghanistan.

When he heard the shower stop in the bathroom, Marls cleared the laptop's recent browser history, logged off, closed it up, and replaced it on the table.

Sylvia stepped out wearing only a fluffy towel, and said, "My feet are killing me."

He smiled at her and flipped down the bedcovers. "We have some time before dinner, my dear. How can we possibly waste a few hours? Come and let me massage those poor feet."

MEXICO

MICKEY'S MARINES WERE THE scouts and protectors as the señora went about her bloody rampage of revenge on the men who had taken her husband's life and violated his rest. Almost every night, Beth shed her natural sparkling personality and went on the prowl to exterminate another target. When the sun set, her mourning dress became a black commando outfit. Her dead husband's private armory provided the weaponry.

They watched her work with a quiet, growing pride. They were all tough men, most had known her for several years, and none had suspected that this Jekyll and Hyde existed. The colonel had never talked about his American bride's past. Now their own eyes gave irrefutable proof that the señora knew exactly what she was doing.

The commandant of the Policía Estatal de Yucatán, the state police based in the capital of Mérida, was at a loss to explain what was happening in the drug world. The peninsula had long been divided into zones of control by the various cartels in a live-and-let-live arrangement. There was plenty of money to go around, as long as a proper share filtered up to the real chieftains. In recent days, the show of equitable sharing had been destroyed. This morning, he had gotten the news that the second of the Beltran brothers had also been murdered—that coming on the heels of a lawyer for the Villareal Organization being gutted like a catfish. The two cartels were heading for war, and he couldn't stop it. He couldn't even investigate it! Neither side would talk to cops. That wasn't totally true, for the deadly crime boss Maxim Guerrera was demanding to know why his people were dying when he was paying so much in protection money to the police.

The government in Mexico City also wanted answers, and all the commandant had was another unexplained dead druggie almost every morning.

The señora had chosen an interesting job for what she wanted to be her final outing for a while. Two marines in an old SUV took her over to the coast and south to a quiet inlet. A warm wind caressed the dunes and the waving high grass provided concealment in the darkness. Tonight, all three of them carried Fire Snakes, the Mexican-made FX-05 assault rifles fitted with thirty-round box magazines.

From their vantage point, the raiders had a clear view of a busy pier on which men were loading packets of cocaine from a covered truck into a sharp-bowed, high-performance Cigarette boat tied at the pilings. Four powerful Mercury outboards hung on the stern. Beth actually smiled. She knew this sort of vessel well. Her first real job in the Coast Guard was stopping these speedy drug runners by shooting them from a helicopter out over the Gulf of Mexico. She knew their strong point was speed, while their weak point was the fact that they were just flimsy boats. On an ordinary mission of yesteryear, she would just take out the motors with a couple of shots, and the classy vessels, worth half a million dollars when empty, turned into a drifting fiberglass hulks filled with drugs. Tonight, she wanted more. She wanted to poke the bosses themselves with a branding iron.

The laborers worked beneath a pair of large lights on the pier, unafraid of being seen. The coke was stowed neatly in waterproof containers inside the hull, so the cargo would arrive nice and dry somewhere along the Gulf coast in the U.S.

"Jamie, you take the truck. Leo, you do the boat, and start by shredding those motors. I take the center." Her voice betrayed no excitement. She checked the automatic rifle. "On a three count, boys. *Uno . . . dos . . . tres!*"

The Fire Snakes erupted in three-and four-round bursts that hit with extraordinary effect. The fiberglass boat was ripped beneath the repeated impacts of the military-grade rounds, and the fast engines were reduced to junk. The truck bucked and jumped, and gasoline spewed onto the wooden pier. While the marines changed magazines, the señora stood with the Fire Snake at her hip. Her boys would do the machinery; she would do the men.

Beth walked steadily toward the pier, giving the surprised workers and crew time to respond, and they went for their guns. She kept moving forward, the sand pulling at her boots, until they opened fire. Her marines were screaming for her to get down. Instead, she started working calmly as bullets zipped around her and splatted in the sand and grass and water. The drug workers toppled like bowling pins as she nailed them with head shots and chest wounds, changed magazines, and swept the deck. She screamed with rage as her rifle barked and she moved inexorably closer to the targets. With a final two-shot burst, she hit the gasoline refueling drums and the pier caught fire. She reloaded and emptied another full clip on automatic into the inferno.

Elizabeth Ledford Castillo stopped moving as the bright cloud bloomed and finished the devastation. She dropped her rifle into the dirt, and for the first time, the marines hurrying up to her saw the señora cry. She fell to her knees in the sand, sobbing, and her entire body shook. Leo gathered all three rifles, and Jamie scooped her into his arms. It was over, and they took her home.

The following day was Sunday, and after church Beth was driven to the airport. The blond hair was neatly brushed and glowing again, her skin was smooth and tanned, and her cornflower-blue eyes showed no sadness. She was actually feeling pretty good by the time she boarded the plane to embark on her trip to Washington.

WASHINGTON, D.C.

THEY FORMED A CONVERSATION triangle on the steps of the Jefferson Memorial. Marty Atkins was seated at the top, with Kyle Swanson and Luke Gibson flanking him, standing a few steps below. No tourists were around, but the security detail remained alert.

"Where in hell have you been?" Gibson snarled at Swanson.

"Doesn't matter. I'm here now." Swanson had flown in from England only two hours ago, just in time for a quick visit home to clean up and put on some old jeans and a sweatshirt.

"I would like to know that, too." Atkins didn't look nearly as miffed as Gibson. "Going out of contact for several days is not cool when a mission is starting."

"Okay. I stopped in London to take care of some Excalibur Enterprises business. Got to protect my cover, boss. Sir Jeff said to tell you hello."

Gibson, in jeans and a black hoodie, started to say something, but Atkins shushed him.

"Won't happen again, Luke," Swanson said. "I've decided to take you on as a partner. If we're going to work together, you need to know everything. If Marty trusts you, then so will I."

That caught Gibson totally by surprise, and the anger drained away, replaced by a boyish grin of satisfaction. "You won't regret it, Kyle."

Jesus, thought Swanson. Toss this guy a bone and he rolls over to get his tummy scratched.

Atkins bowed his head and shook it. "All righty, then. If you two are now past the kissy-kissy stage, let's get to work. I've got something for you."

The snipers stopped talking as Atkins opened a folder. "About twelve hours ago, the police in Paris found the body of an American attorney in her hotel room. She had been beaten to death and left on the floor, rolled up in a plastic shower curtain."

"And?" Gibson crossed his arms.

"The murderer took no precautions. The cops found prints all over the place, then found him on video security footage and talked to the staff. In one part of the video, he's seen flipping the bird at the camera. No doubt, the killer was Nicky Marks."

"He wasn't even trying to hide?" Swanson wondered about that.

"Not at all." Atkins passed the brief report to Gibson, who scanned it quickly.

"He knows that every cop in the world is after him and he's taunting us all," said Gibson.

Swanson read the folder and gave it back to Atkins. "No, he's taunting you and me, Luke. Daring us to try and find him."

"Okay by me. Let's go to Paris, partner."

"He won't be there. He killed this poor woman as a misdirection play. We pour our resources into France and he pops up somewhere else."

Gibson stared above Atkins toward the massive stone likeness of Jefferson. "Afghanistan, then. Nicky has worked there for a long time and has contacts. If we want to get ahead of him, let's go talk to his old special-ops buds."

Swanson liked it. "Sounds like a plan. What about it, Marty?"

The director of intelligence stood and brushed the seat of his pants. "Nicky Marks is a vicious animal. He used this poor woman as cover and then killed her only to force our attention on him. Go shoot the bastard dead."

GIRDIWAL, AFGHANISTAN

THE FARMER FARIDA MASHAAL led his little caravan safely into town and parked in the walled compound of Mohammed Azad, the local opium merchant. The men had tea and spoke of their families and other subjects while the brown-black cakes wrapped in plastic were unloaded under guard and the product was weighed, counted, and sorted in a warehouse. Mashaal's nose twitched at the harsh smell of chemicals.

"You have heard, of course, about the fate of our good friend Mahfouz al-Rashidi?" asked the broker, looking appropriately solemn. "He and all four of his sons went to paradise in a huge explosion recently." He paused.

Both men understood the significance of this: someone else would have to collect the tax for the government. With no one watching, it would be easy to shave the amount due, particularly since the Taliban was already satisfied with its tribute. The farmer proceeded cautiously.

"My crop this year was stricken by an unexpected blight," he said, nodding his head. "That is why it is small. And bad weather. We were also caught at the edge of a battle, and that threw us behind schedule."

"Terrible. Terrible. Such is the fate of a farmer. I am hearing the same from many other farmers. It is increasing my own costs."

"Has a replacement been chosen yet?"

"Yes. In fact, it is a mullah whose son is a close friend of mine. We have already agreed that the tax this season should be thirty dollars per acre of land. Your four acres will be assessed only one hundred and twenty dollars." The broker looked smug. The government's tax this year after the unfortunate demise of the Lion of the Wakham was really $25, but he would pocket the extra five. The rest would be shared all the way up the line. In a country in which the average annual income was less than $700 a year, everybody benefited from the poppy.

The farmer had expected to pay the usual $60 per acre, so this was a financial windfall, although he knew the broker would take some of the difference. The combined total tax to both the government and the Taliban came to only $520! *Praise be to Allah!* "I wish the mullah and his son long life and great success," he said.

Mohammed Azad turned as an assistant came in with the official tally, and he ran the numbers. "To business, then," he said, handing the figures to Farida. "You did very well."

The farmer took a deep breath. All the hard work had paid off. The broker showed forty-three kilos, which meant that at $150 per kilo the farmer would get $6,450, less the taxes and a $500 credit he had borrowed from the broker a few months ago. It was a heart-stopping moment for Farida Mashaal, who was totally unaware that the quality of his pure product would be cut many times and its value increased hundreds of times before it reached the final consumer. The pipeline was full and flowing. The farmer was happy. The broker was happy. The Taliban was happy. The government was happy. And Sergeant Jules Mason of the U.S. Army would be the happiest of all.

BAGRAM AIR BASE,
AFGHANISTAN

JULES HUMMED TO HIMSELF as he headed for one of the dark sections of the fence line toward the dim spot known as Alice's Restaurant, a place where the folksinger Arlo Guthrie proclaimed you could get anything that you want. Same here. Alice was always open for business. An F-16 fighter jet burst down one of the long runways, afterburners sizzling, and leaped into the sky, trailing fire. Jules ignored it. The war was out there beyond the wire, and he had seen more than his part of it. Hell, man. Third fuckin' tour.

The base was huge. Some six square miles and thousands of people, from élite fighting soldiers like himself down to paper-shuffling bureaucrats. He had his M16 on his shoulder, the helmet, and the usual flak jacket, only without the ceramic plates. In fact, he looked like a guard himself.

All he wanted tonight was some relief after being out on a long patrol over toward the tall mountains for the past three days. Not a shot had been fired, but he knew the bad guys were out there, everywhere. The pressure was enormous, for not only did he have to get back safely to base himself; he also had to keep his squad safe. Everybody goes home, he told them.

Once back at the base, it was time to reflect and rest, and deal with the terror he felt.

The first tour had been all business, and he could hack it. In fact, he kind of enjoyed being at the sharp edge of the spear. Second tour, not so much. Scared when he saw American bodies, scared when the mortar rounds came diving down, terrified when he killed his first jihadi—some kid with an AK-47 who ran straight into the squad's fire zone. Third tour was like coming home to hell, and he was introduced to the needle by his best friend, another sergeant.

Dude, what a rush! Made everything better immediately, and he could envision getting through tomorrow. The Army didn't approve, of course, but once Jules broke the code, he found that he was a member of a pretty damn big fraternity. Sometimes he thought everybody on the base was high. After more than a decade of war, the original luster of the mission had tarnished. Nobody wanted to be the last American soldier killed in Afghanistan. Nevertheless, they did their jobs and didn't let the drugs impair their overall combat readiness.

He reached the fence, a spot in the wire where the searchlights that had been put up to deter rapes didn't overlap. A figure stood on the other side, wearing those baggy pants and the funny mushroom hat. "Hey," said Jules.

"Can I help you?" The voice sounded young and confidently experienced in the business.

"Heroin," said Jules.

"How much? Thirty dollars?"

"Do a trade?" Jules Mason was short on cash.

"What?"

"Flak jacket. Worth more than thirty bucks. Give me fifty."

"Not without the ceramics. I see from over here it doesn't have ballistic plates. Thirty dollars top."

"Deal." Jules put down his rifle and shrugged out of the jacket and flung it over the fence. Hell, he'd stolen it anyway, so this was really a freebie.

The dealer picked up the jacket and looked it over. New. "Okay," he said. He pulled a matchbox from a vest pocket and flipped it back to the American. It was filled with heroin.

Jules smiled when he opened it. Perfect piece of heaven. "See you later," he said, and ambled off to find his buddy. Tonight they would do a bit of spoon-cooking, load the syringe, watch the silver needle pierce purple-green veins, and feel the warm, soothing rush. They would ride the dragon for a while and let Afghanistan go away. Tomorrow they would be up in time for reveille, once again the tough noncoms on top of their jobs, backbone of the Army. Neither man considered himself a heroin addict. Just needed a little help now and then until the countdown calendar flipped over and they could go back home.

WASHINGTON, D.C.

JANNA ECKLUND HAD A bone to pick with Kyle Swanson. The Washington office manager of Excalibur Enterprises was feeling disrespected. At six feet, more with heels, and a thick mane of hair, with a stylish cut, that was almost white, the former FBI agent didn't like being overlooked. So when her secretary announced that Swanson was finally back in his office she torqued up her considerable courage and marched in. "I've got a bone to pick with you," she declared, taking one of the padded chairs before his desk.

"Good morning to you, too. Is your worthless husband still with the feebs?"

That threw her off balance. "Of course he is." She had been married to Lucky Sharif for almost three years, a few months after Swanson hired her for Excalibur. The agency frowned upon fellow agents being married. The friendship between Lucky and Kyle dated all the way to Somalia.

"Now listen, Kyle . . ."

"Still in counterterrorism, right?" He swiveled his chair around, got up, and went over to the coffeepot. Held it up. "Want some?"

"No, thanks." This was the problem. Other men sometimes went mute in her presence, but Kyle would look right through her. Sometimes she still missed the badge and the gun.

"Then do me a favor and have one of your assistants make reservations for four of us tonight at a nice restaurant. Something private, not full of tourists."

"Four?"

"Yes. It's time for both of you to meet Beth Ledford. She got in yesterday." The coffee was black and hot. "Now, Janna, what's the problem? What's with the impatient foot-tapping? Why are you letting your problem become my problem?"

Janna stood up abruptly and smoothed her dark skirt, then crossed her arms over her chest. The ice-blue eyes went icier than normal. "I want a promotion. When we started this office, you were the boss and I was everything else. Now we have dozens of people working on two floors of a big building and more business than we can handle. My title is that of 'office manager,' and the corporate bigwigs hardly acknowledge me, much less sign onto a contract for Excalibur. I have to haul along a male lawyer." She tapped her foot harder.

"I meant to tell you," Swanson said, taking his seat again. "We're expanding. When I was with Jeff in London, we okayed a new facility up near Twenty-nine Palms in California. The marines will allow us to test new weaponry on their secure dirt. So that's going to be part of your job now. Hope you enjoy flying back and forth." The smirk was intolerable.

"Dammit, Kyle Swanson! I need more official clout if I'm going to go out there. And who's going to run this place when I'm gone?"

Kyle's eyes held a touch of mirth. "You, I assume. Hire managers for here and in California."

"I *am* the office manager here! That's what I wanted to talk to you about. Please, Kyle, quit playing games and be serious."

Kyle finished his coffee and pushed the cup aside, folded his hands on the desk. "Did I forget to tell you this other thing? Jeff and I decided a few days ago that you should be vice president for North American operations for Excalibur Enterprises. Salary bump and stock. Interested?"

Janna sat back down in the chair. "You are a rat bastard."

"So I'll take that as a yes. You do all the work anyway, Janna, and I'm not interested in sales and contracts. The balance sheet speaks to your success. The company won't suffer if I'm gone for a long spell, which happens now and again. I'll be your show pony anytime you need to trot out a real sniper to talk tech with the military types."

"I'm having a heart attack over here, you jerk. Can I tell Lucky?" The glare had been replaced by total surprise.

"Why not? Sir Jeff and Lady Pat are already spreading the word in England. Your name will be in the *Wall Street Journal* tomorrow. I would give you a hug, but you might break me."

THE PRINCE HAD HIS eye on northern New England. Too many customers up there up in New Hampshire, Vermont, and Maine were getting their dope from unauthorized sources. In urban centers like New York, Dallas, and Los Angeles, he had arrangements with central players, but the small towns were growing their own epidemics without seeking his permission or giving him tribute. He considered that rude. It was easier and cheaper to get a quality shot of China White behind a fast-food joint in Montpelier than to get drunk in a bar. Overdoses were common. The politicians were helpless, and the cops were outmatched. He had to do something. Meth crackheads were another matter entirely. They were like cockroaches who brewed their own poison, then ate it.

He wished Nicky Marks were around, but he was on another mission that was important. Maybe after that he should be dispatched to establish a little lawless disorder up there in Mooseland. If the townships thought they had trouble now, wait until Nicky started tracking the dealers and their bosses, and put things righteous. Right now, a six-dollar bag of heroin purchased in an urbanized place was being peddled for forty dollars in the northern Yankee belt, a bonanza for the dealer and a bargain for the addict. It wasn't just the profit that bothered the Prince, because he had plenty of money. He had to be on top, number one, be the best of the best and spoken of with fear. He craved recognition as the best and the brightest.

The problem was that he didn't have time to do it himself. There was no use trying to straighten out the details of transportation and distribution if he didn't protect the precious poppies themselves. They were the heartbeat. Those jokers in St. Albans, Nashua, and Bath were really no different from any other breed of junky, except that their skins were white. So, he added up the score. The problem in the Wakham Corridor had been solved and a new, reliable man was in charge, protected by the Taliban. Relations were cool with the guy in Colombia, who was both a rival and a business partner of convenience. The Mexican cartels had used Nicky to maximum effect to screw up that government's antidrug plan, and the Prince himself had personally almost seduced that fruitcake congresswoman from Nebraska, who would pull the plug on the CIA and the troublesome Kyle Swanson.

He should leave Swanson alone. The Prince knew that. The man was a legendary sniper in the Marines and had a history that included the Medal of Honor for bravery. He feared nothing. In the space of just a few years after retiring from the Marine Corps, Swanson had enhanced his reputation of being the best special operator on the CIA's payroll. Worse, while Swanson's raids on pressure points had been interrupting the financial and dope pipeline, he didn't even know the Prince existed, much less recognize his superiority. There would come a day when all that would change. The Prince enjoyed having subplots to his main themes.

BALTIMORE, MARYLAND

KYLE AND COASTIE ARRIVED at the waterfront seafood restaurant first, a small and dark place with about a dozen tables spread with white linen, a long bar that had a stripe of ice down the middle of the granite to keep drinks cold, subdued lighting, and dark walls. Kyle was glad to find that it didn't have loading nets and fishing buoys and anchors on the walls. It was the pricey kind of place favored by local VIPs whose hot wheels were babied by valet parkers. Tourists preferred the lower-end crab shacks.

Coastie wore a formfitting but modest dark dress, with a matching shawl across her shoulders, high on her neck, and minimal makeup. Her diamond wedding ring was still prominent on the third finger, left hand, and a small Beretta .380 semiautomatic nested in her purse. She ordered a glass of Merlot, and Kyle had a scotch when the server in a clean white apron greeted them. The reservation had been made for four people, so he didn't rush them, although he leaned in to light a short candle in the middle of the table. "I had just as soon stayed at home. I feel out of place here," Coastie said.

"I need you to meet Janna and Lucky on neutral ground. Plus, the food here is probably better than Chinese takeout, and I can't have you just moping around like you were probably doing in Mexico." Kyle unbuttoned his coat and adjusted the pistol on his hip. His eyes had acclimated to the light, and he looked around as the drinks were served.

"Would you like to see the wine list now, sir?"

"I'm thinking a bottle of champagne with dinner, so you can chill one up. You choose a nice vintage. Our friends will be here shortly."

"Very good, sir," the waiter said, and disappeared. The man hadn't mentioned price. That usually meant a good tip was on the way.

Beth sipped the purple wine and sat the glass down carefully. "Janna is with Excalibur and Lucky is FBI, right?"

"Yeah. She's a piece of work, just like you. She was Lucky's partner and a really good special agent when I stole her. Lucky was an eight-year-old kid in Mogadishu when I was in Somalia, way back in the day. I sort of adopted him and his grandmother, and got them to the U.S. They settled in Minneapolis, and he made a name for himself playing basketball, ex-celled in college, and then again with the FBI."

"How will I recognize them? I'm nervous about this."

"Trust me. That will not be a problem. Did you have a good workout?"

That brought a smile to the glum face. "Three-mile run. Met up with that personal trainer you arranged at the gym, and she ground me down to get an analysis and set a program to 'build up my core'—whatever that means. When can I start shooting?"

"Soon. Ah!" Kyle looked toward the entrance as Janna stepped inside.

"My God, she's gorgeous. And big!"

Janna was dressed in a creamy silk blouse, a long black skirt slit on the side to show maximum leg, and black leather boots with heels. Over her shoulder was slung a bag large enough to carry a cannon, which it did, an M-1911 .45-caliber Colt. Janna didn't like small pistols. She waved and whispered to Lucky, who stepped beside her. "My God, she's *tiny*! And Kyle wasn't kidding about her beauty. Look at those cheekbones."

Lucky Sharif was as dark as his wife was pale, and moved with a quiet sense of total confidence. As they walked to the table, they both swept the place with steely gazes—Janna doing the right side and Lucky doing the left. No threats. Kyle made the introductions, and Coastie extended her small pale hand to welcome them.

The waiter hurried over with the champagne bucket, uncorked the bottle, and poured generous glasses for them all. It took about thirty seconds for Janna and Beth to decide to become friends.

"I'm so sorry about the death of your husband," Janna said, with her palm on Beth's forearm. "It was a terrible thing."

Coastie looked down. She hadn't expected to find a real friend, and tears welled in her eyes. She dabbed them away. "Thank you. It has been hard to handle."

"Then to absent friends and Colonel Francisco Miguel Castillo." Lucky raised his glass in the traditional toast, and they clinked glasses. He didn't ask for information because he had already been briefed on the incident. A real shit sandwich.

"Hey, look," said Lucky, holding up his forearm and grinning. "My rich wife bought me a new watch this afternoon. Claims that her petty tyrant of a boss gave her a promotion." He twisted the wrist so the Rolex caught the light.

Kyle said, "Another toast, then. To Janna, the new vice president of Excalibur Enterprises." Glasses clinked again, and the mood lifted. He noticed a new gold-link necklace at Janna's throat.

The waiter swept by and distributed menus, and by the second glass of champagne the food began to arrive: oysters and scallops and the best the

Chesapeake Bay had to offer. Beth was feeling better, knowing that these three people were totally on her side. They all wore plastic bibs to catch the squirts and splashes of shellfish being dismembered. Laughs erupted, and when it was done the tone changed; coffee replaced wine, and Kyle got down to business.

"I leave for Afghanistan tomorrow, gang, which is the other reason for this meeting. What we say here does not go beyond this table. There's a rogue agent, name of Nicky Marks, on the loose, and I'm going to find him."

"The guy from Mexico?" Coastie was all attention. "Let me go with you."

"Let me finish this, Coastie. I'm being partnered with a veteran CIA guy named Luke Gibson, who was with me in Berlin when the same dude threw a grenade at us. He knows the bad guy, and we'll track him down."

"So? Seems like a pretty straightforward deal now that you know who you're hunting," said Lucky, leaning back and listening carefully. "I know the FBI already has Marks as a high priority over here. He won't last long."

Kyle poured himself some more coffee. "That's not why we're here. It's my partner, Gibson. I don't really know him at all, other than what the agency has revealed, which isn't much. Marty Atkins swears he's a top gun, and I'm supposed to take that for granted. I don't. I can't."

The other three caught it. "You want us to do an independent background check?" Janna asked.

"You got it. Everything from when and where he was born up to today. Don't trust the CIA brief. Lucky, there might be a terrorist angle in this before all is said and done, so you can clear it with your boss to do a bit of independent fieldwork. Go see his parents' headstones, check paper records, follow him as a kid. I want to know everything. The agency thinks highly of him, and I want to believe that. In fact, I really have no reason to think otherwise. Janna, you coordinate things and get one of our trusted computer guys on it."

"What about me?" said Coastie softly.

"You're not ready. But some news on that front, too. Our buddy Orville

Oliver Dawkins is retired from the Marine Corps, but you know he can't sit still."

"I'm going to work with Double-Oh?" Beth felt a tingle of excitement. The former marine master gunnery sergeant had been her mentor in Task Force Trident.

"He's up in Vermont, running a camp for veterans dealing with PTSD and drugs. He'll help whip you into shape again. I want you to be my partner as soon as possible, Coastie. But right now you can help most by hanging with Double-Oh. Let him make the call on when you're ready. The personal trainer can wait until you get back here. Deal?"

"Oh, yeah." For the first time that evening, she actually smiled with genuine joy.

THEY LEFT THE RESTAURANT together, and a pleasant wind along the waterfront closed around them with a smell of brine. This was no war zone but a stretch of the big city that had been renovated, gentrified, commercialized, and made safe over the years. Heavy crime remained on the far side of North Street, a planet away from the showcase extending from Harborplace to Fells Point.

Plenty of foot traffic roamed the area as Lucky and Kyle handed the valets the tickets to have the cars brought around. Girlish trills of laughter erupted from a clutch of teenagers taking selfies in odd contortions. Couples strolled the boulevard, lost in each other's presence. A panhandler in droopy khaki pants, who hadn't yet been moved out by security, approached them, shouting, "Hey, can you lend me twenty dollars for a hotel room?"

The four friends didn't respond. The whiskered man moved a few steps closer, and Lucky growled, "Get lost. Nothing for you here."

The man stopped and lit a cigarette, and the nicotine cloud joined the other smells. Urine. Beer. Grime. He gawked at them. "Rich bastards," he squawked. "Gimme those wallets!" Then he made the move—an energetic dash that belied his original appearance—and dug into his jacket pocket.

Janna had her .45 out in a heartbeat, and backhanded the bum hard across the face, sending him sprawling on the gray concrete with a broken nose. When the attacker's eyes cleared, he got to his knees and was kicked in the ribs by Lucky. After catching his breath, he looked up to see four people standing around him, all pointing guns at his head. Both men were showing badges. His own gun had been scooped up by Snow White.

"Man. Man. Guys! Hold on. Don't shoot. Please don't shoot." He put his hands behind his head, fingers interlocked, and in a moment steel handcuffs bit into his wrists. The guns were put away, although the little woman seemed disappointed that she hadn't pulled the trigger.

The valets had brought out the cars and were standing beside the doors, gawking at the scene. People who dined at the restaurant normally didn't carry an arsenal of weaponry when they sat down for a meal. Lucky showed his FBI badge. "No problem, boys. Just a drunk. I'm going to drop him at the cop shop."

Kyle shoved the man into the back of the silver Lexus and slid in beside him. Lucky got behind the wheel. Janna and Coastie would follow in the Beemer. As the cars moved out, the man was wishing that the cops had shown up. In less than a minute, he had gone from being in control of an easy mugging to being hog-tied in a car with two very unhappy campers.

Kyle ran his hands through the man's pockets, unbuckled his belt and tore open the waistband, snatched off his shoes and threw them out the window. "Hey!" the man protested, and caught an elbow in the mouth.

"Who are you, and what were you doing?" Kyle gave a painful finger jab into the appendix

"Man. Stop it, okay? Just stop it. I want a lawyer."

"Don't blame you for that, but it ain't going to happen." Kyle ripped open the dirty shirt to expose a hairy chest. No wallet. No cell phone. No wire. No listening devices. No dope and no needle tracks. "You're neither a drunk nor a druggie. Good watch, reading glasses, clean fingernails, key ring with a Mazda entry fob, and a wedding ring. You're a player, asshole."

The face changed. He said nothing, and struggled against the cuffs.

An effort to raise his feet and kick at the driver stopped when Kyle nailed him with a hard bash into his balls.

"Do something like that again and I'll put a bullet in your stomach, understand? Now, who the fuck are you, dumbass?"

"Richard Dale. Private detective." The captive closed his eyes and leaned his head back, recognizing that his situation was hopeless unless he gave up everything he knew. Escape was not an option. "Your name is Swanson, right? I've been following you for two days. Took pictures, that was all."

Kyle caught Lucky's eyes in the rearview and saw the slight shake of the head. "You had a gun. You were going to shoot me."

Dale gurgled a laugh. "It ain't even loaded, man. My client said just to wave it around, like, scare you. Said you would get pissed off but not take me down because you're a pro. Now, that Snow Queen—didn't count on her. And the little one was about to cool me out until you stopped her. You guys date weird women."

In the front seat, Lucky got Janna on speed dial and asked her if the weapon she had taken was loaded. "No bullets," he told Kyle.

They were well away from the waterfront, heading north into the darkness. "You from around here, Dale?" Kyle said.

"Jersey," he replied. "Trenton."

"Then you might have figured out that we're heading out on the Delmarva Peninsula, where there are miles and miles of coastline. Many a body has been found out in those rugged dunes. Who's the client, Dale?"

"He calls himself Prince—that's all I know. He pays cash in hundreds, in advance. Baseball cap, sunglasses. No remarkable features. Looks like a million other dudes. I figured you might be screwing his wife or something personal like that. You know, take the pictures and put a scare into you. Routine stuff."

Kyle paused and thought it over. "Dale, have you ever heard of a guy by the name of Nicky Marks?"

The PI shook his head. "Never. Who's he?"

"Never mind. Lucky, pull over and let this asshole out." Kyle unfolded a knife and slit the leather belt. They got him out of the car in the brightness of the headlights from the trailing BMW and made him hobble into the roadside ditch. The pants fell around his feet, which were bare. The handcuffs came off.

"Don't kill me, man." He rubbed his wrists. "C'mon. I don't know how to contact Mr. Prince. He said he would know what happened because he would be watching tonight. I didn't see him. Dude, he may have been there!"

"You get to go home tonight, Mr. Dale," Lucky said. "It is a onetime pass. You stepped into a probable terrorist operation, so Big Brother is going to be watching you from now on. If you report this, your next address will be some cave jail in Africa. Understood?"

"Yuh. Got it, man. Thanks."

Kyle's cell phone chimed before he got back into the Lexus. Luke Gibson's name flashed on the call screen. The voice was neither calm nor excited, just a bit out of breath. "Kyle, watch your ass tonight, pal. Somebody just took a shot at me."

THE WAKHAM CORRIDOR
AFGHANISTAN

THE PAMIR MOUNTAINS AROUND the crossroads town of Girdiwal were pocked with caves, some little more than a few rocks leaning together and others deep and wide. Earthquakes rearranged them from time to time, but, as the Taliban had discovered, they were solid structures that were hidden from the prying eyes of Western satellites. Even if the space birds could somehow see inside, their nations apparently had no interest in doing anything. Anything or anyone could be in those deep holes. The Prince owned a few.

Mohammed Azad, the opium broker, had purchased the crop of gum from Farida Mashaal, packed it with other such harvests until he had a full caravan of plodding, sure-footed mules, and sent it up the scant trails that laced the gray-brown mountains for processing.

A chemical stench permeated the destination, which was the entrance to one of the largest caverns. Despite expensive air purifiers and ventilation, it was still a cave. Workers inside kept their masks on tight, wore white bio-suits and goggles beneath the artificial light. They worked only short shifts in the stifling and dangerous odor of calcium hydroxide, acetic anhydride, ammonium chloride, ether, and other volatile chemicals. No matter that many of them couldn't read, lived in homes without electricity or running water—they cooked and stirred and strained and distilled and performed a miracle every day.

The raw opium paste became morphine, then it was stepped up to low-grade heroin, and, finally, to brown heroin that was ninety percent pure. The final processing stamped it into bricks that each weighed one kilogram, or 2.2 pounds. The product was ready for sale and consumption, and began its trek to the markets of Europe, Russia, China, and America, once again aboard the backs of the mule train, one treacherous step at a time.

The winded donkeys would finally plod into a receiving chute to be unloaded, and the heroin was prepared for onward shipment in secure warehouses at the end of a small dirt airstrip. Donkeys were good, but they couldn't fly, and the Prince had long ago arranged the construction of the critical supply port. Unlike the superlab in the cave, the airstrip wasn't a secret but nonaligned ground where various interests could be accommodated. Everybody used it for their own purposes. Planes brought in chemicals and took out dope. They flew in weaponry and took out dope. Special operators, intelligence agents of various nationalities, back-channel diplomats came in, and the planes flew out dope. They brought in cash, and brought out even more drugs. On all fronts, quality increased and prices fell and global dependency grew.

LANGLEY, VIRGINIA

THE UNBLINKING STATUE OF Thomas Jefferson didn't preside this time when CIA Director of Intelligence Martin Atkins met Kyle Swanson and Luke Gibson in the middle of the night. The lights burned bright in the headquarters building, and security had been heightened after the pair of agents had been tapped on the shoulder by a new person in the game, someone known only as the Prince. By this time, they wouldn't even have trusted Mr. Jefferson.

"Are we suspecting the Saudis now, or one of the royal houses in the Middle East? They have more princes over there than camels." Swanson leaned back against a table with his arms crossed.

Atkins had signaled his own frustration by rolling up the sleeves of his white shirt. "God only knows, Kyle. We're playing the hand we've been dealt—Nicky Marks—and now the game has expanded. Luke, you need some aspirin or something?"

Gibson shook his head. "I'm good. Why would this Prince character do something as stupid as sending a street punk to frighten me? What the fuck is he playing at? Nicky was my recruit, true, and we partnered up a few times, but I took good care of him. Why is this crap washing up on my doorstep?"

Gibson had begun the meeting by describing how he had been running his miles out on the Mall after dark when a skinny kid stepped from between the parked cars only about twenty feet away. The guy was a punk, with a baseball cap turned to one side, a wool hoodie in April, and too large jeans that showed six inches of undershorts. He popped a shot at Gibson, missing by a good distance and pinging a tan Nissan sedan instead. Since Gibson already had momentum, he covered the gap between them before the shooter could adjust his aim. The boy took off in an attempt at escape, but his baggy pants made running impossible. Gibson tackled him three steps later. "Just a piece of junk .25-cal six-shooter. I leaned him against a tire and applied a little enhanced interrogation encouragement until he said some white dude with red hair paid him a hundred bucks to scare me, but not to kill me. He was also to tell me that the Prince was watching. I took the gun, broke his trigger finger, and told him to get lost in a hurry. No police report."

Swanson opened a bottle of water; thought it over. "Basically the same thing that happened to me. Neither was a serious attack."

"Then it was an intentional wake-up call for all of us," Atkins interjected. "Why this man would openly reveal his existence to us is beyond comprehension."

"Maybe he wants us to chase him rather than going after Marks." Gibson had a sudden desire for a cigarette. "We would be running in circles."

Atkins went over to the window. The world outside looked normal, but there in his office things seemed upside down. He stretched. "I want you guys out of the country ASAP. We'll lay on an escort to take you directly out to Andrews, and hook you up with whatever big bird the Air Force has heading across the Atlantic; I'll have somebody meet you on the other end to forward you on to Afghanistan. I'll get the ball rolling to unmask this Prince. You guys still go and find Marks. Unlock this thing before it blows up in our faces."

THE PRINCE WAS ENJOYING himself as his plan unfolded. It was all so easy, with more little events yet to come. Let them hunt all they wanted. He was always a lap or two ahead, and was tying the mighty Central Intelligence Agency into knots.

Tomorrow morning, his latest coup, Congresswoman Veronica Keenan of Nebraska, would arrive at her desk in the Longworth House Office Building and breeze into the day's ritual of being among the power élite. A priority envelope would be delivered to her. Prince figured that she might have bolstered her courage since meeting with him, and he didn't want her drifting off task, so he had sent a reminder via a set of photographs. The instruction was: CHECK REGISTRATION & AREA —PRINCE

There was a small airplane sitting on a dirt runway. Three men and one woman, all in casual work clothes, were clustered around the tail, examining something that dangled downward. The set of letters and numbers N988QQ were in barely visible faint black paint that was hard to see against the gray stripe on the tail of the aircraft.

The congresswoman would share it with her top aide, who would assign another aide to start burrowing into the open electronic files of the U.S. government, including the Federal Aviation Administration. If the assistant had a brain, she would also run a routine Google search and learn that the plane was a DHC Dash-8 multiprop with a checkered history. It had once been seized by the U.S. Drug Enforcement Administration after being forced to land in Florida, when it ran out of gas on a run up from Colombia. It was carrying four tons of cocaine at the time, and the DEA tracked it back through Immigration and Customs Enforcement and back even further through two private front companies. Bottom-line owner was the CIA.

By lunchtime, Ms. Keenan would start putting two and two together again. Apparently, the plane had been rehabilitated. The aide would identify the place by simply reading a handwritten sign the photographer had placed on a rock in the foreground. She had never heard of Girdiwal, Afghanistan. Neither had her boss. A CIA airplane sitting on a remote airstrip in Afghanistan wasn't really earthshaking news, but combined with the earlier tip from Mr. Prince and the plane's bad history of running drugs, maybe there was something there. She would see.

According to the Prince's timetable, the gentlelady from Nebraska would instruct her aide to set up a private meeting by that afternoon with the vice chairman of the House Permanent Select Committee on Intelligence. She wouldn't go straight to the chairman, who was an important figure in the opposition party, without notifying her own team first.

With his puppet dancing, the Prince relaxed, thinking great thoughts. The illegal retail sale of heroin and cocaine was worth about $10 billion in today's market, just in the United States. That figure was dwarfed by the worldwide trade, estimated to be as high as $750 billion annually. He didn't want it all, just a share, because he wasn't a greedy man financially. What he craved was recognition as the man with a chokehold on the trafficking. He was the best. With a turn of his wrist, the drug faucet could be closed and a world filled with addicts would explode into turmoil. To them, their drugs were more important than their lives, or the lives of others.

BETH LEDFORD, JANNA ECKLUND, and Lucky Sharif shrugged off the news when Kyle called from Andrews in Maryland to let them know that he wouldn't be going back home that night. In fact, the schedule was wide open. He gave no details. "He's out of here," Janna said.

They were in Swanson's town house in the exclusive Georgetown area of the nation's capital, ready to work in the middle of the night, but uncertain of what to do to silently investigate Luke Gibson without raising suspicions. Logging into a law-enforcement database might trigger an alarm, since the CIA would be on the alert for any inquiries regarding one of its special operators. After all, the guy had twice been the target of presumed terrorists in recent days.

"Original sources," said Lucky. "We want a hard trail so Kyle can be certain that his partner is as good as advertised."

"Personally, I think dodging a grenade and a bullet are pretty good evidence that Luke Gibson is at risk, too." Coastie kicked off her shoes and flexed her toes.

"We hope for the best and assume nothing," Lucky said, nodding toward the shoes. "We do old-fashioned shoe leatherwork. Real cop stuff."

Janna smiled at her husband. "Just the facts, ma'am."

Coastie looked over at her. "What has Kyle told you about Luke? Who are his mommy and daddy, what was his high-school mascot, anything personal at all?"

"No, he's got a good reputation in the agency. That's about it."

"Facts: Luke Gibson was born. He was given a name. He went to school. Somewhere along the way, probably early on, he was recruited by the CIA. That is our framework."

Lucky asked, "Where did he get his military training? Kyle mention that at all? Army or Marine? Obviously, he got good at the game, but where did he learn it?"

Coastie shook her head and Janna did the same, then said, "Wait, wait, wait. Kyle did mention that he once kidded Luke about his military bearing and Luke answered that it was an old habit left over from his misspent youth at VMI."

Lucky clapped his hands. "That's where we start, then. VMI is in Lexington, Virginia, which is only about two hundred miles from here. I can drive down there tomorrow and check it out."

"Okay," Coastie said in a slow voice. "Only can you tell me first what's a VMI?"

OVER THE ATLANTIC OCEAN

THE FOUR PRATT & WHITNEY jet engines on the C-17 Globemaster III had settled into a harmonic moan once the aircraft reached its cruising altitude of 28,000 feet, heading east. The old U.S. Air Force transport workhorse was carrying a monster M1A2 Abrams main battle tank, pallets of miscellaneous gear, and two passengers: Luke Gibson and Kyle Swanson. A routine puddle jump for the biggest cargo plane in the world, and the seventy-ton tank in its belly was being ferried to the European stockpile that needed to be reinforced because Russian president Vladimir Pushkin was making noise again. The last U.S. tank units had officially left Germany years earlier, but a pre-positioned source of heavy armor was always kept tuned up and ready for battle, if necessary.

Both men had been given olive-drab USAF flight suits with no insignia and settled into an upper-deck compartment for the long flight to Ramstein as easily as commuters taking a train from Connecticut to Manhattan. Swanson uploaded a game on a laptop, while Gibson plugged in the buds of his iPhone and closed his eyes. Swanson soon shut down the computer and pushed it away, dimmed the overhead light, and also began to doze.

Only three crewmen were on board for the routine hop, and the loadmaster looked in on the passengers, saw they were fine, and shut the hatch. "Our spooks are already asleep," he reported to the pilot.

"Wonder what they're up to. We had to hold takeoff for half an hour to let them get aboard," the co-pilot said.

"I don't know, and I don't want to know," answered the pilot. "Let's put this bird on automatic and get us all to Germany."

"They don't look like James Bonds to me," said the loadmaster.

"Staff Sergeant Baxter?"

"Sir?"

"Shut up."

"Yes, sir. Awesome advice, sir."

MARGUERITE DEL CODA, SIXTEEN years with the agency, met them at planeside, heavy sunglasses tilted low on her nose. "I might have known," she said when Swanson and Gibson stepped onto the tarmac. "I received a strange message from Langley that two 'representatives' from the office of the director of intelligence would be arriving. No names, no details other than to arrange transport onward. Welcome back to my little slice of America, guys. Get in the car." She got into the front passenger seat, and the two operatives, groggy from the long flight, climbed into the rear. "Back to the office," she told the driver.

No one spoke during the ride as the driver expertly wove through the complex of roads at the air base in southern Germany. Ramstein was home to the entire USAF headquarters in Europe and teemed with some fifty thousand Americans of various services. Because it was a central NATO point, thousands more rolled in the count. What had started almost a century earlier, when the Hitler regime cleared an airstrip out of dense forests, had grown into a modern military metropolis.

Riding del Coda's pass, they cleared the checkpoints and she led them to her private office. She peeled off a gray jacket and put a big corner desk between them and her. It wasn't neat, and the place smelled of stress. The CIA regional administrator dropped into a chair and fiddled with her dark hair for a moment while staring at them.

"This has something to do with all the scuttlebutt going around, I guess? You guys are being targeted by some fool?" Little stayed secret within the CIA itself, for despite restrictions they were, after all, spies.

Swanson sat in one of the two facing easy chairs, while Gibson took a place on the sofa. "Yup," he said. "We might as well start our hunt by asking you some questions, Marguerite. You've been over here forever."

"Fire away," she said. Her brown eyes were looking past them, as if she were already thinking about other things. Del Coda flexed her hands, folded them on the desk, and brought her eyes back down. She had known both of these operators for a long time, because Ramstein was a central clearinghouse in the war-on-terror intelligence business.

"We're looking for one of our former contractors who went over to the dark side." Gibson thought she seemed a bit off her game. "Name of Nicky Marks."

"Only thing I know is that he was a shooter," she replied. "One of your recruits, as I recall."

"Don't remind me." Gibson flushed. "Anyway, have you picked up anything about him lately?"

She shifted in the chair and the navy-blue shirt she wore tightened on her figure. "Nope, other than he killed some woman in Paris. You're telling me that Marks is behind all this noise?"

Swanson shrugged. "We don't know much of anything right now, Marguerite, except that he's causing us a lot of trouble."

She unconsciously chewed on her lower lip, her eyes drifting to a computer screen on one side of the desk. "Want me to run him through the system?"

Swanson looked over at his partner. "Sure, light him up. He has to know that the French and Interpol are looking for him on the homicide. No harm in us adding him to the watch list, which he would expect. Just don't use our names at all."

"We think he has a source inside the agency. That's why we're moving quietly. Nobody but you and Marty Atkins know we're here." Gibson looked serious, then flashed an ironic grin. "Maybe two or three hundred others."

"Well, *god damn it* all!" She exploded out of her seat, picked up a plastic ballpoint pen, and broke it in half, flinging the pieces across the office. "I've got the drone program raising my blood pressure, the rendition flights still come through here, and thousands of Kraut demonstrators outside the fence line want to close us down. I do *not* need this!"

Gibson laughed at her outburst. The woman was famous for her volatility. "None of us do. Chill out."

The regional station chief stomped around the room, following a faint track in the old Afghan maroon carpet, her mind whirling. "Okay, okay. I'm all right. Is there anything else I can do?"

"Pass the word, person to person, that we want to keep Marks as isolated from fresh information as possible," Swanson said. "The less he knows, the better. You contact Marty directly on any developments."

"Okay. All mission comms will be handled here," she said, making a note.

The three agents fell silent while del Coda cooled down, then she asked, "Why are you going to Afghanistan, then? Why not Pakistan or Iraq?"

Swanson stood up. "He's going home, and he wants us to follow him."

"You realize that you may be walking straight into an ambush?" she said.

"Most likely. It's his turf, but it's our turn, Marguerite. We're getting closer by the day."

Her mental gears had begun turning, which was why she held such a high-ranking position in the agency. Del Coda had the uncanny ability to work multiple complex problems simultaneously, and she was considering options. "Okay, I'll put Marks's name out there, which will make him step carefully, but how about this, too? We tag the two of you for a drone strike?"

Gibson raised his eyebrows. "Offhand, I can think of about a million good reasons why I don't want a drone falling on my head."

"Let the lady talk, Luke," Swanson said, realizing that he was beginning to think of Gibson as an equal, a workable partner. "Why a drone?"

She went back to the desk and brought the computer to life as she flipped through several screens, referring to the latest list of official pass-words. "Most of the birds used in strikes in the Middle East, Africa, and Afghanistan are parked here. The pilots are back in Nowhere, Nevada, but we have the hardware and launch the missions. You know all that, right?" They nodded. It was public knowledge, because a couple of whistle-blowers had wanted their fifteen minutes of fame.

"If I can get clearance from Director Atkins, we can outfit each of you with a transponder to track your movements, and until this thing is done I can earmark a drone for your call. We'll have it circling overhead when you finally move in on Nicky Marks." Del Coda clicked the computer and the screen went black again. "Because of the protests, I got drones to spare, boys. Want one?"

The men looked at each other and nodded. "Okay, thanks," Swanson said.

"Good idea," Gibson conceded. Inside, he brightened a bit at the memory of how a Reaper smart bomb had blown away the home of Mahfouz al-Rashidi right before his eyes not so long ago. This might come in handy.

Del Coda was on her feet again, seeming to drop the stress she'd complained of like an old blanket. She liked actually doing something again rather than being an administrator. "Come on. We'll have some dinner, get you geared up, and you'll be out of here tomorrow morning."

LEXINGTON, VIRGINIA

FOG AND RAIN SLID across the Shenandoah Valley like moving curtains on a stage, forcing Lucky Sharif to keep the wipers going almost all the way as he drove from Washington to the stately layout of the Virginia Military Institute. He did the math in his head on the way down. If Luke Gibson was in his early thirties, as Kyle estimated, then he would have been at VMI between the ages of eighteen and twenty-one, which would put him in a graduating class between 1998 and 2000, give or take a year. The problem was that Sharif didn't want to mention the name by itself, so he would have to plant some misdirection.

The state-run military college prided itself on a long history that had produced such leaders as George Marshall and George Patton. Stonewall Jackson was a professor there before the Civil War. Among the throngs of spit-shined young men and women moving with determined purpose around the grounds today were future officers who might carve their own niches in history, or fall in the line of duty.

Sharif didn't seek out the superintendent—not yet—but made his way to the offices of the archivist, an efficient woman drinking a cup of tea at her desk. He showed his badge, which she examined closely, as if identifying the metal, then took a good look at the identity card.

"This is the surprise of my day, Special Agent Sharif. My name is Clara Cooper." She got up and extended her hand. The mop of red hair was showing signs of gray, and Sharif believed it was due for another henna rinse. "Are we in trouble with the FBI?"

Sharif gave a soft laugh. "No, Ms. Cooper. Not at all. I'm just doing some routine background checks. I would like to see some *Bombs*."

"Why, you could have saved yourself a trip, sir. The yearbooks are all posted online. We have a wonderful electronic archive."

"I'm sure you do. But we prefer not to rely only on electronic copies. You'd be surprised what hackers can and will do. So we double-source whenever possible."

"Certainly, certainly," she clucked like a mama hen. The idea of some hacker rudely disrupting her archives turned her mouth into a firm, straight line. "What year would you like to see?"

"How about 1988, '89, and 2000? Can you do that?"

"Of course. You can look at them right here in my office if you wish privacy. Make yourself at home while I fetch them. Please, have some tea."

She was back in five minutes, cradling three large volumes, which she placed on a conference table beneath bright halogen lamps. Sharif put on some reading glasses, pulled out his notepad, went to work, and struck gold on the first try, in *The Bomb* for 2000.

Instead of looking for individual names, he had fanned through the pages just to get a feel for how the book was organized, and he stopped at a formal portrait of two young men—the top officers of the entire regiment. They were resplendent in full-dress blue-gray uniform coatees and white pants, black-plumed shakos, white belt across the chest, three rows of shining brass buttons, red sashes, swords on right shoulders, and arms laden with gold-lace chevrons. The man on the left, the regimental executive officer, wore five chevrons. The square-jawed regimental CO wore six, plus other markings to signify that he was top dog. He was identified as First Captain Lucas Gibson.

Sharif spent another thirty minutes going through the yearbooks, then handed Clara Cooper a list of six names that included Gibson and asked for their academic records. He had expected her to protest about privacy and confidentiality and that sort of dodge, but Clara had understood that the FBI badge could override all that, so why make a fuss? The cadets from those long-ago classes would by now be rising high in their military or other careers, and that meant higher clearances for secrecy. Why make a bother when the outcome was inevitable? After all, it was a routine background check. The special agent had said so.

"I'll go over to the superintendent's office and get approval and dig these up for you," she said with a wave of the folded paper. "Won't be long."

Sharif took a break and walked outside. Cadets were marching crisply, doing PT, or busy at their other assigned chores around the pristine 200-acre campus. Discipline was evident everywhere; this wasn't the kind of place where a phony would thrive, and Gibson had made it to the top. Sharif talked with a few of them to get a feel for the type of personality that could handle such a strict environment.

Clara came back with the paperwork, and he delved into the files, examining each folder equally, but caring only about Luke Gibson. The rest were cover. Gibson and one of the other cadets had been valedictorians of their high-school classes. The boy had it all—grades, leadership ability, physical fitness, and fluency in two foreign languages—French and Arabic. He majored in international relations and affairs, finishing tenth overall in academics, captained the baseball team, and scored as an expert marksman on the rifle team, taking an individual first in the annual match against West Point. Sharif tapped his pen in thought. Gibson was the gold standard that year, and had made the promotion selection committee's job easy.

He went back to the files. Five of the six cadets became commissioned officers upon graduation: two Army, two Air Force, one to the Coast Guard. There was no such notation on Gibson's transcript. Sharif asked the archivist about that, and she explained that, unlike federal schools like Annapolis and West Point, VMI graduates were required to take the training but didn't have to join the military.

"Ah." This was where the CIA had scooped him up. After this, Gibson was off the official radar.

"Thanks for all your assistance, ma'am," Sharif said. "But, like the old detectives, I have one more question. I noticed that the *Bomb* from 2000 was dedicated to First Captain Gary Smith, who was the regimental commander. That seems to be a discrepancy, because the commander for that year was a fellow named, uh, Gibson. Lucas Gibson. How can that happen?"

Clara frowned. She was puzzled. "I don't know, Special Agent Sharif. There is only one regimental CO at a time. Let me call someone—my predecessor, Millie Hartnett. She knows everything." Clara used her cell phone to dial Millie and exchanged pleasantries, then put her on speaker-phone to include Sharif.

The woman's voice sounded strong. "Oh, my. That was just awful. I recall it. The whole school went into mourning."

"Why?"

"Gary was a wonderful cadet—stood first in his class in academics, and played quarterback for the football team. He had already served two years as an enlisted soldier before coming to VMI and had—let me remember here, he was a paratrooper with the hundred and first."

Lucky Sharif felt Gibson's glow dimming. Maybe he wasn't the gold standard that year after all.

"Well, what happened to him, Millie?"

"It was around Thanksgiving. Gary went rock climbing with some friends over the break and tragically fell to his death. The police said it was a terrible accident."

"So the corps was without its student commander for a while?"

"Not for long. That couldn't be allowed, so the selection committee bumped up the regimental XO to the higher rank so the institute could get back to normal. Gary was a good boy. It was awful."

Clara glanced at Sharif. "Anything else?"

"No, ma'am. Many thanks to both of you. I'll see myself out." When he left, he could hear Clara and Millie turning the conversation to more personal matters as they set a lunch date.

Sharif got into the car and called Washington to get an FBI researcher to investigate the climbing accident that took the life of a VMI student by the name of Gary Smith, including his military record. Then he drove away from the orderly, regimental campus and back into the untidy real world.

ISLAMABAD, PAKISTAN

NICKY MARKS, ONE OF the world's most wanted terrorists, felt safe enough among the teeming mass of more than four million people who lived in the capital federal district of Pakistan and the adjoining city of Rawalpindi. In fact, Islamabad was one of his favorite cities. He was sure that one of the surveillance cameras that webbed the city was probably watching him, but that was no concern. Marks wasn't an enemy of Pakistan; for years he had worked with agents of its intelligence service. One of those agents was on the other side of the table at the café right now, enjoying a cappuccino and watching the attractive women walking outside beneath the tall trees that were bursting with purple and fiery-red springtime colors. Serious cyclists in neon racing tights zoomed by in practice runs along the city's neat grid of streets. The dense green Margalla Hills climbed skyward in the distance.

"I hope you're not planning on staying long in our fair city," said Maroof Sherdil of the Pakistani Directorate for Inter-Services Intelligence—better known by its feared acronym, ISI.

Marks grinned. "Why, Maroof, do you mean that I'm not welcome here in the diplomatic quarter?"

Sherdil, a native Isloo, put down his cup. He was dressed in a fashionable Western-style suit and tie, and had considerable hair that was meticulously barbered, along with a close-trimmed beard—the aggregate giving him the appearance more of an international gentleman than the ragamuffin

Pakistani a bystander might have expected. "You, my friend, are not welcome anywhere right now."

Marks wasn't disturbed. He hadn't been arrested, so he counted himself still to be ahead of the game. "I'm just following orders. How long do I have?"

"A couple of days, three at the most. Nobody knows where you are right now, but you will be pinged on the cameras soon enough, and then the facial-recognition software will identify you and requests for action will start piling up on my desk."

Sherdil looked out at the street, then back at Marks. "I can't believe you would show up here in plain view. Particularly after that stunt in Paris. Damn, Nicky, that was harsh, even for you!"

"Come on, Maroof. You know how the game is played. Sometimes a sacrifice must be made to win the day. She was only an American lawyer, and there's no shortage of those." He seemed not to have a care in the world.

"I'm not talking about the woman. I mean that wave to the surveillance camera. It's gone viral on the Internet."

Marks said he understood, but that in setting a trap you sometimes had to lead the prey to the snare. That was what he was doing now. "I just want you to keep the cops off me for about twenty-four more hours, then I'll be out of here."

"That may be hard to do, with the price on your head getting higher and higher."

"What am I worth now?"

"The Rewards for Justice program is a full million dollars, with France offering just as much. I should arrest you myself and retire rich."

All the play went out of Marks, replaced by a coldness that made the Pakistani wish he hadn't said those words. "The Prince wouldn't like that," he said.

Maroof Sherdil tapped on the small table with his fingertips. "I misspoke. Unforgivable for a diplomat like myself. I would not do such a thing, nor would I intentionally annoy the Prince. You know that."

Marks yawned and stretched. Yeah, he knew that. Mention the Prince and they fold right up. "We're good, man. Give me space for another day and I'll be out of here. The Tribal Areas are calling my name."

"Only if you do no mischief in this country. Do not force me to take action." The ISI man was trying to recover.

"Just passing through, mate. Just passing through."

BURLINGTON, VERMONT

ELIZABETH LEDFORD CASTILLO FELT a cold cube of air enfold her as soon as the flight attendant popped open the hatch after the direct United flight from Washington. By the time she arrived at Burlington International Airport, she was longing for the warmth of the Mexican sun. The light sweater she had brought along was no protection at all as she made her way to the luggage carousel. Long bags of skis were carted in. Skis. In April. People in tufted down jackets looked at her with the annoying smiles bestowed on first-timers to Vermont.

"We only have two seasons up here: winter and August," said a man's voice over her shoulder. "I brought this for you." Orville Oliver Dawkins loomed large and easily wrapped a heavy coat around her shoulders. It was his size, which meant that it swallowed her. Her hands didn't need gloves now, because they didn't reach the cuffs.

She gave him a tremendous hug, squeezing hard. "So good to see you again, Double-Oh."

"Same here. My life has been much duller without Coastie in it. I missed you a lot, girl." Chief Master Sergeant Dawkins, USMC, retired, and Ledford had been close friends when they both worked with the élite and secret Task Force Trident, back in the day. He had been the teacher, and she was his prize pupil. His hair had grown out and was speckled with gray, but the big man was still a rock of muscle and strong as an oak. She noticed that he had on only jeans and a long-sleeved lumberjack shirt, apparently immune to the cold. He held her at arm's length and examined her face. "Listen, that thing with Mickey was absolutely one of the worst things possible. I won't ask if you're okay, because you'll lie and say you are, when you're not. So let's just get your bags and hit the road before we get all weepy."

Coastie looked down at the scuffed floor, shoved her hands deep into the jacket pockets, and didn't react when Double-Oh pulled up the parka's hood. As they walked out together, she looked like a little kid beside him.

A gray Hummer was parked right outside, and when Double-Oh popped the rear door to toss in the suitcase Coastie found herself face to face with two soulful and alert eyes, two pointed ears cocked forward in curiosity, and the furry snout of a large German shepherd that sucked in all her scents in great swoops of breath. "This is Nero, a retired warrior dog who lost that front paw sniffing for us in Afghanistan. He detected an ambush and his handler died in the following firefight." Double-Oh scratched the big dog's head. "Ole Nero has been recovering with us out here in the boonies. He's one of our therapy dogs. Give him a few seconds and he'll lick you to death."

"Hello, Nero," Coastie said in an almost inaudible voice, hurt recognizing hurt. The dog immediately dropped a wet pink tongue to her hand, licked twice, and then pushed his nose flat into the jacket, inviting her to rub his head. "You're the most beautiful dog I've ever seen."

They headed northwest up Interstate 89 for a while before cutting across U.S. 2 toward Lake Champlain, reaching deep into the strange, quiet world of rural Vermont between the Winooski and Lamoille Rivers. Coastie began to cry, pulling herself deep into the parka. Dawkins said nothing, but passed a box of tissue. Nero stepped onto the console and leaned on her. "I can't stop all this crying," Coastie blubbered. "I hate it. When do the images stop coming back?"

"Time," he said. "It's really the only cure."

Nero started nudging around, trying to get his nose into the thick jacket. He sensed the pain of a friend, and pressed with his right front leg. Coastie gave in and helped the seventy-five-pound dog into the spacious seat with her, wrapped both arms around him, and held on tight, her tears wetting his fur. Nero sat strong and loving as the countryside passed, contentedly sniffing her uniqueness and listening to her heartbeat. She was part of the pack now. He would protect her.

When she spotted the lake's broad expanse of shining water, she finally asked, "Where are we going?"

"I have some property up here, about a hundred acres surrounded by forest, and we've built up a private retreat for special operators like ourselves who are having problems. Coming back from a war is never easy, and for folks like us the nightmares can be even tougher. We get some grant and foundation money, but Excalibur Enterprises is the main sponsor."

"Kyle and Sir Jeff and Lady Pat do this? I hadn't heard of that."

"None of us are big on publicity, Coastie. The results are what counts. You can rest here for a while, fully protected, and we'll help each other. We've all lost someone."

"Kyle promised you'd train me up again."

"He lied, girl. He's trying to keep your existence on the down-low, so we'll do some exercises and stuff, and maybe some shooting. Hell, there's nothing I can teach you about shooting, Coastie. Not a damn thing. We'll just plink some targets. No heavy stuff."

"So what's the plan?" She felt Nero shift beside her, detecting the sudden uneasiness.

"I'm supposed to determine if you have your head screwed on straight. If you have a couple of loose bolts, we'll tighten them up. After what happened with Mickey, there's bound to be some trauma." He drove along a narrow road, through a desolate stretch that had its own dark beauty. They reached a fence line, and a wooden sign nailed to a tree announced PHOENIX FARM. A polished brass ship's bell hung beside the opening in the fence, because there was no gate.

Coastie began to glimpse outbuildings through the trees—stables, a main house and some smaller bungalows, horses, other dogs, and a few people. "I'm okay," she insisted, not believing it herself.

"Nero and I disagree. That mutt and I both think you're pretty fucked up right now. The good news is that we can fix it."

WASHINGTON, D.C.

SPECIAL AGENT LUCKY SHARIF drove straight back to his office in the Hoover Building when he got back to D.C. to plow through the file that the FBI had hastily compiled on the late VMI First Captain Gary Smith.

The young man's biography was truly impressive, but irrelevant, and Sharif skimmed through it to learn about the fatal accident. A few brief newspaper articles sketched the overall story. Smith had been free-solo climbing, which Sharif knew meant not using any ropes, helmet, or safety harness. In fact, the authorities reported that Smith was clad in only a pair of green Jockey boxers, a rock-band T-shirt, shorts, and climbing shoes, with a small flask of water and a bag of chalk around his waist. No tubular rope, no snap carabiners, no bashies, no cams to help him get out of a tough situation. The coroner found no indication of intoxicants or drugs in the system. The abrasions and broken bones and violated organs were consistent with a hard fall onto stone. He ruled that it was a tragic accident.

Sharif let that percolate for a few minutes as he went to get a soda and some crackers. Free-soloing was an inherently risky business, but Smith, a former paratrooper, would have had no fear of heights and would have been in splendid physical shape. Smith against the mountain; the irresistible force against the immovable object. Sharif felt that was reasonable for such an overachiever. A normal picnic wouldn't be enough.

Virginia boasted plenty of rock-climbing routes for more traditional adventurers. The death site in the New River Gorge wasn't one of them. A ranger said the climb apparently started at a virgin spot reached only by off-roading and a bit of luck. It hadn't been certified for public use because of the obvious danger of the hard climb over loose scree to a range of boulders and then up an apparently sheer cliff face that crested at a small space known as the Buzzard's Beak.

An addendum contained a brief report from the sole witness, Lucas Gibson, a classmate of the victim at the Virginia Military Institute. The cop wrote that the witness was emotional but showed self-control. It was the witness who had summoned rescuers by using a radio in the climbers' truck.

In the terse language of police reports, the account said: "The witness stated the victim was climbing well and showing no sign of distress. The witness began his own ascent about three minutes after the victim and was positioned below the victim. The witness said the victim put his weight on his right foot while edging to a new position, and slipped. The drop was an estimated seventy feet onto rocks."

The mourning would take place elsewhere. To the authorities, the incident went into a "shit happens" file. There was no further investigation.

Lucky Sharif packed up, turned out the light, and finally went home. Janna was still awake, waiting, and they went over the file again together, working until dawn as they threw questions back and forth, just as they had done when they were FBI partners. The picture was complete, but the pieces didn't fit.

KAISERSLAUTERN, GERMANY

THE TWO SNIPERS HAD dashed away from Washington so fast that, a day later, they needed everything from toothpaste to shoes. A big base like Ramstein and its nearby German towns had it all, and more. After letting their body clocks adjust to the time change, Swanson and Gibson went shopping off-post for certain civilian gear, because they didn't know what would be their next step in pursuing the elusive killer Nicky Marks. That he might be going to Afghanistan was only a hunch.

They went for medium prices in buying a few lightweight shirts and slacks similar to what the Germans and tourists in town were wearing, because it would be ideal to conceal themselves as Europeans and not be tagged as Americans at first glance. The sundries were available off the shelf, and they quickly filled their backpacks. Back at the base, the two split up and interviewed other special-ops types who had been in the area for a while. Swanson took the marines and the SEALs, while Gibson did the Army. They found nothing of interest, and morosely drifted over to Zur Big Emma for schnitzel and beer and maybe to pick up some gossip.

"Gonna have to run a lot tomorrow to work off this meal," Gibson said, devouring a forkful of soft spaetzle. "No wonder Germans are so big."

Swanson drank some beer from a tall mug. "I can tell you don't like it. Remember, this is the land of the Hindenburg blimp."

"It blew up."

"That's my point," said Swanson, cutting into his meat. "Our rule is to eat when you can because you don't know when your next meal will be, right?"

Marguerite del Coda was suddenly at the table, pulling up a chair and brushing her hair back from her eyes. "Islamabad," she said. "The sonofa-bitch just pinged the Net in Islamabad. The sighting has been confirmed by the Pakis."

Swanson wiped his mouth with a white napkin and tossed it on the remains of the food. He looked at Gibson. "Let's go to work, then. You ready?"

Gibson looked longingly at the half-eaten dinner and grinned. "I was born ready, podna."

VERMONT

COASTIE AWOKE TO A series of quick wet slurps on her ear from Nero. The dog had slept with her all night, a warm, comforting, and hairy presence that she would bump a hip into or rest her arm across to keep from feeling so alone. The morning light was bright, and Nero was telling her that it was time for him to go outside and attend to important dog stuff. "Got it," she said, sitting up with a big yawn, then pushing off the bed. Nero made the transition to the floor smoothly, despite his missing paw, and when she opened the door he hopped out, propelled by his strong hind legs. The remaining front leg balanced him, and the big foot landed surely. He had adjusted to his new lifestyle, felt no pity for himself. It was what it was.

She went into the bathroom and brushed her teeth and combed her hair into a hasty ponytail, then laced on her sneakers and did some stretches. She had slept only in shorts and a loose T-shirt, so she added a warmup suit before going outside for a run around the frosty Phoenix Farm. Other people were also up, mostly doing chores. A few waved to the newcomer. What could be more normal than feeding chickens and grooming horses while happy dogs gamboled about? What could be more safe? What could be quieter? She found a path and loped into the forest shadows.

Double-Oh explained it last evening during the evening meal, which was eaten on long wooden tables with attached benches so that a group could share the food that was prepared by a kitchen staff. Three men and another woman shared their table—the mashed potatoes, the salad bowl, the meat, the iced tea, and the conversation. All were special-ops types of one form or another who had found out about Phoenix and come for a stay during their personal journeys back to normality. Years of military service back in the day had placed them in extreme danger, over and over. They had lost friends and seen terrible things, and, often out of necessity, had been forced to do things they would never discuss. And it was hard to just walk away when the enlistment was up. Thanks a lot for playing, sign these papers and go back home and climb the corporate ladder, or go to hell. Ghosts didn't like to stay behind doors. The blaze in the large stone fireplace helped burn them away.

Coastie found a comfortable jogging pace, and her lungs adjusted to the altitude. Is this place all uphill? she wondered. She ran automatically, as Phoenix Farm residents had been doing on this path for years. The sweat came with the deeper breaths. There was a quiet presence behind her. Nero was striding along at half speed without effort, his tongue hanging out like a wet pink shoe, and they went into a small valley with a swift-flowing brook.

If someone wanted to come to Phoenix Farm, all he or she had to do was ring the bell and walk on in. It was intentionally the direct reverse use of the bell that was clonged when a defeated and demoralized trainee decided to leave the Navy SEALs. This bell marked an arrival at a destination, not a failure. Residents could leave at any time, without shame or remorse, whenever they felt their time was done and they were ready to rejoin the civilian world. No private guns were allowed, just as no booze is allowed in an Alcoholics Anonymous meeting. The only drugs were in the first-aid kit. Dawkins kept some weapons in an off-limits safe for his personal use. He said they were just a couple of shotguns.

It all made sense, she thought. A noble effort to help troubled vets traverse the dreaded PTSD chasm. Good on Excalibur for sponsoring it. Good on the horsies. Good on Nero. Good on everybody. Good on her for being here.

"I hate it," Coastie said to herself. "There's nothing wrong with me. I didn't ring that damned bell."

WASHINGTON, D.C.

THIS WAS GOING TO be a good day, Veronica Keenan thought as she finished her own one-mile run in Rock Creek Park with a flashy sprint, then walked around with her hands on her hips, breathing hard and not even trying to hide the joy that she felt inside. She was going to make her mark with the House Permanent Select Committee on Intelligence. There were many people who thought she didn't deserve that committee assignment, but today they would change their minds when she took on the CIA.

She had been nervous the previous afternoon when she had the private meeting with her party's senior member on the committee, but that eased when the wise old congressman lit up like a Christmas-tree bulb as she presented her findings. He could see it all unfold in his head even as she spoke: a congressional hearing about a rogue CIA agent running a big drug operation out of Afghanistan. Keenan was promised a place on the investigating subcommittee that would hold the hearings. Sticking a needle in the CIA would show their determination to hold the secret agency accountable to the public. It wouldn't hurt the reelection chances of either member of Congress when the news leaked to the press.

Her aide caught her on her smartphone before she reached the office. There was going to be an emergency meeting of the committee leadership before lunch, and Keenan was to present her findings once again. The aide also explained that she had been able to dig up the astonishing background of the agent involved—Kyle Swanson, an expert sniper who had been around for years—and that would be juicy new meat for the conference. Instead of a vague description of the operation, she would have a precise target. It didn't matter to her whether or not this Swanson guy was actually a bad guy, as he was just a tool to be used to pry into the CIA's dirty little world.

"Is there going to be a CIA rep there?" Keenan needed to know before walking into a buzz saw of criticism. This investigation, if it got off the ground, could make her career. It could also end it in a hurry if she was wrong. She wanted the CIA person to know that she was really on the agency's side, pointing out a piece of dirty laundry that could perhaps be handled internally.

"One of the big names is coming over," the aide responded. "Martin Atkins, the director of intelligence."

"The CIA director himself is going to be there?"

"No, Congresswoman. This man is one level away from the big chair, but he is the one in the know about all the cloak-and-dagger stuff."

Keenan paused. She was only ten minutes from the office now and could see the white dome of the Capitol looming ahead, crowning the hill at the end of Pennsylvania Avenue. "Okay. Put together a backgrounder on him, too. I don't want to be blindsided."

"Yes, ma'am. See you in a few."

AS FAR AS THE Prince could see, everything was in order.

Nicky Marks would soon be out of Pakistan, while the CIA hunters were yet to arrive. They had left the Ramstein base in a rush when the Pakistani intelligence service reported that their quarry had been sighted in Islamabad. Instead of a lumbering USAF transport plane, the two could now make shorter hops aboard aircraft owned and flown by the Central Intelligence Agency. They would be too late to nab Marks, but everyone involved would be buoyed by the feeling that they were closing in fast. One step behind is still second place, Marks thought.

That headlong dash to complete their mission was resulting in a lack of caution and a lowering of awareness of what was really happening. And as the agents swam deeper into his net in Pakistan, the Prince was already tightening things behind them.

Back in Washington, the politicians were about to haul in the CIA director of intelligence, who would obviously stonewall any questions about an ongoing operation. That would make the politicians angry, and they would retaliate by expanding the circle of knowledge. He'd always found it fascinating that a single pebble tossed into a pond could cause ripples that would go on and on. In this case, the pebble was the ambitious widow from Nebraska. Within twenty-four hours, the rumors that the CIA was running drugs out of Afghanistan would be in the briefing papers of power-wielders from the White House on down. Nobody wanted to be unprepared for the coming barrage of media questions.

And questions there would be. Some reporters would start receiving leaks from pet sources: There's something weird going on over at Langley. Congress is asking for answers, but not getting any. The Prince gauged that it would be fresh meat for the TV talking heads by tomorrow evening.

And then the name would be dropped. Kyle Swanson would be outed as a secret agent who had gone bad. Then the average man and woman, boy and girl with an iPhone would start constructing the social-media noose around Swanson's neck. No proof would be offered, but speculation would be more than enough.

As if with the snip of a ribbon by sharp scissors, that would be the end of the top-priority hunt for Nicky Marks. The agency, having been tarred with scandal, would terminate the mission and all support of Swanson even without admitting or denying anything. Supplies would stop. Intelligence wouldn't reach him. Friends would become enemies, and co-workers wouldn't trust him. Marty Atkins would be forced to recall the sniper from the field and place such a distance between Swanson and Langley that it might never again be bridged.

Swanson's reputation would go up in flames, and he would be fortunate to get out of this without being arrested by his own people. The Prince didn't really want him arrested. Ruining his reputation was important, but he had a more unpleasant fate in store for the man.

For now, just leave things alone. Every ingredient of the trap was simmering nicely on a low heat. He turned his attention to other matters.

ISLAMABAD, PAKISTAN

EVERYBODY DOES IT. EVEN Maroof Sherdil of the Pakistani ISI had dreams. As an important man in Joint Intelligence X, which coordinated and processed everything from the other three branches, Sherdil carried the rank of an army full colonel. For most men, that would have been enough. Not only did he have a decent salary; the agency provided a free car, a furnished home, medical care, schools, and other attractive benefits. The colonel wanted more.

Climbing the ladder of rank and power simply didn't pay enough in these days of economic uncertainty, and he had to be on the lookout for a way to increase his savings if he was ever to achieve his dream of moving out of the grim government-sponsored lodgings and into the commodious home whose construction he'd been watching in the capital's prestigious F-10 Markaz area of Zone 1.

He frequently played the Internet lotteries, but that was a waste. Petty blackmail would land him in prison. Special-mission bonuses and the usual bribes had helped. They simply weren't enough. The new four-bedroom home close to McDonald's and Pizza Hut and the golf course and excellent shopping was priced at a bit over fifty million rupees.

He toyed with a scratch pad. One strong American dollar was worth about a hundred and four rupees on the exchange today, so fifty million rupees was equal to roughly half a million U.S. dollars. The colonel had saved only half that amount, even when he factored in the special breaks that the seller would grant to a rising ISI official who could make him disappear.

He fed the paper into the shredder beside his desk in the ISI central headquarters. Enough worrying for one day. He put on his uniform jacket, checked his appearance in a bathroom mirror, then went upstairs to the Office of the Director General.

The suave Lieutenant General Zahid Ali Khan was polite enough to stand and shake hands when Maroof Sherdil entered the office. Khan had the cut of an Egyptian film star and was unfailingly mannered in his dealings with others. He invited Sherdil to have a chair. "I regret not having much time for you today, Colonel. How are Sarah and the children?"

"God has blessed me, sir. My family is well, and I wish similar good fortune for yours."

"My thanks," said Kahn. "Now, is this unfortunate business done?" He leaned back in his chair and folded his arms.

"Yes, sir. The Americans should be on the way even now. They sounded pleased to find the exact location of Nicky Marks."

"The man is a danger to all around him, including us, and it is time for his exit. The Prince was agreeable?"

"It was his suggestion, sir. Marks has apparently become a liability for him, too. There will be no blowback from that direction."

The lieutenant general slid his right index finger across his bristly mustache. "The U.S. Rewards for Justice Program?"

Nicky Marks had a million dollars on his head. Sherdil and his boss would split it evenly. Tomorrow, he would have the needed cash for the house, his superior officer would be even richer, the drug money would continue to flow, and the American government would have its terrorist scalp. Everybody wins. Almost everybody.

Maroof saluted and left the building through the lobby, adjusting his black beret once he was outside. As he walked across the manicured grounds to his silver Volvo, he thought about Sarah, their two boys and one daughter, and how they would be opening a new chapter in their lives. *Insh'Allah.* God willing.

He tapped his blinker and moved smoothly into the traffic, heading up to see the house once again. The cement foundation had been braced with steel girders and deep pilings as protection against earthquakes, and the wooden frame was far enough along that the workmen were able to work beneath the roof they had put on. Greenery would be plentiful.

At the turn on the Ibn-e-Sina Road, traffic began to flow better. Five cars back was a black Audi, with Nicky Marks at the wheel, listening to music and cool in the air-conditioning. He knew exactly where the ISI officer was heading, for hadn't the colonel been jabbering non-stop about finding this special house? Lost in his fantasy, Sherdil had hardly checked his mirrors during the trip from the ISI headquarters to the little lane that angled up to the new home, and then into what would become his private driveway.

"Bye now, Maroof," Marks said with a quiet laugh as he hit the Send key on a pre-dialed cell phone number, triggering the bomb beneath the Volvo. It went off in splash of flame and clouds of smoke, scattering chunks of metal and flaming debris. The house caught fire as Marks wheeled about and drove away.

SAVANNAH, GEORGIA

LUCKY SHARIF DROVE TO Savannah because flying down from Washington meant changing planes in Atlanta, an experience that most sane people tried to avoid. Of course, following the interstates also meant going through Atlanta. It was believed down South that when you die there will be a stopover in Atlanta on the way to heaven or hell. Instead, he meandered down the older coast routes, through miles of pine trees and azaleas that ran wild and the choking tendrils of green kudzu vines; he smelled the stench of the Union Bag–Camp Paper Corporation plant and slapped his first mosquito before he'd crossed the Talmadge Bridge and dropped downtown.

So this was the hometown of Luke Gibson, he thought, nosing slowly down Broughton Street, once the busy heart of commerce before the white residents started to migrate to the suburbs and out to the islands to build mansions on salt marshland. It had a feeling of decay and wasn't in the same antebellum league as Charleston, just up the coast. He turned toward the water and bumped over the cobblestoned street down to the tourist area along River Street, and up again through the squares, where the old city was flashing its April glory of bright flowers and mighty oaks. The tourists enjoyed the historic area during the daylight hours. At night, strolling among the magnolias was not a good idea. Too many places for danger to lurk, his cop instinct told him.

Following his nav system out of the tourist zone and down the long, palm-lined Victory Drive, he found a little restaurant called Carey Hilliard's, on Skidaway Road, and worked on his laptop while tackling a barbecue sandwich and a cup of Brunswick stew and sweet iced tea. He sent his wife a selfie to make her jealous. Back in D.C., she would be having a tasteless salad at her desk.

Back in the car, with a refill of tea nestled in the console, he cruised the final mile to 2134 East Fortieth Street, circled through the working-class neighborhood that was laid out in a grid, and finally pulled up in front of the corner lot. It was an innocuous place, much like the other homes: three bedrooms, kitchen, bath, living room, and a garage in the back—a baby-boomer suburb built after World War II as ordinary Americans began riding the economic engine into the middle class. The clapboard had been repaired over the years, but the paint was fresh. The roses were trimmed and the lawn was cut. On a cracking sidewalk, a boy of about six and his little sister leaned on their bikes and stared at him when he got out. "Hi," he said.

"Mommy!" the little brown-haired girl screamed.

"Are you LeBron James?" the boy asked, never having seen a black man this tall.

Sharif squatted to get smaller and showed his badge. "Don't I wish? I'm just a policeman. Can you get your mommy for me?"

A neat woman with a pretty face and a dishtowel draped over one shoulder appeared at the front door, shooed the children aside, corralled a yapping spaniel, and said, "You're a cop?"

"FBI, actually. My name is Lucky Sharif," he said quietly, extending the cred pack. "May I ask your name?"

"Maureen Alonso. Those are my kids, Bobby and Lisa. Did he do something wrong again? Did he break another window with that dang baseball?" She stepped aside. "Come on in here, Special Agent Sharif. My husband, another Bobby, is at work, and the neighbors are nosy as hell. Now, what can I do for you?" Her eyes sparkled with wit and curiosity.

Sharif ducked his head to clear the doorframe. "Just some routine inquiries that don't involve you or your family. I don't know anything about Bobby's baseball felonies. He looks like he can hit pretty good."

Without asking, she went into the small kitchen and returned with some cold sweet tea. Sharif thanked her and felt his kidneys starting to ache. "You and your husband bought this place about three years ago, right?"

"Sure did. We got a really good deal on it. The widow woman that lived here died and the family wanted to dump it in a hurry. Neighborhood changing and all that rot. Truth is that it was run-down and dilapidated because she couldn't take care of it. She went into a nursing home and rented it out, and the renters were slobs. Place was a mess, believe me. Why?"

At his peril, he tasked the tea. It was cool and delicious, and he could feel his arteries beginning to clog with sugar. "Did you ever meet her?

"Mrs. Gibson? Oh, no. We dealt only with the Realtors. The papers were signed by her son, but it was all done by mail. I think he's a soldier off somewhere." Mrs. Alonso twisted the napkin while she thought. "You know, Mr. Sharif, she did leave behind a box of stuff that we didn't throw away yet. We thought maybe the son might want it, but he never replied when we told him about it. So I'm more than ready to get rid of it. You can have it if you want."

VERMONT

AFTER LUNCH, COASTIE BORROWED the Land Rover and drove sixteen miles to the town of Clarke, where she bought an AR-15 rifle and a box of 5.56 ammo from a private collector for less than nine hundred dollars and no paperwork. "It's for my husband," she explained to the seller, who had posted an ad on the Internet. When she returned to the ranch, she hid the waterproof case near the bell.

ISLAMABAD, PAKISTAN

KYLE SWANSON FELT THAT if he had been a bloodhound his sensory intake would have been quivering from overload. Nicky Marks was here, his presence almost the light touch of a bug on the arm. The vibe was that tight. "You feel it?" he asked Gibson after they deplaned.

"Oh, yeah." Gibson removed his sunglasses and took a slow look around. "Not *here*, here, but somewhere."

The Gulfstream had flown them more than three thousand miles, from Germany to Rome to Istanbul, and finally to the Pakistani military air base in the capital. Even aboard the executive jet, with all its comforts, the two special operators were exhausted and unsteady when it slid to a stop. Bones creaked, crotches itched, and armpits smelled sour.

"Like Grant told Sherman after the first bloody day at Shiloh, 'We'll lick 'em tomorrow,'" Gibson quoted with a weary roll of his shoulders.

They walked side by side to a waiting sedan that ferried them to the CIA compound, where a briefer informed them that the man they had come to see, the ISI officer who had fingered Marks, had been blown up in his car two hours before they landed. Marks was in the wind again.

"That *fucker!*" Gibson snarled.

Swanson shook his head. "Doesn't matter, Luke. He's still here. This will be the end of the road."

SAVANNAH, GEORGIA

SHARIF DUG TWO BOXES of memorabilia out of Maureen Alonso's dusty garage, and Bobby helped load it into the car. There might be jewels in them, or just trash. Wouldn't know until he went through it. He was leaning toward jewels.

"You ever shoot anybody?" Bobby asked.

"Oh, you saw my weapon? I just use it to scare bad guys."

"I bet you shot a bunch of guys. How tall are you?"

"Do you always ask so many questions?"

They went back to the house so that Sharif could say goodbye to Maureen Alonso, but the perky woman suggested that he go across the street, one house down, and talk with old Mrs. Boykin, who had lived there forever and had probably known the late Mrs. Gibson very well. "Bobby, take Mr. Sharif over yonder and introduce him to the nurse, then you come right back home."

"Before we go, could I use your bathroom?" Sharif asked. "All this iced tea is killing me."

Bobby was waiting in the branches of a chinaberry tree in the front yard when Sharif came back out. He was delighted to escort his new best friend, the tall black man with a badge and a gun, and he hoped Rodney and Teddy would see them crossing the street together. He rang the bell, and the door was opened by a middle-aged black woman in comfortable clothing who radiated an aura of gentleness. "Hey, Miz Adele, this is Mr. Sharif from the FBI, and he wants to talk to Miz Boykin."

Sharif showed his identification. "Bobby, you go on back home now and guard the car, okay. Don't let anybody steal my boxes."

"If I do that, will you let me hold the gun?"

"No. It's not a toy. Now scoot."

"He's a handful," said the woman as she invited Sharif inside. "A normal boy. I'm Adele Anderson, an extended-care nurse for Mrs. Boykin. You caught us at a propitious moment; she's just up from a nap and is quite chirpy. Can I ask what this is about? I don't want her upset if we can avoid it."

"I only want to ask what she might remember of a former neighbor, the people who lived in what's now the Alonso home."

"Good. She's ninety-six, but she has a pretty good memory for someone her age. Just be gentle. Can I get you some tea?"

Lucky blanched. "No, thanks."

Clara Boykin was in a sunny little parlor, with a white lace shawl thrown over her shoulders. She was in a wheelchair, and blue slippers peeked from beneath the hem of her cotton nightgown. She studied Sharif from head to toe as Adele made the introductions and motioned him to sit down. The small room was filled with loaded bookshelves, and a Garfield cat glared at the intruder.

"You read all those books, Mrs. Boykin?"

"I certainly did. Those and many more." Her voice was soft but clear. "I was an English teacher for thirty years. But age took my eyesight and all I can do now is listen to audiobooks. I don't get the same flavor that the writers wanted to convey from audio. Do you read?"

Sharif grinned. "Not as much as I'd like. Mostly I'm wrapped up in work, and official forms aren't very literary."

"You look smart." She appraised him. "Play ball in college?"

"Basketball at Marquette. Majored in criminal justice, and a master's in psychology."

The woman nodded approvingly. "Ask your questions then, young man, before Adele forces more pills down my gullet."

"This is just routine background information-gathering because a former neighbor of yours is being considered for a high-ranking position in the federal government. He lived right across the street. His name is Lucas Gibson."

The levity drained out of the old woman, the eyes sharpened, and her mouth went grim. "Luke. I should have figured that out. Well, Special Agent Sharif, I remember him well and have absolutely no use for that imperious little shit. Do not trust him. Do not give him the job. Let me tell you."

Sharif was surprised by the vehemence in her voice. "May I record this?" he asked, putting his cell phone on the table.

She smiled. "Yes, you may."

WASHINGTON, D.C.

DIRECTOR OF INTELLIGENCE MARTIN Atkins got a kick out of meeting Janna Ecklund in a McDonald's out beyond the beltway. He was long past his clandestine days as a CIA field agent, but there was always something about hiding in plain sight. They were in a corner booth, and his security detail occupied the surrounding tables. The yells of kids back in the play area would overwhelm any listening device.

He had a chicken salad, while Janna had a Big Mac with fries. An agent placed the order and delivered the red trays to their table. "You're not really going to eat that, are you?" Marty asked.

"Maybe a little. I want to send a picture of my meal to Lucky first. He's down South eating like a pig and torturing me with his food. I hope he gains a hundred pounds." She snapped, clicked, and sent, then pushed the meal aside except for a single French fry to nibble on. "So, what's up?"

Atkins drew in a deep breath. "We have some potential problems, and I wanted to give you guys an early warning. Word is going around Capitol Hill that the agency is running drugs again, that Kyle is involved, and that, somehow, Excalibur Enterprises and Sir Jeff are behind it all."

Janna pushed back against the hard bench and chewed thoughtfully. "Bullshit." She swallowed, then smiled. A shark smile. "Utter bullshit, Marty."

"I know, I know. It's a political thing that came out of nowhere. A congresswoman from Nebraska, of all places, is trying to tear a piece off the agency's hide to earn some Brownie points."

"Where does it stand now?" She picked another fry from the carton.

"The chairman of the House Permanent Select Committee on Intelligence says he's concerned. Nice choice of words there, eh? Means nothing either way. So I have to go to a private meeting to explain things, which I will not do. Next step will be for the minority committee members to leak it to the press to force something."

"Ouch," said Janna. "This have anything to do with Kyle being out chasing Nicky Marks?"

Atkins pushed the salad aside and helped himself to an oily fry. "No such thing as a coincidence in this business, Janna. You're FBI-trained and know that. For protection, I'm going to have to shut down the Marks thing and get Kyle and Luke Gibson back under cover until the political flap blows over."

"You think Sir Jeff should also hunker down? He's not the type to hide from some politician. He'll go after them with everything we've got—and we've got a lot."

"I cannot advise you to do anything. Excalibur is your business, but none of us want to put a light on the help the company provides on special operations. Tell Sir Jeff what's going on and get Kyle back on safe ground. I'll get around to Nicky Marks later."

"Good enough. Thanks for the tip, Marty. You're a good friend."

Atkins wiped his hands on a few little paper towels and slid out of the booth. A coterie of security men and women stood at the same time, like flowers blooming in a group. "Right. Be careful what you say about this."

Janna nodded and her snowy hair kept its shape. She made no move to get up. "Yeah. The hell with Lucky, I'm going to finish my Big Mac after all."

PAKISTAN
2:30 AM LOCAL
2230 ZULU

U P! UP! GET UP!" Kyle Swanson had gone for a run to get some exercise, choked down a sandwich, and collapsed on a bunk in the special-ops dorm at midnight, a new day in Pakistan. He groaned now as some worthless SOB pounded on the plywood door. "What?" he called out angrily, and the voice answered, "Briefing room SAP." Swanson looked at the blue numbers on a digital clock. Two-thirty in the morning. Not enough sleep. Not nearly enough. He heard the man pounding on Gibson's adjacent door and shouting the same instruction, followed by the thump of something, probably a boot, hitting the door in response. Gibson was awake, too.

They met in the hallway, two bleary-eyed operators in wrinkled T-shirts and boxers and flip-flops. Gibson stretched and yawned, and reflex made Swanson to the same. They stumbled down the short hallway, out the door, across a patch of pavement, and into the command center, where young men and women in front of computer consoles and projected maps ignored them. Operators came and went through this room, and no one raised an eyebrow. A man with a shaved head waved them into a side room and they flopped into chairs.

"What?" Swanson asked, glancing at the three clocks mounted side by side on the wall: 0230 local time, which meant that the calendar had flipped from Tuesday to Wednesday. It was still Tuesday in England, where the Greenwich Mean Time—called Zulu by the military—was 2230.

Washington lagged behind, at 1930 Tuesday, five-thirty in the afternoon, which meant that offices all across the capital were closing.

"Coffee," Gibson said. "I demand coffee." The man pointed to a sideboard where a squat Mr. Coffee pot was full. Gibson poured two cups and handed one to Swanson.

"Your target popped up again," the CIA briefer said, lighting up a map. "Got into a shoot-out at a border crossing and killed two—one Paki and one Afghan—and wounded two more. Cameras caught it all, so the ID is positive. You want to watch it?"

"No need," said Swanson. The coffee was hot and strong, but he still felt as wobbly as a duck. "Where did he trip up?"

The officer enlarged the map several times, then used a red laser pointer. "Right here. A lightly used road, way off the main highway. More of a village road than anything."

"Why didn't he just go around it?" Gibson asked.

"We don't know."

"The bastard wanted us to see him again." Gibson told the briefer. "Draw a straight line from Islamabad to the border point, then extend it on up."

The officer tapped some keys and a thick black line appeared that crossed flatlands and mountains alike.

"I know where he's going," Gibson said with certainty. He stood and walked over to the map, where he tapped a specific area with his fingertip. "Nicky plans to get beneath the Taliban umbrella in the Wakham Corridor."

Swanson was at his shoulder, the briefer forgotten. The pros were at work. "And you know this how?"

"It's a big drug town. He and I did a hit on the warlord there some time ago—a major player in the drug trade. If he gets to the poppy fields, he'll have an army of fighters and informers around to protect him."

"International drug trade, you say?"

Gibson nodded. "Big-league growing, processing in superlabs, and shipping. Your friend, down in Mexico—that was drug-related, right? I'll bet it's all tied together somehow."

A fever rose in Swanson's chest. "So we have to stop him before he gets there." Turning to the CIA briefer, he asked, "How quickly can you scramble up a bird?"

"How about a Blackhawk? By the time you guys get dressed and geared up for the mission, I'll have the crew warmed up and waiting."

Gibson put down his coffee. "No, not this time. Chopper is too slow. I'm through chasing the sumbitch. Let's get ahead of him for once, Kyle. I think I know exactly where he's heading—an abandoned safe house where we staged for that raid. Let's get there and wait for him."

"Okay." The briefer thought for a minute. "Something bigger. Something to haul you all the way if you can give a GPS point."

"I can do that. You get us there, and we jump."

SAVANNAH, GEORGIA

LUCKY SHARIF FINISHED INTERVIEWING the wrinkled old woman with the sharp mind and sharper temper in the late afternoon. He checked his watch: 5:30 PM in Savannah meant that Kyle was probably sound asleep in Pakistan. No use sending up distress flares yet, because he had some gaps yet to fill. After all, Clara Boykin was almost a hundred years old; her facts would have to be double-checked. She had given him a hurricane of information. He was unsure how much was fact and how much was just her remembrance of "Get off my lawn" commands.

At the recommendation of the nurse, Adele, he wound his way back onto Victory Drive and headed south toward Tybee Island in search of a down-home crab shack on Wilmington Island. He followed the nav system right to the crushed-shell parking lot, got a table in the rear, and ordered a combination platter. "You want tea with that, hun?" asked the waitress. "Why not?" he replied, noting that she hadn't used the "sweet" adjective because it was superfluous. When his order arrived and was arranged on the thick paper that covered the table, he snapped a picture of the spread—fresh salad, crabs, oysters, shrimp, hush puppies, fresh bread, butter, tartar sauce, coleslaw, and tea—and sent it to Janna, texting, "Call you later. Got some good stuff."

As he ate, he let his mind roam to find the weak points and the work he needed to do. For starters, Luke Gibson wasn't really Luke Gibson, according to Mrs. Boykin. The boy's original last name was King, but his mother divorced his father early on, remarried, and assumed the new name. Mrs. Boykin had no use for the first husband, Thomas, who was apparently wealthy, arrogant, and generally no good.

That little house didn't look like the home of a rich guy, Sharif had noted, and the neighbor gave a little laugh. That wasn't King's place, she said. Daddy lived overseas primarily but kept a huge place up at Hilton Head and used that when he came back to America to visit Luke.

"How did he make his money?" the FBI agent asked, and she said the magic words: "Oil. Construction. Saudis. The Arabs, all over." The first thing on Sharif's list would be to get the office to run a full background on Thomas King and determine any links he had with the players in the oil game.

"Now, that Perry Gibson—he was a real gentleman," Mrs. Boykin had told him. "Right as rain, a good Christian man who worked out at the shipyard, manufacturing machine parts. He was good to Luke, but the boy detested him. Luke and his biological daddy had a strong bond. The child idolized the absent father, who showered him with praise and money. When Luke was about ten years old, he started spending his entire summers with his important daddy, who took him all over the world."

Sharif made a mental note. Ah! That's how Gibson learned to speak Arabic—a big question that the VMI résumé had introduced. Odd, but nothing weird once he found a logical explanation. Sharif worked on a crab cake while he considered how rich little Luke Gibson must have felt when the summer ended and he had to go back to the modest white home with all its financial constraints. He must have been miserable.

But the money and, more important, his father's influence, kept flowing like a running faucet. The best prep school in town, Benedictine Military, started him down the military road, and he excelled in all things, as if touched by destiny, and was the cadet colonel brigade commander in his senior year.

Mrs. Boykin said the boy became insufferable around the neighborhood, strutting as if he was better than everybody else. The other kids shunned him, and he withdrew into the country-club life of his richer friends. In a sad tone, she related that the death of Luke's stepfather during his junior year at Benedictine devastated his mother but almost put a skip in the boy's step. A real little bastard, Sharif thought, seeing it unfold in his mind. He pushed the remains of the meal away and called for the check. A hotel room down on the waterfront was waiting, and he was tired, so he would call Janna and then hit the pillows. The puzzle that was Luke Gibson could wait another few hours.

CLARKE, VERMONT

AT ABOUT ELEVEN O'CLOCK, Coastie once again cadged the Land Rover from Double-Oh Dawkins, saying that she just wanted to drive around with Nero for a while, maybe along the lake, and do some alone-time thinking. She tossed a cushy down sleeping bag into the back, Nero took the passenger seat, and they headed out, stopping briefly near the bell to retrieve the AR-15.

The dog stuck his head out the window to get the wind in his face as Coastie headed toward the lake. Few places were as dark and haunting as the Vermont North Woods in the middle of the night, and they were alone on what felt like a silent, foreign planet that was both forbidding and comfortable at the same time. Nero's ears were up, the nose busy, the eyes piercing the woods. She felt better with him around.

They picked up the main road, and after ten minutes of traveling north a steeple of light tore away the gloom and a red neon sign marked the oasis of Trapper's Bar & Grill. She drove by slowly, taking a look. The main building was long and low, with a broad parking lot of packed dirt off to the right. She could hear the sounds of music and people inside. Nero watched impassively. His owner wasn't stressed, so neither was he.

Coastie drove for another mile, turned around at a crossroads, went back, and entered the lot. Trapper's was busy tonight, but the dinner crowd was already gone. The night people were taking their turn, chasing away the blues in a variety of ways. She parked nose first in the back row, left the windows partially open to contain the dog, told Nero to stay, and gave him an ear scratch. "Be right back, big guy."

Even in faded jeans and a hoodie sweatshirt, with a billed Toronto Blue Jays cap pulled over her upswept hair, she still turned heads when she walked in. Eyes were on her. Several couples were dancing to a country song, groups of men and women congregated at tables, and there was hardly an empty spot at the bar. She stepped to the side, and a waitress found her. "Can I help you, sister?"

"Do you have a place for just one person? I want to get a burger."

The waitress, a round woman who had seen a lot of people, detected sorrow in the new customer. "Sure, I got a small table back by the kitchen. The guys won't bother you much back there. C'mon."

"Thanks." Coastie followed her, conscious that she was being examined as a stranger intruding into a familiar environment. "Cheeseburger with no onion. A cold draft beer."

The first pickup artist ambled over before the beer even got there. He had on his best blue Walmart T-shirt, made in China, and jeans that were tattered at the heels of his workboots. His eyes were deep and a bit unfocused. "Hey, you," he said. "I'm Steve."

"I'm Marie," she replied softly, looking directly at the triangular face. "Where can a girl score some dope around here?"

Steve sat down uninvited, and the waitress returned with the beer. "That didn't take long. If this asshole starts to be a problem, you let me know." She went back to the bar.

"You a cop?" Steve wasn't a stupid man. At least, he thought so.

"Absolutely. You got me," Coastie said, and blinked a smile. "I'm working undercover for the government, and I'm here to take your guns."

"You ain't really, are you?" Steve was in love. "Can I buy you a drink?"

She lifted the full mug of beer. "I have a drink, you idiot. What I need is some good dope. Not marijuana. Coke. H. The sort with a heavy kick. You got any, or do I move on to somebody else?"

He screwed up his face in puzzlement. This conversation wasn't going as he'd hoped. "How about trading for sex?"

"How about I stick this fork in your eyeball?" Coastie used the table knife to slowly saw the burger in half. She took a bite and a sip. "I got the money. You got product?"

Steve slowly looked around the bar. "See that big guy in the camo jacket? Looks like a fuckin' dogwood tree? That's Moose, and he's a *gooood* friend of mine. He's the best dealer around here. Me and him can meet you out by his truck—big black Dodge, left side of the lot—in ten minutes. You bring the money and he'll give you whatever you need. Good shit, too. But what do I get for all this help?"

Coastie had another sip of beer. "Okay. After I get the heroin, I'll flash my boobs. Good enough?"

Steve was thinking that, once out of sight, out there in the dark with the woods for cover, out there with his big pal Moose, more than that might happen with this smart-mouthed girl. Coastie was thinking that it was too bad she was going to have to kill this one, too.

She finished half the burger and half the beer, dropped two twenties on the table, and left through the kitchen door. Back at the SUV, Nero was waiting, smiling his toothy dog smile. Coastie got in, gave him a smooch, and they drove to a better parking spot on the opposite side of the parking lot from the big Dodge, shut down the engine again, and climbed into the back. With the seats out of the way, there was more than enough room for her to roll out the sleeping bag, and she used the space to give the rifle a final check. The grip and stock were a bit oversized for her, and it wouldn't have been her weapon of choice, but it was okay. She racked in a thirty-round Magpul magazine.

She rolled half of the sleeping bag over her and called Nero, who came and lay beside her. Rifle ready, she pushed the button to lower the back window. The sight line from her to the Dodge was clear. Any expended cartridge would be contained within the truck bed. Coastie took a deep breath, rested her face on the rifle for a moment, thought of Mickey, then said, "Easy, Nero. This won't take long."

Two men came out of the bar, down the stairs, and walked, laughing, toward the truck. Steve was on the right, and a fat guy was on the left. Coastie could see the bulge of a pistol beneath his tight jacket. They went to the rear, and Moose unlocked and lifted the lid, then propped it open. He had a wagon full of dope, she concluded.

She breathed easily, let her heartbeat slow, clicked off the safety. Moose filled the sight picture of the scope. Nero whined softly and turned his head just as a big hand reached in, grabbed the barrel of the AR-15, and yanked it aside.

In his deep voice, Double-Oh Dawkins said, "Coastie, my friend, the bad news is that I can't allow my guests to roam around murdering people on my turf, even if the targets are ignorant scumbuckets like Moose and Stevie. How long do you think it would take for the cops to figure out how a real sniper might have come into our midst? I would have to turn you in, testify against you in a murder trial, and send you to prison." He gave Nero an easy head rub. "The good news is that you passed the test. Let's go home."

17

ISLAMABAD, PAKISTAN
9 AM, WEDNESDAY
0500 ZULU

HURRY UP AND WAIT. It was a military mantra that everyone hated but no one could avoid. That, plus Murphy's Law: If something can go wrong it will go wrong, and at the worst possible time. So a daring plan that had seemed so possible only a few hours earlier—Gibson's idea for a lightning-strike parachute drop onto the likely hiding place of Nicky Marks—had eventually come to a jarring, complete stop, like a drunk walking into a lamppost. The arrival of the dawn forced a scrub.

Kyle Swanson stared into the cloudless blue morning sky above yet another runway. Perfect visibility for miles. Adjusted his sunglasses. "It ain't going to happen, Luke. A daylight drop would be suicide."

Gibson took a deep drag on his cigarette, then agreed. "Shit happens, but this mission is still worth doing. We'll try again tonight." For the first time, Swanson detected a note of urgency in Gibson's voice, as if he were under some new pressure.

The CIA logistician, who had been having hourly heart attacks as the wheels fell off the original plan, asked, "Why don't we just drone the sumbitch and be done with it?"

"We need to take him alive to answer a bunch of questions. Who's he working for, why are they doing such lunatic things? I want those answers." Swanson removed his sunglasses and wiped them on the tail of his T-shirt. Smears and scratches.

The frustrated CIA man chomped on a wad of gum. "Answer me this, Swanson. We're stuck here in a puddle of Gorilla Glue and you get a FedEx package from London via overnight delivery. How the hell does that happen?"

"My company is very efficient."

"I thought we were, too."

"Both Excalibur and FedEx have to make profits, so they outperform any government better on routine stuff like on-time deliveries. I called and they answered."

"What's in it?"

Swanson lifted the lid on the long box that lay on the metal table. A titanium gun case winked in the sun. Opening that, too, he lifted out the latest version of the Excalibur sniper rifle and matching scope, hefted the lightweight .50-caliber weapon a few times, whipped it up to his cheek, then back down. "My personal weapon, molded and balanced to my features and grip, with electronic sensors to make sure only I can fire it. Wrong fingerprints or optical features and it won't shoot."

Gibson laughed. "He's got a Death Star and I get a stick that goes bang. Doesn't seem fair," he said nervously, and flicked away his cigarette. "I want to get this show on the road. We're running out of time, and the longer it waits the harder it's going to be on the other end."

"I know," sympathized the CIA man. "We're working on it."

AZAD, KASHMIR
PAKISTAN
NOON
0800 ZULU

"SO ARE YOU KEEPING the baby?"

"He's two years old, you moron." Ingmar Thompson kept his eyes in the game, watching the doorway of a multistory apartment house a mile away through a pair of binos.

"You going to marry the girl, then, are you?" Bruce Brandt was watching the same portal, only through the 25x scope above the long barrel of a big rifle.

"Been married coming on three years now. You were at the wedding. Several gentlemen exiting and taking defensive positions."

"Right," Brandt confirmed. "The guards. I'm just making some conversation to pass the lonely hours, Ingmar."

Commanders had learned long ago that an élite sniper team was a terrible thing to waste on an ordinary terrorist. Pick off one and the victim would be hauled away for a glorious burial beneath a flag, with a lot of chest-beating, and some other guy would pick up the gun and carry on. Brandt and Thompson were helping change that equation. The two-man CIA sniper team were specialists, and dealt only with high-value targets.

While terrorist groups like ISIS and Al Qaeda don't have traditional military ranks or organization, somebody has to be in charge of the other fighters. Religious zeal isn't enough to ensure sustained operations that are sometimes years in the making. Even the most dedicated terrorist needs shelter, food, training, communications, and intelligence, no matter how screwed up an organizational chart might be. There are always leaders and followers, and the CIA team was a go-to pairing for use against insurgents whose standing was equivalent to that of a colonel or better. Killing someone in such a position left a hole that was much harder to fill.

"I count three dudes down there, all with weapons out of sight," Brandt said, devoid of emotion. "The fourth must be bringing out the car. They seem relaxed enough. No sign of He Who Must Not Be Named."

"He will be right along." Ingmar glassed the busy street, which appeared totally normal. "Everything looks good."

This was the payoff for months of hard intelligence work that had identified and tracked down Mohammed al-Jaboun, an ISIS supply master who roamed about making deals for beans and bullets. Kashmir was one of his frequent stops, since the city had long been a key trading route on the Pakistani border with India. The world came to make deals in Kashmir, and some of the negotiations ended in gunfire when the parties couldn't agree. In a total security lapse, the ISIS merchant of death had made the mistake of establishing a regular apartment in the city, with a regular routine.

Brandt and Thompson had found it easy to come into the area, thanks to the lingering influence of the British Raj, which had left its imprint on both sides of the border. Everyone of worth spoke English, trade was normal, and the little office of a couple of British lawyers drew no special attention when it was established two months ago. The lawyers, who were actually veteran counterterrorism operatives, left last week and the snipers moved in, wearing business suits. The office had been outfitted properly, with facilities for tea and toilet, cell phones, food, and cots. Thompson was the larger of the two, an enormously strong man who stood six feet even and weighed two hundred pounds, with arms and legs that seemed to have been carved from tree trunks. He carried in the large suitcase containing an L118A1 rifle, scope, and suppressor.

"Mary, is it? Her name?" Brandt was on the gun now, feeling comfortable, letting it tell him it was ready. At five feet nine, he was as lithe and purposeful as a panther, and usually wore some sort of cap on missions to cover his bright-ginger hair. At a party, Thompson would anchor a table with pitchers of beer while Bruce freely went after every girl in sight, knowing that if it came to a brawl he had the strongest guy in the bar at his back. In the field, they worked together like twins wired to the same brain. After moving into the office, the pair had spent a lot of time out in the open, mixing with people of every nationality, eating at European and local restaurants, hiding in plain sight by becoming familiar faces in the community.

They had laser-ranged the target property and had even mounted a small flag atop an adjoining building to read the wind. The doorway was exactly 310 meters away, and the guards had conveniently shooed foot traffic to the far sidewalk. The space was clear.

"Here comes the car, turning now." A black SUV maneuvered smoothly up to one of the guards who was holding a space for it. "No, her name is Laura. Tend to business."

"On it." Bruce checked the settings and the wind and the scene and the sun, factored in time, motion, and angle of fire, and logged them into his busy brain, then extended his right index finger to caress the trigger. "This guy is a real dirtbag."

Mohammed al-Jaboun came through the door with confidence, without a care in the world. He was wearing dark slacks, an open-necked white shirt, and a blue sports coat; he had luncheon reservations at an upscale restaurant on Residency Road, where he usually ordered mutton curry. As he pulled a pair of sunglasses from his jacket pocket, he turned slightly to say something to the young woman behind him and, in doing so, presented the back of his head to Bruce Brandt and Ingmar Thompson. A good sniper never hesitates to shoot a target in the back. The focus was so razor-sharp that Brandt could see the brush marks in the thick black hair.

"Fire, fire, fire," Thompson whispered.

Brandt was already exhaling, and he pulled back steadily on the trigger until the rifle barked and slapped his shoulder with a hard recoil. The ISIS man's head exploded forward in a spray of blood, brain, and bone; the body stayed upright for a moment, then spun lazily to the sidewalk while his companion screamed and the stunned guards froze in their tracks.

The gunshot was still echoing around the streets, but it wasn't attracting much attention. This was, after all, Pakistan. The guard detail started to freak out, caught between trying to protect their leader, who was already dead, dealing with the screeching and blood-soaked woman, and looking for the origin of the single lethal shot.

By then, Brandt and Thompson had finished a quick breakdown of the weapon, stowed it in the carrying case, and slid it into the closet. They put on their suit jackets, adjusted their ties and briefcases, and walked away from the scene, just two more people working to make a deal in Kashmir.

"You do know that I'm not married and that I have no children, don't you?" Thompson asked. "Or are you just getting senile at an early age."

Brandt shrugged. "Just makin' conversation, man. Let's get some lunch."

PAKISTAN
2 PM LOCAL
1000 ZULU

THE PRINCE DRUMMED HIS fingers rhythmically on the tabletop. Time was running out. Was it his fault? Not really. He couldn't preordain every single detail in such a complex scheme, but perhaps he could have built in a little more time, more of a cushion.

Still, he was confident that Nicky Marks would size up the situation and make an appropriate adjustment in the field. Just be patient, he told himself. It will all work out, then he could do his own part and snatch the prize he most wanted. Swanson would die, and the CIA would go into a death spiral of its own.

It would be a beautiful thing to watch unfold on the news channels. Like an evil magician, the Prince would disappear—*poof*—and exit into an entirely new life. His intricate empire of drugs, intrigue, and violence would collapse and he wouldn't give a damn, because it had always been only a vehicle to prove to himself, over and over, that he could succeed with such an audacious plot. In the months to come, his contacts would start wondering where he had gone. In a few years, he would be a legend, a name to be whispered in conspiracies.

So don't blow it all because of a few minor setbacks. Stay cool. The fun part was just ahead.

LONDON, ENGLAND
NOON LOCAL
1200 ZULU

SEVEN TIME ZONES TO the west, Sir Geoffrey Cornwell was on a Skype call, and Janna Ecklund was at the other end in Washington, seven in the morning her time. The gray-haired Englishman rubbed his neck, frustrated but maintaining his composure. "It is preposterous, Janna. I have three messages on my desk from news organizations asking for my comment."

Janna was in total agreement. "I'm fielding a lot of queries, too, Jeff. The story is on the morning news shows over here: the CIA caught running drugs with the help of Excalibur, and our company promoting terrorism. Kyle's name is being made public. We can't let this stand, sir. We have to issue a statement."

"Rubbish! That's my statement, Janna. It's all rubbish."

She smiled. The old warrior looked ready to leap from his chair, locked and loaded for battle. "Actually, that is a perfect official response, sir. One word that leaves no room for interpretation. Should we give interviews?"

"No, absolutely not. We're not going to cooperate with these vultures. Our public-relations people will release the statement, not us. Let their lawyers talk to our lawyers. Have you heard from Kyle?"

"No, sir. He's pretty much off the grid on that manhunt. Director Atkins says the agency will probably call it off today and bring the team back. I suggest that we get him back into the office here, let him carry on normal work, and we stick with the 'Rubbish' comment. Kyle will demonstrate that he has nothing to hide."

Sir Jeff paused. "That could be dicey, given the situation."

"The other side is going to have to show proof and some solid evidence in order to move this thing forward, Sir Jeff. Months will pass before it gets a hearing on the Hill and subpoenas are issued. Meanwhile, we stay our course, as if the problem doesn't exist. Rubbish. We will cooperate with any legal requirements, but we keep to the high road."

A slow smile creased Cornwell's weathered face. "Many things may happen during such a long time."

Janna shook her finger at the camera. "Do not start thinking about interfering in a congressional investigation, you old rascal."

He laughed. "And you don't forget that it's not my Congress, young lady. I am a citizen of Great Britain, and Excalibur Enterprises is a privately held company with many friends. The United States Marine Corps will be very unhappy to learn that we have changed our minds about opening that test facility at Twentynine Palms and putting it instead in Ireland because of a friendlier tax structure."

"You won't do that, and you know it. Remember, this is an unsecured line."

"I'm just considering our options, Madam Vice President, and, as you Yanks say, we play hardball. We are legally innocent of all charges, and I will not stand by and let political fools freely besmirch our reputation."

"Jeff, calm down," she warned.

"No. I look forward to this fight, and to finding out what's behind all of this. But first things first. Issue the news release—*Rubbish!*—and get Kyle back. If Director Atkins thinks we can help on that front, we will happily oblige."

18

CIA HEADQUARTERS,
LANGLEY, VIRGINIA
8 AM LOCAL, WEDNESDAY
1300 ZULU

MARTY ATKINS, THE DIRECTOR of intelligence, was alone in his office, elbows on his desk and his head in his palms early Wednesday morning. How in the hell had this thing jumped from a small deal to a big deal? One minute he was working quietly to put down a mad dog named Nicky Marks and here he was, a few days later, with a political inferno waiting for the touch of a match. A steaming mug of coffee was his only solace.

Atkins had barely mentioned the situation to the man in the White House during the president's daily security briefing, but had brought the national-security adviser and the chief of staff up to speed on the summons from Congress. Both had already heard about it on the morning news, and would tell the president what he needed to know only when he needed to know it. He hadn't asked about the plan to abort the mission, either, because the decision wasn't appropriate for a White House intervention.

Still, the decision wasn't his alone. Marty Atkins wasn't at the top of the CIA pyramid and needed to get the final stamp from the director himself, who wouldn't be in for another few hours, about eleven o'clock. The chiefs of all the alphabet agencies were spending the morning in a conference about the overall global-terrorism situation and homeland security.

His talk with Janna Ecklund over at Excalibur Enterprises had left him with a headache. Sir Geoffrey Cornwell wasn't going to back down from a confrontation with anybody; that just wasn't who the old commando was. Instead, her report that he was rethinking an important project in California meant the possible loss of American jobs while also throwing a wrench into Pentagon out-years planning.

Killing Nicky Marks had become a small-potatoes project. Atkins wanted to tamp down the sudden threat and get his snipers back under cover. When the director arrived, Marty planned to meet him at the door and get his autograph on the shutdown order, then hunker down before the coming storm.

PAKISTAN
6:30 PM LOCAL, WEDNESDAY
1430 ZULU

THE STUBBORN RED SUN that had hung in the sky all day finally settled behind the mountains, painting the underside of the drifting clouds with dusty golds and purples. By six o'clock, it was dim enough for Gibson and Swanson to get down to business.

Their ride turned out to be neither a swift jet nor a quick helo, but an updated USAF C-130 prop plane, as common as a piece of toast, older than members of its crew, and trusted as a workhorse. The four-engine turboprop could grind out almost any job. It had come in early in the afternoon and was immediately assigned for the snipers' run up to Afghanistan.

By six-thirty that evening, the briefings had been completed, the weather and the target had been examined in detail, and the aircraft commander and the primary jumpmaster had run their final checklists. Swanson and Gibson climbed the ramp, which closed behind them as they strapped themselves into their seats and stuffed plastic plugs into their ears as the engine began to whine and roar. With final clearances, the aircraft began to move. Everything was a go. Swanson checked his watch. Outside, darkness gathered. The drop zone was two hours away.

SAVANNAH, GEORGIA
9:30 AM LOCAL, WEDNESDAY
1430 ZULU

SPECIAL AGENT LUCKY SHARIF read the thorough biography that the FBI had assembled overnight on Tom King as if delving into a spy novel rather than doing a normal dull backgrounder. The most interesting thing was that the man wasn't even the star of his own remarkable life. The analysts had to look higher up the family tree to discover the patriarch, Sir Horatio Kingsley, who was born in Alexandria, Egypt, on November 11, 1873, the son of a British Army officer. At the age of twelve, the boy had been packed off to England to get a top-tier education in public school and then at Oxford. He graduated with honors eight years later. At twenty-one, he followed his father's footsteps back to Egypt as a lieutenant in the Royal Engineers. In 1894, Kingsley distinguished himself in battle at Omdurman, where befriended the young Winston Churchill, and later fought in the Second Boer War, during which he was wounded. Retired from active military service, Kingsley continued working for the government as an engineering consultant along the Nile Valley and the Suez Canal at the dawn of the twentieth century.

A son, Horace, came along in 1903, and a daughter, Margaret, the following year, and when the Great War began the family moved back to Alexandria, where the engineer was recalled to active service on the General Staff. There he met the enigmatic T. E. Lawrence, who milked Kingsley for every drop of information he had about Arabia and, in the process, became a lifelong friend. After the war, when it was time to draw the boundary lines of new countries in the Middle East, Brigadier Horatio Kingsley was named to the Sykes-Picot Commission. Nobody was really satisfied with the outcome, but Kingsley was knighted for his service and exited the military. At this point, he knew almost every leader of consequence in the region, plus his influential friends Churchill and Lawrence.

Sharif stopped leafing through the family tree and walked around his hotel room to gather his thoughts, calling for room service to bring up a second breakfast with plenty of coffee. *So shouldn't Luke Gibson be a Brit?* He took a short bathroom break and hurried back to the next chapter.

THE WAKHAM CORRIDOR
AFGHANISTAN
6:45 PM LOCAL, WEDNESDAY
1445 ZULU

NICKY MARKS REACHED THE rendezvous point first, with time to spare, and was greeted warmly by the elderly couple who kept the hideaway ready for visitors. They had been expecting him, so the generator was on and providing electrical current. He gave the shabby place a quick walkthrough inspection. Everything was in order. The woman prepared a small meal for him, then she and her husband chuffed away in an old Fiat to spend the next several days with the man's family. It was understood that anyone staying at the house was a guest of the Prince and was not to be bothered. Patrols of Taliban fighters often came by to ensure security.

It was a small, square place girdled by a head-high adobe wall that was almost concealed by a grove of hardy junipers and wild-olive and pine trees. There was a narrow bedroom, a large main room, a kitchen, and a bath; the high windows in each room were curtained. A scatter of cheap rugs and pillows gave color to the wooden floor. The building plan was the most common in the community of Girdiwal, a village of about a thousand souls.

Once the old couple left, Marks pushed aside the rugs in the main room to find a metal handle that was set into the floor. Beneath the trapdoor was a small cache of weapons and explosives, and he picked out what he anticipated he would need for the coming night. One flash-bang grenade, a Glock handgun, a compact Israeli Tavor bullpup 5.56 rifle for close-quarters firepower. He didn't stack up extra magazines, because whatever happened here tonight was going to be over in a hurry. He turned the lights off and settled down to wait in the gathering gloom.

SAVANNAH, GEORGIA
10:00 AM, WEDNESDAY
1500 ZULU

WHAT HAPPENED NEXT? THERE was a time gap in the King family tree, and Sharif burned up Google and the FBI's private databases hunting it.

Brigadier Sir Horatio had been in the British Army at its zenith, when the nation was rich and influential and ruled the oceans, with colonies around the globe. The bloodbath of World War I ended that marvelous era, and Kingsley could see over the time horizon that Britain was in decline and the United States was ascending. So the old boy adjusted the family's gears accordingly and did not send his son to Sandhurst to learn soldiering. Horace came back to Egypt from Oxford as a businessman, and shrewd Arab traders replaced the university dons at just about the time oil was discovered in Arabia by another Englishman, who had been hired to look for gold. He started a family of his own, with a proper British wife, a daughter and a son.

Lucky thought that was interesting but still couldn't see how or why they jumped the pond when they were doing so well in the Middle East, where ARAMCO was leading the oil boom. Oil didn't just spring from the ground; it had to be pumped and refined and transported, which meant that roads and infrastructure and entire new cities were going to be built. The Kingsleys got rich, but not sweaty, by being go-betweens who could connect the eager buyers with willing sellers.

That was where the veil was drawn. Horace and his own father, the brigadier, saw war clouds gathering again over Europe as Hitler took over Germany. It was time to shift to a safer base. Horace's daughter Margaret was already in the United States, married to a Boston banker. The son, Royce, who had grown up among Egyptian aristocracy, was dispatched to attend Harvard and live with Margaret. The brigadier died when a U-boat torpedoed the passenger liner *Athenia* in 1939. Horace remained in Egypt as an allied intelligence officer and vanished behind the iron walls of British official secrets.

So, then, on to Royce. How did a young man in his prime get out of serving in World War II, since he graduated in 1945? And why was there no Royce Kingsley listed in the graduating class? Sharif needed another bathroom break and a talk with Janna.

OVER AFGHANISTAN
7:15 PM LOCAL, WEDNESDAY
1515 ZULU

SWANSON AND GIBSON UNBUCKLED and stood up in the noisy, quivering cave of the C-130 cargo hold. The jumpmasters swarmed around them like seamstresses attending a couple of debutantes, studying even the smallest details. Missing something could cost a jumper his life. The two snipers swayed with the rhythm of the plane as the Ram Air Parachute Systems were fitted and tightened and checked and rechecked until the fussy jumpmasters were satisfied.

"You guys are good to go," said the leader after he went over the work done by his assistants. He had the power to terminate the mission but, after a final discussion with the pilot, declared that the conditions were acceptable. "You hop-and-pop at ten thousand feet, so you won't need helmets or air cans. Your altimeters will be recalibrated in thirty minutes. Green light in about forty. Any questions?"

The two operators nodded. "Any messages from home?" Gibson asked. The senior jumpmaster said there had been no radio traffic concerning them since takeoff.

Swanson took firm hold of the cargo webbing and started to loosen up. No traffic from anybody. Nothing was a good thing at this point. He glanced at his partner and saw that Gibson was doing similar stretching exercises, his face calm and expressionless.

WASHINGTON, D.C.
10:30 AM LOCAL
1530 ZULU

CONGRESSWOMAN VERONICA KEENAN OF Nebraska had been expecting some pressure for rolling out the CIA scandal in the name of the House Permanent Select Committee on Intelligence. It was pleasant to discover that things were smooth in her office on Wednesday morning. Requests for press interviews were coming in, and she would pick and choose among them, because a national cable television news show would reach more voters back home than any *New York Times* ink.

The CIA was stonewalling under the pretext of national security. The Englishman who was president of Excalibur Enterprises had been dismissive with his one-word reaction that her charges were "rubbish." Keenan made a note to remind the reporters that she had proof to back up her charges. Of course, the CIA and Excalibur would deny it all, just as tobacco-company executives once pledged that their products weren't poison. A congressional committee would get to the truth.

Keenan's administrative assistant rapped on the door and entered with a smile. "Get your lipstick on straight, girlfriend. You've been summoned by the House leadership."

"That would be the White House checking in to assess damage control," Keenan said.

"Right. You can say that to the media, too. If there's nothing to this, why is the president meddling?" The assistant studied her smartphone. "Call from the State Department, too."

"More administration interference in the overwatch role of Congress?" Keenan cocked an eyebrow.

"Exactly so," replied the aide, who was the political professional in the office.

"Anything from home yet?" Keenan asked.

"It's too early for the press back there," the aide replied. "I've alerted staffers from other members of the Nebraska delegation about what's going on. They can put together statements of their own."

The congresswoman found a lipstick tube in her desk, got a small mirror, and organized herself. "Let's go see his highness the Speaker," she said.

CLARKE, VERMONT
10:45 AM LOCAL
1545 ZULU

"COME ON, ORVILLE. I can take anything but your silent treatment." Coastie was propped against a thick old maple tree that still bore slashing scars from the years during which it had produced syrup. Nero was sniffing the ground nearby after finding the faint scent of muskrats. "You've hardly said a word since the parking lot. Tell me where we're at. What did you mean that I passed some test?"

Double-Oh Dawkins was watching the dog get around, unaware that it had lost a leg. The retired marine had a thermos of coffee for himself and a plastic-wrapped bone in case Nero couldn't find and finish some unlucky varmint.

"Why did you want to kill those two characters, Coastie? Seems a little extreme, you ask me."

"They were drug dealers," she replied simply.

"Oh, so you're a self-righteous vigilante now? Out to scour the world of drug dealers? God knows we have enough of them in Vermont to keep you busy for a while." He scowled. "Now, try telling me the truth."

Coastie peeled a thick leaf and returned his hard look. "You won't like it, Double-Oh. After what they did to Mickey, yeah, I wanted revenge, sure. Who wouldn't? I can't take down a cartel by myself, but I can take them off the board one asshole at a time. I hold each of them personally responsible."

"So this wasn't your first time. You started before you got here."

She nodded and straightened her shoulders. "Yes. Down in Mexico, I made them start killing each other because they assumed it was a turf war, when it wasn't."

"Nobody up here yet, right?"

"Those two at the bar would have been my first."

"So you haven't committed any crime in the U.S."

"No."

"You can't have both things now, you realize that. You cannot be the partner of Kyle Swanson and go around helter-skelter murdering drug peddlers."

"And if I don't want to stop?"

"Then you get the hell out of here and don't look back. You were little league last night, Coastie. I've had you under surveillance since you got here. Everybody here is a former special-ops type, and you painted a bright line straight to your hide. In other words, my dear, you aren't ready for prime time again. And you were really going to use a little AR-15? Jesus H. Christ."

That stung. She hadn't seen anybody trailing, and Nero had been a lousy guard dog because he knew everybody who was following her. "Oh."

"Yeah, 'Oh.' So no more freelancing." He leaned forward and put his big hands on his knees. "Do you think Kyle and I have forgotten about Mickey Castillo? Can you really be that dumb? We wanted you to come with us, train up, and eventually we'll make whoever was responsible for that abomination pay in full. Think about landing the whale, not the minnows."

Beth Ledford willed herself not to cry. Nobody would make her cry, ever again. "Nero, come on," she said. The big dog wheeled around and loped over to her. "Okay, Orville. Maybe I just needed to purge some demons from down there, you know? No more minnows, I promise."

"You wanted to know about the test? Well, Kyle and I wanted to see if you had the guts to still pull the trigger and take life. You answered that." He polished off the last sip of coffee and screwed the lid back on the thermos, unwrapped the bone, and tossed it to Nero. "But you're a lying little bitch right now, lying straight to my face, pulling your pretty little lost-girl act. If we can't believe you, we sure as hell won't trust our lives to you. So you go somewhere else and run your little scams and get over yourself, Beth. Anyway, Kyle already has a guy who looks like he might make a good partner. Too bad it couldn't have been you."

OVER AFGHANISTAN
7:55 PM LOCAL, WEDNESDAY
1555 ZULU

THE SENIOR JUMPMASTER WAS in constant radio contact with the aircraft commander as he worked the ramp-control panel to open the paratroop door, and the 120-pound hatch slid back on its rails to expose the night sky beyond. When all systems had stabilized, a hard wind hammered through the door, whipping against Kyle Swanson, who was firmly in the grasp of another jumpmaster. Luke Gibson was right behind, held by a third crew member.

Both snipers were weighed down with equipment, but in a few seconds that would no longer matter. The senior jumpmaster stepped aside and snapped his hand toward the door, and Swanson stepped into the profound abyss, ten thousand feet up and ten miles east of the target landing zone.

He clamped his arms at his sides and tightened his legs together to knife forward at terminal velocity, as fast as he could fall, counting off fifteen seconds before adjusting to bleed off airspeed and pop the chute. The canopy of the RAPS gliding system came to life with a smooth flair instead of a jaw-breaking jerk after he gained control of the free fall. The plane had already disappeared from view, beyond any threat of detection, leaving two dark shapes falling through the inky sky. Swanson tugged on his risers to make a tight pivot, picked up the faint blinking red light attached to Gibson's backpack, and flew toward it. Gibson was also successfully deployed under canopy, and they swung into a tandem glide toward the sprinkled lights of Girdiwal, passing through nine thousand feet and skittering along at about thirty miles an hour as gravity pulled them back toward the planet.

Swanson almost smiled in pleasure during the drift through the night sky, swinging like a pendulum beneath the silk, reading the compass, clock, and altimeter. Somewhere down there was Nicky Marks, who needed to die tonight after answering some questions. Swanson's normally impassive face tightened into a grimace, despite himself. He knew some very creative ways of making men talk and wouldn't hesitate to use them if Marks started getting brave with his answers.

Down through eight thousand feet, coasting over the Wakham valley. Getting ready.

SAVANNAH, GEORGIA
10:55 AM LOCAL, WEDNESDAY
1555 ZULU

THIS REMINDED LUCKY SHARIF of the "begats" in the first book of the Bible. By scraping away the details, the authors of Genesis were able to trace the big picture, starting with Adam and Eve and quickly begetting through many generations. In his own search, he now had Brigadier Sir Horatio Kingsley, who begat Horace Kingsley, who begat Royce Kingsley, who hadn't begat anyone, because he stopped existing somewhere along the way.

"I want you to come home so we can try to begat a baby," his wife, Janna, teased while he explained the search by telephone.

"You hear anything from Kyle?"

"Not a peep," she said. "Chances are he's gone dark on the job until it's done."

"I saw on the TV that Sir Jeff called the charges against Excalibur rubbish. That your work?"

She laughed, and the sound was the most pleasant thing he had heard all day. "It was all him, Lucky. Excalibur is clean and he knows it, so he's going to have some fun with them. The Congress critter from Nebraska will rue the day. When you coming home, big guy?"

"I shouldn't be more than another day. I got a hunch about Royce."

"Tell me?"

"Not on this line. I really just called to hear your voice."

There was a pause, and she said, "I'm always here for you. You know that."

"Yeah."

"Then go get 'em. Bye."

His new theory in the Kingsley saga related to the changing times of World War II, when the look of the postwar world was being mapped alongside active battle plans from Salerno to Okinawa. West Point produced the generals, Harvard turned out the young government types, and Yale was the school for spooks. Sure enough, there was no Royce Kingsley among the Harvard graduating seniors, but there was a Roy King coming out of Yale with academic honors, and, like many of his fellow graduates, firmly plugged into the Office of Strategic Services, the the CIA's predecessor. Royce returned to the Middle East, this time as Roy King, and took over the family spook business, and also begat a son of his own, Thomas.

That closed the loop, as far as Sharif was concerned. It was impossible for the King family not to succeed with so much backing from so many quarters. Royce steered it further into the shadows by not being a competitor for the lucrative contracts but gathering secrets and doing favors for individuals and governments and skimming a piece of the transactions. Father and son took the business through the Vietnam War and the Cold War years, expanded its fortune and its influence, and along the way Lucas was begat, to the new King was groomed from birth to someday lead the family firm.

Sharif found the old obituary of Thomas King in the *International Herald Tribune*, read it, printed it out, and suddenly knew that he had forgotten to ask an important question of the neighbor lady, Mrs. Boykin. He dialed and got the attending nurse, who gave the phone to the old woman. Lucky made his apologies for disturbing her, but Mrs. Boykin couldn't be more pleased.

"When we spoke yesterday, you mentioned that Luke Gibson seemed almost happy when his stepfather died, right?"

"That is correct, Special Agent Sharif." Her voice was crisp, her memory sharp as it was the previous day.

"Exactly how did Perry Gibson die, Mrs. Boykin?"

There was a momentary lull. "Why, we didn't discuss that? How negligent. Shame on us both."

"Was it anything unusual?"

"Quite so, Mr. Sharif. Mr. Gibson was killed in a hunting accident. The boy shot him."

Now it was Sharif's turn to be silent. "You sure about that, ma'am?" The copy of Tom King's obit was shaking in his hand.

"Of course I am." She didn't like being challenged on something so obvious. "There was a police investigation, and they decided it was an accident during a quail hunt. The boy blew the back of Mr. Gibson's head off with a double-barreled shotgun. You can look it up in the *Savannah Morning News* if you don't believe me."

"I believe you, Mrs. Boykin." Sharif was on his feet, pacing. "I believe you. Thanks for your time."

"I think Luke murdered him, but he was a juvenile, and it was all hushed up."

"Okay. Thanks again. I have to go now."

"Anytime, Special Agent Sharif. Goodbye."

Sharif hit the speed dial to get Janna. "We need to get word to Kyle to get away from Gibson as fast as he can. The guy is a total fraud and a psycho."

"Are you sure?" She seemed worried.

"He killed his stepfather in a hunting accident. He killed his VMI friend in a climbing accident. And he killed his real father in a shooting accident while hunting big game in Africa. I have the obit in the *Herald Tribune*. A double patricide. God knows how many people he's killed legally for the CIA."

"I'll call Sir Jeff and Marty Atkins right away," Janna said.

"Tell them I'm cold certain about this. The first two were written off as accidents, but the third one—Tom King in Africa—wasn't. By that time, Gibson was a sniper for the CIA, and knew exactly what he was doing when he pulled the trigger. Removing his father gave him total control of the family's riches. He's a killer and a freakin' psychopath, Janna. Get Kyle out of there!"

OVER AFGHANISTAN
8 PM LOCAL, WEDNESDAY
1600 ZULU

ALMOST DOWN, SLIDING EASILY under the whispering cones of the parachute, working the risers to keep the little red light Gibson wore in front and below him. Swanson had given him the lead because Luke had been to this section before and was heading toward a precise GPS pinpoint familiar to him. He was pleased that the private investigation of Gibson's background hadn't turned up anything, and Gibson had the seasoned attitude of a veteran. Apart from the man's irritating sense of humor, they got along fine.

The bright array of village lights became clearer and more individualized as they navigated closer, stacked one behind the other. Swanson could see a few headlights moving on a road. He looked at the altimeter again and mentally ran through the checklist of gear—from ammo to food, guns to survival gear, and satellite phone. No surprises in the inventory. Nothing to do but pay attention to everything. He could feel the ground climbing up to greet him.

They were in a final gentle curve to get a better airflow, and at about two hundred feet up Swanson made out a rectangular field that reflected the overcast moonbeams and came together like a painting of soft colors. He adjusted for landing, dumped the air to kill all the speed, and dropped into a waist-high field of opium poppies. Gibson was about fifty feet away, already gathering his collapsed parachute.

"You okay?" Swanson asked.

"Best day of my life," Gibson responded. "Let's go do this thing."

Swanson dug the sat phone from a cargo pocket and hit the Send key that would transmit a numerical code, meaning that the snipers were in position and proceeding with the mission. Then he turned it off. No one could contact them until the mission was done and he called for extraction.

KAISERSLAUTERN, GERMANY
8:15 PM LOCAL
1615 ZULU

A CIA ANALYST INVOLVED in drone targeting was seated at his messy desk deep in the bowels of the agency operation at Ramstein Air Force Base in Germany. When the machine began to flash an alert code, he was facing away and didn't see it for a while. There were open books, sheaves of paper, and other screens vying for his attention, and in his job it was hard to assign priorities because everything was important, so at present, Ryan Winters was getting his butt kicked by a Rhydon in a Pokémon Go turf war.

The computer behind him clocked off the passing seconds, and when Swanson's landing confirmation wasn't recognized, the machine began a steady beep that broke through the game-brain trance and shook the analyst back to the real world. He called up the data and said to himself, "Weird."

But CIA computers don't often make mistakes in processing data, given that they're very expensive electronic number crunchers. The landing alert had been expected, but a second alert had also begun to beep. It shifted him over to an identical set of GPS coordinates from an entirely different channel. That wasn't normal. He banished the Rhydon game and started earning his paycheck again, did verifications, and printed out the results. He tossed the brown bag of chocolate M&M's and tucked in his shirt. At the age of thirty-five, and with no life beyond his desk, Winters had started noticing how his belt was getting tighter.

"Got something for you, boss," he grumped as he marched uninvited into the office of Marguerite del Coda.

"I was just leaving, Ryan. Can it wait?" She badly needed a glass of wine and some sleep.

"You better look at it." He gave her the matched coordinates.

"What's it mean?" she asked, and sat down again.

"Beats me, Marguerite" He put his finger on the top line. "This top one is from the GPS sky file on where emergency caches of equipment and gear for agents are located. We have them all over the world."

"And . . . ?"

"The second set is the precise location of the two operators who just went in. Same, same."

Del Coda thought about Swanson and Gibson, who had passed through Ramstein only about a day ago, flown down to Pakistan and were now being inserted into Afghanistan. The team communications were monitored at Ramstein, codename "Checkerboard" for this mission. The landing zone had been designated by Gibson for the CIA liaison man in Pakistan who had been tasked to scramble up the covert insertion flight.

"So they have dropped right on one of our safe houses?" Winters asked.

"Looks like it." She gathered her purse again.

"No shit? We're attacking our own place? How cool is that? Now let me show you the kicker." Winters dialed up a third piece of information, an automatic alert that was triggered when the secure safe containing all of the goodies was opened. "Someone was messing around in there just a little while ago," Ryan said.

"Before our guys got there?" She knew that ordinary procedure would have dropped them some distance away to avoid exposing the exact location of the secret hideout. Instead, Gibson chose to land almost in the back yard. That was peculiar, but not a deal breaker. However, someone else being inside the target house and in the weapons storage area could not be just a coincidence.

"Dig out the background on this cache, then send everything we have back to Langley, with the addendum that we're are running diagnostics to rule out a systems glitch. This exact match made me uncomfortable, and I definitely don't like the unknown factor that is showing. After sending our data back home, try to contact our boys to make sure they both know what's going on."

"I'll try, but they are probably in radio silence. You have a good night."

"I will. You start losing some weight, my friend."

LANGLEY, VIRGINIA
11:20 AM LOCAL
1620 ZULU

MARTIN ATKINS WAS FLOORED by the call from Janna Ecklund over at Excalibur. They had run an independent background check on Luke Gibson, a longtime CIA operative, one of the best, and found things the agency's own exhaustive background check years ago hadn't turned up. Lucky Sharif of the FBI had sent a summary by email.

When Atkins had come to grips with this latest development, the Office of the Director called to tell him the big man was finally back in the building and wanted urgently to meet. Atkins took the elevator up to the top floor of CIA headquarters. Everything was going sour. He was waved directly into the office of Director Richard Burns, who was standing at the window, gulping down a glass of water.

"I've just spent more than an hour in a room with a bunch of people who jumped all over me about things I didn't know. Are we really running drugs again?"

Atkins sat down uninvited. "Rick, the truth is that I don't have any answer for you on that. I can't believe that some renegade agents have started up a narcotics business on their own, but proving a negative is impossible."

"It's all over the news. Talking heads on the radio are howling for some scalps, Marty—our scalps."

"About all we can do is stall for time and run an internal investigation—"

Rick Burns's face flushed in anger. "Can't even do that. Who would believe us? An independent counsel would have to be in charge, and that woman from Nebraska is pushing for open congressional hearings."

"Which is impossible. Secrecy would go out the window."

"What's so urgent that you have tracked me down? What else is going on?"

Atkins took in a deep breath. Exhaled. "That's why I wanted to see you as much as you wanted to see me. I want to shut down an operation that's just been launched. Kyle Swanson is on it, teamed up with Luke Gibson."

"Aw, Jesus! Swanson is the drug lord? Sir Jeff was quoted as saying that it was all bullshit. I know Swanson is no traitor. Congress will want him back anyway. Can the termination of the assignment wait until it's done? He and Gibson are after that Nicky Marks nutcase, right?"

"As of about twenty minutes ago, they reported being on the dirt in Afghanistan. And Swanson isn't the problem—at least, not all of it. The other guy is. Luke Gibson. He's been fooling us for years, Rick. At best he's a crazy killer, and at worst he's a traitor. Reading the tea leaves now, it looks like Marks works for Gibson and they have set a trap for Swanson."

"Crazy? We both know Gibson is as smart as a fox, which is one of the reasons he works for us."

"He's also crazy enough to have killed both his father and his stepfather."

The CIA chief rocked back, took off his glasses and rubbed the bridge of his nose. Not even lunchtime, and his world was crashing. "And Swanson may be walking into an ambush? We know all this how?"

"Sorry, Rick, but first things first here. I'll give you everything I've got, but right now I need your permission to stop that operation, extract Swanson, and grab Gibson."

Burns nodded emphatically in agreement. "Of course. Do it, do it now. Get the department heads into the conference room and fill us all in at the same time. We've got problems on our hands, brother."

THE PAMIR MOUNTAINS ARE a surging upheaval of the earth that extend from the lowlands in Afghanistan into the steep ranges stretching across western Asia and up to the roof of the world. They were carved by aeons of earthquakes, storms, and mighty moving glaciers that shoved gouging boulders along riverbeds. The mountains are forbidding fortresses, but in the lower elevations lush valleys become fertile with the melting snow and ice before descending into the high desert. Every time Kyle Swanson experienced the area, he was startled that people lived in such a climate, not only as stubborn individualists but also as organized communities that were once way stations on the old Silk Road trade route. Such was this little speck on the map called Girdiwal.

Flat on his belly in the dirt, Swanson unlimbered Excalibur from the protective casing across his chest while Gibson, angled out to his left, glassed the area with small binoculars. They seemed like two big black cats patiently watching for prey. The .50-caliber Excalibur rifle was built to do one thing, and that was to kill the enemy. Resting in its protective sheath or viced tight to a workbench, it was a compilation of parts, none of which were deadly by themselves. Assembled and loaded with thick high-powered rounds longer than a man's trigger finger, Excalibur transformed into a piece of war waiting to happen. With Swanson snuggled against the personalized fiberglass stock, the weapon seemed to breathe along with him, slow and measured.

"I ever tell you about my father?" Gibson asked in a quiet voice.

"What?" Swanson, startled, hissed, "Shut the hell up." Here they were on a covert operation and this guy suddenly wants to talk about dear old dad?

"First time I ever saw this place, he showed it to me. It's an agency safe house."

"God damn it, be quiet, Luke. Maintain noise discipline. Marks might hear you." Swanson took a moment away from the powerful telescope on Excalibur to have a hard look at his partner. "You brought us in right on top of a safe house?"

"Don't sweat it. Marks ain't here, Kyle. I can feel it." Gibson crawled forward a few feet. "Nearest neighbors are about two hundred yards off to the west, an old couple who live alone and take care of this place."

"I don't care. We should be looking at this from far away. Treat it like you've never seen it before. Your casual familiarity could get us killed. Clear?"

Gibson grinned and put the binos back up to his eyes. "Yup, you're the team leader."

Swanson swept the area with his scope, trying hard to maintain mental focus. That this was a safe house was a guarantee that there would be access to weapons, gear, and money. But the walls would be thicker than normal, the courtyard could be a killing zone, entries could be booby-trapped, and sensors and cameras could be hidden, along with tricky alarms. Luke should have told him about this before they came. And his father was a spook, too? *Slow down. Improvise. Carry out the mission.*

He motioned for Gibson to spread away and skirt the big outer wall to the left while he went right; they would meet in the rear. Gibson nodded and snake-crawled away, fading from sight within seconds. Swanson moved closer, extending a hand to touch the wall. It was just the usual brick-hard clay found around most houses in the region, a way to maintain privacy and safety while keeping predators from the animals. It was about eight feet high and no doubt topped by broken glass along the lip to discourage anyone from climbing over. He slowly worked his way forward, finding no trace of alarms or cameras. The wall was aged and patched, and Swanson thought it was more for show than anything else. He neither heard nor smelled any animals, and there were no tracks. Maybe Gibson was right and nobody was home.

Step by step, he moved along until he reached the far corner, where he pressed against the wall before doing a peekaboo that exposed his head for only a moment. Gibson was right there, leaning against the wall, waiting with his snubby Heckler & Koch MP5KA submachine gun dangling from one hand. Gibson gave a thumbs-up, and Swanson moved closer as they both took a knee.

"Clear back that way," Gibson reported.

"I assume you know the way in?" he whispered, face to face. If it was a safe house, there would be some emergency ingress and egress points.

Gibson motioned directly above where they stood. "No obstacles at that point up top. Same on the front eastern corner. Soft landings on the other side. A tunnel leads from the bedroom out to the goat pen for a fast getaway."

Made sense, Swanson thought. "We'll go over here. You first." He hung Excalibur on his shoulder and laced his fingers together to make a stirrup. "Give me your foot."

Gibson gave him a funny look, slinging his HK. "It's only eight feet, Kyle," he said, and jumped. His fingers snared the clear spot and he hauled himself up in one smooth motion, confident of what was up there. Swanson handed up the long sniper rifle and pulled himself up while Gibson dropped into the courtyard with hardly a sound. As promised, there were no shards of glass or embedded nails to slow their progress. Swanson went over, picked up his rifle, and strapped it over his back. The barrel length would be of no use in close, so he slid his preferred sidearm, a Colt .45 pistol, from its nylon holster.

Snipers are creatures of their surroundings, and the courtyard was an entirely different environment than beyond the wall. Although the enclosure was open to the sky, it was essentially cut off from outside influences. Their night vision had to make some adjustments, too. Slowly, things began to materialize and take shape in the vague light; the open space was no nest of junk, but neat and orderly. Solid black became deep purple. A slight breeze outside might be unfelt inside. Noise would be amplified or reduced on different sides of the wall, and it was so quiet that he heard a small flotilla of birds flutter overhead. Humidity would be different. While making the necessary physical adjustment, Swanson grabbed Gibson hard on the shoulder in an urgent warning.

When Gibson turned, Swanson gestured as if he were puffing on a cigarette and pointed toward the house. He had smelled cigarette smoke. Gibson dropped all pretense of laziness and went on point, steady as a bird dog. He could smell it, too, and brought the HK to his shoulder as he studied the shadows. The aroma was familiar. It was Marks's favorite brand. Gibson nodded that he understood.

Swanson fought back his anticipation. This was no time to get stupid. They communicated with hand signals, deciding to make a two-direction entry: Swanson in the back door and Gibson bursting through the front as soon as he heard Swanson yell. No matter how good Mr. Marks was, he couldn't take out two professional CIA shooters hitting at the same time.

Swanson had been doing this sort of thing for years, so stalking a target was thoroughly ingrained in him. Back on his belly, he started the crawl toward the rear portal, inching over the approximately twenty feet to his goal. Survival depended on remaining invisible. A bucket was in the way, and he wormed around it. The earth pressed against his body. Excalibur was an added weight and rode at an awkward angle, and although he would rather not take it off, it would be a hindrance in any close-quarters dance. He silently removed the rifle and propped the barrel against the house. Picked up the .45. Back to crawling. Slow, small, precise movements would get him where he wanted to go.

The smell of smoke lingered in the air like a sour, tantalizing perfume as Swanson worked his way forward. Their quarry must be in the front room. No lights were on. Swanson made it to the single poured-concrete step and studied the door. It was open about two inches. *Why?* To catch some night breeze, or an invitation to a trap? In an instant, Swanson voted for a trap. This was too easy. A seasoned operator like Nicky Marks smoking a telltale cigarette and leaving a door unlocked and open?

The unexpected, deafening crash of a flash-bang grenade tore the silence, followed by a lightning-bright burn of incandescence. It sparkled Swanson's night vision for a few heartbeats, and he wondered why Gibson changed the plan so abruptly. He shook his head and charged inside, stumbling over a chair as he bolted into the room swirling with acrid smoke.

"GET YOUR HANDS UP, SWANSON! GET 'EM UP! DROP YOUR WEAPON!"

Swanson saw a shadow in the smoke transform into a full figure and he recognized Nicky Marks, rooted in a shooting stance, both hands around the butt of a Glock pistol with a laser sight mounted on the rail. The pinpoint scarlet streak cut through the smoke and danced on Swanson's face. *An error!*

Swanson didn't hesitate. He did a halfback juke to the left and the red dot followed, then he planted his weight on his right foot and leaped directly at Marks with a war cry of his own.

Marks pulled the trigger and a single shot rang out, but the bullet buzzed past wide to the left, missing by no more than an inch and splintering the chair where Swanson had been a moment earlier. Marks had screwed up. *Overconfident.* Swanson felt no fear as he closed in, piloted by instinct.

The pistol swung back as Swanson tackled Marks around the waist, beneath the gun, slamming him against the wall, off balance and back on his heels. Marks got off another wild shot before Kyle smashed down on the gun hand with his own pistol. Both weapons flew away in the collision. The red streak spun crazily, and Swanson logged that information away: *Both guns out of the fight.*

The aggressor now, he grabbed Marks by the collar, feeling the man squirm as he searched for a hold of his own. Swanson freed his left hand just long enough to smack a sharp elbow strike aimed at the nose, but Marks turned his face aside. It was only a glancing blow.

Marks drove a hard flat hand just below Swanson's sternum, and although there was no room for a follow-through, he dug into the abs as if trying to pull out the liver. At some other time, in some other situation, the strike might have been painful, but with the adrenaline pumping it was no more than an insect bite to Swanson. Still, it was enough of a technical score to force him to *oof* out a breath and lean away.

They threw simultaneous knees at groins, but succeeded only in tangling legs, losing their leverage and falling, taking down a crash of crockery as they toppled. They landed hard, and Swanson cartwheeled away while Marks rolled in the opposite direction.

Both men got back on their feet, panting hard. Staring at each other, they reached for their belt knives as they warily began round two. Swanson's thoughts flashed back to his Marine Corps days and how to fight with a knife. He'd never practiced the arcane art much, preferring to shoot his enemies from a distance. But it is what it is. He was armed with a dark and heavy SEAL knife, which was designed to do everything but algebra, while Marks pulled a Fairbairn-Sykes commando dagger, built for close-quarter blade work. Advantage: Marks. Nicky saw that, too, and began a little shuffle to get close enough to strike.

Physical conditioning was about even, Swanson thought. The superior equipment was more than offset by the fact that Luke Gibson should be bursting through that front door any second now. All that Swanson had to do was not get killed until help arrived. *Where the hell is he?* Swanson looked for his gun, but it was lost in the rubble. The ruby laser beam was gone, too.

"Give it up, you surly prick," Swanson snarled, noticing that Marks's gray eyes actually held hope instead of gleaming like those of a trapped animal. "My partner is coming in."

Marks struck with a rattlesnake-quick thrust, in and back, and the Fairbairn-Sykes nicked Swanson's forearm, leaving a red trail behind. Marks didn't appear to be in a hurry to finish it. "You're a dead man if that's what you think."

Swanson tried a side-kick sweep, and although Marks dodged it, the move bought a few extra inches of space, a few more seconds off the clock. But it seemed that Marks was the one buying time.

A short rattle of automatic gunfire shook the tight room and a dozen 9-mm. bullets stitched Nicky Marks from legs to torso. As he fell backward, blood oozing from multiple wounds, a look of surprise crossed his face. "My prince," he coughed in a death rattle, staring at Gibson. Gibson stepped up and shot the man three more times, all in the head.

Gibson looked over at Swanson, who was breathing hard. "You okay?"

"Yeah." He wiped away some of the blood running from his forearm down to his wrist. "Why the hell did you throw in the flash-bang?"

"I didn't." Gibson pointed toward the sprawled body. "He popped it. I saw him through the window, and maybe he saw me, too, and decided to start the action on his own terms. Once again, Nicky knew our movements."

"Impossible." Swanson went to the corpse and rifled through the pockets. No paper. No phone. "You shouldn't have killed him, Luke. We needed answers from this guy."

"Well, you're welcome very much for saving your life, asshole. Those were the orders. I believe the exact words from Marty Atkins, our superior officer, were 'Find him and shoot him dead.' That's what we did. Anyway, he didn't leave us much choice."

Swanson looked hard at his partner. "Why did he call you 'my prince'?"

"Well, that's something I've been waiting to discuss with you."

Gibson swung the H&K submachine gun around like a baseball bat and struck Swanson hard across the back of the skull. Swanson's legs buckled and he went down like a bale of hay, unconscious before hitting the floor.

21

GIRDIWAL, AFGHANISTAN
9:18 PM LOCAL
1518 ZULU

HEADACHE. POUNDING AND PAINFUL, and a thirst that begged for moisture. The roar of a machine. Kyle Swanson sensed movement, then fell back into blackness. The machine roared again. Close by. It scared him, and he took the fright back into dreams.

The Boatman was leaning on the oar of his long canoe, waiting. "I told you," the ragged specter said in a voice dry and sandy. "I tried to warn you. 'This cannot be done alone,' I said."

Swanson groaned. Somebody working with a hammer. "I don't remember."

"Try." The nightmare figure spoke quietly, in contrast to the noise elsewhere.

"Water. Please give me some water."

"Think about it."

Swanson heaved, but his arms wouldn't work, and he collapsed again. "Did you come for me? Is it finally my time?"

"No. Just this one, although my work is just starting this night." The Boatman gestured toward the front of the bateau, where the corpse of Nicky Marks sat mute. Splotches of dried brown blood crusted his wounds. He had no head.

The Boatman stirred the imaginary pond and the boat sluggishly moved away, toward the carmine glow on the faraway horizon. "Try to remember," the figure called out before disappearing. "It is the answer."

SWANSON SLEPT AWHILE, THOUGHT he heard someone calling his name. He tried to force his eyes to open, but he couldn't see anything beyond an intense brightness, so he closed them again. His body shook. Another spell of blackness enveloped him, then he heard different voices, real ones this time. Words he couldn't understand. So thirsty.

LUKE GIBSON WAS BEGINNING to believe that he had popped Swanson too hard. That wasn't his intent. He had patched up the wound and hoped there was no concussion. He checked the restraints and stepped away, got a cup of water and poured some into Swanson's mouth, and heard him gag and cough, then gave him a little more.

"Are you finished yet?" he asked in Arabic.

One of the three rugged young men who had come up from the village said the work was complete, and Gibson went over. "Let's see how you did."

Nicky Marks's body hung upside down, tied by the ankles, from a hook in the ceiling above a blood-stained bathtub. It was messy. They had been in a hurry, because blood pools in the lowest part of the body after death, and Gibson needed the postmortem wounds to pump out a profuse amount of blood. It streamed from the deep gouges made on the back and thighs, from the spikes driven through the palms and into the walls, and flowed from the neck, where a chain saw had removed the head, and at the groin, which was missing the testicles and penis. He nodded approvingly. That should do the job. "Smile, Nicky," Gibson said, and started taking pictures.

THE WATER TRIGGERED A recovery, and Kyle Swanson felt as if he were landing in a hot-air balloon as his senses quickened. Where am I? He opened his eyes, but the vision was fuzzy. He saw dark figures and blinking bright light. The headache squeezed him again, and his body tightened in a spasm to compensate. The green field where he had been about to land vanished again.

Gibson, checking the pupils with a flashlight, thought Swanson would be coming around in a few minutes. It was only ten o'clock at night, so there was plenty of time to finish the email and make the calls.

Rep. Keenan:
Forwarding these pictures made today at secret CIA rendition house in the Afghan village of Girdiwal, the site of the drug airfield. This torture is the bloody hallmark of special operator Kyle Swanson. You must put a stop to this.

He didn't sign the note, but attached the grisly photographs in a slide-show format and sent them to Veronica Keenan in Washington. When the transmission had been completed, Gibson broke the burner phone apart, crushed the SIM card beneath his boot, and threw the pieces on the plastic sheet in which two of the men were wrapping the remains of Nicky Marks. "Take it all back into the mountains and burn it," he ordered.

Then he activated the sat phone and called the CIA contact in Germany. "Checkerboard, Checkerboard, this is Player Two."

Contact was instantaneous. Ryan Winters had been waiting for this call. "Player Two, this is Checkerboard. Send your traffic and stand by for new information."

"No time to wait, Checkerboard. Mission failed. Repeat, mission failed. Player One has gone berserk. Swanson tortured Nicky Marks to death and turned on me when I tried to stop him. Gunfight. I am hit and trying to egress. He is following me."

Winters was stunned. He was supposed to pass along the urgent instructions for Swanson to break off the mission because his partner might be unstable, and return to base on the double. This radio call from Gibson flipped everything. "Player Two, Checkerboard. Are you all right?"

"Bleeding from a shoulder wound. I'm in cover for now. I need orders." There was a moment of static, but before Winters could say anything, Gibson was talking again, louder and in a rush. "Gotta go! Gotta go! Aw, Jeez. He's coming. . . ."

Well, that should keep them busy for a while, Gibson thought as he turned off the sat phone and trashed it, too. Two of the men lugged Marks's body out the door and tossed it into the bed of a pickup truck, then covered it with canvas, tying the corners. The Toyota pulled away from the house and headed away from civilization.

KYLE SWANSON SAW SHADOWS that firmed into shapes as he awoke, bound to a chair. "What?" he croaked, his throat aching and parched.

"Ah. Back from nappytime, are we?" The jovial voice of Luke Gibson registered. "You're okay, Kyle. Just a little bump on the head. Here's some more water."

A firm hand gripped his jaw and a plastic bottle bumped his lips. He drank, swallowed, drank again, stopped. "What happened? Grenade? I don't remember anything after Marks went down."

"That's because I knocked you out. You never saw it coming."

"What the fuck, Gibson? Why am I tied up?"

Gibson put the bottle on a table and rocked back in a chair of his own. "You're tied up because otherwise you would do something stupid, like try to kill me before I explain the situation. You're a dangerous man, Kyle, so I can't take that chance."

Swanson tested the bonds. Duct tape was strapped around his chest, his hips, and probably his legs, because he couldn't move his feet. His hands were loose in front of him, but handcuffed, and his watch was gone. He reached for the bottle, looking at Gibson, who made no move to stop him. He drank. A packet of aspirin was on the table, so he opened it and took two tablets, chasing them with another sip. "You contact Checkerboard yet?"

"Sure. Brought them up to date."

"I thought I heard somebody talking. Marks?"

"Dead and gone."

Kyle looked around the room. No body. He saw lots of blood in the open bathroom door. "What . . . the . . . hell . . . is . . . going . . . on?"

Gibson spread his hands as if to calm him. "Don't sweat it about Marks. He was a rotten bastard anyway. As for you, I didn't bring you here to hurt you, Kyle. To kill you, yes, eventually, but not for torture. In fact, I want you in top shape."

Swanson's head still hurt, but he was thinking more clearly as he sat back in the chair, seeming to relax a bit while taking a physical inventory. He raised his hands to his head and his fingers found a square bandage compress that had been taped over a small cut that still oozed liquid. He clenched his hands, his toes, and did isometrics to be sure everything still worked. He was tied in a peculiar way, but otherwise it seemed he was fine. "I never trusted you, Gibson. Not from the start."

Gibson laughed as if he was truly amused and slapped the table a couple of times. "Yet here we are! I win!"

"You win? Win what?" Swanson flicked his eyes to a young man sitting in a shadowed corner. Slight, with an expressionless face that carried only a fuzz of beard. Age no more than fifteen. A Kalashnikov was propped next to him.

Gibson got to his feet and began to pace. He was in full flow, and Swanson didn't interrupt. Let him talk and give away some nuggets of intelligence. Swanson kept his own mind busy on other things, looking for possible weapons, possible advantages. He stretched against the tautness of his bonds. There was little give to it, and he knew the fibers of duct tape were incredibly strong. He couldn't bust his way free. A slow anger boiled inside, but he fought it back in order to remain calm. Somehow, someway, there had to be an exit.

"I was telling you about my father, remember? Well, he was a CIA guy, too, as was his father before him. I come from a long, long line of spooks, Kyle, dating back to the days of the British Raj. I was actually bred and trained from childhood for this kind of work. Just like some dads spend their afternoon training their sons to be professional athletes, mine taught me tradecraft."

Swanson gave a small laugh. "Whoopie for you. Must have been a lot of fun." Then he paused. "You're crazy, Luke. You know that, right?"

"That depends on your definitions. Crazy enough to dream big dreams and then go out and make them come true. Crazy enough to be the best at everything I do."

Swanson checked the kitchen. It was small, with a counter and some cabinets that seemed about to fall from the wall. He saw a small stove, which meant that the place was actually used for preparing meals. That meant a knife or two, perhaps some glasses or plates and other stuff. He inhaled and caught a whiff of stale food, and assumed it had been cooked, which meant that fire was available, probably with propane gas. He turned his attention back to the babbling Gibson. "What's the plan here, Luke? Why didn't you shoot me out there? You had plenty of chances?"

"Didn't you hear me? Listen up. I've always been the best at everything. The CIA, through my family connections, first recruited me back in high school. If they could take a kid—the right kid, of course, not just anybody—and mold him through his formative years, they could create a professional of exceptional talent and possibilities."

Swanson couldn't let that curveball pass without a swing. "Kids lie about their age all the time to get into the service. Discovering a sixteen-year-old soldier isn't a rare occurrence. They get trained fast, and a high-school dropout might become a combat medic or learn to speak Russian in six months. You aren't so special."

Gibson didn't take the taunt. "By the time the recruiters hit the college campuses for juniors and seniors, they may find some with unique skills, all of them very bright, but some ten valuable years of learning have been wasted. By the time I was a junior, I was already running missions and helping my dad."

Swanson nodded his chin toward the young fighter crouched in the corner, who apparently didn't understand a word of English. He seemed bored. "You and I both have seen guns on boys in Africa who should have been in about the third grade. And how about your little punch boy over there, Luke? Doesn't the fact that he's probably illiterate kind of blow your élitist theory out of the water?"

"Children can be useful tools, that it true. Even a mosquito can bite. I created a group of boys called the Lions of the Caliphate. They cannot think and plan or see beyond tomorrow, and then they die as cannon fodder. Anyway, I don't have to prove myself to you, Swanson. I've already beaten you several times."

Water? The word made him look at the bottle on the table. This place had water and food supplies. A scan of the walls showed old nails and random screws sticking out. Propane plus nails equal bomb? Possible. A couple of lightbulbs showed that there was electricity. A broom and who knows what other housekeeping supplies would be around. In the right hands, this place had a lot of possibilities. Although he was bound like a chicken, he was beginning to feel better.

"You said you came here, to this house, as a boy, Gibson. Why did dear old dad haul you to such a dump? Some parents take their kids to Paris or London or New York, but you end up in the ass-end of nowhere?"

Gibson moved to the kitchen and came back with a fresh water bottle. He opened it and drank. "One of the family assignments was to establish safe houses for the agency in interesting places when the Middle East started to heat up. Along the way, we created some rabbit holes where we could also hide."

Swanson grunted, as if in admiration. A safe house meant weapons, money, comm gear, identity papers. Probably under the rugs. Also, his Excalibur sniper rifle had been laid on a nearby table, along with his other gear and ammo.

Gibson turned a chair around and straddled it to face Kyle. "I know what you're doing, Mr. Secret Agent Man. You're noting things you might be able to use in an escape. We went to the same schools on that shit, remember?"

"I'm tired of your bragging about your weird family business," Swanson snapped. "What's the point? You get me here, then you kill Marks . . ."

He stopped in midsentence. The words of the Boatman came back, and things started to snap into place.

"*This cannot be done alone.*" All the while, Swanson had believed the subconscious voice was urging him to take Gibson on as the partner he needed for a complicated mission. No, it had been about the partner and the target working together in a complex ballet of death to lure him into a kill zone. "You and Marks were a team!"

"Almost. I need specialized help now and then. He was handy when I decided to reel you in and teach the CIA a lesson." Gibson opened a tall armoire and tossed a couple of bundles of clothing on the table, then undressed while continuing to talk. "It was the damned agency, you see that? I worked for them all my life, as my family had for generations, then they betrayed me. I was the one who did the high-value targets, I was the one with the best assignments and rewards, I was the loyal soldier who could go anywhere and do anything. Anything! So what did they do to piss me off so much? You, Kyle Swanson, Marine Corps legend and top shooter for Task Force Trident, became available—out of the corps and still in your prime, plus your connections to Excalibur. That's a helluva weapon, I gotta say. But, presto, you were number one from the day you walked in the door." The belts and boots and jumpsuit were thrown into a pile, and he donned loose pants, a tunic, and sandals like those worn by the kid in the corner. Changing into local garb; getting ready to fade away.

"No such thing, Luke. I'm pretty much full time with Excalibur and only do occasional contract work for the agency. There is no rating system of who's who in the sniper world. The number of kills is a media fantasy. You know that."

Gibson pointed a finger at him, the smile gone. "And YOU know that they always turn to you first in a clutch. That fucking Marty Atkins thinks you're a god of war. Atkins is the one who promoted you over me."

"So you're going to ruin Marty? That's silly. He's a bureaucrat, and someone just like him will take his place. It isn't a personal judgment, Luke—just who he has available and where at the right time. I hardly know the man."

Gibson was growing agitated as he adjusted his new clothing for comfort. "So I decided to set things straight, once and for all. Top of my list is that you have to go. I've already ruined your reputation. Understand? Next, Marty has to go. Then I'll send the whole fucking CIA right down the sewer."

Swanson cocked his head and said, "Gee, Luke, you seem upset."

Gibson slapped him hard across the face and the chair tumbled to the floor, with Swanson bouncing along with it.

22

THERE WERE MOMENTS IN her job when Marguerite del Coda knew it was best to act on her own. That not only got things moving faster but also shielded her superiors in the event something went wrong. This was one of those moments.

The situation in Afghanistan had deteriorated from a somewhat unusual but still routine job to a potential catastrophe faster than a flash flood fills a Texas ditch. The news had caught her in the middle of her first glass of wine, and she pushed it away as Ryan Winters filled her in.

A weird radio message had been picked up from Luke Gibson, deep in Afghanistan, and it made no sense whatsoever. Two veteran operators were trying to kill each other, and a third one had been tortured? No way.

"We put a drone overhead, didn't we, Ryan?"

"Yes, boss. It was for attack purposes, however, with only tactical vision. We don't have an eye in the sky."

"Let's change that, then. Get a camera overhead." She knew Langley would have no problem with that, since flying drones was a big part of her job. The next part was more of a roll of the dice.

"Do we have anybody else in the general area?" she asked.

Winters played his keyboard for about thirty seconds. "The closest option would be that other sniper team, Brandt and Thompson. They're just coming off that successful assignment in Pakistan."

"Let's get them saddled up as soon as possible to get to that location, find out what the hell is going on."

Winters hesitated and gave a little wince. "Are you sure you want to do that, Marguerite? Langley may not like it."

"My call, Ryan. Easier to ask forgiveness than to seek permission, and we need to sort out some details. Crank it up. I'm on my way back to the office. This may end up as a full-blown search and rescue in a hot zone, but we're not abandoning our people on the ground."

CLARKE, VERMONT
NOON LOCAL
1700 ZULU

COASTIE SULKED HER WAY through a long talk with herself, then called Mexico, and she and Mama Castillo shared a long cry across the miles. "I don't know what to do, Mama," she confided between sobs. "I can't get over what happened to Mickey. I'm doing and thinking crazy things." She stroked Nero, who stretched beside her.

"Miguel is gone, my sweet Beth. We cannot bring him back."

"How did you get over it when Papa died? What's the secret?"

There was a brief silence, then Mama quietly replied, "Only time, my dear. One dawn at a time. The hurt fades away, although the ache of such a lost love stays forever. Miguel loved you with great passion."

"I know. Just as I loved him." She snatched another tissue from the box and wiped her nose and eyes. "It was special."

Mama's tone changed a bit, kind but sharper. "However, we both knew he was in a very, very dangerous business. He risked his life every time he went out. That was the kind of man he was when you first met him, remember? He didn't change. He couldn't."

"Damned drug cartels!" Coastie said, gripping a handful of Nero's fur. The dog looked up, startled, and she went back to petting him.

"Beth, remember that you were in that same line of work. You understood him in ways that no other woman could." Her tone softened then.

"You're not meant to be a housewife, Beth. Miguel often told me that you could conquer dragons. You need a cause, something bigger than yourself."

"I should just come back to you and the family."

"NO!" Mama was adamant. "There's nothing but trouble for you now down here, Beth, and a drug war is under way in the region. The family is fine. I'm getting better. I won't let you come back and sit around and wilt away wrapped in black lace and sorrow. That isn't who you are. Is Kyle helping you out?"

"I haven't seen him for a while," Coastie said. "Don't know where he is. I'm up in the state of Vermont right now, and some old friends are trying to help. Apparently, they find me to be a heavy load to carry. I miss Mexico."

"And I miss you, too. Stay busy, Beth. Keep your mind occupied. Count yourself fortunate to have known true love in this lifetime and to have good friends. Now, let go of the past and look toward tomorrow."

When they hung up, Coastie sat still for a while, thinking hard. Mama was right. She should postpone her rampage against the cartels for a while. Not quit; just take time off. She washed up, brushed her hair, put on clean clothes, and hunted Double-Oh. He was unloading some bales of hay from a pickup, picking them up without effort, his big forearms bulging as he tossed them.

"I'm back," she said, looking up at him, her arms across her chest.

"Yeah?" He threw out another bale and took a break, with his hand on his hips, looking down at her, detecting an internal change in the pint-size killer. This was the girl he knew.

"Yeah," she said. "I am."

GIRDIWAL, AFGHANISTAN

SWANSON CONTINUED TRYING TO get his bearings. He spat out some blood, and Gibson lifted the chair upright. "Why the Mexico attack on the grave, Luke? Mickey Castillo had nothing to do with any of this. That was really out of bounds."

"Castillo was a pain in the ass for the drug chiefs. Those constant raids on the labs and the caches had become a bother, and his commandos had taken out a lot of their most reliable gunmen." Gibson wandered over to the window and looked out, then back at Swanson. "Worse, he couldn't be bought off. So when he got killed—that was a lucky shot, by the way—Maxim Guerrara wanted to send a message to dissuade other righteous idiots. He did not know exactly how."

"I still don't get it." Swanson was being truthful about that, and the longer he could keep Gibson talking the better. Something might happen.

"When I heard about the colonel's death, I saw my chance, Kyle. It was common knowledge that the two of you were close friends, so here was an opening to start you along the path that has brought you here. I offered Nicky to go in and do something dramatic to resolve their problem. I also told him to be recognized, so the chase could begin. It had to seem to be your idea, Swanson. You had to want to take the next step. Avenging your friend's grotesque end was a perfect reason."

Swanson filled his cheeks with air and blew it out slowly. "You're a deranged animal," he said as he did some more isometric flexes, creating wiggle space.

"And you were so easy to catch," Swanson snapped. "Once Nicky's name and picture were in play, you couldn't be held back. So we met in Berlin, not by coincidence but because I wanted it that way."

Swanson looked quizzical. "The grenade that Marks threw almost took you out, too."

"We had worked it out beforehand, dumbass. We even practiced with rocks that afternoon before dinner. The thick foliage provided cover, and the rollaway down the slope took us under the blast. It was choreographed, and I signaled him by lighting that cigarette, then flipping it away. Remember, I was the one who identified Marks as the villain that time, right?"

Swanson had to agree. The man had done some work on this, and Swanson was ready to kick himself for not recognizing the hurry-up scenario.

"After that, Nicky and I stayed in touch by phone to keep him one step ahead. At the same time, I pushed you and Marty Atkins to hurry, hurry, hurry. The cherry on top? You'll love this."

"What?" Swanson noticed that the boy in the corner was falling asleep, bored by the foreign words and not caring. No attention to his weapon.

"I hooked a member of Congress into launching an investigation of the agency. She's a fool, but useful." He stopped talking and went to the doorway and looked outside when the buzz of a small airplane sounded overhead in the darkness. Gibson checked his watch. "Too early for a rescue party, Kyle. They may not send anyone at all. Sorry about that. May be my own ride out, or just another little plane coming in late. We get plenty of traffic here."

"A congressional inquiry? On what?" Why was a plane flying so low? A busy little airport? He kept his eyes on Gibson. Flexed his calf muscles.

Gibson was showing off now, proud of his machinations. "The gentlewoman from Nebraska received information that the CIA is running drugs again, along with some photographic proof. The thing that will interest you even more is that she also believes Excalibur Enterprises is involved in the scheme." Gibson poked a finger at Swanson. "You've been identified as a rogue agent. Your cover is blown and your reputation will be ruined no matter what Congress decides."

Swanson couldn't hold back a laugh. "Bullshit, Gibson. There's nothing like that going on. Excalibur will eat her for lunch if she takes on Sir Geoffrey Cornwell."

"Oh, that will eventually become clear, but in the meanwhile the Permanent Select Committee on Intelligence will enjoy a field day with televised hearings, and my pet congresswoman will get lots of free TV time. Your friends at the agency will sacrifice you to save their own butts, partner."

Swanson shrugged and put his manacled wrists in his lap. "You're not my partner, and you're dumber than a box of rocks to try something this looney. Cut to the chase, Gibson. What happens next? How is this fairy tale of yours supposed to end, you delusional moron?"

KASHMIR, PAKISTAN

"MY GOODESS," SAID INGMAR Thompson with a slight tsk-tsk of surprise as he read the screen of his phone.

Bruce Brandt frowned. "I don't like to hear you say that." He was eyeing a cool silver belt buckle the size of a saucer as they passed a shop in the bazaar.

"We have to go to a car that's waiting for us a block from the office. Right now."

Brandt kept his frown. "I hate to bring this up, but won't that area be crawling with cops because we killed that ISIS dude?"

"Apparently, it isn't, and please keep your voice down."

"But I'm bargaining for that buckle, man. And the fleshpots are one street over. We have many things to do right where we are."

Thompson reached out and wrapped a big mitt around his friend's left biceps and gave a pull. Trying to stop Bruce from talking occasionally required direct and decisive action.

"Five dollars U.S.! Not a penny more. Last offer," he called to the shopkeeper holding the intricately carved silver belt buckle and watching as the big American almost pulled the customer almost off his feet.

"Ten! It is worth twenty-five," he responded, following them.

"Seven," Bruce shot back, trying to break his friend's grip. Ingmar propelled him forward.

"Seven is good," the shopkeeper said. "But by the beard of the Prophet it is worth fifty dollars."

"Let me go, Ingmar. Let me pay and we're out of here."

"Hummph," Thompson grunted with dissatisfaction as he loosened his hold on his fellow sniper.

The dark sedan with glazed windows was waiting, the engine running. A Pakistani policeman shooed other traffic around it. Thompson ducked into one rear door and Brandt slid in the other, saying, "Look what I just bought!"

"How much did you pay?" asked Khan Dajani, the driver, looking back in the mirror. He was an American of Pakistani heritage and had the local accent and looks.

"Stole it for seven bucks."

"You paid too much," Dajani said, laughing. "I could have gotten it for three."

"Well, you weren't there, were you, Kahn?" Brandt snapped. He held up the big chunk of polished silver and looked at the design. Worth seven, easy. Probably more.

"Why are we here?" Thompson asked the man in the front passenger seat, a black man with a high hairline.

"Kyle Swanson is in trouble and you're going in to get him." Roger Lincoln sketched the situation verbally as Kahn pulled into the traffic and a police motorcycle moved in front as an escort.

Brandt and Thompson were silent during the quick update.

"Things are moving fast on this one, guys," Kahn said. "The buzz is that another Benghazi is unacceptable."

"So Ingmar and I are going in to take on the Taliban, the ISIS goons, any Afghan Army soldiers and pissed-off civilians who may be standing around and rescue Swanson and Gibson and that crazy Nicky Marks. All by our lonesome we're going to do this? We just got through killing a guy a few blocks over."

Khan looked in the mirror again. "You was volunteered again, mate. If you get killed, can I have that buckle?"

23

GIRDIWAL, AFGHANISTAN

"Y OU LOST ME SOMEWHERE along the line," Swanson said, easing his lower legs against the chair, feeling for advantages while keeping his eyes locked on Gibson. "Your whole story seems pointless. You kill me, the agency kills you, and other operators take our place. There is never a number one."

"There is! I've always been the best. Always better than you."

Swanson gave a chuckle. "It doesn't matter, Luke. Can't you understand that? Nobody but you cares, and you're laying it all on the line out here in a mud hut in the middle of Afghanistan, where nobody will ever hear about it."

"You'll know what happened out here. I'll know what happened. That alone would be enough."

Swanson raised his handcuffs level with his eyes. "And this is how you prove it? You with a gun and me taped to a chair and without a weapon. Where's the glory in that? Anyway, get on with it."

"The people will know, Kyle. The ones around here and up and down my network. Those are the ones who matter. They know me as the Prince, and that I run a tight kingdom. When they hear that I killed the top CIA shooter in one-on-one combat, my legend will be at its zenith." Gibson's eyes had taken on the unusual sparkle of a serial killer.

"A prince." Swanson cracked a smile. "Honor without honor. What a crock."

Gibson checked his watch, getting antsy, ready to go.

Swanson guessed that he only needed a few minutes alone, but Gibson wouldn't stop his spiel of self-glorification. "There's one big problem with your idea, Luke. It's all built on the premise that you kill me. Unless you pull the trigger right now, it won't happen. I will kill you, and, deep down, you're afraid because you know it's true. So let's do it . . . partner."

Gibson snapped on the bait. "Yes, I'm going to leave now, and Hamid will remain as a guard until three o'clock. At that point, he will put the key to the cuffs on the table and also leave. If I come back at dawn and you're still here, I will shoot you on sight."

"And if I get out, you hunt me down."

"Exactly."

"Luke, you're more trouble than you're worth. Go already. I'll see you again in a few hours."

Gibson was upset that Swanson didn't seem angry or worried. He turned, removed the key to the handcuffs from his pocket, and motioned for the boy to go outside with him. "I'll give him a few instructions in private. Just understand that he may be young but he's just fine with a gun. One order is to shoot you if you try to cause trouble."

"You know I'll have to kill him," Swanson said as Gibson and the boy exited into the night.

"It's your only hope," Gibson said, throwing a protective arm around Hamid's shoulder as he closed the door. "He is one of my young lions, however, and is tougher than he looks. He might even be able to take you out."

TICK. TICK. TICK. SWANSON counted fifteen seconds before moving. He didn't care why Gibson had taken the boy outside, only that they'd left him alone. The handcuffs rattled when he made his move, inching the chair away from the table using the toes of his boots and rocking his body.

He lost his knife when he was knocked cold by Gibson, the pistol had been stolen, and the Excalibur was propped against the wall next to the AK-47. It might as well have been on the moon. This didn't mean that Swanson was without assets, though.

He was tightly taped to the chair, but by stretching his arms down and pushing his legs up he was able to snag the left leg of his trousers and pull it out of the boot; the tape held the cloth and not the flesh beneath, which made for a minuscule bit of freedom. He wiggled his feet as high as they could go. Inside of thirty seconds, he had his hands between his calves, searching blindly with his thumbnails for a different piece of tape. No one had ever said he could take only one knife with him on a mission. Screw fairness.

The thumbnail caught the top edge of a strip of easy-pull medical adhesive that stretched vertically up the back of his left leg. A casual pat-down normally touched only the outside of the feet, searching for an ankle holster. An amateur might even rub the crotch area, but the back of the calf was seldom touched.

It was there that Swanson had secured a folded straight-edge razor. Almost a minute had passed by the time he worked it free, and there were still no sounds from outside. He hoped that whatever the boy was doing to serve his prince would last for a while. No bets on that.

Swanson held the razor at lap level before opening it, and it glittered. Holding it with his forefinger and thumb, braced in his palm, he went to work. The old-fashioned blade cut though the individual sticky strands of tape with a minimum of sawing and he was able to part the bands of tape across the top of his right leg, then his left, until they barely hung together.

That allowed him just enough freedom to extend the razor to his ankles and slice those bands, too. To the naked eye, he would appear to be as immobile as before. Two minutes had passed. He folded the straight blade and pushed it far up the sleeve of his left forearm. Then he pulled the chair back near the table and sat and waited, hands in plain sight on the wood, cuffs in place, trying to look resigned to his fate and not sweat the details of the coming attack. There were too many unknowns. Just let it flow.

HAMID SEEMED A BIT unsteady when he reentered the house and shut the door. The truck engine that was fading away was evidence that the boy was now alone with the prisoner, and, despite apparently having all the advantages, he was nervous. The Prince had told him not to worry. Hamid took the chair facing Swanson at the table and placed the AK-47 between them, with the barrel pointed at Swanson and a finger near the trigger, then plopped the small key for the cuffs beside it. When the prisoner hardly looked up, more confidence flowed into the young captor, who ranted a few Arabic curses. Swanson just sat there, unmoving.

Long minutes passed. Swanson knew that his silence and his manner would foster the illusion that the boy was in control, and the young fighter wouldn't be able to maintain that baleful glare and menacing attitude for long. Swanson yawned, planting in the other man's mind the suggestion that he, too, was sleepy so late in the night.

Hamid adjusted his position in the chair, leaning back to a more comfortable position, hands pulling farther away from the Kalashnikov. There was no danger evident in the room. He was in control.

Swanson slowly rotated his hands and put them on his thighs, so that the palms faced upward, then rested again. No reaction. With a mighty surge, he grabbed the table by the edge and threw it at Hamid as hard as possible, following with a leap that was powered by his legs as the few remaining threads of tape parted. The gun spun away, and the astonished boy cried out as the table crashed into him, followed by Swanson's full weight. The connecting links of the steel handcuffs were jammed across Hamid's throat, and Swanson pushed down viciously to crush the windpipe and simultaneously head-butt Hamid under the bridge of the nose. Physics and biomechanics did the rest. The nose shattered on impact, and the resulting hemorrhage sent a torrent of blood spewing outward, but because the victim was on the floor, more blood also poured back down the throat and into the lungs, further stressing the fractured larynx. The boy flailed wildly at the table, the strangling handcuffs, and Swanson. Death closed in fast and with a lot of pain. It sounded as if he was calling for his mother.

Swanson kept the pressure on until he was sure that Hamid was gone, then crabbed away from the debris. *Luke knew something like this was going to happen. He threw the boy to me as a sacrifice to buy time because he really wants the one-on-one stalk and kill. This was just to tire his prey.* Swanson banished the thought as fast as it had appeared, because there was no use dwelling on the past, even if was only a minute ago.

The razor had remained in his sleeve during the attack, so he slid it out, spread it open and cut through the tape that still bound him to the chair with easy strokes. The chair fell away with a clatter, allowing him to peel off the sticky strips one by one.

When it was all off, he stretched his muscles luxuriously. Truly free, and still alive.

HE DUG THE AK-47 from the debris and gave it quick check. The banana clip was fully loaded. Then he recovered the Excalibur, which had been severely damaged. Gibson had taken the time to waste the weapon so that it couldn't be used against him from a distance.

Sand spilled from the barrel, the trigger housing had been battered with a hard object, and the magazine was gone. The front scope lens was cracked. No .50-cal ammo anywhere to be seen. Swanson would take it along all the same to keep the technology secret, and also because the Big E wasn't yet out of the game.

After a drink of water and answering the call of nature from having sat tied up for so long, Swanson moved to his next task, which had come to him while he was bound to the chair. Somewhere high above, a drone was circling with a load of high explosives, but he had no direct control over it. The reverse was true, because electronic beacons had been sewn into the clothing of both members of the sniper team before they had departed, which meant that a missile might be coming down the chimney if Gibson decided to rain down some hellfire.

Swanson cut the small tracking device from beneath his collar and tossed the gizmo into a bucket of water to drown it. Gibson had probably already gotten rid of his, too, leaving the drone as blind as a really big bat. Step two was to get the heavy drag bag that protected Excalibur on an active mission. The weapon itself was what caught the eye of someone curious, not its cloth container. A strong zipper ran the length of the case, with an inch-round fob for opening and closing the metal teeth. Swanson pried the metal fob open and extracted another round object that rested inside like a Russian nesting doll. Carrying it over to the damaged rifle, he plugged the button into a tiny slot beneath the battery pack normally used to power the scope. It activated with a soft beep and began sending signals to the blind drone. Swanson was back on the grid.

With the AK in hand, he toured the little house, memorizing directions and moving about slowly, aware that Gibson's hint that he would return at dawn was worthless; he might be standing outside right now. The man-to-man stuff was a crock, too, and Swanson didn't want a trip-wire booby trap to ruin his day.

But he needed to gather supplies, and he had to have some food. In a quick sweep, he gathered up carbohydrates, sugar, liquid, a spoon, some cord, plastic wrapping, and anything else that might prove useful, including the needle and thread he found in the bedroom. The half-used roll of duct tape spoke for itself. Some first-aid stuff. A cloth bag to carry it all. On the kitchen counter was a half-eaten plate of stew. On the stove was a covered pot of the same. Somebody had had a meal, so odds were it was probably safe to eat, and he wolfed it down cold.

The one thing that was guaranteed to be in a safe house was weaponry, stored somewhere out of sight. Swanson looked around. It had to be under the rugs, but if Gibson was going to plant an improvised explosive device anywhere, it would be where Swanson was sure to look for some armament. Forget it. With the AK at the ready in his right hand, the bag of goodies in his left, and Excalibur across his back, he went out through a window.

24

KAISERSLAUTEN, GERMANY

T HIS MAKES NO SENSE." Ryan Winters grabbed a yellow no. 2 pencil, scratched his scalp with the eraser, then stuck the pencil behind his ear. The streams of data on the screen didn't lie, but neither did it add up. Things just didn't work that way. He sighed and headed in to see Marguerite del Coda again.

"Boss?" It was more of a sorrowful plea than a question.

Del Coda had the look of a pit viper after giving up any hope of a quiet evening. "What?"

"It's that thing in the Wakham Corridor again."

"Is the new drone in place?"

"Getting there."

"And the backup team? Brandt and Thompson?"

"Also still getting there. Not about any of that."

She fingered the small, spiky necklace of orange coral at her throat. Clapped her hands once and stared over the rim of her glasses. "I have no time for riddles, Ryan. What is it?"

Winters said, "Watch this." He activated a large screen on the wall. "Before Gibson and Swanson left, we attached tracking beacons on their clothing, remember?"

"Of course."

"Here's the imagery after they dropped into Girdiwal." Two bright green dots appeared on the magnified screen in the middle of a grid map.

"Both beacons going strong and being read by both the gun drone and the cargo plane that delivered them. Signals are loud and clear."

"I see them." She was impatient, but Ryan Winters was a supremely logical person and would spell it all out at his own pace.

Winters made a fluttering motion with his fingers and the screen clock spun faster. "Time passing. Time passing." The clock slowed, as did the finger dance, and he said, "Watch."

One of the tracking signals disappeared. "That was Luke Gibson. No communication was made to explain why."

"Whoa!" Marguerite said. "We got a distress call from him that Swanson was chasing him. Did Swanson bring him down, you think? Kyle killed Luke?"

"Swanson's beam is still strong in that frame. But according to the beacon he hadn't moved. Neither had Gibson, at the time his signal was lost. They were still together at the target safe house."

"So Gibson was not on the run. He is alive? He lied?"

Winters fluttered his fingers again. "Time passing." The clock rolled ahead. Suddenly the second tracking beacon pipped off the screen, leaving it blank. "That was Swanson."

Del Coda almost wilted. "All contact has been lost with both of them?"

"That's what I thought. That's exactly what happened. Had to be."

"Gotta call Langley."

"Not yet. Watch." He had let the screen unroll its mystery in actual time. In the blank grid, another dot suddenly appeared, blinking at odd intervals. "That is neither of the original devices."

"So what the hell is it?"

"According to the databases, the serial number is listed as being part of a special-weapons development unit belonging to Excalibur Enterprises in the U.K. and is currently in the possession of Kyle Swanson."

"Swanson is alive, then?"

"We don't know. All we have is that the new beacon has been activated and the signal, while strong enough, is coming through intermittent microburst transmissions being read by the drone's standard frequencies. My guess is that it's battery-powered and whoever's using it wants to conserve the energy source."

"Now can I call Langley?"

"Sure. And tell them that whichever of them is transmitting is beginning to move."

GIRDIWAL, AFGHANISTAN

SWANSON STASHED HIS GEAR near the courtyard gate and hurried over to the humming generator. Two five-gallon jerry cans of gasoline stood near it, and he lugged them to the house. After he'd closed the door to the kitchen, it took only a few minutes to saturate the rest of the place with one can, sloshing it over the rugs, the weapons cache, and in the corners. Luke Gibson had probably left behind a booby trap; Kyle intended to return the favor. The strong vapor irritated his nostrils and made his eyes water, and he placed the second full can in the front room, amid all the debris. The tricky part— not blowing himself up while arming the device—came next.

In the kitchen, keeping the door closed, he dumped the remaining stew from the pot on the stove and dropped in a handful of rounds that he had taken from the AK-47's magazine. Then he carefully lit the propane burner and set the heat on low. Taking a deep breath, Swanson threw open the kitchen door and ran for his life, grabbing his gear as he passed through the courtyard and dashing through the front gate.

He covered about a quarter of a mile, roughly four football fields, before the fire roasting the bullets in the metal pot ignited them and gunfire rapped through the night air. An instant later, the fire and hot shrapnel and burning gunpowder ignited the heavy cloud of trapped gas fumes. The nightmarish *whoosh* of the gasoline was followed by the explosions of the propane tank in the kitchen and the jug of gasoline in the front room. A booming detonation shook the area, and Swanson felt the heat against his back but didn't waste time looking behind him. Legs pumping, he headed for his chosen ground.

The detonation rolled across the valley and shook the town of Girdiwal, and many residents rushed outside to see the roaring fire and the rising smoke. Luke Gibson slept through it, but one of his young followers, a fifteen-year-old boy, was soon pounding on his door at the little inn.

"What is it?" he called out in Arabic.

"Sir, your home has just blown up," the boy said, almost beside himself with excitement. "It is on fire!"

Gibson rolled over and checked his cell phone: 0300. Damn, Kyle, that was pretty quick. Leave that guy alone for an hour and all hell breaks loose. He laughed aloud. His personal hunt would start at dawn, but, in the meantime, he should keep Swanson guessing.

The boy was startled by the laughter. He had expected Gibson to burst forth fully rigged for battle, but instead there was only the sound of amusement.

"Okay, you Lions go get him," came the order. "Be careful. This American is a prime enemy of the caliphate and there's a reward for his head. May Allah guide your quest."

The boy turned and hurried downstairs to get his partner, another fiery teenager. Upstairs, Gibson rolled over and went back to sleep. Cannon fodder.

WASHINGTON, D.C.

THEY COULD WAIT NO longer. Throughout the day, the pressure had been building on several fronts, and they had reached the point where the White House had to be brought into the loop. By six o'clock that afternoon, President Christopher Thompson was at the head of the long table in the Situation Room, flanked by almost every heavy hitter in Washington. He had been through many crises since assuming the job six years ago, and could smell the possibilities of this one. He had handled the others competently enough, and he would get through this, too. To ease the tensions, he slipped into his blue windbreaker with the presidential patch on the left breast and encouraged the others to shed their coats and ties and high heels and get comfortable. His paternal smile imbued his team with confidence. "Let's get through this in time for dinner, huh, folks? Bring me up to speed." Ignoring the images on the flat-screen monitors on the walls, the president thumbed through a two-page summary as his national-security adviser, retired marine Lieutenant General Bradley Middleton, went through an even shorter version.

"Three CIA operators are missing—or maybe not—around the Afghan village called Girdiwal. One or more tried to kill the others at different points. Two more operators are on their way in. You've seen TV reports about a possible congressional investigation into accusations that the CIA is running drugs again—through an airstrip in the same place, Girdiwal."

"Deal with the operators first, General Middleton. Politics can come later."

"Yes, sir."

Middleton, CIA director Rick Burns, and Martin Atkins, the director of intelligence, took turns explaining the background, and the president peppered them with questions. "It all started with a tragic bombing in Mexico, but it goes deeper than that," said the general. "We have stories and accusations, and little proof of which is correct."

The president rubbed his fingers together, as if he had glue on them. "I cannot believe Kyle Swanson has gone rogue. Impossible."

"Mr. President, until recently, I would have said the same about the other two guys, Luke Gibson and Nicky Marks. Solid, reliable pros. Now I've ordered a re-examination of everything concerning them."

"What's the best guess right now?"

The Situation Room watch officer took her cue from Middleton and put up the screen. A blue circle was immobile on the background. "That is an overhead satellite view, sir. We believe this transmitter belongs to Swanson, although both he and Gibson had other signals gear, but on different frequencies, when they went in. All of that was lost."

"The bright area nearby?"

"Looks like a hot spot. Maybe a fire, sir. We'll know for sure when the camera drone arrives, in about thirty minutes. All we have on station right now is a gunship and this satellite, which is going out of range."

Thompson paused in thought. "Bad stuff. Get to the politics now. Briefly, please."

Rick Burns, coat off and sleeves rolled up, took over. "A congresswoman from Nebraska has made the charge against the CIA. By the way, sir, we're not running drugs—emphasize 'not.' One of her few pieces of evidence shows a CIA plane on the ground there at Girdiwal." He put down his notes and took off his glasses. "That's a lie."

President Thomson lifted a thick eyebrow. "A lie?"

"That specific plane actually did belong to the agency at one time, and was utilized as a drug ferry now and then, under our predecessors in another day. We wrote it off after a crash and sent it to the junkyard, or so we thought. Someone bought and rehabilitated it and sold it back into service. That aircraft is now the property of a Russian Mafia outfit. Girdiwal seems to be a high-traffic zone for moving heroin. We have indeed used it ourselves to get supplies to our allies fighting the Taliban in that region."

"So this congresswoman is fanning the fires of an already bad situation with false information." The president leaned forward, elbows on the table. He drummed his fingertips on the wood.

"The bipartisan leaders of the House are already planning a come-to-Jesus meeting with her later tonight, sir. The last thing they want is a highly publicized hearing based on bad information. She's being used. By whom we don't know, but our friends in the FBI are going to find out."

"Most likely it's going to lead right back to Girdiwal." General Middleton's voice was more of a growl.

"What assets do we have in the area, General?"

"Everything. It's Afghanistan, sir. We've been there for quite a while."

Thompson put a palm on the briefing sheet and slid it aside. "Okay. Girdiwal is the source of the problem, somehow, and our missing operatives are there. Can we get that drone gunship over to the airstrip and work it over?"

"Yes, sir." Middleton looked around the room. "That won't do much but put some holes in the ground."

"To be followed by a full air strike, ladies and gentlemen. And *that* is to be followed by an airborne assault to subdue and secure it until our people can sort all of this out. You folks take care of the tactical details, but as of right now I want Girdiwal closed for business. Get it rolling. Now, about the operators. Help is on the way for them?"

Director Burns braced himself. "We've dispatched another two-man sniper team to bring them out, Mr. President. It was to be low-profile."

"Not anymore. Two men isn't an option. Get them all the support they need. More than they might need, including additional boots on the ground."

Middleton raised his hand to his chin, rubbed it, and spoke. "Sir, I have to bring this up. We have to consider the possibility that this might be a trick just to sucker us in, a few men at a time, then start a major battle in mountainous terrain, ambush terrain."

"I understand that, General. I truly do. Given the circumstances, I see no other choice. If they choose to fight, the United States will wipe them out. I want our teams safely out of there, I want Girdiwal secured, and I want the head of a certain congresswoman. Are we clear?"

Silence filled the room. "Good. I'm having a private dinner with my wife tonight, and I do not want to be disturbed. Thank you all."

There were murmurs around the Situation Room as they all stood, and General Middleton followed President Thompson out. "One last thing, sir," he said privately when they'd passed the threshold.

The president didn't break stride. "What is it already, Brad?"

"Your son is one of the CIA operatives on the way in to Girdiwal right now."

President Thompson fought the jolt to his thought process. What had been a purely logical decision was now a personal dilemma. Could he— would he—even tell his wife? It was always different when a politician had to send his own family members into harm's way.

"Thank you, General. Keep me posted, will you? The orders stand. Ingmar knows what he's doing."

GIRDIWAL, AFGHANISTAN

THE LIONS OF THE Caliphate, two teenagers in a small, battered pickup truck, raced out of the village and down the road toward the burning building. Mohammed was driving and yipping like a puppy, while Hamid was standing in the bed, behind the mounted .50-caliber machinegun. For the pleasure of feeling the power, Hamid loosed a long burst of fire into the heavens and several gold tracers flew upward toward the stars. The roar made the light truck tremble, but Mohammed kept up the speed. The boys were warriors in their own minds, although the families wouldn't let them join the Taliban, or ISIS, or anyone else, because they were needed in the poppy fields. The Prince, however, gave them weapons and created the Lions of the Caliphate so they could perhaps see some action after their chores were done.

When they pulled to a stop, they saw that the place was an inferno. Both jumped from the truck with their AK-47s in hand and advanced side by side toward what had once been the gate, trying to see into the flames. That destroyed their night vision. They stepped over the roadside ditch and moved on, heat strong on their faces.

"Let's walk all the way around," suggested Hamid. Kyle Swanson rose from the ditch behind them and swatted Hamid hard in the kidneys with the butt of the AK-47, then spun and kicked Mohammed's feet out from under him. He knocked the guns away, and cracked the rising Mohammed on the nose, sending him back into the gravelly dirt. Swanson duct-taped the boy's wrists and ankles and across his mouth and eyes, then dragged him over to the ditch and dumped him in.

Young Hamid was still spasming in pain as Kyle stripped him of his long white tunic and baggy pants and took the wool *pakol* cap. He would be dressed like the locals now, plus he had the truck. He trussed up Hamid and tossed him beside the other boy.

Gibson had sent a couple of kids to keep him busy, but hadn't come himself. There was no time to waste thinking about that, though, so Swanson started changing clothes.

He didn't hear the flutter of the silk parachute as a large figure suddenly appeared right behind him, landing erect, and said, "Hey, Kyle. Got any beer?" Ingmar Thompson was peeling out of his straps, grinning like an idiot.

"No, I don't have any goddamn beer."

"Want some?" A second parachutist plopped down ten feet away. Bruce Brandt was busy collapsing his chute. "Ingmar, shouldn't we point a damned gun at him or something?"

"Why? We're on the same side—as of a few minutes ago, I think. Besides, it's Kyle."

"Well, there is that," Brandt conceded as he unhooked his rifle. "Where are Gibson and Marks? We've come to bring you all out of this shithole."

Swanson was overjoyed to see his old friends and fellow snipers but kept in the moment. "Marks is dead. Gibson is over in the village. I'll explain it all, guys, but let's get out of here first. Into the truck. Ingmar, you take the .50 cal in back."

"Ah, that's what it was." Thompson laughed. "Whoever was on that gun almost got us coming down. Tough to hide up there when you're hanging from a piece of cloth. Tracers went right between us." He climbed into the bed, checked the belt of ammo, declared the gun filthy but usable.

"Where we going?" asked Brandt, sliding into the passenger seat and adjusting his gear. "You need anything right now? Medical, water, whatever? I gotta tell you, this whole thing is a major pain."

"No, I'm good. I want to drive down the valley about ten miles, away from the village, toward the Mehtar Gap, as if we're trying to get a road to Kabul. Hide the vehicle and double-back to get into the high country."

"Misdirection, got it. But listen up, pal, because things have changed mightily since you and Gibson came in. Ingmar and I were tasked early on, so we're the first in, but now it seems that the whole damned cavalry is on the way to take that village and knock out an airstrip. Lots of political stuff going on."

Swanson was making decent speed on the twisting old road but slowed when he saw movement ahead, dark shadows against light shadow. He slammed the brakes as he yelled, "Ambush!" Automatic weapons fire erupted from a roadside barricade. Thompson immediately returned fire with the .50 cal as Brandt and Swanson jumped from the cab and joined the fight. With Thompson providing cover, Swanson ran about fifteen feet and dropped to the ground to provide cover for Brandt, who leapfrogged past him. It sounded as if a pair of automatics were hidden in the rocks, but the ambush was already collapsing under the heavy return fire. Brandt sprinted a final leg and tossed a grenade, and the firing sputtered to a halt.

Swanson ran up and gave each enemy fighter a double tap just to be sure. He used Brandt's flashlight to examine them. Two more kids. "That damned Gibson," he said to his teammates. "He knows us. Thinks like us, so he counted on me coming down here and planted these two guys to block me. He probably has a few more stashed away up higher."

Brandt took the light back and stuffed it away. "He wouldn't have been expecting Ingmar and me."

"He expected a rescue party of some sort. He told me that. So stay chill, boys. These are amateurs, but Gibson is the real deal, and he'll be coming out to play soon."

Thompson said, "Then he'd better get his ass in gear."

KAISERSLAUTEN, GERMANY

"OKAY, PEOPLE, LISTEN UP," Marguerite del Coda barked into her headset. "This is real-time action, and lives depend on it, so keep your mind in the game."

She was at the rear of the drone central control room, standing on a pedestal that helped her survey her kingdom. "You ready here, Mr. Winters?"

"Yes, ma'am. Two birds in the air." Ryan Winters was hunched at a keyboard.

"Major Fox, are you ready?" Jill Fox of the Forty-second Attack Squadron was overseeing the mission out of Creech Air Force Base, not far from Las Vegas, Nevada. She had a pilot and a sensor operator running each of the drones. Her targets were in Afghanistan. Her family home was an hour's drive away from the base. "We're ready," she said.

"Very well, Major. Roll on that airstrip. Dump your full ordnance load on targets of opportunity, then peel out of there to make room for new traffic."

"Roger that." Fox nodded to the pilot of the MQ-9 Reaper, and the huge drone broke from circling over Girdiwal into an attack run. The sensor operator calmly worked the data controls, and the Reaper homed in on a dusty area in the surrounding hills, darkened by night but visible enough on the multiple computer-console screens. There was stuff down there, although visibility was poor and so late at night there was little movement

"Do two runs, guys. Put the Hellfires on that boxy building with a flagpole on the first pass. It must be the control tower. Then come around and walk the bombs down the flat area that has to be the runway."

As everyone watched, the cameras tilted and reacquired, the exterior narrowed in its computer-game reality view, and the picture jerked as the Hellfire missiles tore away on streams of fire in the night. The drone whizzed by at a speed slow enough for everyone to see the rockets destroy the building in a sudden flash that banished the night. Nobody spoke. The pilot took it in a wide curve and brought it back. The sensor operator adjusted and dropped four Enhanced Paveway II smart bombs, each weighing five hundred pounds, and the Pamir Mountains trembled with the shock of the quadruple explosions.

"Bring her home, boys. Good job. Ms. del Coda, the Reaper is exiting. Our MQ-1 will be on station in a few minutes." The new arrival was an intelligence-reconnaissance bird with enhanced camera capabilities that could see in the dark and read the date on a dime from ten miles up.

"Very well, Major Fox. We'll link up again, then." She went to the internal circuit and asked her chief analyst, "What do you think, Ryan?"

"Probably woke everybody up. Damage will be insignificant, because the target was insignificant."

"And our boys?"

"Brandt, Thompson, and Swanson are all grouped together, moving slowly to the north. We'll be able to see and talk to them when the MQ-1 arrives. I'm taking a bathroom break."

Del Coda chewed on a fingernail.

GIRDIWAL, AFGHANISTAN

THE ROCKET AND THE bombs woke Luke Gibson and he stretched out before looking at his clock. Less than an hour since the Lion had knocked on his door. He hadn't heard any gunshots, but the series of hard explosions left no doubt that things were getting serious.

Since he had been the one to give up the airfield as an international smuggling site, it was logical for it to be attacked in any attempt the CIA made to extract him and Swanson. He got up and went to the bathroom to wash his face, then sat on the side of the bed, thinking, as he had breakfast—an apple, some raisins, thick slices of paneer cheese, some bread going stale, and tea. That done, he pulled on his clothes, laced his boots tight, checked his weapons, and called for another Lion to bring a truck around front.

As he left the inn, the air carried the scent of smoke, and orange fingers of fire reached up beyond the ridge to the north. It had all happened too fast for the attack to be anything other than the Reaper guard drone Marguerite del Coda had put overhead. "Let's get out to the airport," he told his driver, and they sped away.

The question, now, was what had happened to Kyle Swanson? He asked the driver if he had heard anything from his friends who had gone out earlier to the burning building. The answer was an indifferent shrug of the shoulders. He had planned to start his hunt at dawn, but that was no longer an option. Swanson had cost him a couple of hours of good sleep by escaping from the house so soon, and was already on the run. But Swanson had no contact with the agency, so the Reaper drone strike was likely a onetime attack to warn the locals that Uncle Sam was watching.

Gibson wanted to make a quick check of the airport, and then make a round of the ambush sites before settling down to the business of the day. Swanson is toast, he thought.

WASHINGTON, D.C

WHITE HOUSE PRESS SECRETARY Sam Rausch had won the battle with his CIA counterpart, and, for a change, everyone agreed that the press might be of some help in the situation. Now all he had to do was find a qualified journalist in a hurry, someone who knew how to jump out of a plane.

His argument had been simple: the TV talking heads were being brutal with the tip that a congressional hearing was brewing because of CIA drug shenanigans. The 24/7 news boulder was rolling downhill, gathering steam, and the CIA's official denials were being portrayed as a cover-up. Rausch believed something must be done to stem the tide of bad news.

"So let's flip it," he said. "We embed one good media type to go in with the first troops and even help with his communications. No censorship. He can go where he wants, ask what he wants. We have nothing to hide. Our talking points will say that we were all shocked by the unfounded allegations, which endangered ongoing operations and troop movements. Therefore, we moved on Girdiwal in force to close the drug-shipment point and rescue our undercover operatives. We do not believe Congresswoman Keenan's allegations, but the House of Representatives can proceed any way it wishes on the matter, with our full cooperation."

He already had a reporter in mind. It wasn't unusual for a military man to go into the media after his service, bringing his unique knowledge to the dicey job of being a war correspondent. One who had done so was a decorated Delta Force warrior who had gotten banged up by an IED and retired more than two year agos. Since then, John "Tilt" Foster had returned to the war and filed remarkable coverage, first as a freelancer and then as a writer of thoughtful magazine articles, with occasional appearances on TV. Yesterday he was on an evening news segment about the drawdown of American forces at Bagram Air Base in Afghanistan.

Rausch had his secretary call the network's news editor and describe the offer: If you want to be inside on tomorrow's biggest story, get Tilt Foster out to Bagram right now. An escort will meet him at the gate. He'll be the pool reporter on a sensitive and important mission. No, I won't tell you what it is. Call me in fifteen minutes or I go to my second choice. The call came back in ten. The job was on. Foster was already at Bagram.

Tilt was a lean fellow, almost stringy, who stood five feet ten and weighed about 175 pounds; he kept his brown hair short. A square jaw and an easy smile and a disdain for self-promotion had helped his transition to becoming a writer and reporter, and his Delta links kept him in touch with the military grapevine. He had that strut, that bored been-there attitude, and a reserved personality, but he was nobody's pushover.

"Where are we going?" he asked the lieutenant from the public-affairs office who showed up in a Humvee to collect him.

"Hell if I know, Tilt. I'm just taking you out to the flight line." The young officer liked the calm man. While other media types could be pests, Tilt was a laid-back dude, and his stuff was always good. When Foster wrote a piece, it left marks.

Foster was ferried across the base to a giant C-17 cargo plane, where long lines of helmeted men in parachute gear were bumping their way inside. A captain greeted him when he unfolded from the vehicle. "Mr. Foster, I'm Jim Sanchez, Company B, Third Ranger Battalion. Glad you could join us. Heard a lot about you."

"Rangers, huh? Dropping in somewhere, are we?"

"Yep," said Sanchez. "You remember how?"

"Sure. I cry like a baby until a jumpmaster throws me out?"

"That's about it," the captain replied. "These guys will get you suited up. I'll brief you once we're airborne. Still sure you want to go?"

"Always a privilege to be asked to jump with the Rangers. Let's do it." Two enlisted men approached, and Foster changed clothes on the runway, exchanging his jeans and T-shirt for a full-camo combat rig. He carried a camera, a notepad, and pens instead of a gun.

THE THREE SNIPERS ALL faced northeast, listening to the roar and rattle of the attack at the airfield. "I like that sound," Thompson said. Bruce Brandt agreed. "Has a certain ring to it," he conceded. They could see the glow of fire dancing in the distance. Swanson was on one knee, reloading and wondering what to do next. "Ingmar, you said we have a Blackhawk inbound to pick us up?"

Thompson forced his eyes from the attack zone and back into the darkness, looming above Swanson like a big bear. "Yep. At least one of those stealth jobs—probably a backup, too. A couple of snakes will escort them."

"Can you communicate with them?"

"Yep. It's kind of scratchy and all, but the closer they get the more the comms will improve."

Swanson thought about this as he tore open an energy bar, falling silent as he chewed. The situation had changed dramatically in the past hour. He was no longer tied to a chair, listening to Luke Gibson brag. The man had actually left the house believing that he was the best shooter the world had ever seen, and had devised an elaborate scheme to bring down the CIA to prove his point. He also wanted to kill Swanson in some kind of Wild West shoot-out at a thousand meters or so, hunting and stalking. Gibson was nuts. However, at the time, he thought he held all the cards: more than enough firepower, extra men, and his enemy tied up in a little house in the middle of nowhere. Even if Swanson managed to escape, there was nowhere for him to go, nothing to stop Gibson from tracking him down and killing him like a helpless gazelle. Well, that had all changed. Swanson now had the winning hand, but Gibson didn't know it yet. Although Swanson hadn't acknowledged it even to himself, Gibson's crowing about being the best had gotten under his skin, and a small candle of revenge had started burning in his stomach. "And a lot of other stuff is on the way, too, right?" Swanson dragged himself out of his thoughts.

"Like I told you before, Kyle, it's going to be a full package."

Blackhawks and AH-1Z attack helicopters were a potent and mobile asset, particularly following the noisy drone hit. "How about calling and getting them to hang back for a while. We're not in danger now, and if a bigger strike is coming that will give us even more cover."

"I can't do that, Kyle. Bruce and I were sent in to extract you, so you're going to get your ass on that Blackhawk."

Brandt cut in. "Ignore him, Kyle. He just wants to go home and get a cold beer. What's on your mind?"

"The orders, as you explained, were to bring back me and Gibson and Nicky Marks. Well, Marks is dead, but Gibson is still out there. He's the mastermind behind this mess, and calls himself the Prince out here. Let's go get him, then leave."

Brandt looked around, then stared down at Kyle, waving his hand at the vast, dark expanse. "We don't know where he is. There's a whole galaxy out there."

"I got an idea," Kyle said.

"So instead of arresting your skinny butt for treason we disobey orders and work with you?" Thompson scanned the road back toward the ambush site.

"You're not a SEAL anymore, dumbshit. We specialists are supposed to wing a lot of this to meet changing circumstances. Otherwise some butter-bar lieutenant will be having you fetch his laundry." Swanson smiled, knowing that Thompson never liked taking a hint, much less a direct order.

"What's your idea?"

"It's a good idea," Swanson said, and told them.

Bruce Brandt said, "That's a good idea. I'll see if our truck still runs."

Thompson got on the radio and in less than two minutes the quartet of inbound choppers settled into holding orbits, making gentle, lazy circles to the left some twenty miles out. While he stood guard, Swanson and Brandt dug the jack-and-tire changing kit out from behind the seats, lowered the spare tire, and put it all in the bed, then slammed the tailgate. Kyle said the tire should remain flat for the time being.

THE TOYOTA PICKUP HAD taken quite a bruising. The windows had been shot out and the body and bed were punctured by scatterings of bullet holes. Headlights were gone, paint ruined, and the right rear tire was flat. None of that was fatal for the little warhorse, though, and the engine turned over on the first try. Brandt drove it gently through a circle and pronounced it ready. The two other snipers piled into the back, and Thompson got the .50-caliber machinegun, still warm from the firefight, back in operation and fed in a fresh belt of ammunition. Swanson rested his elbows atop the cab, with his rifle pointed ahead. "Go," he called down to the driver, and the truck limped away, retracing the way it had originally come.

The fire at the house had settled down quite a bit while they were gone, and although it was outmatched by the carnage erupting at the airstrip, it was easy to find, glowing like a burned stack of hay. Thompson swung the mounted machinegun in various directions, but there was no opposition as Swanson jumped from the back and Brandt cut the sputtering engine and got out. They walked toward the smoldering ruin and found the two young Lions still bound and tied, right where they'd been left in the roadside ditch. Swanson put down his weapon and drew his knife.

Brandt walked back to the truck, cursing the vehicle. He opened the hood and cursed at what he saw. He kicked the bumper, rammed a large shard of glass from the passenger door window, then pulled his pistol, took aim, and shot the rear tire twice. He walked to the front and put two more shots in the engine, still cursing the vehicle as if it were responsible for all the evils in the world. Thompson remained silent.

Bruce went back to the ditch. "That useless sonofabitch is dead, Kyle," he said in Arabic. To the captives, he added, "Next time get a Dodge Ram. Should I kill these dudes?"

"Nah. They're just kids." He sliced through the bonds. "Get out of here, you little assholes, before my partners light you up. Go on home to Mommy." Swanson slid the knife back into the scabbard and, ignoring the two boys, called to Thompson: "Come on down, big guy. We're humping out of here." Brandt had GPS with a bright little screen, and the commandos gathered around it, arguing among themselves about which way to go.

Hamid and Mohammed muttered prayers of thanks to Allah as they skittered away from the soldiers. Hamid was almost naked, so his buddy lent him a heavy vest. He thought about getting into the truck, but the Americans were abandoning it because it was useless. The crazy one had pumped two bullets into the engine, which had already sounded wheezy when it came up, and the numerous bullet holes bespoke other internal damage. It could be reclaimed come morning, but for the moment it was best to escape before the crazy one changed his mind. They ran. Looking back, Mohammed saw only that the Americans had disappeared.

"They're gone," said Brandt, who was watching the boys through high night-vision goggles. He began jogging quietly down the road to keep them in sight, his automatic weapon pointing the way.

Thompson jumped out of the ditch and hustled to the truck, flinging out the spare tire and the changing tools. Swanson stomped on the pry bar to loosen the nuts while Thompson got the jack in place and started cranking it up. Swanson pocketed the nuts so they wouldn't get lost. It was one of those take-your-time moments, because a mistake in such a routine chore could amplify a simple error into a gigantic problem, and that could kill time and them as well. It wasn't the first time either of them had to change a flat in hostile territory, and they did it as smoothly and swiftly as a dirt-track pit team.

Swanson rolled the flat into the ditch, closed the hood, took the wheel, and got the truck running again. Brandt's two shots into the engine compartment had been aimed to miss everything and to convince the frightened Lions that the motor was dead. And the shots into the already flat rear tire reinforced that impression. Thompson resumed his position behind the gun, slapped the top of the cab, and Swanson eased forward, slowly and quietly, but steadily gaining a little speed. It had taken no more than five minutes to change the tire, which meant that the boys would have had to be world-class runners to run a mile in that time. More likely, they had tired and were walking fast, slowing down all the time, feeling that safety was straight ahead in the first outlying lights of Girdiwal.

Brandt had been expecting the truck and was waiting a half mile down the road. He waved them down and climbed in. "Game on, guys. They're straight ahead, no more than five hundred yards. Slow and quiet."

THE AIRFIELD

GIBSON FOUND WHAT HE had expected: a minimal amount of actual damage to the small airfield but a lot of smoke and fire and borderline chaos. Rockets and bombs can do that to a place. It confirmed his suspicion that the attack was only a dump of munitions from the drone, which had then fled. The sky was empty.

He toured the runway and found that it still serviceable, as long as there were markers identifying the few craters. There were no craters in the middle, because there was no middle line on a landing area made up of a square mile of dirt. Lithe small planes could approach from almost any direction. The control shed was ruined; again, no surprise, as it was the largest building there. One small Cessna was flipped over and wingless. A pen of donkeys had been savaged, and the smell of their seared flesh befouled the air. Over to one side of the airstrip, a jumbo pile of heroin and opium remained unharmed. On the other side, a fuel depot that was under camo shelter had also escaped harm. Gibson counted three other planes dispersed far from one another, all looking ready to fly. Bombing blind at night had negated much of the effect, although the shock and awe factor had been superb.

Men were already on the field putting out the fires, and Gibson figured the pilots were on their way to get the planes out of the danger zone. In other words, it was under control and, without further disruption, should be back in operation soon and they could clear out the product. He wasn't needed at the field, so he swung to a side road that led uphill for more than a mile to a cavern set back from a broad, flat apron. One of the Lions stepped from the gloom with his AK-47 and the truck flashed its lights.

Gibson identified himself and walked to the cavern. Barrels of aviation fuel were stacked to one side of the entrance. It was cooler inside, and dim light cast weak shadows. "Is he here?" he asked the boy.

"Yes." The youngster was jittery from the fury of the attack, and his finger lingered near the trigger of his gun.

Gibson told him to stay calm, that everything was fine. The Americans had just sent in a drone, that was all, and he had come up to make sure nothing had been damaged. The Prince's calm and reasonable tone cast a balm over the boy. Gibson patted him on the shoulder.

"Tell the pilot to get ready, but to keep the bird in the cave until I come back," Gibson said. He looked over at the vintage UH-1E helicopter that his dad had stolen back and stashed here after the Vietnam era. It wore the olive-drab paint job of the U.S. Army, complete with black numerals, and it was kept in flying condition with constant maintenance and a full-time throttle jockey on hand. The big rotor tilted down, idle. "This is the way out, Luke, if there is ever a true need for that sort of thing," his father had explained. "Always plan at least one escape route when you move into a place."

Wise counsel from the old man. Gibson stroked the smooth skin of the old Huey helicopter and walked back to his truck. It was time to go hunting.

"FAST MOVERS NINETY SECONDS out," Brandt called out from his position in the bed of the truck, hands pressed to his helmet to better hear the radio transmissions from an EA-6B Prowler electronic surveillance plane high up and far away, but assigned to control the battlefield traffic. "Pair of jarheads."

Swanson, on the machine gun, gave a thumbs-up. The truck was at the edge of the town, and his bet was that the boys were headed straight for Luke Gibson's overnight lodging to report what had happened. Still wearing Hamid's clothing to better blend in with the locals, he bounced out of the pickup to follow on foot in case they dodged down some alleyway.

Thompson let his speed fall off even more and followed. Bruce moved up to the big gun. They both still wore the black jumpsuits, and in the poor light could easily be mistaken for Taliban troops, but it was best for them to stay out of sight before someone became too curious. Swanson was off the vehicle, trotting ahead, and saw the boys moving toward a multistory building with bright lights aglow on the lower floor, where a few people had gathered to discuss what all the explosions had been about. A hotel.

The camera drone had arrived on station and fed an overhead view of the scene live and in color all the way back to Germany, and also to Washington. The signal was clear, but the visibility sucked.

A pair of F/A-18 Hornets swirled into the opening at the lowland front of the Wakham Corridor, flying only five hundred feet off the deck and guided by the Prowler upstairs and the all-weather-terrain systems aboard each jet. The land rose higher on each side, but marine aviators train to fly low just for missions like this, in support of their guys on the ground. The lead pilot noticed a pair of headlights on the road as he rushed through the corridor, but ignored the vehicle. The planes were loaded for bear, having been off tending to business elsewhere in Afghanistan before they were recharted to complete the work on the airfield. There was no incoming anti-aircraft fire, no golden braids of tracers carving the obsidian darkness, and, as always, no enemy aircraft, so they lowered their altitude even more and received permission to go weapons-free. They would be in and out twice before any joker down there woke up and found a Stinger missile to shoot at them. The weapons-systems operator activated the bombs, missiles, and guns and looked for specific targets. In a few more seconds, it was going to be party time around Girdiwal.

LUKE GIBSON SAW THE wingtip lights suddenly appear out in front of the truck, coming fast from nowhere, then two jets thundered overhead. He couldn't really see them, but the force of their exhausts shook the little Toyota like a puppy with a chew toy. He ordered the driver to park and turn off the lights, and when the Toyota halted he stepped out and looked back to watch the light show. No drones this time. Those were big boys. Well, that ain't fair, he thought.

GIRDIWAL, AFGHANISTAN

KYLE SWANSON BROKE INTO a gallop when the two boys scuttled into the hotel, brushing past a knot of people gathered outside in the street, whose attention had been drawn to the new attack on the airfield. Panic had gripped them, because the old warlord Mahfouz al-Rashidi and all his sons were dead, and his replacement hadn't yet asserted control. They were without leadership among their own people, but they knew that the Prince was still around. Surely this esteemed man would stop the assault. The poppy fields were burning from rocket strikes. The airfield was being pulverized.

The young Lions swung into a second-floor hallway as Swanson bounded up the stairs at their heels and heard them pounding on a door, calling out, "My prince! My prince!" Just as a five-hundred-pounder exploded on the approach road between the village and the air terminals, Swanson knocked them aside and kicked in the door. The boys were in shock. It was the same man who had captured them earlier and then released them. They rolled onto their bellies, then got up and headed back down the stairs.

The cheap lock tore from the frame under the force from Swanson's boot, and the door flew open and banged against the wall as he charged in with his AK-47 extended, sweeping the two small rooms, left to right, eyes following the barrel. A little cheap furniture and an empty bed, so he looked for possible hiding place as hell broke loose in the Wakham Corridor. Gibson had been there but was now gone.

Keeping his finger on the trigger, Swanson pointed the Kalashnikov down along his side and leaned wearily against a wall. His head pounded, his neck ached, arrows of pain crept through his back. It was delicious to rest for a moment, but there was no time for that, so he forced himself to retreat. The boys might come upon a little bravery and raise the alarm if he stayed, and, with Gibson once again on the move, there was no point in hanging around. He made his way easily through the frightened crowd, didn't see the kids, and walked back to the waiting truck. "Let's get out of here," he told Thompson, and the big commando put the vehicle in gear, made a U-turn, and took the road back toward the old, destroyed house. They could call for the extract helicopter from there.

THINGS WERE SLIDING SIDEWAYS and Gibson's choices were narrowing. Where was Swanson? Were the strikes at the airfield a limited response, or was Washington going to throw more stuff into this nothing place? The people back in town would be looking for him, but he had no answers for them. Every minute that passed brought him that much closer to dawn, which would cost him the cover of darkness. It was time to get out of Dodge.

The small truck careered down the road away from the safe house, and he told the driver to get back on the side track to the lair of his Huey helicopter. He would just have to give Swanson a pass on this one; live to fight another day. The game wasn't over. It had just gotten more unpredictable and interesting. Gibson didn't spend a lot of time dwelling on what had gone wrong, or how. Safety first, and gather the pieces later.

Another truck was on the road, coming from town. Gibson used a night-vision monocular to get a better look, and the image changed from a dark shadow to a mounted machinegun with a man on it. Had to be Taliban, running around with no plan, looking to shoot down a chopper or just unleash ribbons of bright tracers toward the sounds of the passing planes, which were long gone. He didn't need the Taliban tonight, and didn't want them to know his destination, so he told his own driver to keep moving.

When the vehicles were side by side, heading in opposite directions, Luke Gibson locked eyes with Kyle Swanson in the opposite truck, and they were both momentarily stunned. Gibson pounded his driver on the shoulder and yelled, "GO! GO! GO!" The Afghan driver stomped the accelerator.

"It's him!" roared Swanson, bracing against the dash as he turned in his seat. "Gibson is in that truck!"

Thompson slammed the brakes hard and twisted the steering wheel sharply to the left, sending the vehicle into a hard skid. In back, Brandt hadn't expected the sharp change of direction and was almost thrown overboard by the centrifugal force, saved only by his handhold on the .50-cal. Swanson was jammed against the door, and the truck stopped abruptly when the drift was done. The engine stalled and died.

Gibson stared back at the little truck Swanson was in, bewildered to discover that the man was not only still alive but apparently also had help. Whether they were Delta, SEALs, or CIA did not matter. Their very presence decided the issue. His original plan of hunting down Kyle Swanson, all by himself in a war zone, was in tatters.

They were approaching the intersection at which the diagonal road from the chopper's cave intersected with the main road. "Slow down, my friend," Gibson said with an easy grin to buoy the man's confidence. "Do not use the brakes, just slow down enough for me to jump out. I will go up the road on foot, while you go back into Girdiwal as fast as you can to bring back help."

"Yes, my prince," the driver replied, and removed his sandaled foot from the accelerator to let the truck coast. Gibson waited a few seconds, picked a landing spot, and rolled out, his arms cradling his long gun. The grit scraped him like sandpaper as he bounced into the scree before coming to a stop on his back, chewing dirt and rocks. When he looked up, the truck was just a tiny shape, although he could hear the engine straining with effort.

Turning around, he could hear the second truck cough back to life.

Swanson was coming, and would be at this spot in less than thirty seconds. Gibson got to his feet, wiped his face, and trotted up the diagonal road, hugging the side and crouching in the inky dark when the Toyota went tearing past. All three men in it were looking straight ahead for their target.

"OPEN FIRE IF HE'S in range," Swanson yelled up to Brandt, who was hunched behind the powerful automatic mounted in the truck bed.

"I don't see him! I don't see him!" Brandt called back. There was a faint dust cloud in the distance, but the target truck was on the other side, invisible.

They drove onward, but it was too late. "Stop," Swanson said about a minute later. "He'll make it to the town before we can overtake him, and we can't go back in there again."

Ingmar slowed and pulled to the side. Sweating heavily, he crossed his hands on the steering wheel and leaned forward to take a few deep breaths. His face remained impassive, but his forearms were burning: the strain of driving, staying on the road and not ending up in a tangled heap. "So now what?"

"Let's call in the birds and get the hell out of here," suggested Brandt, who had hopped down out of the bed and was leaning in the window.

Swanson slid out of the seat and walked around, rubbing the back of his neck. "I don't want to give up on him."

"As usual, we don't know where he is," Brandt retorted, his voice hardening. "We barely even know where *we* are! Let me call the Blackhawks, Kyle. Don't make this a personal thing with this asshole. Stay professional. Luke Gibson is just another fugitive now, and every cop on the globe is going to be looking for him. He'll turn up sooner or later."

"Bruce is right," said Thompson, still breathing hard. "Luke can't stay here in Girdiwal, because the Afghan Army will be searching it within a few hours. There are mountains all around, and we own the skies. Road-blocks will be strung out on every goat path. Cops everywhere will be looking for him, and the agency won't rest until he's bagged. Let's go home, pal."

Swanson understood the logic. Everything they said was true. But giving up the hunt when he had the momentum grated on him; he wanted not only to be in on the Gibson kill but to be the man who nailed him. He tossed off the itchy *pakol* cap and ran his fingers along his scalp. "Yeah, you're right. He made me look bad, and I hate that."

"Chill, bro," said Brandt. "He made the entire intelligence community of the United States look bad. We'll get him next time. Right now, I want to get you out of harm's way for a thorough debriefing back at Langley. That's the best chance of beating Luke. Now that we know he's an outlaw, we'll sic all the dogs on him."

With a deep sigh, Swanson gave in and turned toward the flaring sky above the airport. The bombing and strafing had stopped, leaving behind a field of embers. "Okay, let's get on up to the airport and have the extract birds meet us there. I've got an idea."

"Of course you do," Brandt chided.

GIBSON WAS ALMOST THERE, grinding along the uphill path with his heart beating fast and his breath hot and ragged, when he heard the sound. He stopped to listen more closely and catch his breath, thinking at first that it might be Swanson and his guys coming up behind him. But it wasn't a four-cylinder Toyota engine; it was a multiengine heavy turboprop approaching from the east.

The plane wasn't at all stealthy, because a brute that large didn't have to be quiet. There were probably escorts in the sky above and in front of it, looking down for possible threats, and the crew was highly trained in flying at night and in mountainous terrain. They were unafraid, and snapped on the blindingly bright landing lights that made Gibson feel that the lowering aircraft was heading straight for his nose. It passed overhead at about six hundred feet, and Gibson saw shapes falling from it in a long trail that blossomed into strings of paratroops dangling beneath canopies.

Tilt Foster's heart was pounding a tattoo in his chest, and his belly clinched when he stepped through the door and into the Afghan night to be greeted first by the shock of wind blowing sideways and again by the jolt when the rip cord pulled out the chute. He grabbed the toggles and looked around, seeing no one else, although he was surrounded by Rangers. It was impossible to relax when he knew the ground was down there somewhere, rushing up to crunch him like a peanut.

Luke Gibson sprinted with what little energy he had left in the tank. Then he saw the opening in the hillside, where his pilot, Pavel Gagarin, was already running the checklist and his assistant, Ivan Nagurski, was aboard the little tractor that had pulled the Huey out to the flat pad. The Russians knew their jobs well, and had gotten the old helicopter ready without being given final instruction. By the time Gibson gasped to the pad, Nagurski had disconnected external support and jumped into the co-pilot's seat to help Gagarin set the buttons and the dials. Gibson jumped in through the open door, strapped into a canvas seat, and fitted an intercom headset over his ears.

"Where should we go?" asked Gagarin. The long rotor blades slowly began to move as the engine whined in sympathy with the effort of gears to chop the air.

"Stay low and head north for a few valleys, then land at that abandoned geological survey station for a little while. Ivan, you pull that chart that will get us to the easternmost end of the Wakham Corridor. We're heading for China."

Gibson recognized that one planeload of airborne troops wasn't enough for a meaningful battle. They would have light machineguns and little mortars, good for securing a tiny place like the scoured airfield, but heavier stuff and more troops were needed to undertake any serious offensive action. That meant more troops and equipment were on the way, probably aboard helicopters and overland by trucks. The timetable for the raid had obviously been put together in a hurry, which guaranteed that things would stop running like clockwork as more people and machines became involved. A chopper might crash, a fight might actually break out, someone might misunderstand an order. The troops would hardly look up at the sound of another helicopter. And the electronic world on the surveillance plane high above was about to get very tangled, as radar blips would be flowing every which way, exiting and entering the area. That was all Gibson needed to get lost in the traffic.

THE SNIPERS SLID IN some rubble and covered themselves as the Rangers toppled from the sky and drifted down to the plateau. They didn't want to exit from cover until the soldiers had some time to get organized. Popping up out of nowhere in the landing zone of a bunch of heavily armed paratroopers was a good way to draw a lot of gunfire, even if they were expected.

The soldiers dropped their heavy harnesses, and their sergeants collected small groups and organized defensive points around the heart of the field. A team of specialists got the radios going and a command post was soon up and running, with aerials marking the spot. Medics set up an aid station nearby, and a few soldiers hobbled over, or were helped, from drop-related injuries. For a moment there was absolute quiet, and the Rangers offered silent thanks for the cold landing, then hunched over their weapons, ready for anything.

The two Cobra gunships dashed overhead with floodlights nosing into the surrounding area, and then came the extraction Blackhawk and it's twin backup, settling down at one end of the slowly expanding LZ, but inside the perimeter. Bruce Brandt raised the pilot on his own frequency, and the chopper relayed the call to the CP.

An officer and a sergeant emerged from the command center, looked around, then called out for the men near the choppers to hold their fire because three friendlies were coming in. The crew chief of the lead helicopter joined them.

Actually, the snipers were already inside the perimeter, which had surged past their hide without detecting them. Swanson, Thompson, and Brandt stood slowly, hands in the air, mysterious and shadowy figures who weren't there one moment and, the next, they were. Swanson hailed, "Friendlies coming in."

The officer stepped forward. "Captain Sanchez, Company B, Third Ranger Battalion," he said, extending a hand.

"Good to see you, sir," said Swanson. No names were given, or expected, from the operators.

"You boys been having a good time?"

"Best day of my life," Thompson answered.

"Well, much as I'd like to hear about it we've got no time for chitchat. Let's hustle you all out of here. Lot of material and troops on the way to this little spot of dirt. We'll be moving into the village at daybreak."

"You know to keep a lookout for our missing target?" Swanson asked.

"Fully briefed, sir," said Sanchez. "Luke Gibson is dead meat."

"Right, then. We're out of here." Swanson turned to the helmeted crew chief. "Lead on."

"Back to the world. Warm bed, hot chow," said Brandt, moving toward the waiting Blackhawk.

"Beer," said Thompson, and they walked away, back into secrecy.

28

THE WELL-COIFFED NETWORK ANCHORWOMAN in a blazing red dress did the intro. Twenty-four hours a day, seven days a week, the cable network churned out news and opinion, so there was always an anchorwoman, or an equally charming anchorman, to read the teleprompters mounted on the studio camera they faced. To be an anchor at any hour was considered a major achievement for a television news reader, and somebody was always in the makeup room backstage, preparing for the next hour.

"We have a major story developing in Afghanistan right now involving American soldiers," said Jennifer Holland. "A single pool reporter was allowed to accompany the troop movement. We switch now to John Foster, the embedded correspondent, who is on the ground in the town of Girdiwal." She blinked her eyes once. "John, what can you tell us?"

"Hello, Jennifer." Tilt Foster looked weary and sweaty as he did his fourth interview in an hour. "Elements of the U.S. Rangers parachuted into an airstrip in northeast Afghanistan early this morning. Let me emphasize that I am reporting with the full knowledge and permission of the Pentagon, so we are not endangering our troops. In fact, an Army communications team is my camera and sound crew.

"The attack here came as a total surprise to almost everyone, including me, because I wasn't briefed until we were airborne." Some of the pictures he had taken while flying rolled onto the screen: young men weighted down with weapons, chute packs, and other gear were seated inside the plane in two long rows, and had waved for the folks back home.

"The mission was to secure the airfield just outside the town of Girdiwal, which has become a crossroad in the international drug trade. From where I stand, I can see scorched fields of opium poppies that were a major source of the heroin and opioids that challenge all countries." Pictures came of daylight breaking over flat fields and sheer mountains, and of dim rooftops below.

Foster took a breath, counting the ticks of the clock in his head. On TV, time was money. "As most people now know because of recent developments in Washington, the CIA was accused of running drugs out of this place. The CIA has denied that charge, and I've seen no evidence here to substantiate that accusation." A pause to toss the ball back to the anchor. "Jennifer?"

The studio director told her through an earpiece to go another fifteen seconds. The video was good, and he didn't want to have to wait in line for another hour or two before getting another report from this guy half a world away.

"John, was the mission a success?"

"Let's ask one of the men in charge. This is Captain Jim Sanchez. Captain, the question is whether the mission was a success."

The handsome, equitable, calm face of Sanchez came on camera, a war paint work of camouflage oils. His hair was high and tight. "It most certainly was, Tilt. It was a multiforce, multinational operation, and the Air Force and the Army and the Marines obliterated most of the opposition before we even arrived. After a few minor skirmishes, we took absolute control with minimal casualties, just a couple of broken legs. Very little collateral damage, since the town was asleep when we hit the airport. Now the Afghan Army is rolling in to secure the village."

"Did you find any evidence of a CIA drug-running operation, Captain?" Fostert asked.

Sanchez kept his pleasant demeanor and shook his head. "Nope. Nobody here but us chickens."

Tilt didn't mention the three men he had watched get on the Black-hawk and disappear. It was obvious they were spooks. Enough of a scoop is enough, and he didn't want to burn the bridge of letting the CIA owe him a favor. Delta boys knew when to call in favors, and when to shut the hell up. "Thanks, Captain Sanchez." Camera back on Foster. "Jennifer."

"John." She maintained a serious face, and the dark eyes bored into the big lens. "We'll be right back with an exclusive story about a sixth grader in Ohio who has an amazing memory."

WASHINGTON, D.C.
MIDNIGHT

CONGRESSWOMAN KEENAN WAS SERIOUSLY considering getting drunk. Her big ex-posé of the CIA had boomeranged and smacked her right in the head. It was all over the news. The Leadership wanted to see her first thing in the morning, although she didn't want to see them. She didn't particularly want to see anyone, except maybe that Prince character who had opened this can of worms. Her staff had all left with their tails between their legs. They were probably in the pubs of Georgetown and around the Hill, spreading gossip and looking for new jobs, since her ship was going to sink at the end of her term. She took a bottle of Chardonnay from the sideboard and poured a glass so full that it almost brimmed over. She was bending over, sipping away the excess, when the ringtone of her private cell phone broke the silence: ABBA's "Dancing Queen."

She carefully picked up the glass, took a sip, and noticed that the caller ID was blocked. "Hello," she said, impatient. Victoria Keenan hated all anonymous callers, who usually only bombarded her with long strings of profanity.

"It's Mr. Prince, Congresswoman." The voice sounded faint and far away.

"How did you get this number?" She spat the question as anger rose inside her. She toed her way out of her heels and sat at her desk.

"We'll make this short." His voice seemed normal, in total control of himself. "How are you holding up?"

"Everything has fallen apart and you dare ask me that? I'm going to be skewered, thanks to your lies. You can be sure that I will cooperate fully with the authorities to prosecute you."

He laughed. "Don't be too quick to judge, Congresswoman. I know what happened at Girdiwal, because I was there. Don't believe the press reports. That's just the government covering its ass."

"You were there? How?" She placed the glass on a piece of paper so as not to leave a wet ring on the wood.

"Never mind. Your next move is to point out that the raid was nothing more than misdirection. It confirmed that Girdiwal was a drug highway, but that's all. They're dodging the question of the agency being a cult of covert corruption that has run amok."

Keenan sucked in a sharp breath. "That Kyle Swanson guy isn't a rogue, as you said. I just watched on-the-spot reporting that there was no sign of CIA involvement over there."

"That's why I called, ma'am. Don't be so sure about Swanson being in the clear. Keep the pressure on him. His partner, Luke Gibson, has also turned out to be a rotten apple."

Keenan was hoping for a rope of help, but instead she was getting more cloak-and-dagger stuff that couldn't be proved. "That's not enough. They're going to crucify me," she said with a slight moan.

The man's voice was lower, more confidential and soothing. "No, they're not, Vicky. May I call you that? When you have them all going on record as saying nothing happened, you can drop the anvil. Have them look into the outgoing traffic at Girdiwal immediately after the raid. A Blackhawk helicopter extracted a three-man CIA team—Swanson and two others. They had killed several Afghans, so deal that card when they brag about no collateral damage."

"Are you sure about that?"

"I was there, Vicky. I saw them leave. U.S. troops were already on the ground and helped them."

"Okay," she said. "That's good."

"Then play your ace. Shortly after that Blackhawk departed, another helicopter belonging to the CIA took off and headed east."

A gulp of wine. "You saw that one, too?"

"No doubt about it. Hang tough on this, Vicky. You're the hero in this drama, not them. I'll contact you again later." The call terminated.

Keenan poured another glass, and her mood was entirely different. She could go home and sleep tonight, because she had the mother of all whistle-blowers in her pocket.

KAISERSLAUTEN, GERMANY

ANOTHER TAKEOFF, ANOTHER LANDING. Kyle Swanson felt like a piece of lost luggage, being shuttled around until it arrived wherever it was supposed to be. He had gotten aboard the helo at Girdiwal and had immediately huddled with the waiting medic, Thompson, and Brandt. Then he gave out.

"I've got a bad one back here," the medic said on the Blackhawk internal intercom system. With sharp scissors and help from the other two men, Swanson was stripped to his skivvies by the time the bird was flying. Stethoscope, blood pressure, oxygenation, temperature, light in the eyes—a full airborne quickie physical. The crew chief unfolded a silvery blanket for the patient. The medic noted the conditions and had the pilot raise a doctor. The word came back to hydrate the patient, keep him warm, administer a strong sedative, and put on a stiff cervical collar to help immobilize the neck and spine.

Swanson relaxed through it all, and when the needle poked into a blue vein, the first drops put him out like a light.

The rest of the long trip was a bounding dream, things happening to him just below the surface of consciousness—being strapped down, hearing muted conversation, being placed on rolling litters, given a more thorough examination at a base aid station, then swaddled up again and locked into a bed aboard a Gulfstream executive jet belonging to the CIA. Brandt and Thompson rode with him, keeping him apart from everyone other than the original medic. The new assignment was to protect him and keep him from talking to anybody until they reached the CIA station in Germany. He made the trip in a pleasant twilight zone.

When he was allowed to surface again, Marguerite del Coda was at the foot of his bed, which itself was a haven of white cotton sheets and warm blankets with cool air-conditioning. She was watching him curiously. He flopped a hand in druggy recognition. "'Lo, Marjrit . . ."

"Hey, your own self, Kyle," she said. The voice was pleasant, but cool with a touch of worry.

"Luke?" Breathing came hard. Splitting headache. "Catch Luke?"

"No, but we'll talk about that later. He played us all for fools and we were really worried that he'd have you trapped in Afghanistan." She squeezed his big toe hard. He flinched. She smiled. "You've been unconscious since they brought you in yesterday, so they want you to have some rest and recovery. You did a great job out there, Kyle."

"Bruce and . . . Ingmar?"

"Already debriefed and gone. They told me about your idea, but I have my doubts. I'll try is all I can say. Meanwhile, you're being sent over to the Landstuhl medical center. An interrogation team flies in from the Death Star to dig around about what happened. After that . . . we just have to wait and see. Kyle, I don't know if what you want to do is possible. It could do serious harm."

"Try." His voice was hoarse in a raspy throat. Swanson balked for a moment about the briefers. They would be building a book on Luke Gibson and kicking over a lot of stones hat had never been exposed. He didn't like the exertion that would be required to answer their questions, but he would just have to endure. He closed his eyes and breathed evenly. He couldn't move his head. Opening his eyes again, it seemed as if he were looking through the face guard of a football helmet. Tried to reach, but his wrist was lashed.

"Okay." She gave another squeeze and studied the darkening bruises that covered most of his face and arms, and the tubes feeding in the meds. A bad cut on the back of his head required stitches, and the helicopter medic reported that while checking for a possible concussion he had discovered a possible skull fracture and spinal trauma. She wondered if Swanson had finally pushed himself beyond his limits. He was now headed for X-rays and CAT scans.

She stepped away and two nurses swept into his room, while two others pushed in a gurney. They read the charts and machine screens, and one punched the morphine feed. Swanson's eyelids closed and he was gone, heading down deep to where the nightmares lurked, fully anticipating another spitting match with the Boatman.

Instead, he found himself feeling comfortable on a wharf that he recognized, a pier of heavy pilings extending from a concrete walkway. Somewhere on the Massachusetts north coast. Lobster boats canopied with nets bobbed at anchor, and frilly ice floes decorated the small, restless waves. A figure stood waiting for him, but it wasn't the dreaded Boatman. It was a small blond woman in a thick white wool sweater with a rolled collar and tight jeans tucked into black leather boots. Coastie? When she turned, the smile on her face lit the sky with gold. In the dream, he walked toward her, she reached out her hand to grab his, and they fell together in an embrace that he never wanted to end.

HONG KONG

LUKE GIBSON HAD FOLLOWED the Chemin du Roy, the King's Highway—the old family footsteps—from the Chinese border with Afghanistan all the way to the best watering hole in Asia, the Hong Kong Foreign Correspondent's Club. It was an area where friendships required generational ties, and his tribe had been passing through Honkers since long before it ceased to be a British colony. They knew people.

He had made his way by helicopter, automobiles, small planes, junks, and powerboats. Once the border guards entered his cover name and code into the system, he was vouched for by intelligence officers in Beijing; the way was cleared to the family's privately owned flat on the thirteenth floor of an apartment building on Cloud View Road. The harbor below had a bronze look in the setting sun and was crowded with ocean-tough freighters, some warships, and the reliable old Star Ferries that still churned from the island over to the Kowloon side, packed with people, despite the highway bridge. The flat was almost an heirloom, and he felt the presence of his forefathers there, all the way back to the Brits, and was almost sorry he had murdered one of them. It was kept clean by an amah, who had telephoned ten minutes after he arrived offering to cook dinner. He smiled. Talk about networks. He hadn't been in town for almost a year, and the amah was already on the job. He declined.

The noise of the city roared up the heights—car motors and yells, and the eternal slapping of mah-jongg tiles. Furniture from all over the Orient had been collected here and tastefully arranged in strong, dark patterns and curves. Gibson pushed back a thick bamboo chair and used a knife to pry up a square of parquet floor: two pistols, Canadian passport, press badges, credit card and cash in various currencies. He removed the new identity, some money, left the guns, covered the square again.

After a shower in the master bedroom, he pulled a tailored gray suit from the closet. The amah kept his wardrobe fresh. A generous absentee foreign landlord was a gift for the whole family, and was pampered, no matter the nationality. After all, Hong Kong was about money.

A taxi ride down to Central and he found Detective Inspector Susannah Lai waiting at the Great Bar. The FCC had always adapted with the times, and since the Vietnam years, when it had been a playground for rowdy war correspondents, it had slewed back into the grasp of the Old China Hands, the diplomats and public-relations and businesspeople— a two-way mirror into and out of Communist China.

Lai waved him over, and he gave her a light kiss on the proffered cheek. "Long time no see, Luke. You have been a naughty boy." She was elegant in her mid-forties, with shining hair and a figure that demonstrated that she exercised daily. Dainty and dangerous, Lai was an agent of the Beijing government's intelligence service, with a detective's badge in Hong Kong.

"Great to be back, Susannah." A pair of cold gin and tonics appeared before them, and he toasted her. "We must fight malaria every day."

She signaled a waiter and they went upstairs to a quiet table in the corner, windows on two sides and the Bank of China hulking like a giant among the business buildings. Lai ordered a salad, and Gibson chose a chicken curry.

"I can give you seventy-two hours on the island, Luke." Her hands folded on the table. "You are radioactive-hot, my friend."

"Works for me. Many thanks for expediting the trip from Afghanistan."

"No problem. That's a big public-relations black eye for Washington, so we're glad to help. I can offer to move you deeper into China, even Beijing or Shanghai for a while, until they lose interest."

Gibson drained his glass and ordered another. "Thanks. The CIA may lose interest in me, but I still have unfinished business with them. So I must decline, although I appreciate your having my back."

She smiled. "My help is not free, you know."

Gibson was ready. He took a flash drive from his shirt pocket and put it beneath the folded linen napkin. "This is a proposed merger deal between two major software companies in Silicon Valley. Completion would open the way for advancement in military laser technology—specifically, airborne weaponry. You may want to wreck that partnership. I understand that not all the board members on either side are happy, because they don't want to share that Pentagon pie."

Lai drew the napkin toward her and dropped the thumb-size memory bank into her designer purse. "Good. Anything else you need from us?"

"Get me on a cargo plane full of toys, or some such, heading for Canada."

"Sure. But why Canada? What's in Canada?" she asked.

"Safety," he said. "Moose and safety."

CIA HEADQUARTERS
LANGLEY, VIRGINIA

WHAT PRICE SUCCESS? MARTY Atkins pondered that question at his desk. Back when he was a young man, he considered the world to be his oyster. By going to work for the Central Intelligence Agency, he believed that he could do anything: be stronger than a locomotive, or fly across entire continents in a single bound. He was in line to eventually become director of the entire agency. That was now probably out the window. Superman was a make-believe cartoon, and Atkins lived in the real world, which was why he'd been mentally drafting a letter of resignation. Before this was all over, somebody at the CIA was going to have to fall on his or her sword. He was the likely scapegoat.

The quick and hard military attack to secure the drug town of Girdiwal in Afghanistan had worked with precise efficiency. The world saw the results on television. The CIA proved it had nothing to hide and wasn't running a Middle East drug bazaar.

So why was that pesky congresswoman from Nebraska hanging so tough with her accusations? Perhaps the agency wasn't out of the woods of public opinion yet.

Added to that public relations problem was the loss of two of his best operatives. Luke Gibson was a total asshole of a traitor who had fooled them for years and was still on the loose. God alone knew what damage he'd done, what secrets he'd compromised, how many lives he'd cost. Atkins already had an internal investigation under way.

Kyle Swanson, the indestructible sniper, was immobile in traction, shut off from his own senses in an induced coma at the Landstuhl Regional Medical Center outside Ramstein Air Base in Germany. His condition was listed as critical, with a seriously injured neck.

"How soon can he be evacuated?" asked Willa Kent, one of the interrogation specialists on the internal investigation team. She was a quiet, unthreatening brunette who had earned her psychology degree at Purdue and developed her interviewing chops down in Guantánamo.

She and a second psychiatrist, Tom Hughes, had been invited to Atkins's office in Langley so that Marty could deliver the news personally. "He cannot be moved right now, so you guys have to go over there."

"If he's in a coma, what's the point?" asked Hughes, a thin man in his mid-thirties. Far from being a beard-pulling shrink, Hughes ran Ironman competitions and had piercing steel-gray eyes that missed little.

Which was why Atkins didn't look at him. "If not an actual interview at this point, you can provide an accurate assessment of his condition. Kyle cannot be moved for several more weeks, according to the med staff in Germany. And his parents want to put him in a first-class private facility in England, not back here. So you have to go there."

Hughes, who was also a doctor, read the brief Army medical report. "He had a brain concussion and herniated disks and still carried on with the mission? Ouch. The pain must have been excruciating."

Atkins was of the opinion that continuing the mission would probably have been impossible for a normal human being. Tom Hughes understood how a body could be forced to work beyond its limits. "The two guys who brought him out said that Swanson collapsed as soon as they got aboard the extract helicopter. Like all the wind escaped from a balloon," he said.

"Adrenaline dump," Willa Kent concluded. "He was so pumped up during the action that it overrode the pain. When it was over, he had no reason to continue blocking it, and it all slammed him at once."

She tapped the arm of the chair. "The family is still going to demand that he be moved. We'll have to talk them out of that so we can keep him in secure custody."

Atkins reminded them both that Kyle Swanson was not some terrorist and would not be treated as one. "He will remain sedated and immobile right where he is for a couple of weeks to give his body some time to heal and rest. Sir Jeff Cornwell might send in a private specialist, but I've informed him there's no real need for that. This hospital has handled casualties from the war for more than a decade. They've seen it all before and know what they're doing."

"So, a month?"

"I'm not a doctor, guys. It is what it is. Maybe getting a civilian specialist in there to take a look would be a good idea."

"Silly question, but is Swanson safe?"

"Yes. He's listed as a John Doe in the intensive-care unit of a Level III Trauma Center at an American military base. Nobody is going to bother him. Security is tight." Atkins kept his face devoid of anything but sympathy and worry.

Hughes asked, "Why doesn't this file include the latest X-rays? I could tell a lot more about his condition."

Atkins dodged. "You should have a fresh set made when you get there. Your prime assignment is to examine the overall situation and find any clues that might lead us to our traitor, Luke Gibson. Beyond that, figure out when Kyle will recover fully and how we can help."

Kent said, "Healing is one thing, but combat is another, sir. Beyond the physical damage, which appears substantial, there will be severe psychological challenges—maybe a lifetime of PTSD. I think our boy may soon be looking for another line of work."

Marty hated lying to these good people, but he had a story to tell. *What price success?*

CLARKE, VERMONT

NERO SAT STILL AS a rock, the big head cocked to one side, watching his Alpha lying almost as still on the forest's verdant floor twenty feet away. Elizabeth Ledford Castillo was in a Ghillie suit that she had spent the morning making from local vegetation, and she looked like a bush. Coastie glanced over at the German shepherd, who didn't break from the command to remain still. His nose picked up her scent, magnified it, and he knew she was okay although he could barely see her. The bush extended her hand, flat and with a downward motion, and the dog dropped to his belly.

Coastie had thrown herself into training after being read the riot act by Double-Oh. She had been behaving like a fool; she knew that now. The loss of her husband had almost sent her around the bend with grief, excused her inexcusable decisions, and left her feeling lost and vulnerable. The only thing she was really good at was shooting a weapon and killing bad guys, and it was impossible to find solace in bloodlust. It was hard to forget.

She dug her toe into the damp soil and hauled her bushy self a few inches. Her goal today was to approach the camp without being seen, but that was going to be impossible as long as Nero thought she might need his guard-dog skills, big white teeth, and muscled frame. He stuck to her like glue. She pushed another foot forward and scanned the area, seeing nobody. Coastie was invisible, but sneaking around undetected in the woods of northern Vermont wasn't exactly rocket science.

The suit was itchy. She ignored it. Part of the challenge of being a scout/sniper was being able to put up with a few inconveniences, such as mosquitoes and rain and cold. All part of the training, which seemed meaningless in their individual parts but, taken together, could cost or save a life. Today was better than yesterday, and Mexico seemed very far away. Confidence was seeping back into the sniper, and courage would follow.

"Hey, Coastie! Double-Oh wants you at the office." Lieutenant Nina Blume, whose truck had been kicked around by an IED in Afghanistan, was at the camp trying to make sense of what had happened to her on that lonely, dusty road two years earlier, and how and why she survived when the others died.

"How did you find me?" Coastie asked, irritated at being discovered. "My suit is pretty good."

"I didn't." Nina pointed to the dog. "He's never far from you. Hey, Nero," she said, squatting and rubbing the big nose.

"He's a lousy guard dog. Everybody around here can find me, and he doesn't do a damn thing to stop them. He should be ripping your throat out, Blume."

"He guards us all, girlfriend. Anyway, Get out of your leaves and branches and hustle up there. I'll let him know you're on the way."

Coastie struggled to her feet. "What's he want?"

"No idea," the lieutenant answered, limping away.

Nero remained lying obediently in the dirt, grinning because everybody was okay.

BAGRAM AIR BASE,
AFGHANISTAN

BRUCE BRANDT AND INGMAR Thompson wandered into the mess hall after a shower and a snooze. They were in a somber mood and took their trays of chow and coffee mugs to a table favored by special-ops types. Two other guys were about, though. The snipers sat. Said hello.

"Rough night?" asked a Navy SEAL.

"Might say that," replied Brandt. He started on his steak and eggs.

"Classified?" the SEAL continued.

"The mission is all over the news now, so no, it's no longer classified." Thompson put two fried eggs and hash browns between two slices of Texas toast and smothered the sandwich with Tabasco and a handful of jalapeño peppers. "That drug place up in the Wakham Corridor. Not much there now but a lot of show-and-tell for the folks back home."

The other man wiped his lips and settled with his coffee. He was a PJ, an Air Force parajumper. "So that's where all the Rangers went in such a hurry. Good on them. So how is that bad?"

"Not the mission. Swanson."

"Kyle?" the SEAL was suddenly attentive, as was the PJ. "He catch a bullet?"

"They have him up at Landstuhl. Took a hard knock to the back of his head and neck, and the docs think it may be a spinal break."

"Good Lord," said the PJ. "That's gotta hurt."

"Critical condition," said Thompson, around chewing the giant sandwich and staring at the man. "Total coma."

"Hard to imagine Kyle getting banged up like that," said the SEAL, following with a burst of cursing.

"Shit happens," Brandt said.

The PJ lifted his coffee cup. "To Kyle," he toasted, and the others joined in clinking the ceramic mugs.

The SEAL and his PJ buddy moved to the bar, fell into serious conversation, and would point back toward the table as if for confirmation. Little salesmen making the rounds friend by friend, spreading the word that the great Kyle Swanson had been wounded and was hospitalized in a full traction rig because somebody or something broke his back. A gasoline-fueled fire couldn't have spread faster than the news, which would soon spill beyond the special-ops community and out into the force in general, and then beyond.

LONDON, ENGLAND

SIR GEOFFREY CORNWELL SUMMONED his personal physician, Sir Patrick Whyte, who rushed from his private surgery to attend to his richest client. He was relieved to find that the emergency didn't involve Cornwell directly.

"Are you ill in any way, my friend? The leg is causing problems?" the doctor inquired, accepting a brandy from Lady Patricia in the sitting room of the town home.

"No, Patrick. I'm in excellent health, thank you, and I apologize for taking you away from your work. Please have your office bill me for the time." The older man was seated in a firm, ergonomically correct chair.

"And you, Patricia?" Whyte asked. He was puzzled.

"Good." She inhaled deeply from a seven-inch Lancero cigar and exhaled with slow pleasure.

"You must stop smoking those cigars, m'lady," he chided.

"Maybe when I get through with this latest box from Nicaragua. Probably not." Her smile was amused.

"So, now, why am I here?" asked the physician.

Cornwell had called Whyte because the surgeon, one of the best in the U.K., was also involved in helping servicemen and women who had been injured in the line of duty and, as such, he was covered by the required strict security demands. What he saw or heard around those patients would never be repeated.

"Patrick, we need your assistance on a very sensitive matter. I'm afraid it's a D-Notice affair, and I want to let you choose whether to undertake it. There is no problem if you do not wish to do so." The Defense Notice was technically used to keep state secrets from being reported by the media, but it had become slang for many circumstances that were bound by the nation's need for security.

Whyte waved it away. "Of course. You didn't need to ask. How can I help? One of your SAS boys need patching up, does he?"

Sir Jeff clicked a keyboard and a large screen on the wall came to brilliant colored life, then he changed it to brilliant fluorescent white and a series of X-rays slid into place.

"Our lad took a hard blow to the back of the head. The doctors in Germany say there are also some herniated disks at the top of his spine and cartilage is seeping out and pressing on the nerves in his neck. Based on these X-rays, would you agree?"

Patrick Whyte stood and moved closer to the screens, studying the pictures. He traced his forefinger around, put his hands on his hips, and laughed. "No, I most certainly would not."

Lady Pat interrupted, her face reddening. "Why, Patrick? This is a serious injury."

"And one that can be repaired with a single level anterior cervical fusion."

"Speak the King's English, for God's sake, Patrick," snapped Sir Jeff.

"Basically, I would slit the throat, go to the spine, and screw in metal plates that would strengthen the vertebrae. It's not the injury, my dear, it's that ludicrous cover story. You're going to have to bring me in all the way if you want my help. This is a hoax. It isn't even your patient."

The Cornwells exchanged looks. "Tell us," said the knight to the member of the Royal College of Surgeons.

Whyte resumed his seat and crossed his legs, becoming professorial. "You said several times that our wounded warrior was a man. That X-ray is the skull of a woman. Now, let's start at the beginning. May I have another brandy?"

CLARKE, VERMONT

COASTIE KNOCKED ON THE solid door of Dawkins's cabin, some fifty yards from the main building. She had never been to his private quarters before, because Double-Oh tried to maintain a distance between himself and the others. He called out, "Come on in, and close the door."

It was as if she were stepping into another dimension. This was no sloppy man cave but an immaculate three-room suite. No beer cans or pizza boxes, and soothing instrumental music was playing. It was dark, but her eyes adjusted quickly.

"How good are you as a salesperson?" he asked in a gruff voice that had shriveled the testicles of many a marine.

"I worked retail during the summers in high school. It wasn't much more than pushing buttons on a computer screen and asking if the customer wanted cheese on the burger." She leaned against the door, not in the least wary of Double-Oh, who was almost twice her size. Another woman might have quailed before him because he gave such an overpowering sense of being larger than life.

"Too bad. You're going to have to do the sales job of your life in about five minutes. Beer's in the fridge if you want one."

"I'm good. You keep a nice place, big guy. What's up?"

He came into the light so that she could see him better. "Kyle's got himself into some trouble and needs our help. You think you're ready?"

"Yes, I am. What kind of trouble?"

He straddled a kitchen chair and told her the story. "That's the secret, girl. Now, I've called a meeting of our people in the great room, and will announce to that our good buddy Kyle Swanson has a broken neck and is in a coma. At that point, you break down crying as if your soul had been torn out. Everyone already knows the stress and grief you've suffered because of Mickey, and now it's being compounded by the horrible fate that has befallen Kyle. You gotta sell this, Coastie. Make them believe. Can you do that?"

Beth Ledford knew she could do it. The very thought of losing Kyle or Double-Oh or any member of the old Task Force Trident was enough to bring on the tears. "Yeah. Then what? We just stay here among the maple trees? With Kyle hurting?"

"Of course not. Pack your bag. We'll leave for London immediately."

SUSANNAH LAI LIED. GIBSON would repay her for that someday, and he had murder in his heart as he leaned over the starboard railing of the Russian trawler *Dalny Atlantica*, puking into the Sea of Okhotsk. The Chinese operative in Hong Kong had promised to get him to Canada, but hadn't said how she would accomplish that.

The day after their meeting at the Foreign Correspondent's Club, Lai gave him a packet containing a new identity, including a well-used American passport that had been doctored after being stolen by a hotel bellboy. She hadn't arranged a first-class airline ticket. Luke Gibson was, for the time being, a marine biologist from the Woods Hole Oceanographic Institution on contract with the Maritime Stewardship Council. She included a book on commercial fishing that he could read during the trip to get some useful details and terminology. His new name was Daniel Cabot McCabe, which carried a hint of New England aristocracy.

An Air China flight got him far north into Russia, where he had been cleared in advance, and then a frightening series of puddle jumpers got him over to the oil boomtown of Sakhalin Island, which bustled with foreigners doing business. Late that night, Daniel Cabot McCabe boarded a 330-foot trawler. The calendar turned to May, and the snow was falling hard as the trawler shoved off. Three days later, it was still snowing as he wretched up his bowl of food.

"Daniel, you should be over this sea sickness by now," observed Pyotr

Koshemyako, the burly first mate, offering a bottle of vodka. "We expect the weather to worsen. Some ice floes are on the radar."

Gibson gripped the ice-covered rail with thermal gloves and still felt the cold. "Oh, fuck me, Pyotr. I hate this." He smelled like fish. The whole boat smelled like fish. Gibson swore that he would never eat another fish.

"Drink, anyway, before I do this thing to you," said the mate. "I don't understand it, but I will obey."

"No booze. Go ahead." Gibson turned toward his new friend, who immediately popped him the in the face with a fist. Every night, the same ritual.

The weather did worsen, and the quick beatings continued, even after he changed to a larger factory ship. When it finally broke to clearer skies and seas, the wide, welcome mouth of the Columbia River loomed off the port bow. America had never looked so good to him.

The bureaucratic folderol required to get a foreign vessel into an American port had reverted to pre-9/11 practices. There was just too much traffic for the border-protection officers to handle on a detail-oriented task. The captain of the ship prepared the manifest and the necessary personnel papers, but the customs agents had no desire to spend all day pawing through holds carrying tons of pollock.

The ship had dropped anchor to allow the inspection team aboard before docking in Astoria to unload. A tight knot of sullen sailors stood near the gangway, as if to block the aft deck.

Suddenly, a man burst out of a forward hatchway and ran to the U.S. customs officer, grabbing him by the arm as the sailors began to move about with unexpected anger. "I'm an American, and I need to get off of this fuckin' tub before they kill me," the man shouted to the federal agent. "My named is Daniel Cabot McCabe, and I'm a scientist out of Woods Hole. The captain has all my paperwork."

"You're a mess, man," the officer exclaimed. The face was badly bruised, black and blue. A broken nose was covered with plastic splint taped crossways. His bottom lip was split, and crude stitches closed a gash above his scabbed eyebrow. His clothes were filthy, and he reeked of fish. "What the hell happened to you?"

"I was sent out as a representative of the Maritime Stewardship Council, which has had a lot of complaints about this old bucket. The crew didn't like my findings, so almost every night they made certain that I stepped on a bar of soap or fell down a ladder or got in a fight. The captain didn't do anything to stop it. Look, Officer, I'm supposed to stay out here for two more weeks. I can't take it. They will kill me. Can I get a ride back with you guys?"

The sailors remained nearby, muttering Russian curses. The American stared back. "Not my fault their fishing fleet is obsolete and falling apart and they won't fix it. They're taking dangerous shortcuts to keep their catch numbers up. That's going to be in my report."

One of the sailors pointed and yelled, "Is not true! He lies!"

"Get down the ladder and into our boat, Mr. McCabe," the officer said. He didn't know why, but something about the name Cabot rang a bell. Something about history that commanded respect. "You guys back off."

Gibson scrambled from the deck into the customs officers' patrol boat, turned, and shot a middle-finger salute to the milling Russians, then winked.

LANDSTUHL REGIONAL MEDICAL CENTER
GERMANY

WILLA KENT AND TOM Hughes had a couple of problems arranging the transatlantic flight to Germany. The CIA travel office, generally very efficient, had hit a couple of snags, blaming weather on the other end, computer glitches, and housing. Finally, things came together three days after their meeting with Marty Atkins, the director of intelligence. Neither considered it a big deal, since the patient was still in a coma.

The personable regional agent in charge, Marguerite del Coda, met their plane at Ramstein Air Base and took them to a nice hotel to rest up after the long flight. They graciously accepted the offer, then she took them out to dinner.

The following morning, they went to see the patient and knew the trip had been wasted. Kyle Swanson lay in a chilly private room, unconscious beneath light-blue cotton sheets. His head, neck, and upper body were encased in a halo vest—a metal ring that encircled the head and was held in place by screws into the skull. His skin was sallow and slack.

"My God," whispered Kent upon entering the room. Del Coda introduced an older man and woman, the parents of the patient, and the CIA agents offered their heartfelt sympathies. An Englishman in a tailored suit, eyeglasses dangling from his neck, was at the bedside, checking Swanson's pulse. His name was Sir Patrick Whyte, and he was now Kyle Swanson's private physician of record.

Del Coda took Sir Jeff and Lady Pat over to the cafeteria for some food and to give the professionals some time alone with the doctor and his patient.

"Can he hear us?" asked Hughes.

"Very doubtful. He's been heavily sedated for almost a week."

"What's your diagnosis, Dr. Whyte?" Kent moved around the bed and felt Swanson's cold hand. *This guy is dying.*

Whyte slapped a couple of X-rays on the light board. Hughes moved close to study it as the British surgeon walked them through the injury. Things were worse than originally thought, he told them. He pointed to the crushed skull at the neck, and the angled bends of the upper vertebrae.

"Imagine a terrific whiplash effect from the trauma inflicted at that exact spot. The brain bounced around like a rubber ball in the skull, then, instead of being immobilized, he made things worse by carrying on with an arduous mission. You see, right there—that's the only slice of bone connecting the spine to the skull. If that gives way, he'll be paralyzed."

Hughes found no fault with that conclusion. Neither did Kent. The pictures proved it. "What happens now?" she asked.

"There is nothing more to be done here in Germany, so at the request of his parents I'm having him transferred to my private clinic in London. We'll try a single level anterior cervical fusion for the disk herniation in a few weeks to stabilize the spinal injury." The Englishman spoke with authority.

"So there's no chance of interviewing him until after that?"

The surgeon lowered his voice. "Quite frankly, I'm not certain he'll make it that far. We'll see where we are in two weeks."

"Damn bad luck," Hughes said. "Kyle Swanson was quite the warrior."

"Yes. I will do everything possible for him." Dr. Whyte took down the X-rays and put them in a thick folder, along with the medical history he'd prepared. "Everything you need is in there."

"A pleasure to meet you, Dr. Whyte. Good luck." Hughes led the way out of the room, and they were scooped up by del Coda and put back on a plane to Washington. On the flight, Kent went through the folder. "I know Whyte's reputation, Willa. He is one of the best in the business, and I have the same conclusion. Kyle's out of the game," she declared. "He'll never see another day of active duty."

Kent ordered a Bloody Mary. "You mean if he lives."

ASTORIA, OREGON

THE MAN KNOWN TO the U.S. Immigration and Customs Enforcement officers as Daniel Cabot McCabe was taken to the CMH Urgent Care on Exchange Street. They made him take a shower to wash away the fish stink, then put him in a powder-blue set of scrubs and got him on an examination table.

He was in better spirits once he was off the ship, and vowed that his report would probably force the boat out of service when it returned to Russia. He carried on about international-fishing laws and compacts and standards even as the ICE officer questioned him about the rough treatment. Assault on the high seas would be almost impossible to prove, he said. McCabe agreed. "Don't worry. I'll put it all in the reports," he said.

The officer whistled as the doctor fluttered about. With McCabe's shirt off, the bruising around the ribs was clear, as was a big one across the kidneys, and a yellowing stripe down one shin.

"They did a job on you, Mr. McCabe. You ought to go to a hospital," the doctor said, and the ICE agent, a friendly guy named Jack Myers, agreed.

Gibson refused. "No broken bones except the nose, and nothing to do for the ribs. They were careful with the violence, attempting to scare me off, which they did very well. I'm not even pissing blood." He winced when the doctor reset his nose, then gave him some antibiotics before reluctantly pronouncing him fit to leave. "Keep the scrubs," he said.

"Burn my other clothes."

"I guarantee that has already been done."

He had retrieved his notebooks, tablet, and cell phone, wallet and identity papers. "Can you recommend a place where I can rest up for a couple of days?"

"I'll run you over to the Hampden Inn and Suites. Pretty nice hotel," Myers said.

"Let's go," Gibson replied, stepping gingerly into the paper hospital slippers. "I can order some new clothes from there. Thanks, Doctor. I appreciate it."

"You'll be fine. Just take things easy."

"What are you going to do next, Mr. McCabe?" the ICE man asked as they left the urgent-care facility.

Gibson pulled out his wallet and showed the lawman the small, credit-card size laminated U.S. passport that was good for crossing all borders in North America. "I'm still on the government dime, Jack, just like you. The taxpayer is going to replace my stuff with better stuff, including new fishing tackle. Then I plan to rent a car and fish my way across Canada to the East Coast, thinking up really horrible things to say about that goddamn boat."

"Sounds like a plan," Myers said, laughing. "Safe journey. Meanwhile, my boss says we're going to take a special interest with that boat before letting it into our ports. It will take quite a bit of time and it will be a real shame if those tons of pollock rot in the holds because some forms weren't filled out properly."

ABOARD THE *VAGABOND*

SIR GEOFFREY CORNWELL WAS pleased with the newest version of his yacht, the *Vagabond*. It was bigger, brighter, and had far more toys than its illustrious predecessors, which had been world-class in their day. What really stood out about the gleaming vessel was its odd shape and pointed edges, closer to the U.S. Navy's *Zumwalt*-class stealth destroyer than to a potentate's plaything, more of a fighter than a lover.

The *Vagabond* had been a joint operation of Cornwell's Excalibur Enterprises and the American and Royal navies, with invisible funding siphoned through the Pentagon and the Ministry of Defense. Just as the CIA had its own air arm, the intelligence services occasionally needed secret help at sea. The hull was laid down by the warship builder Vospert Thornycroft at Southampton as the lead yard, then Brooks Marin, in Lowenstaft, installed the military-grade material, and a succession of other yards finished making it look like a white-and-gold luxury vessel ready for the blue water. It stretched almost 512 feet in length and was 77 feet wide, and its power plant could push the 15,906 gross tons of ship at speeds better than 25 miles per hour. It could handle up to thirty passengers and carried a crew of seventy-five, all of them military veterans with a surprising array of skills.

A helicopter with the matching Excalibur corporate color scheme hovered above the landing pad and carefully touched down with hardly a quiver. When the blades finally stopped, a medical team emerged, wrangled a gurney through the open hatch, popped down the wheels, and set off for the aid station. Lashed atop the conveyance was Kyle Swanson, still out like a light and wrapped in his steel cage. There was silence on the vessel when the crew members saw him so still and wan.

Lady Pat and Sir Jeff stepped off the helicopter. They had a beaten air about them.

Elizabeth Ledford was on the bridge of the *Vagabond*, held in check by Double-Oh Dawkins to keep her from getting in the way on the helo deck. When Swanson was safely in the aid station, he let her go, and she ran down below until she reached the hatch with the red cross painted on white.

Lady Pat gave her a hug. "Stand here by me, dear, until Dr. Whyte can get him out of that contraption. It looks a lot worse than it is, which was the purpose."

"He's still unconscious?" Coastie asked.

"All part of the plan, girl," Dr. Whyte said as he unfastened the straps. Unnoticed by the CIA interrogation team, the small screws that appeared to secure the halo to the skull actually had been tiny bolts with soft rubber tips that didn't even penetrate the skin. The steel frame had simply been a misdirection play—as had the horrific X-rays, which Whyte had dug up from a terrible motorcycle accident. With a bit of digital legerdemain, those pictures became X-rays of Kyle Swanson's head.

Whyte tossed the cage aside, and the orderlies transferred Swanson to a fresh bed with a new IV drip. The doctor filled a syringe and pumped in a dose of medicine that would allow Swanson to slowly emerge from the back depths to which he had willingly consigned himself. "He's fine," Dr. Whyte said. "He'll be waking up in a few hours and the orderlies can care for him during that twilight time. Now, let's have some dinner, shall we—Pat, Jeff?"

Coastie stepped to the bedside and ran her palm along Kyle's damp forehead, then kissed him on the cheek. "You all go ahead. I'll just stay here with him for a while." She took the sniper's hand in hers and perched on the edge of the bed.

ABOARD THE *VAGABOND*

SWANSON BECAME AWARE IN increments as his mind slowly adjusted to the lessening grip of the chemical sleep. Where nothingness had ruled for days, things now began creeping into his consciousness. Coastie, Lady Pat, Sir Jeff, and Double-Oh were clustered in a loose semicircle as Dr. Whyte brought him up through the final stages. An orderly monitored his vital signs.

A dreamlet was forming in the patient's idle brain. He was underwater, coming up from a surfboard spill, held down by the force of churning water and the strong outward rush of a retreating wave. Swanson sat on the drifting sand as the ocean surged all around and through him, looking up like a seabed plant. That was interesting. There was light up there. He watched the bubbles rising from his nose and mouth being drawn automatically to the surface. He decided to follow them. It seemed nicer up there.

Breathing wasn't a problem, even beneath the water; he thought this was very odd. He coughed several times. New air replaced the old, and his lungs filled with the fresh taste of life. Sounds filtered in, a cacophony of babel that he couldn't understand. A powerful light stabbed into his eyes, so sharp that he jerked his head away from it.

"Waddah," he moaned as his first word, and a cup was at his chapped lips, giving him a few sips of liquid gold. "Ahhh."

"All good," the orderly told the doctor.

Swanson heard, but didn't understand. "Watter?" The cup visited again. His hearing improved and a cold wet cloth wiped gently at his eyes. He was in a room with other people.

"Kyle?" The man's voice was an easy baritone. "Kyle, can you hear me? Shake your head if you understand me."

"Hear." He coughed. Sir Jeff and Double-Oh did a fist bump, while Lady Pat and Coastie hugged each other. Coastie took Kyle's hand again. Dr. Whyte decided that tactile contact was a good thing, and that he could work around her.

"Very good." Whyte continued. "You're waking up from a very deep sleep. You're safe and in good condition. There's nothing wrong with you except for a lot of drugs that will work their way out of your system. Do not fight that."

"Uh-hunh."

"Good. We are aboard the *Vagabond*. Do you know what that is?"

"Boat." Another cough. A bad dream crashed through his head, a deadly and roaring red demon, and he began to thrash, but his arms and feet were still secured to the bed. Coastie jumped away as if shocked by a bolt of electricity. Lady Pat grabbed her as if gentling a spooked pony.

"You're okay, Kyle. That was a normal reaction. Relax." The doctor pursed his lips and nodded to the orderly to let the morphine drip resume. "We're going to let you rest a little while longer, until you adjust at a slower speed. There's no hurry. No more nightmares."

He faded again, but seemed comfortable, safe, and serene. "I love my Coastie," he said to himself, bringing his mind to bear on life. But she heard it, and tears came.

LIVINGSTON, IDAHO

LUKE GIBSON WAS IN no hurry. Having cleared U.S. Customs through the ruse of shipboard persecution, he was now able to go where he wished, and America was a very big place. Time was his buddy. As long as he didn't break the law or draw undue attention, he was good.

Using a Maine credit card provided in Susannah Lai's packet of goodies—maybe he wouldn't kill her after all—Gibson rented a well-used pickup truck for a week in his alias of Daniel Cabot McCabe. It had a bold round National Rifle Association sticker on the rear window. At a sporting-goods store, he outfitted himself with a camo cap and jacket and big aviator non-reflecting sunglasses. At Walmart he found underwear, jeans and four shirts, plus toiletries and other items—sneakers, work gloves, a small shovel, a flashlight, and a large backpack. Then he set out to see America on a leisurely cross-country drive aboard his 2010 Dodge Ram V8 with four-wheel drive. East, over to Interstate 5, then south to I-84 and east again into majestic landscapes dominated by national forests and by Mount Hood far to the left. A man in camo cap and shirt, his face shaded by large sunglasses and the tinted window of a pickup truck with a few dings and an NRA sticker was unlikely to draw a second glance from any cop or camera.

He somehow managed to stay awake for eight more hours and rolled safely into the mirror border towns of Clarkston, Washington, and Lewiston, Idaho. The rush was on him now, sleep tugging but unimportant. Hot coffee and a few uppers were his fuel.

The smokestacks of the Potlatch and Clearwater Lumber factories regurgitated stinking clouds into the darkening sky as Gibson got his bearings in the Lewis and Clark Valley. He crossed the old drawbridge spanning the Snake River, got to East Main in Lewiston, and headed into the industrial sprawl—a rolling carpet of trash, junk, and scrap in a land with no zoning laws that might prevent a man from doing as he wished with his property

The tires crackled against the gravel of Shelter Road, and from the gloom he found the ruins of the old Sacred Heart Chapel. Its stones were slimy with moss and lichen, and it was isolated behind a rusty barbed-wire fence and a field of waste and thorns. Instead of being a place of worship, the chapel seemed to be trying to hide.

Dear old Dad, thought Gibson. The King had recognized value when he saw it, and dilapidated churches had been high on his list of hidey-holes. Local governments were reluctant to condemn them, and the religious community liked having them around. Sacred Heart had survived. Gibson shut down the truck and went in.

The senses were quick to react. The place stank of urine and feces, piled and rotting for decades. Obscene painted words had obliterated any sign of respect. The pews and the pulpit were gone, as was the roof, which had let the weather come inside. The place was a lot worse than when his father had discovered it. It was not just dilapidated, it was dead. He showed the light around, dancing it over the slag, and saw nothing. "Hey! Anybody here? Show yourself!" he hollered. Only silence came back.

Gibson held the shovel like a weapon as he moved toward the back of what had once been the nave. He walked directly to the west wall, then back five paces. One more flash around, and he started to dig. The covering of trash and debris was easy to clear, but he had to pry and pick hard to remove the joined rock of the floor.

He paused to catch his breath, then dug hard to finish. It was either still there or it wasn't. The blade struck metal, and Gibson chipped around it, then used his fingers to extract an old metal ammunition box. Originally designed to hold several hundred rounds of .50-caliber ammo, the box had been retooled by King for his own purposes: beneath the pop-top metal lid lay a neat set of interior compartments sealed with wax. The contents were refreshed every ten years, so there was a new usable identification set, two credit cards, a thousand dollars in hundreds, fifties and, twenties, a dull silvered Ruger 9-mm. pistol and fifty clean rounds. He squatted on his boot heels and read the new ID: he was now Craig D. Abrams of Charlotte, North Carolina, a sales rep for an international computer-chip manufacturer. The only problem was that the King's photo was on it, not that of the Prince. Gibson could alter that easily enough. He thanked his father and his grandfather, too, for having the foresight to install these little emergency caches everywhere they had put a CIA secret stash, which in this church was counted from the west wall. He pocketed the money, loaded the Ruger, and replaced the box, making a mental note to replenish it later.

With the debris haphazardly stacked back in place, Gibson gave Daniel Cabot McCabe a small, fiery sendoff.

He left the truck where it was, with the keys in the ignition. The last trace of the marine biologist who had passed through the port of Astoria would be stolen and gone by morning. Gibson flung the shovel as far as he could, and it bounced and came to rest amid the beer cans and junk. Shouldering the backpack, he made the easy walk back into town, paid a hundred dollars in cash for a nice, bland room at the Holiday Inn Express, showered, brushed his teeth, and went to sleep feeling like a new man.

The following morning, he slept late and missed the complimentary buffet, so he wandered downtown and found a real restaurant that fortified him with eggs, ham, hash browns, fresh biscuits, and strong coffee. Back to the Holiday Inn Express, and the crowd was gone, off to wherever their big recreational vehicles would travel. Gibson slid into a chair in the semi-private travelers' business suite and logged into one of his accounts. He had been out of touch since Hong Kong, but struck gold in the first chat room, where a coded message awaited. The source was an old-timer inside the CIA:

> Regret to report that your good friend Kyle Swanson suffered catastrophic head and spine injuries. Condition critical. Prognosis grim, probably fatal. He is paralyzed neck down and on life support in the care of a private clinic in London. Condition entered in personnel file by on-scene observers who interviewed physician. I share your grief.

Gibson sucked in a sharp breath. *Damn. I got him! Or did I?* He had butt-stroked Swanson pretty good, but to this extent? Still, what extra damage was done in the following action? Good news indeed, but inconclusive. He called up a second secret site, a private message board from a source buried within the élite community of special operators, and his heart began to sing:

> Swanson is finished with a broken neck. Source the two snipers who brought him out, plus helo medic that treated him on extract.

Luke shut the computer down, erased the history, leaned back, and snapped his fingers with controlled joy. *I got him. Not the shoot-out I wanted, but I got the bastard.*

He returned to his room, gathered his belongings, and checked out of the hotel into a bright and glorious Idaho day. *Number One!* He stuck out his thumb beside the highway and headed east, toward Big Thunder.

ABOARD THE *VAGABOND*

THE SUN WAS HIGH when Kyle Swanson awoke again, this time with a gentler emergence back into the real world after his drug-enforced hibernation. His lids fluttered and he coughed. There was some mild disorientation, but it gave way as life resumed. It felt as if he were being reborn, leaving a comfortable place of which he now had no memory.

Hands were holding his, Coastie on the right and Lady Pat on the left. He smiled at them. "Welcome back, boy," called out Sir Jeff, leaning on the foot of the bed. The big frame of Double-Oh Dawkins shadowed behind them.

He just looked at all of them for a moment, taking in their presence. "Did I make it okay?" His voice was a croak.

"Don't make such a big deal out of sleeping for a while," grumped Dawkins. "You still have all your fingers and toes."

Coastie leaned forward and kissed Kyle lightly on the forehead. "Everything is good," she said.

"Hey, you really are here," he said, taking a long look at her. "I thought I saw you earlier. Can I get some water?"

Sir Jeff told him that he'd been attended by one of the finest physician-surgeons in London, who was now on his way home. "You looked like hell, and we have pictures to prove it, but you're fine. You may have a headache for a day or two, and an upset stomach. Otherwise, it went well."

"Let's not do that again, shall we?" Lady Pat squeezed his hand.

Kyle drank some water. "Did it work?"

"Who knows? We sure planted enough hard evidence and rumors.

Everybody but a tight handful of friends believes you are crippled with a broken neck and expected to die." Double-Oh crossed his arms. "We are ready to go hunting whenever you are."

Kyle felt the gentle sway of the yacht and knew they were aboard the *Vagabond*. His stomach felt a bit queasy, and he closed his eyes again. "Where are we?"

Sir Jeff spoke again. "We've passed out of the North Sea and are nearing the Channel Islands. The captain says we'll be in the Atlantic sometime overnight."

"Anything on Gibson yet?" He looked at Double-Oh.

"He got away aboard an old helicopter in the Afghan fracas. Marty Atkins thinks the agency may have a lead on him in Hong Kong, but he hasn't pinged the system."

"So we don't know if he's taking the bait." Kyle was tiring.

"Not for sure. But we certainly provided a convincing show."

Kyle faded again, and the medical orderly stepped in to instruct that he should be left alone for a while. Reluctantly, the four of them trooped out of the cabin. The patient asked weakly, "Can I get something for sea sickness?"

"No problem," replied the orderly. "All your vital signs are stable. You might be on your feet tonight."

"I may puke."

"Basket's at your right hand." She gave him a shot of Dramamine, then turned off the light and left the room.

32

WASHINGTON, D.C.

THE CONGRESSWOMAN FELT THAT her star-spangled universe was closing in on her. She had wrapped herself in the flag and called it patriotism, and now it was strangling her. She was seated in the immense office of the Speaker of the House, and he looked at her as if she were a bug that had splattered the windshield of his limousine. The same look came from her boss, the minority leader. There were four people at the conference table, and the third was Marty Atkins, the CIA director of intelligence. The welcome hadn't been cordial.

"We'll get right to it, because we all have more important things to do today," said the Speaker in an icy tone. He nodded to the minority leader.

"If you were in a private company, you would be fired for cause and incompetence, Congresswoman Keenan. We, however, are the Congress of the United States and cannot do that. So here is the offer you can't turn down: You are out of politics at the end of this term. Do not run for reelection."

Veronica Keenan opened her mouth to say something, but the Speaker shut her down. "If you do not heed the advice of your party leader, we will all crush you. Go back to the farm, Veronica. You're done in Washington."

"This is a cover-up!" she squeaked, and turned to Atkins. "Your agency is riddled with corruption and you're trying to lay the blame elsewhere."

The professorial civil servant had seen hundreds of these characters in a lifetime with the agency. Flailing for support, their first instinct was to throw a stink bomb at the CIA. This one had caused more trouble than most because of the congresswoman's membership on the House Permanent Select Committee on Intelligence.

"You brought us a scandal, Ms. Keenan," said Marty Atkins. "A scandal with no proof. As a result, the media had another field day at our expense. We investigated everything thoroughly and found nothing."

"I don't believe you, sir," she snipped.

"We do," bellowed the Speaker. "In the process, you endangered our men and women, compromised operations, and broke your oath of secrecy. You should be going to prison, but we don't need even more bad public relations from your tawdry power grab."

"Two of our field agents are dead and a third is missing, thanks to you."

"What about that drug center in Afghanistan? I saw that military takedown on the news. I forced the action on that."

Atkins wearily responded, "There are hundreds of places like that around the globe, ma'am. Little hubs for the opium trade that are used by dealers. You know that from the confidential briefings, and that the United States is focused on a shooting war in Afghanistan. You forced an attack on a place that will be back in the dope business as soon as the troops leave. We keep an eye on them, but have bigger fish to fry."

The Speaker, growing impatient, pointedly looked at a big grandfather clock on the wall. "You were used," he declared. "We know your source. Tell us how you contacted Luke Gibson, the man you know as Mr. Prince."

Keenan gathered her waning strength. They knew! "Have you been listening to my calls?"

"Yes," replied Atkins. "Where is he?"

"I think this meeting is over," she said. "I should get a lawyer."

Her party boss reminded her, "You are not a private citizen, Keenan. You go that way, and you'll be looking at a prison sentence for certain." He leaned forward on his elbows and said, softer, "It's over, Veronica. You were played by a professional and got in over your head. Help us catch this traitor, and save yourself in the process."

He was right. Fighting it would lead to her personal destruction. She sat back against the deep seat, shut her eyes, and caught her breath. "What do you want me to do? I don't know how to contact him."

Marty Atkins closed a folder. "I have a team waiting in a private office who will debrief you. You hurt us bad, Ms. Keenan, and a killer is on the loose because of your actions."

The Speaker smacked the table. "We're done here. No press statements from you, Veronica. Not one fucking word."

ABOARD THE *VAGABOND*

THE DOUBLE CHEESEBURGER WAS a heart-attack special, but Swanson wolfed it down and polished off two cold beers. He was feeling almost like his old self, and was hungry as hell after being tube-fed. Dessert was a big slice of Boston cream pie. The medical checkup was done, and that alone was cause for celebration. His neck and skull were normal.

"That coma was an idiotic thing to do, Kyle," said Lady Patricia Cornwell. "You put yourself in mortal danger."

"Nah. It might have been a stroll on some thin ice, but I knew you all would take care of me." He smiled at the crusty Englishwoman. "And you did."

The *Vagabond* was chopping into the Atlantic swells, headed southwest. The motion no longer bothered him. "Well, let's hope Luke Gibson bought the story, and that it holds long enough for us to find him. After all, that's the goal."

In Afghanistan, Swanson's thoughts had been focused on killing Gibson not so much because of that "I'm the best" bullshit as because Swanson didn't want to have to keep looking over his shoulder for the rest of his life. And after they had actually seen each other passing in those trucks, Swanson knew that neither would give up until the other was dead. After he had drawn that unshakeable conclusion, the question became how to reach Gibson first, and the solution to the puzzle came in a blinding flash before Thompson, Brandt, and he reached the helicopter; he was able to share the details over the thumping blades.

It was an accepted fact that Gibson had sources on the inside, so the job of gathering information on his location had to be done without mentioning his name. It was the same trap that Swanson and Gibson had discussed together, of having too many people in the logistical tail. This time, only the few people who absolutely needed to know what was happening would know. He instructed his fellow snipers and the medic about who was needed, what they needed to do, and when. No one else would be allowed within the circle.

It had all become so clear when he analyzed the situation, even while the fighting was under way. If Gibson went off the map again, and he would, they had to find someone who had links to him. One name stood out from all the others—the powerful Mexican drug lord Maxim Guerrera, who had ordered the attack on the gravesite. How did Guerrera contact Gibson? According to Gibson, as he sounded off back at the house, he had been called directly. That meant the drug lord had a private number for his American fixer.

So while Swanson had slept, both Marty Atkins of the CIA and Lucky Sharif of the FBI had personally gathered the background on Guerrera, never mentioning the name of Luke Gibson. The Drug Enforcement Agency, ICE, and Homeland Security all had files, and the NSA furnished some recorded conversations. It was all forwarded to the *Vagabond*, which was on a course to the Gulf of Mexico. For the next five days, as Swanson healed, the team labored over the data.

"There has to be a pressure point that will draw him out," said Coastie during one long afternoon session. She was openly excited to once again be going after the man responsible for the death of her husband

"The man loves his ponies and his boat, but there's no opening, no weakness, beyond those," Double-Oh added. "Goons with him all the time. I doubt that a snatch is possible."

Sir Jeff chimed in, "I quite agree. Even when he's out on the water, a patrol boat of guards is lurking nearby. We could destroy them all, of course, but that would be messy. A good shooter might bop him. Anybody here know any good snipers?"

"Quite," said Lady Pat, laughing as she lit one of her little cigars. "Killing him is not the goal, however, may I remind you all."

"That will come eventually. His scalp belongs to me." Coastie's tone was cold. "So where is the pressure point? How do we get him alone?"

"Keep workin' the problem, gang," Kyle said when they briefed him. "The answer is right here in front of us. I can feel it. Something in what Double-Oh said about the horses and boats. I'm going to get some ice cream." He disappeared toward the galley.

ISLA MUJERES, THE ISLAND of Women, was part of Maxim Guerrera's safe sailing zone. About eight miles off the Yucatán Peninsula, the rocky outcrop was a popular tourist designation, but also maintained a good harbor to support the bigger private craft, and not many questions were asked by the local authorities. Guerrera had been out all afternoon with his sweetheart, a hundred-foot sloop-rigged fiberglass racer he had named for his daughter, *Valeria*. The big cruising yacht was named for his wife, *Maria*, and was anchored on the other coast of Mexico.

For the past two days, Guerrera had put the smooth *Valeria* through its paces, tightening things up for the upcoming Havana to Cancún regatta. She wasn't an expensive boat, having cost less than a million dollars, but he had poured at least that amount into making it less of a showpiece than a genuine racer. In all things, Guerrera intended to win. The *Valeria*, with its ebony fiberglass hull and scarlet-and-gold spinnaker, was going to do just fine, and he took her to the dock after the workout.

Wind-lashed and ruddy-faced from the sun, his shorts and his shirt still damp and salty, Guerrera strolled with a single bodyguard over to his favorite crab shack facing the water. The owner had kept the table open, and a cold beer and a plate of lobster tacos laden with spices and peppers was served immediately. He dug in as the sentinel kept watch. Guerrera was on his second beer and reading some newspapers when the guard handed him an envelope and motioned toward the open veranda, where he could make out the silhouette of a small woman with shining blond hair. The note was brief, written in a feminine hand:

I am unarmed and alone, and wish a private word with you.
Sra. Elizabeth Castillo

There was a momentary shock of recognition, then he took another slow drink and told the guard, "Bring her over, then call for some more men."

Coastie wore low black heels, black slacks, and a gray top, with no jewelry except a Samsung Gear S2 Smartwatch. She allowed a quick pat-down by the guard, who then escorted her to the table. Guerrera didn't get up, or offer a hand in greeting. "I am the widow of Colonel Miguel Castillo," she said, sitting uninvited directly across from him.

"I know who you are." Most people trembled in his presence, but not this one. In fact, she made *him* nervous. "What do you want?"

"A telephone number for Luke Gibson, the American," she said, her eyes hard and level. "Give it to me now and I walk out and nothing more will happen."

"Go away, woman," he snapped. "I have never heard that name, and I would never hand anything over to you. I know of your past life and exploits, señora. My guess is that you are currently an agent of the U.S. government." He was starting to sweat because she remained so calm.

"I represent no one but myself. You and Gibson took something precious from me—the life and reputation of my husband. I offer you this chance for redemption."

Guerrera laughed. "How generous. Or what?"

"I begin taking precious things from you. Last chance."

"Go fuck yourself, cunt."

She glanced at her wristwatch and tapped the small screen several times. "Sorry to hear that answer. It was crude. So now we have to wait a few minutes."

Two miles from them, on the leeward side of the island, a lightweight torpedo had been idling two hundred meters from the *Vagabond*. On her computerized command, the six-hundred-pound beast that had been brought along for testing surged forward, the course adjusted from the bridge of the yacht.

"You are wasting my time."

"Just another minute. I understand that my husband was in a dangerous business, but why the desecration of his grave?"

"Business. I had to send a message to the government that they should ease their efforts." He shrugged.

"You are an animal." Her watch blinked red. "Now say goodbye to your *Valeria*."

The torpedo slammed a hundred-pound warhead into the sailboat with thunderous results. The explosion rocked the waterfront, set several other boats aflame, and rained debris like hard, sharp snow. Maxim Guerrera jumped up, spilling his beer, and stared like a stricken child. The *Valeria* was gone, leaving behind nothing but smoking and burning wreckage. By the time he sat back down and stared at Coastie, she had laid another note on the table.

"You bitch! You murdered my crew!"

"Just business," she replied. "Read the note. Every five minutes now, something else belonging to you, something you hold dear, will disappear, just like your little sailboat. Give me Luke Gibson's number and I will stop it all now. Otherwise, the clock continues to tick. Let's see, Maxim, the next target is Espada. Four minutes."

She sat back, contented. The smoking ruin of the sailboat was an inspirational view.

"How?" he gulped. Espada was his favorite polo pony, an Argentine-bred champion with a bold personality. Polo was another game that Guerrera loved, a game for the rich, and he owned a whole string of ponies, but Espada was a bruiser on the turf. He didn't believe her; this had to be a bluff. How could these people harm the ponies, which were stabled at a mountain ranch several hundred kilometers away?

"Never mind that. After the horse, the next item on my list will be your boat on the far side, the *Maria*. The bomb is already aboard. Then we move on to real people, starting with your son, Carlos, in California. As long as you want to play, Maxim, I have targets enough for an hour. I really don't want to kill those horses. Give me the number. Two minutes."

"Like hell I will. You wouldn't dare. I will see to it that every drug lord in Mexico declares war on you. Stop this madness or I will kill you right here."

"The program goes on automatically and cannot be stopped if I am harmed in any way. Time is up. Say goodbye to poor Espada."

They sat locked in mutual hatred until the cell phone rang in his pocket. He listened quietly, asking only, "All of them?" When the answer came, his grim face fell apart. The supervisor of the mountain ranch had reported that a missile with multiple warheads had struck the facility, killing the ponies and wrecking the training complex.

"After we are done with the physical things, we will dismantle your operation, freeze your funds, and make a deal with your bother drug lords to put your ass in a maximum-security federal prison. Or just kill you. I haven't made up my mind yet. The *Maria* in four minutes."

Guerrera retrieved his telephone and went to the list of contacts, selected one, and spun the screen to face Coastie. It was listed as the Big Thunder Ranch, with a U.S. calling code. "That's the answering service. I call him and leave a message. It is all I have, señora. I don't know where he is. Please make this stop. Please."

She tapped her wristwatch phone and read the address and number to Swanson. "Hold on further attacks until I return safely," she said, then walked from the restaurant without another word.

33

KYLE SWANSON WAS TWO blocks away, in an overwatch position buried deep in the tangled shadows of a second-floor corner room. An Excalibur sniper rifle was braced on a bipod anchored to a table and snug against his shoulder. O. O. Dawkins was at his side, getting a larger view than Swanson had through the big weapon's scope. Both saw Coastie walk away from the dockside restaurant. Swanson remained locked to the entranceway to the restaurant she had just left. So far, so good, but Swanson doubted it would stay that way.

Maxim Guerrera had been stung badly by Señora Ledford, and his fiery temperament would not let such an insult stand. He would rather lose everything than be disrespected. Guerrera had given up the Big Thunder information because he didn't give a damn about Luke Gibson. Now he had to strike back hard and fast, or word would get out that the drug lord had been bested by a woman.

Some members of Guerrera's guard detail had been killed in the boat explosion, but others were rushing to shield him. The single close bodyguard heard the boss yell, "Grab her!" Guerrera was gambling with fate, but if he could get his hands on her now she could be used as a hostage. "Alive!" he shouted.

Double-Oh dropped the binos and bounded down the stairs with a compact H&K MP7 in one hand and a flash-bang grenade in the other. Swanson didn't move, except for controlling his breathing and toucing his finger to the trigger.

Coastie broke into a sprint when she heard the shouting behind her. Looking back would be a waste of time. By lunging forward to chase her, the perimeter bodyguards abandoned their protective posts, but were still scattered, so she slowed a bit to let them catch up.

For that instant, Swanson's world was sniper silent, a private place in which he was alone with the target, and Maxim Guerrera, with a sun-reddened, angry face, stood still, awaiting the capture of the woman. Swanson caressed the trigger, pulling straight back, and the broad, loud voice of Excalibur spoke in its definitive .50-caliber vocabulary. Maxim Guerrera, one of Mexico's most vicious criminals, took the shot in his broad chest, and it destroyed his insides. He slumped to his knees and held the position long enough for Swanson to take a second shot that snapped the man's skull as if it were an egg.

The bodyguards froze at the booming sounds that rolled out over the bay, and Coastie reached the hide house, passing Double-Oh, who was exiting. Dawkins flung the grenade into the street and ducked back into the doorway before the detonation. Then he tossed a smoke grenade, just to confuse things even more. "You ready?" he shouted back to her.

"Yeah, go." Coastie had picked up a waiting MP7, and they both charged out through the curtain of dense, swirling smoke. A guard appeared, coughing, and Double-Oh downed him with a three-shot burst.

Swanson hadn't altered his sight pattern for new range and distance readings, because any new action would center around the body. A man with a pistol jumped from a car and Kyle blew him away instantly.

Another burst of fire blasted when Coastie ripped a guard. Then she and Dawkins emerged from the smoke cloud and were beside the corpse. Double-Oh turned and took a knee, firing selective shots now, as Coastie searched Guerrera and grabbed the cell phone, with all its information, and took the wristwatch and the wallet, too, in case they might also contain information.

"Gimme!" she yelled, reaching out to Double-Oh. Without looking back, he tossed her a small bar of Composition C plastic explosive. She ripped a sticky strip off one side of the malleable claylike block and inserted a pre-set fuse, then shoved the device beneath the body. "I'm done here," she said with a prankish grin. "Thirty seconds. Go!"

They had sprinted almost clear of the smoke cloud when the C-4 exploded and bits of Maxim Guerrera sprinkled along the waterfront like dirty red rain. "That's for Mickey, you asshole!" she hollered, and Double-Oh grabbed her by the arm and yanked her inside the doorway of their hide.

Swanson was poundiging down the steps, cradling the Excalibur. "Let's get moving," he said, leading the way to the back, where a couple of the *Vagabond*'s crew of ex-special-ops veterans had a Range Rover waiting. They were gone in thirty seconds, without another shot being fired.

ABOARD THE *VAGABOND*

THE YACHT HEADED DIRECTLY east, away from Isla Mujeres, at a leisurely pace. There was no link between it and the attacks. The yacht crew had been visible to observers doing strange things like launching weather balloons, scuba diving, fishing, and partying. The torpedo had been launched unseen through an underwater port, and the double launch of the sea-to-land missiles appeared to be part of a gigantic fireworks display. Many luxurious private boats came to the island for a few days, spent a lot of time playing, then sailed away again. The *Vagabond* was no different. After the gunfight in town, several other boats also had hauled anchor.

With the shore team back on board and everything secure, a council of war was held in the day cabin, fueled by celebratory champagne. Coastie looked as if a thousand-pound burden had been lifted from her mind and her shoulders. Punishing Maxim Guerrara had been worth the risk, although she felt sorry about killing the polo ponies.

"Did we get some good stuff?" she asked. The material she had taken from the drug king was sacked in transparent plastic evidence bags that were sealed and labeled. Not that it would ever see the light of day in any courtroom, but the government labs would pick it apart and suck out every molecule of information.

"I certainly think so!" Sir Jeff crowed. "The call directories and histories on the phones should lay out a big map of Señor Guerrara's empire."

Swanson poured himself a refill. "I called Lucky to pass that Big Thunder number along, and we fly out first thing tomorrow to hand-carry this cache to Washington and maintain the chain of custody. I will give it to Marty and he'll unleash the alphabet agencies on it. Meanwhile, Lucky will have the data on Big Thunder. So, yeah, it's some good stuff."

"Only thing I want is the intel on that Big Thunder place." Double-Oh was as calm as if he were reading a comic book. "That's where we're going to find Luke Gibson. By the way, Coastie, you done good back there. Cracks me up when somebody underestimates you."

Beth Ledford sank into a deep cushion. "No prob. It had to be done if I ever hoped to put my husband at peace. Sad about the horses, though."

Lady Pat walked over and took her hand. "Think, instead, of all the people you've saved by getting that monster out of the way."

Dinner was a leisurely affair of cold cuts, cheese, fruit, and wine, then the Cornwells retired to their cabin after the long day. Double-Oh was also weary and went to binge-watch Netflix. Coastie and Kyle sat side by side in deck chairs on the stern, watching the Gulf waters flow by. The engines were a monotonous, quiet hum.

"So what now?" she asked. Red wine had helped the events of the day slide into perspective. She felt better than she had in a long, long time, comfortable and protected and without worry.

"We go get Luke."

"Of course we will. That's not what I'm asking, you silly boy."

Kyle blinked at her. The lovely hair and tanned skin, the curve of her cheeks and the compact body in tan cargo shorts and a loose white shirt. "Well, that's a tough one, isn't it?"

Coastie reached over her chair and touched his right hand lightly. "I love Mickey, you know that. And I miss him terribly."

"Yeah, so do I. Think about him all the time." He turned. The moonlight seemed to halo around her. He gently squeezed her hand. Could he say the words?

She squeezed back, leaning against the cushion, her eyes soft. "But I love you, too, Kyle. I never really stopped."

He broke the spell and got out of the chair, walked to the rail, and left her alone. Several deep breaths made his shoulders heave. Then he spun about and turned to see not a pixie with the soul of a stone-cold killer but the warm-hearted woman with whom he wanted to spend the rest of his life. He slowly lifted her to her feet. "I never stopped loving you, either, Coastie, and now I love you more than ever," he said. The hug led to a slow kiss, which led to her stateroom.

MONTANA

LUKE GIBSON WAS TROTTING through the sagebrush and trees on the thousand-acre spread of the Big Thunder Ranch, letting the horse lope along at a gentle pace on an old cattle trail. The big black could go anywhere it wanted to and still be on the Big Thunder. Five hundred acres on the U.S. side of the border and another five hundred across the invisible border in Canada. The ranch had been carefully crafted over the years onto the national land of both countries, and blended into even more protected acerage.

Checking with his GPS would have been a waste of times; he knew he was about equidistant between Plentywood, Montana, and Crosby, North Dakota. Over the border, Regina, up in Saskatchewan, lay to the north and the south was desolate all the way down to Wyoming. It had been planned that way to create an oasis in the middle of nowhere. The only place to really avoid was the customs border checkpoint in Regway.

The border literally ran right through the living room of his beautiful log ranch house, and he could walk unimpeded into either country. The family had carved out the idea decades ago, and it had given law enforcement fits on several occasions, but the CIA connections scared away the local badges, although they thought it might be a central point for transporting heavy drugs across North America.

Ragged brush whipped against his leather chaps as he rode up a rise

282 / Jack Coughlin and Donald A. Davis

that gave him a big-sky view for miles, and he pulled the horse to a stop beside a watering hole. The saddle squeaked as he dismounted, took a drink himself, and estimated his position and the time, with neither compass nor watch. He was the best sniper in the world, and those skills had become habits. Gibson scratched at a mosquito and settled in the shade.

He had beaten Kyle Swanson, and now he would take a few months off, stay near the ranch, and let the manhunt furor cool down. He was about as far from the action as he could be, safe in the family fortress, while Swanson was, at best, a caged vegetable with a broken neck and a crushed spinal cord. His source in the agency had sent a digital photo of the X-rays, and there was no doubt that most men would have been dead from that injury. Swanson always was a stubborn one. At any rate, the quest was over, and victory was sweet.

Gibson let his thoughts travel back through time, replaying almost every day, and was proud of the complex amount of planning and personal bravery he'd demonstrated, and of recognizing his destiny so early in life. He didn't regret a thing. The day was cool, the water trickled up from an underground reservoir, and he went to sleep.

It was coming on to dusk when he rode back to the ranch, the sky painted purple and gold, and the sounds of silence telling him that everything was fine. He had given the staff a few days off, so he stabled the horse himself, then went inside and checked the security room. The sensors showed no alerts. Taking a shower, he saw a lot of improvement in his battered face, and he felt strong. Maybe tomorrow he would take a drive into North Dakota, where the atmosphere of the oil boom still existed in some places. Maybe. Maybe not. Decide tomorrow when he rode over to look around.

WASHINGTON, D.C.

HE'S IN THERE SOMEWHERE, said Special Agent Lucky Sharif, running a red laser dot over a vast square of more than a thousand acres that straddled the U.S.–Canadian border at the juncture or Montana and North Dakota.

"Back on our turf right now, but able to sprint into Canada at a moment's notice."

The area on the satellite map had been pieced together through a massive search of documents in both countries, from current tax payments to old land deeds written in flowing script by long-dead clerks who made entries in leather-bound record books. The combined high-resolution sat shots showed the big ranch house, a stable and barn area, and two small airstrips, one on each side of the border. Roads were narrow but navigable. "This place didn't spring up overnight. It took decades of foresight, and the cost must have been monstrous. A bunch of rogues," said Chief Superintendent Matthew Fox of the Royal Canadian Mounted Police, who was coordinating the search in his country.

"Money was never much of an object; they made a fortune by selling information, weapons, and drugs in the guise of secret government operations. This family goes back a long way, and they built the Big Thunder Ranch as an ultimate hideaway." Marty Atkins was at the conference table, and not a happy man.

"The important thing is that we're closing in on him, and he doesn't know it. So long as he doesn't creep through the outposts around Big Thunder before we go in, he's a walking dead man." Kyle Swanson sipped some coffee, and the bitter taste told him that he needed a fresh pot.

"You're speaking figuratively, of course," reminded the Mountie. "We're not assassinating him."

"Of course. My goal is to crush his spirit, not to kill him, and let him spend the rest of his miserable life in some cold, dark cell moping about his failure."

"I know a few such places," said Atkins. "Much worse than Club Gitmo. We have a long interrogation process ready for Mr. Gibson—all perfectly legal, but secret."

Sharif took over again. "So the F Section Mounties out of Regina have been reinforced and are in position—right, Matt?"

"Yes."

"Highway Patrols are ready in Montana and North Dakota, plus some

284 / Jack Coughlin and Donald A. Davis

locals. So, Big Thunder is sealed," Sharif concluded. "We have an FBI Hostage Rescue Team staging fifteen minutes away from the ranch house. On signal, we all go in at once and meet in the middle. Temporary border crossings for law enforcement have been authorized by both sides."

Matthew Fox drummed his fingers on the table for a moment. "Then what are we waiting for?"

"Just the clock. We hit him at four o'clock tomorrow morning."

34

BIG THUNDER RANCH

THE ALARM SCREECHED LIKE a wounded wildcat, tearing Luke Gibson from a sound sleep, and he rolled off the mattress before his eyes were even open, groping for the shotgun under the bed. The unmanned security control room was running on automatic and had piped the unvarying, piercing whine into every room. An instant later, warning sirens began to hoot outside. Gibson scrambled to his feet and headed for the control room. Every light in the house flashed on. They were coming.

He threw open the security doors and saw that every screen was lit with alert signals. Sensor dots to pinpoint unwanted guests flecked the computers like measles, and coming from every direction. He took a moment to collect his thoughts, then dashed back to grab jeans, boots, sweatshirt, and the bug-out bag that was kept topped off for just such a situation. When he ran outside, shotgun in hand, he heard the rattle of approaching helicopters and motorcycles and trucks—a cacophony of bad news.

Gibson reacted like a test pilot in a spin, ticking off options one after another as disaster drew ever closer. The airstrips were of no use, and neither was a big 4×4, because the roads would be blocked. A horse was too slow. The encircling force meant that the Canadians were in on this, which wiped out the usual border trails.

Gibson took off for the trees. Darkness and cover were his allies now, and, in addition, his attackers wouldn't know about the tunnels. He broke into a hard run, pounding down the driveway. A haze of headlights rose above the distant treetops, moving his way. The chopper was closing in fast. He reached the tree line just as some unlucky cop hit a hidden claymore mine off to the east, and the explosion shook the night.

He felt a momentary surge of euphoria as the victory virus swept through him. The ranch was full of surprises that only he knew. His path to the tunnel entrance would be clear when the automatic defenses took their toll on the unsuspecting policemen, most of whom could arrest speeding drunks but had no training in tactical combat scenarios. A white phosphorus grenade exploded up where the Mounties were coming in. He ran.

The main threat was that helicopter, probably an FBI HRT unit. Those were bad boys. He recalled hearing one pass by in the distance during the night, but had given it little notice. Choppers and small planes were frequent modes of transportation across the immense distances up here, particularly over toward the oil patch. This new one, however, was heading for the ranch house, and he saw the brilliant cone of its searchlight combing the forest and the ground. It came toward Gibson fast, and he ducked against a boulder, letting the bird pass overhead.

The tone of the attack was already changing as the ranch took its defensive toll, and Gibson knew the momentum had shifted. What had looked like an overwhelming force on the attack plan only moments ago was fizzling into disarray. There was another boom in the south, and he heard someone cry out. Breathing hard, he hunkered down beside another boulder to catch his breath. The pain in his lungs indicated that he'd probably been running dangerously hard for about a mile. He knew the tripwire locations, but if he stumbled and broke a leg or ran into a tree the game would be over. "Hell it will," he told himself, and a smile creased his face as he inhaled deeply and put down the weapon to take a drink. "This game is already over. I'm number one."

"Hello, Luke," a voice said softly in the darkness.

Gibson looked out in disbelief as a silhouette broke from the shadows and moved toward him at a lazy pace. Luke screamed and grabbed for his gun, and Kyle Swanson unloaded a blast of his own 12-guage, unleashing a swarm of miniature flechettes. Some of the needles broke on the rocks and shredded trail brush, but about a dozen punched through the clothing and skin of Luke Gibson with the power of a mad surgeon. He had never felt such searing pain, and he screamed as it immobilized him; the tiny syringes had been packed with enough chemicals to bring down a gorilla.

Swanson charged. The result was certain, but a few heart pumps were required for the drug to circulate to the brain and vital organs; until then, the victim would be able to resist. Swanson kicked Gibson in the ribs and sent him sprawling. "How you doin' down there, Number One? You look like a porcupine."

Gibson tried to crawl, but Swanson stomped on the back of his knee, then kicked the shotgun away as he reloaded his own weapon—a test model of the anti-personnel, multiple-projectile, remote drug-delivery system straight from the Excalibur laboratories. It was supposed to be nonlethal, but dosage was a still a problem. At the moment, Swanson didn't care. He had been dropped off six miles from the house early this morning and found a hide on a ridge from which he could see most of the spread. When Gibson ran out, Swanson trotted up the trail behind him.

"You're dead." Gibson croaked as his energy evaporated. The bright cone of the helicopter light came back and painted a circle around them. "You're dead!"

"Oh, go to sleep," Swanson said. He punched Gibson hard in the temple as FBI black-clad fighters slithered down long ropes to the forest floor.

AN ANESTHESIOLOGIST AT THE Kalispell Regional Medical Center efficiently brought Luke Gibson back. The patient was secured to a hospital bed in a guarded part of the facility, where he had been flown while still unconscious. A doctor had plucked out the quills and closed the little wounds. Blood work had taken a while, because of the complex formula used as ammunition in the darts, but the recovery was relatively swift. Dose like that, delivered by a shotgun blast, could kill a man.

When Gibson finally became aware of his surroundings, he saw two women standing on each side of the bed. One was a nurse in pink scrubs who had a lousy bedside manner as she shook him awake. The second wore a brown uniform with blue shoulder flashes and a duty belt.

"Hey! Hey! Can you hear me?" the cop barked. She also gave him a shake. "Wake up." Her voice was young but firm.

Gibson was irritated and still groggy, close to barfing. "Yeah. God damn it, I can hear you. Where's Kyle?"

"I don't know any Kyle," she said. "My name is Danielle DeLaittre of the Montana Highway Patrol, assigned to District Five. Do you understand that?"

She came into better focus. Lean and muscle-toned, with a turtleneck sweater beneath her shirt, and looking very young. "How old are you?" he asked.

DeLaittre had been expecting such a comment. She had been briefed by her training officer to emphasize her lack of law-enforcement experience with the prisoner. The federal officials who had brought this guy in wanted him to be treated like a common criminal. "I'm twenty-five years old and a member of the most recent graduating class of the Montana Law Enforcement Academy. Before that, I worked my way through college by cleaning motel rooms and making sandwiches at a Subway over in Billings. Now, are you coherent?"

"You're a damned rookie!"

"Lowest of the low, sir. They made me leave my .357 Sig outside because you're some kind of bad dude. However, I consider you somewhat special because you're my first arrest."

"And I'm fresh out of nursing school," chirped the nurse. Both cop and nurse grinned in amusement.

While Luke Gibson groaned at the intentional insult of being treated like pond scum, Danielle DeLaittre took a small card from her pocket. "I will now read you your rights," she said.

BILLINGS, MONTANA

THE LAWYER FROM MANHATTAN looked out across the plains and felt nervous. This was cowboy-and-Indian country, and probably not a decent bagel within a hundred miles. He had flown out yesterday and spent the night in a hotel, hoping not to be scalped. As Leonard P. Flagler climbed the steps of the federal building, he felt that he was reaching the safety of a frontier fort, and put on his business face.

He presented his card and was ushered directly into the office of Melissa Jacob, an assistant U.S. Attorney in the Criminal Division for the District of Montana. She was an attractive woman, dressed in blue jeans and a flannel shirt, plus Western boots. No, this was not Manhattan.

She apologized for the casual look, but said it was a paperwork day for her, just to clean up some loose ends; she could have worked from home had she not made this appointment. She put on a pair of rimless glasses and read briefly from a file. "So you're the attorney of record for Mr. Lucas Gibson?"

"I am." He read the body language. This woman wasn't cowed by his courtroom reputation. In fact, it looked as if this might be a short meeting.

"And Gibson wants to make a deal?"

"I visited with my client earlier today, and he is willing to become a fully cooperative government witness in a number of important investigations in exchange for . . ."

Melissa Jacob leaned back and crossed her arms. "Whoa up right there, Mr. Flagler. I'm afraid you've made a long trip from New York for nothing. There will be no deal. Period."

Flagler felt a trickle of sweat on his back. He might be out in the badlands but he knew how to make prosecutors crawl. "That's highly unlikely, Ms. Jacob."

"Tell your client he does not have a single thing we want. Nothing at all. In fact, we're finishing up the paperwork today, declaring him to be an enemy combatant and a national-security threat; he'll be transferred into military custody. Any trial will be in secret, and he will not be allowed a civilian lawyer."

"That's preposterous, madam! On what charge?"

"I cannot tell you that because you do not have proper clearance for top-secret material. Just assume we start with treason and murder and work our way down. I suggest that you get your payment up front, Mr. Flagler, because we're seizing all of Mr. Gibson's assets as soon as possible."

"He's an American citizen and has constitutional rights!"

"Read the fine print in his employment contract with the CIA. Oh, sorry, you don't have clearance for that, either." Melissa Jacob came around the desk and extended her hand. "Look, Mr. Flagler, I'm doing you a favor here. I know your firm defends drug dealers and other such criminals, and everyone deserves a robust defense, but you do not want any part of Luke Gibson. We intend to bury him. Spend your time elsewhere."

Flagler was being dismissed. He sputtered, "My client demands to confront his accuser, a man named Kyle Swanson."

"Ain't gonna happen," she said. "Go tell your client what I said, and that he will be transferred tomorrow to the United States Disciplinary Barracks at Fort Leavenworth, down in Kansas. His future after that is unknown. You will never see him again. Have a nice trip back to New York, Mr. Flagler. Thanks for dropping by."

Epilogue

SWANSON AND GIBSON NEVER met again. Gibson was convicted in a secret trial of the single charge of murdering fellow CIA contract worker Nicky Marks, a cover that kept intelligence issues off the table. He was on a long, slow, never-ending road to nowhere.

The man whose reputation meant everything to him was ruined. Guards were ordered not to speak to him except to give orders. He was allowed one hour a day in an exercise area, alone, then back to his small single cell. His bed was made up at eight o'clock in the morning, and he was not allowed to sit or lie on it until nine that night. There was a single chair and a steel desk bolted to the wall. A steel commode and a small sink was in a corner. His only visitors were occasional federal investigators, never senior in rank or experience, who practiced their interrogation skills on him concerning various things. The information the government had gleaned from the one-time friends of the Prince, who had been tracked down through a drug lord and a careful perusal of his family history, had brought down a dozen major criminal enterprises and rolled up the few rogues inside the CIA, and the investigations were ongoing. The result was that Luke Gibson became a practice dummy for trainees to question; always men, never women. After a few years, even they stopped coming.

ABOARD THE *VAGABOND*

A BABY SNUFFLED INTO a cry and was swept up into the protecting arms of its grandmother, Lady Patricia Cornwell. Kyle Swanson and Beth Ledford were married a year after the death of her first husband, with the blessing of Mickey's mother.

Lady Pat had been planning Kyle's wedding for years, just waiting for him to settle down enough to pick a bride, and Coastie was a darling. But the plans went for naught when the bride and the groom threatened to run off to Las Vegas and be married by an Elvis impersonator if Lady Pat didn't calm down. The ceremony was held not in a castle or a cathedral but on a private, rustic estate in Maryland, with a few intimate friends. The ceremony was performed by the president of the United States, Christopher Thompson, who had lent the couple his Camp David retreat for a few days as a token of respect for their unspecified services to the country.

The baby arrived ten months later, and was named Jeffrey Michael Swanson, and soon was given the nickname Rocky, because he often punched out with his rolled fists. Lady Pat couldn't keep her hands off him. She had thought these precious moments would never come.

"Oh, *DO* give the lad some breathing space, Patricia," Sir Jeff said over the rim of a glass gin and tonic. "You don't need to come running every time he burps."

The yacht was cruising off the Azores, and the family was enjoying the scenery and the calm waters. A baby who cried now and then was the only emergency, and a full-time British nanny was in attendance.

Coastie kept both of the older women within hailing distance where anything to do with the child was concerned. They could play with him and change his diapers and feed him stewed carrots, but she was his mother, and made certain there was no question about that. She and Lady Pat had gone toe to toe a couple of times before the issue was settled and ended in hugs.

Kyle drank from a bottle of beer, leaning back against the rail on an upper deck, facing Sir Jeff. Coastie, Lady Pat, and Rocky were below decks, and the ship's crew had everything running like clockwork. There was no emergency in his life. Not a single one. A three-legged German shepherd basked in the bright sun.

"I know that you dislike the idea, dear boy, but Mommy and Daddy simply cannot continue running around being assassins anymore," Sir Jeff said, continuing an argument that had been ongoing for months. Coastie and Lady Pat agreed with the new grandfather. Kyle was still unsure.

"It's the only thing I really know," he said, and it sounded lame even to him.

"Time to get off the helicopter, lad," Sir Jeff replied. "It comes to us all. Your new job is to get home safe and sound to your family at night."

"You just want to retire. Lazy old man."

"You're dead right about that. A wise fellow once asked me, 'After your make your first dollar, read your first good book, have your first adventure, and make love to your first woman, what do you do next?'"

"And the mysterious answer is?"

"I haven't figured that out yet, Kyle. But I'm working on it. We've built an empire, you and I, a couple of tired old soldiers who had a bit of luck. Then we both snared a couple of exceptional and beautiful women. We've served our nations well, and can continue to do so, just not on the front lines or sneaking around with Excalibur sniper rifles and that sort of thing."

The plan that had taken form was for Sir Jeff to retire and for Kyle to assume the job of president and chief executive officer for Excalibur Enterprises. Janna would run the North American operations from Washington, and Kyle would live in London and handle the U.K., NATO, and Europe. Money would never be a problem. Not a bad way to handle middle age, Kyle decided.

What disturbed him was the thought that he would be retreating from a world in trouble. Evil was still out there, and always would be, and it needed to be confronted and fought. He was just unsure whether, sitting behind a big desk, he could still get that rush of finding a good hide and bringing a bad guy into the crosshairs. Coastie had already made the transition; the instincts of a killer had been drowned by love for her family. She would never go back.

Coastie came on deck, and the breeze hugged a light sundress to her figure and blew her golden hair over a tanned shoulder. In her arms was Rocky, clucking and flailing, while Grandma Pat, trailing behind, warned that the child would catch its death out there in the breeze.

Kyle knew the argument was over. It made sense to at least give it a try. He gathered his wife and child into his arms. His son punched him softly. "Good left hook, kid. You're going to be a great marine."